Earth and Elsewhere

KIR BULYCHEV

SEVER GANSOVSKY

OLEG KORABELNIKOV

OLGA LARIONOVA

ARKADY STRUGATSKY
AND
BORIS STRUGATSKY

Translated from the Russian by Roger DeGaris

MACMILLAN PUBLISHING COMPANY
New York

COLLIER MACMILLAN PUBLISHERS
London

Macmillan Publishing Company
866 Third Avenue, New York, N.Y. 10022
Collier Macmillan Canada, Inc.

Library of Congress Cataloging-in-Publication Data
Main entry under title:

Earth and elsewhere.

Contents: The way to Amalteia / Arkady Strugatsky
and Boris Strugatsky—A part of the world / Sever Gansovsky—Another's memory / Kir Bulychev—[etc.]
    1. Science fiction, Russian—Translations into En-
glish.   2. Science fiction, English—Translations from
Russian.   I. Bulychev, K. (Kirill)
PG3276.E27   1985   891.73'0876'08   85–18946
ISBN 0-02-518240-4

10 9 8 7 6 5 4 3 2 1

Printed in the United States of America

Contents

The Way to Amalteia

ARKADY STRUGATSKY
AND BORIS STRUGATSKY

PROLOGUE: AMALTEIA, J-STATION

Amalteia, the fifth and closest of Jupiter's satellites, rotates about its axis about every thirty-five hours. In addition it makes a full revolution around Jupiter every twelve hours. Therefore Jupiter slides over the nearby horizon every thirteen and one-half hours.

The rise of Jupiter is very beautiful. To appreciate it, however, you must take the elevator up to the top floor, under the transparent spectrolite bubble.

When your eyes get used to the darkness, a frozen plain is visible, stretching in a hump to the rocky ridges on the horizon. The sky is black, and in it are countless bright unblinking stars. From the shining of the stars dim reflections lie over the plain, and the rocky ridge seems a deep black shadow against the starry sky. If you look closely, you can make out even the outlines of individual jagged peaks.

It happens sometimes that the spotted sickle of Ganymede hangs low over the ridge, or the silvery disk of Callisto, or the two of them together, although that happens comparatively rarely. Then from the peaks across the glittering ice of the entire plain, even gray shadows spread. And when the sun is above the horizon—a round spot of blinding flame, the plain turns blue, the shadows become black, and every crack in the ice is visible. The charred smudges on the rocketdrome resemble huge ice-covered puddles. The sight arouses warm, half-forgotten associations, and you feel like running out onto the field and sliding down the thin skin of ice to see how it crackles beneath your magnetic boots, how the cracks race over it, like the skim on hot milk, only dark in color.

But all of this can be seen elsewhere as well.

It really becomes beautiful when Jupiter rises. And the rise of Jupiter is truly beautiful only on Amalteia. And it is particularly beautiful when the rise of Jupiter overtakes the sun. First a green glow burns beyond the peaks of the ridge—the exosphere of the gigantic planet. It glows brighter and brighter, slowly creeping up to the sun, and one after another the stars in the black sky go out. And suddenly it attacks the sun. It is very important not to miss this moment. The green glow of the exosphere instantaneously, as though by sorcery, becomes bloodred. You always wait for that moment, and it always comes startlingly fast. The sun turns red, and the icy plain becomes red, and bloody rays flash on the round navigation tower on the edge of the plain. Even the peaks' shadows become pink. Then the red gradually darkens, becoming chestnut, and finally, the huge red-brown hump of Jupiter crawls over the rocky ridge on the near horizon. The sun is still visible, and it is still red, like heated iron—an even cherrylike disk against the brownish background.

For some reason it is felt that brown is an ugly color. That is what a person who had never seen the brown glow of half a sky and the distinct red disk on it might think. Then the disk disappears. Only Jupiter remains— huge, brown, shaggy, it slowly climbs above the horizon, as though it were swelling, and occupies a quarter of the sky. It is streaked with black-and-green ammonia clouds, and sometimes tiny white dots appear and immediately go out—that is the way exospheric protuberances look from Amalteia.

Unfortunately, watching the rise of Jupiter from beginning to end is hard to do. Jupiter rises too slowly, and you have to go to work. During observations, of course, you can follow the entire rise, but while taking observations you don't have time to think about beauty.

The director of J-Station looked at his watch. Today the rise had been beautiful, and would soon be even more beautiful, but it was time to go below and think about what had to be done.

In the shadow of the ridge the mesh skeleton of the Big Antenna started to move, turning slowly. Radio opticians had set about their observations. The poor, starving radio optics. . . .

The director looked at Jupiter's brown cupola for a last time and thought how good it would be to seize the moment when all four large satellites— the reddish Io, Europa, Ganymede, and Callisto—were hanging over the horizon, and Jupiter itself, in its first quarter, was half orange, half brown. Then he realized that he had never seen Jupiter set. That, too, must be beautiful: The glow of the exosphere slowly dies out, and one after another the stars flash on in the darkening sky, like needles of diamond against velvet. But usually that time was the peak of the workday.

The director entered the elevator and went down to the bottom floor.

The planetological station on Amalteia was a research city on many levels, cut into the ice layer and poured out of metalloplast. Around sixty persons lived, worked, studied, and built here. Fifty-six young men and women, fine people, with excellent appetites.

The director glanced into the sports room, but no one was there, just someone splashing in the round pool, and the echo was ringing from under the ceiling. The director walked on, moving without haste in his heavy magnetic boots. On Amalteia there was practically no gravity, and that was highly inconvenient. After a while, of course, you get used to it, but at first it seems that your body is filled with hydrogen and about to leap out of your magnetic boots. And it was particularly difficult getting used to sleeping.

Two astrophysicists went past, their hair still damp from the shower, said hello, and quickly walked on, to the elevators. One of the astrophysicists apparently had something the matter with his magnetic soles—he was hopping along awkwardly. The director turned into the dining room. About fifteen people were having breakfast.

Uncle Valnoga, the cook—the station's gastronomic engineer—distributed the breakfasts on a cart. He was gloomy. He had been gloomy since the unfortunate day when they had radioed from Callisto, the fourth satellite, about an accident affecting the food supplies. The food storehouse on Callisto was destroyed by fungus. It had happened before, but this time the whole supply was wiped out, down to the last cracker, and the chlorella farm had been lost, too.

On Callisto it was very hard to work. Unlike Amalteia, Callisto had a biosphere, and no one had found a way to prevent the fungus from invading the living quarters. It was a very interesting fungus. It would penetrate any wall and devour everything edible—bread, canned goods, sugar. It was particularly fond of chlorella. Sometimes it would infect a human being, but that was not at all dangerous. At first everyone was very much afraid of it, and even the boldest were concerned when they found the characteristic slightly slippery film on their skin. But the fungus did not cause living organisms pain or harm. It was even said that it had a tonic effect. But food it destroyed in nothing flat.

"Uncle Valnoga," someone called out. "Are we going to have crackers again for dinner?"

The director did not manage to see who had said it, because everyone turned their heads toward Uncle Valnoga and stopped chewing. Handsome young faces, almost all deeply tanned. And already pinched-looking. Or did it just seem that way?

"For dinner you will get soup," Uncle Valnoga said.

"Great!" someone exclaimed, and once again the director did not notice who.

He walked over to the nearest chair and sat down. Valnoga wheeled the cart over to him, and the director took his breakfast—a plate with a small pile of crackers, a half a bar of chocolate, and a pear-shaped glass of tea. He did it very skillfully, but all the same the crackers jumped up and hung in the air. The pear of tea stayed still—it had a magnetic bottom. The director caught one of the crackers, took a bite, and grabbed the glass. The tea was cold.

"Soup," Valnoga said. He spoke softly, addressing only the director. "Can you imagine what soup is anymore. And they probably think I'm going to serve chicken broth." He pushed his cart away and sat down at a table. He watched the cart roll down an aisle slower and slower. "But on Callisto they are eating chicken soup."

"Not likely," the director said absentmindedly.

"What do you mean, not likely?" Valnoga asked. "I gave up one hundred seventy cans to them. More than half of our reserve."

"Have we eaten up the remaining reserves?"

"Of course we have."

"Then so have they," the director said, crunching his cracker. "They have twice as many people."

You're lying, Uncle Valnoga, he thought. I know your tricks, gastronomic engineer. You've already set aside twenty cans for the sick.

Valnoga sighed and asked, "Is your tea cold?"

"No, it's okay."

"The chlorella on Callisto just won't take," Valnoga said and sighed again. "They radioed for another ten kilograms of ferment. They reported that they had sent the planet ship."

"Well, we have to give it to them."

"Of course we have to!" Uncle Valnoga said. "Of course. But I don't have a hundred tons of the stuff, and I have to let it grow. I'm probably ruining your appetite, aren't I?"

"It's okay," the director said. He was not hungry to begin with.

"Enough!" someone said.

The director raised his eyes and immediately saw the confused face of Zoya Ivanova. Alongside her sat the nuclear physicist Kozlov. They always sat next to each other.

"That's enough, do you hear?" Kozlov said in anger.

Zoya blushed and bent her head. She was embarrassed because everyone was looking at her.

"Yesterday you shoved your crackers at me," Kozlov said. "And today you do it again."

Zoya was silent. She was almost crying from shame.

"Don't yell at her, you ass!" the atmosphere physicist Potapov barked from the other end of the dining room. "Zoya, why do you sacrifice for him, that animal. Give me your crackers, I won't mind. I won't even yell at you."

"No," Kozlov said, calmed down already. "I'm healthy even without them, and she needs to eat more than I do."

"Not true, Valya," Zoya said without raising her head.

Someone said, "How about a little more tea, Uncle Valnoga?"

Valnoga stood up. Potapov called across the whole dining room, "Hey, Gregor, how about a game after work?"

"You're on," Gregor said.

"You'll be beaten again, Vadim," someone said.

"The law of averages is on my side," Potapov asserted.

Everyone broke out laughing.

An angry face poked itself into the dining room.

"Is Potapov here? Vadim, a storm on Jupe!"

"Well!" Potapov said and jumped up. And the other atmosphere experts got up hurriedly from their tables. The angry face disappeared and then reappeared suddenly. "Grab me some crackers, okay?"

"If Valnoga will give them out," Potapov said. He looked at Valnoga.

"Why not?" Uncle Valnoga said. "Mr. Konstantin Stetsenko, two hundred grams of crackers and fifty grams of chocolate."

The director stood up, wiping his mouth with a paper napkin. Kozlov said, "Comrade Director, what's happening with the *Takhmasib?*"

Everyone fell silent and turned to the director. The young tanned faces, already slightly pinched-looking.

The director answered, "Still no news."

He walked slowly down the aisle between the tables and headed for his office. The whole problem was that the "food epidemic" on Callisto had come at a bad time. It still was not a real famine. Amalteia could still share its chlorella and crackers with Callisto. But if Bykov did not come soon with food. . . . Bykov was already close. He had been spotted, but then he fell silent and had remained so for over sixty hours already. I'll have to cut the rations again, the director thought. Here anything could happen, and the base on Mars was far away. Strange things could happen. It happened that planetologists from Earth and Mars were lost. It happened rarely, more rarely than the fungal infections. But it is very bad that it happens at all. A billion kilometers from Earth strange things did happen, worse than ten epidemics. It was famine. Perhaps it was death.

1. THE PHOTON FREIGHTER *TAKHMASIB*

1. *The planet ship approaches Jupiter, and the captain argues with the navigator and takes sporamine.*

Alexei Petrovich Bykov, the captain of the photon freighter *Takhmasib*, left his cabin and neatly closed the door behind him. His hair was wet. The captain had just taken a shower. He had even taken two showers—a water shower and an ion shower—but he still felt unsteady after his short sleep. He wanted to sleep so much that his eyes just would not open. During the last three days he had slept perhaps five hours total. The flight had turned out to be tricky.

The corridor was deserted and light. Bykov headed for the control room, trying not to shuffle. He had to go through the lounge to get to the control room. The door to the lounge was open, and voices could be heard. They belonged to the planetologists Dauge and Yurkovsky and sounded—it seemed to Bykov—unusually irritated and strangely hollow.

Once again they're up to something, Bykov thought. There's no getting around them. And I can't even curse them out properly, because they're my friends and are terribly happy that we all are on this flight together. That hasn't happened that often.

Bykov strode into the lounge and stopped. The bookcase was open, the books had tumbled onto the floor and were lying in a messy pile. The tablecloth had slipped off the table. Yurkovsky's long legs, wrapped in tight gray pants, stuck out from under the couch. The legs were waving wildly.

"I tell you, she's not here," Dauge said.

Dauge himself was not to be seen.

"You look," Yurkovsky's smothered voice said. "It was your idea, so you look!"

"What's going on here?" Bykov angrily inquired.

"Aha, there he is!" Dauge said and climbed out from under the table.

His face was happy, his jacket and shirt collar unbuttoned. Yurkovsky backed out from under the couch.

"What's the matter?" Bykov asked.

"Where's my Varya?" Yurkovsky asked, getting to his feet. He was very angry.

"Scoundrel!" Dauge exclaimed.

"Good-for-nothings!" Bykov said.

"It was him," Dauge said in tragic tones. "Just look at his face, Vladimir! Murderer!"

"I am speaking absolutely seriously, Alexei," Yurkovsky said. "Where's my Varya?"

"You know, my planetologist friends," Bykov said, "you can both go to hell."

He stuck out his jaw and strode into the control room. Dauge said as he left, "He incinerated Varya in the reactor."

Bykov closed the hatch behind him with a thud.

It was quiet in the control room. The navigator, Mikhail Antonovich Krutikov, was sitting in his usual position behind the computer desk, resting his double chin on his chubby fists. The computer was humming softly, the neon lights on its panel blinking pensively. Mikhail looked at the captain with a friendly expression and asked, "Did you sleep well, Alexei?"

"Yes," Bykov answered.

"I took bearings on Amalteia," Mikhail said. "They've really been waiting. . . ." He shook his head. "Imagine, Alexei, their rations are two hundred grams of crackers and fifty grams of chocolate. And three hundred grams of chlorella soup. It tastes terrible."

You should be there, Bykov thought; you might slim down, my chubby friend.

He looked angrily at the navigator but could not help himself and broke out in a smile. Mikhail, sticking out his fat lips in an expression of concern, was studying a sheet of blue graph paper.

"Here it is, Alexei," he said. "I wrote the finish program. Please check it."

Usually checking one of Mikhail's course programs was a waste of time. Mikhail remained the fattest and the most experienced navigator in the interplanetary fleet.

"I'll check it later," Bykov said. He yawned sweetly, covering his mouth with his hand. "Enter the program in the cybernavigator."

"I already did," Mikhail said guiltily.

"Aha," Bykov said. "Well then, all right. Where are we now?"

"In an hour we come out onto the finish," Mikhail answered. "We will pass over the north pole of Jupiter"—the word *Jupiter* he pronounced with evident pleasure—"at a distance of two diameters, two hundred ninety megameters. And then the final arc. We're as good as there, Alexei."

"You're calculating the distance from the center of Jupiter?"

"Yes, from the center."

"When we come out on the finish, you will give me the distance from the exosphere every quarter hour."

"Yessir, Alexei," Mikhail said.

Bykov yawned one more time, wiped his drooping eyelids with his hands, and walked alongside the accident signal panel. Everything there was in order. The engine was working without interruption, the plasma was proceeded at the appropriate rate, the tuning of the magnetic traps was holding perfectly. The flight engineer Zhilin was responsible for the magnetic traps. Good work, Zhilin, Bykov thought. You've got them humming.

Bykov stopped and tried to throw off the tuning by slightly changing course. The tuning was not thrown off. The white fleck on the transparent plastic disk did not even budge. Good work, Bykov thought again. He skirted a protruding wall—the photoreactor housing. Zhilin was standing by the reflector controls with a pencil between his teeth. He was holding onto the edges of the panel with both hands and barely noticeably doing a little tap dance, his powerful shoulders bulging.

"Hello, Ivan," Bykov said.

"Hello, Captain," Zhilin said, turning around quickly. The pencil slipped from between his teeth, but he caught it dexterously as it fell.

"How's the reflector?" Bykov asked.

"The reflector is working fine," Zhilin said, Bykov still bent over the panel and picked up the dense blue ribbon of the control system record.

The reflector is the most important and most fragile part of the photon drive, a gigantic parabolic mirror covered with five layers of superstable mesomatter. In the technical literature the reflector is often called a sail. At the focal point of the paraboloid, millions of bits of seuterium-tritium plasma are transformed into radiation every second. The flow of the pale purple flame strikes against the reflector's surface and creates a force. During this process enormous temperature changes occur in the mesomatter layer, and the mesomatter gradually, layer by layer, is burned up. In addition, the reflector is constantly corroded by meteorites. And if the engine is on and the reflector breaks at its base, where the fat horn of the photoreactor joins it, the ship becomes an instantaneous, soundless flash. Therefore the reflectors on photon ships are changed every hundred astronomical units of flight. Therefore the control system is constantly measuring the condition of the working layer over the reflector's entire surface.

"So," Bykov said, twirling the tape between his fingers, "the first layer has burned away."

Zhilin was silent.

"Mikhail!" Bykov called out. "Did you know that the first layer is burned out?"

"I know, Alexei," the navigator responded. "What can you do? It's oversun."

Oversun occurs rarely and only under exceptional conditions—like now, when there was a famine at J-Station. In oversun, the sun is located between the takeoff planet and the finish planet—a situation highly unfavorable from the point of view of direct cosmogation. The photon engine must work at maximum, the ship's velocity reaches sixty-seven thousand kilometers a second, and nonclassical effects begin to affect the instruments, effects that are still poorly understood. The crew gets almost no sleep, the expenditure of fuel and reflector is colossal, and to top it all off the ship, as a rule, approaches the finish planet from the pole—very inconvenient for the landing.

"Yes," Bykov said. "Oversun. It's oversun, indeed."

He returned to the navigator and looked at the fuel gauge.

"Give me a copy of the finish program, Mikhail," he said.

"One minute, Alexei," the navigator said.

He was very busy. Blue sheets of paper were scattered over the desk, and the semiautomatic attachment to the computer was humming softly. Bykov plopped down into his chair and let his eyes close halfway. In a blur he saw Mikhail, without taking his eyes off his printout, reach out to the panel, his fingers dancing over the keyboard. His hand began to resemble a large white spider. The computer hummed more loudly and stopped, flashing on the stop signal.

"What do you want, Alexei?" the navigator asked, still concentrating on his printout.

"The finish program," Alexei said, barely managing to force his eyelids apart.

A tabulogram crawled out of the output device, and Mikhail grabbed it with both hands.

"Right away," he said hurriedly. "Right away."

Bykov felt a sweet buzzing in his ears, a yellow flame appeared beneath his eyelids. His head dropped against his chest.

"Alexei," the navigator said. He reached over his desk and slapped Bykov on the shoulder. "Alexei, here's the program."

Bykov shuddered, shook his head, and looked from side to side. He took the print-covered sheets of paper.

"Heh-hmm," he cleared his throat and massaged the skin on his forehead. "So then. . . . The theta algorithm again. . . ." He sleepily fixed his gaze on the printout.

"You should take some sporamine," the navigator advised.

"Hold on," Bykov said. "Hold on. What's this? Have you gone crazy, Navigator?"

Mikhail jumped up, ran around the desk, and leaned over Bykov's shoulder.

"Where, where?" he asked.

"Where are you flying to?" Bykov asked bitingly. "Maybe you think you're flying to the Seventh Testing Grounds?"

"What is it, Alexei?"

"Or maybe you imagine they've built a tritium generator for you on Amalteia?"

"If you're talking about fuel," Mikhail said, "why, there's enough fuel for three programs like that one."

Bykov woke up once and for all.

"I have to land on Amalteia," he said. "Then I have to take the planetologists into the exosphere and land on Amalteia again. And then I have to return to Earth. And that will be an oversun again!"

"Hold on," Mikhail said. "Just one minute."

"You dream up an insane program, as though stores of fuel were waiting for us."

The hatch to the control room opened partway, and Bykov turned around. Dauge's head appeared in the crack. The head ran its eyes around the room, then said pleadingly, "Listen, guys, Varya wouldn't happen to be here, would she?"

"Out!" Bykov barked.

The head disappeared in a flash. The hatch closed quietly.

"Good-for-nothings!" Bykov said. "But look here now, Navigator! If I don't have fuel for the return oversun, you're in big trouble."

"Don't shout, please," Mikhail answered indignantly. He thought for a second and added, blushing deeply, "Damn it anyway."

They were both silent. Mikhail returned to his spot, and they looked at each other, sulking. Then Mikhail said, "I've calculated the flight into the exosphere. I have almost calculated the return oversun." He put his hand on a pile of papers on his desk. "And if you are chicken, we can very easily stop off at Antimars."

Antimars was the cosmogator's name for an artificial planet in Mars's orbit but on the other side of the sun. In essence, it was a huge fuel reservoir, a fully automated filling station.

"And there is absolutely no reason to . . . yell," Mikhail said. The word *yell* he pronounced in a whisper. Mikhail stood there, cooling off. So did Bykov.

"Well," Bykov said, "forgive me, Mikhail."

Mikhail immediately broke out into a smile.

"I was wrong," Bykov added.

"Ah, Alexei," Mikhail said hurriedly. "It's nothing. Absolutely nothing. . . . But just look at what a remarkable circuit we'll have. From the vertical"—he began to gesture—"to the surface of Amalteia and over the exosphere itself on an inertial ellipse to the meeting point. And at the meeting point the relative velocity will be only four meters a second. A maximum overload of only twenty-two percent, and only thirty to forty minutes of weightlessness. And the errors in computation are very small."

"The errors are small because of the theta algorithm," Bykov said. He wanted to say something nice to the navigator: Mikhail had been the first to develop and apply the theta algorithm.

Mikhail gave out a vague sound in reply. He was pleasantly embarrassed. Bykov looked through the program, nodded several times in succession, then put the printout down and began to rub his eyes with his huge freckled hands.

"To be honest," he said, "I didn't sleep a damned wink."

"Take some sporamine, Alexei," Mikhail repeated. "I take a tablet every two hours and don't feel like sleeping at all. So does Ivan. Why torture yourself?"

"I don't like messing with chemicals," Bykov said. He jumped up and started pacing the room. "Listen, Mikhail, what's really happening on my ship?"

"What do you mean?" the navigator asked.

"The planetologists again," Bykov said.

Zhilin explained from behind the photoreactor casing: "Varya has disappeared."

"So?" Bykov said. "It was bound to happen." He paced again. "Children, very old children."

"Don't get mad at them, Alexei," the navigator said.

"You know, comrades,"—Bykov sat down—"the worst thing about a flight is the passengers. And the worst passengers are old friends. Give me some sporamine, Mikhail."

Mikhail quickly pulled a box out of his pocket. Bykov watched through sleepy eyes.

"Give me two right away," he said.

2. *The planetologists look for Varya, and the radio optician learns what a hippo is.*

"He chased me out," Dauge said, returning to Yurkovsky's cabin.

Yurkovsky was standing on a chair in the middle of his cabin and feeling the soft matte ceiling with the palm of his hand. A crushed cookie was spread out on the floor.

"She must be up here," Yurkovsky said.

He jumped down from the chair, shook white crumbs off his knees and called out pitifully, "Varya, light of my life, where are you?"

"Have you tried sitting down unexpectedly on the chair?" Dauge asked.

He walked over to the couch and stiffly collapsed on it.

"You'll kill her!" Yurkovsky shouted.

"She's not here," Dauge reported and settled in more comfortably, putting his feet up on the back of the couch. "We should perform this operation on all the couches and easy chairs. Varya likes curling up in something soft."

Yurkovsky dragged the chair closer to the wall.

"No," he said. "In flight she likes hiding behind walls or ceilings. We'll have to go through the ship searching the ceilings."

"Lord!" Dauge signed. "What planetologists won't do when they have no work!" He sat up, glanced at Yurkovsky and whispered sinisterly, "I'm sure it's Alexei. He always hated her."

Yurkovsky started at Dauge.

"Yes," Dauge continued. "Always. You know it. And why? She was so quiet . . . so gentle."

"You're a fool, Grigory," Yurkovsky said. "You're clowning around, but I'll really feel terrible if she gets lost."

He sat on the chair, his elbows on his knees and his head in his hands. His high forehead with a receding hairline gathered in wrinkles, and his eyebrows fell tragically.

"Come on, now," Dauge said. "How is she going to get lost on this ship? She'll turn up."

"You say she'll turn up," Yurkovsky said. "But it's time for her to eat. She never asks to eat herself, so she'll die from starvation."

"She's not going to die," Dauge disagreed.

"She hasn't eaten anything in twelve days. Since takeoff. And that's very dangerous."

"When she feels like it, she'll come," Dauge said confidently. "That is a characteristic of all life forms."

Yurkovsky shook his head.

"No, she won't come, Grigory."

He climbed up on the chair and began to feel the ceiling again, inch by inch. Someone knocked on the door. Then the door slid to the side and the small black-haired Charles Mollart, the radio optician, appeared.

"Will I come in?" he asked.

"A good question," Dauge said.

Mollart threw up his hands. "*Mais non!*" he exclaimed, and smiled joyously. He was constantly smiling joyously. "*Non* 'will I come'—I wanted to know 'will I came?' "

"Of course," Yurkovsky said from his chair. "Of course, came right in, Charles. Why not?"

Mollart entered, closed the door behind him, and looked up with curiosity.

"Voldemar," he said, "you are learning walk on ceiling?"

"*Oui, madame,*" Dauge replied with a terrible accent. "Or *messyur.* Actually, *il cherche la Varya.*"

"No-no," Mollart exclaimed. He even waved his arms. "Not that way. Not French. I want not to speak French."

Yurkovsky climbed down from his chair and asked, "Charles, have you seen my Varya?"

Mollart threatened him with a raised finger.

"Oh, you always joke me," he said with a strong accent on the "me." "You joke me twelve days already." He sat down on the couch next to Dauge. "What is Varya? I many times hear 'Varya,' today you look her, but I see her not one time. A?" He looked at Dauge. "Is bird? Or she is cat? Or a . . . a—"

"Hippo?" Dauge asked.

"What is 'ipo'?" Mollart inquired.

"*C'est* like a lirondel," Dauge answered. "A swallow."

"O, *l'hirondelle!*" Mollart exclaimed. "Ipo?"

"*Mais si!*" Dauge said. "*Natürlich.*"

"*Non, non!* Not other *langues!*" He turned to Yurkovsky. "Is Grégoire speaking truly?"

"Grégoire is laying it on thick," Yurkovsky said angrily. "It's nonsense."

Mollart looked at him attentively.

"You are upset, Voldemar," he said. "I can help?"

"No, not likely, Charles. Just have to keep searching. To feel everything with your hands, the way I am."

"Why feel?" Mollart said in surprise. "You tell me what are her looks. I become search."

"Ha!" Yurkovsky, "I'd like to know myself what she looks like right now."

Mollart leaned back in the couch.

"*Je ne comprends pas.* I do not understand. She has no looks? Or do I not understand?"

"No, that's right, Charles," Yurkovsky said, "She 'has looks,' of course, but different ones. When she is on the ceiling she looks like the ceiling. When she is on the couch, like the couch."

"And when on Grégoire, she likes Grégoire," Mollart said. "You still joke me."

"He's telling you the truth," Dauge interposed. "Varya keeps changing color. Mimicry. She camouflages herself incredibly. Mimicry."

"Mimicry with a swallow?" Mollart asked sarcastically.

Someone else knocked at the door.

"Come in!" Mollart called out joyously.

"Come in," Yurkovsky translated.

Zhilin entered, huge, rosy, and a little shy.

"Excuse me, Vladimir," he said, leaning forward slightly. "I—"

"O!" Mollart exclaimed, his smile sparkling. He was like the flight engineer. "*Le petit ingénieur!* The little engineer! How are things, good?"

"Good," Zhilin said.

"And the girls, is it good?"

"Good," Zhilin said. He was already used to Mollart. "*Bon.*"

"Beautiful pronunciation," Dauge said with envy. "By the way Charles, why do you always ask Ivan about girls?"

"I like them very much," Mollart said completely seriously.

"*Bon,*" Dauge said. "*Je vous comprends.*"

Zhilin turned to Yurkovsky.

"Vladimir, the captain sent me. In forty minutes we will be approaching the exosphere."

Yurkovsky leaped to his feet.

"Finally!"

"If you want to observe, I'm at your disposition."

"Thank you, Ivan," Yurkovsky said. He turned to Dauge. "Well, my friend, onward!"

"Oh, lovely brown Jupiter!" Dauge said.

"*Les hirondelles, les hirondelles,*" Mollart sang out. "And I go to prepare the dinner. Today is my turn, and for dinner will be soup. You like soup, Ivan?"

Zhilin did not have time to answer, because the planet ship tilted suddenly and he fell out the door, just managing to grab onto the jambs. Yurkovsky tripped over Mollart's outstretched legs and fell onto Dauge. Dauge groaned.

"Oho," Yurkovsky said, "it's a meteorite."

"Get off!" Dauge responded.

3. *The flight engineer admires great heroes, and the navigator discovers Varya.*

The cramped observation compartment was jammed with the plane-tologists' equipment. Dauge squatted down in front of a large, shiny piece of equipment that resembled a television camera. It was called an exospheric spectrograph. The planetologist had high hopes for it. It was completely new—right from the factory—and was synchronized with a bomb-release mechanism, whose dull black breech ring filled half the compartment. Alongside it, in light metal shelving, the flat clips of bomb probes shone dully. Each clip held twenty bomb probes and weighed forty kilograms. In theory the clips were supposed to be fed into the bomb-release mechanism automatically, but the photon freighter *Takhmasib* was poorly equipped for scientific research, and there was no room for the automatic feed. Zhilin handled the bomb-release mechanism.

Yurkovsky commanded, "Load."

Zhilin opened the cover on the breech ring, grabbed the edges of the first clip, lifted it with effort, and placed it in the firing chamber's rectangular opening. The clip slid silently into place. Zhilin fastened the cover, clicked the lock, and said, "Ready."

"I'm ready, too," Dauge said.

"Mikhail," Yurkovsky said into a microphone. "Will it be soon?"

"Another half hour," the hoarse voice of the navigator said.

The planet ship tilted again. The floor dropped from beneath their feet.

"Another meteorite," Yurkovsky said. "That's the third one."

"A little thick, isn't it?" Dauge said.

Yurkovsky asked into the microphone, "Mikhail, are there many micrometeorites?"

"A lot of them, Vladimir," Mikhail answered. His voice was concerned. "More than thirty percent more than the average density. And still increasing."

"Mikhail, my friend," Yurkovsky asked, "Measure them a little more often, okay?"

"The measurements are going at three a minute," the navigator responded. He said something aside, and then Bykov's bass was heard: "Yes."

"Vladimir," the navigator called, "I'm switching to ten times a minute."

"Thanks, Mikhail," Yurkovsky said.

The ship tilted again.

"Vladimir," Dauge said softly, "this is hardly trivial."

Zhilin also felt that it was hardly trivial. Nowhere, in none of his textbooks or manuals, had anything been said about an increase in meteorite density in close proximity to Jupiter. However, few scientists had ever been in close proximity to Jupiter.

Zhilin leaned against the bomb-release mechanism and looked at his watch. Only twenty minutes now, no more. In twenty minutes Dauge would release the first round. He said it was an unusual sight when a round of bomb probes exploded. The year before last he had studied the atmosphere of Uranus with bomb probes. Zhilin looked at Dauge. Dauge was squatting in front of the spectrograph, holding onto a handle—dry, dark, sharp-nosed, with a scar on his left cheek. From time to time he stretched out his long neck and glanced with one eye into the eyepiece of the videosearcher, and each time an orange reflection played over his face. Zhilin looked at Yurkovsky. He was standing with his face pressed against the periscope and was leisurely shifting his weight from foot to foot. The ribbed egg of the microphone dangled from his neck on a black band. The famous planetologists Dauge and Yurkovsky. . . .

A month before, Chen Kun, the deputy director of the Advanced School of Cosmogation, had called in Ivan Zhilin, a graduate of the school. The interplanetaries called Chen Kun Iron Kun. He was over fifty, but he looked very young in his blue jacket with the overturned collar. He would have been very handsome if it had not been for the gray-pink spots on his forehead and chin—the traces of an old radiation exposure. Chen Kun told him that the Third Section of GKMPS had urgently requested a good flight engineer and the school's council had selected graduate Zhilin (graduate Zhilin felt chill from the excitement: During his five years in school he had been afraid of being sent as an apprentice on moon flights). Chen Kun said that it was a great honor for graduate Zhilin, since his first assignment was to a ship going oversun to Jupiter (graduate Zhilin almost danced for joy) with supplies for J-Station on Amalteia, the fifth satellite of Jupiter. Amalteia was threatened by famine, Chen Kun said.

"Your commander will be the well-known interplanetary, Alexei Bykov, also a graduate of our school. Your senior navigator will be the well-experienced cosmogator Mikhail Krutikov. In their hands you will receive a first-class apprenticeship, and I am very happy for you."

The fact that Grigory Dauge and Vladimir Yurkovsky would also be on the flight was something Zhilin found out later, only at the Mirza-Charle spaceport. Christopher Columbus and Jacques Cartier! The terrifying and beautiful semilegend, familiar to him since childhood, of the men who had thrown a forbidding planet at humanity's feet. Of men who in the antediluvian *Chius*—a photon slowpoke with a single layer of mesomatter on its reflector—broke through Venus's wild atmosphere. Of men who found amid the black primal sands the Uranian Golkonda—the crater from the impact of a monstrous meteor of antimatter.

Of course, Zhilin had known other famous people. For example, Vasily Lyakhov, the interplanetary and test pilot. During the third and fourth years in the school Lyakhov taught the theory of photon drive. He organized a three-month practicum for graduates on Sat-20. Interplanetaries called

Sat-20 the Little Star. It had been very interesting there. They were testing the first direct-point photon engines. From there automatic sounding scouts were launched into the zone of absolutely free flight. There the first interstellar ship, the *Chius-Lightning*, was being built. Once Lyakhov had taken the students into the hangar. In the hangar only a recently arrived automatic photon tanker was hanging; it had been launched into the zone of absolutely free flight a half year before. The tanker, an enormous clumsy construction, had reached a distance of one light-month from the sun. Everyone was struck by its color. The hull had turned emerald green and fell apart if you touched it. It was crumbling like a loaf of bread. But the control system had remained in working order; othewise, of course, the scout would not have returned, as three of the nineteen scouts launched into the AFF zone had not. The students asked Lyakhov what had happened, and Lyakhov had answered that he did not know. "At large distances from the sun there is something we still don't understand," he had said. And then Zhilin had thought about the pilots who in a few years would take the *Chius-Lightning* out where there is something we still don't understand.

It's great, Zhilin thought. I already have something to remember. Like during my fourth year during my trial flight in the geodesic rocket when the engine failed and the rocket and I landed in a farm field near Novoyeniseisk. I wandered for several hours among the automatic high-frequency plows until I bumped into a human being in the evening. He was a telemechanic operator. We lay awake the whole night in the tent watching the plows' lights moving in the dark field, and one plow came quite close, roaring and leaving the smell of ozone behind it. The operator treated me to the local wine, and there was no way I could convince the happy-go-lucky guy that interplanetaries didn't touch the stuff. In the morning a transporter came for the rocket. Iron Chen really chewed me out for not bailing out. . . .

Or my diploma flight, Earth Sat-16—Moon Cepheus, when the member of the examining commission tried to confuse us and right after giving the initial data yelled out, "Third-magnitude asteroid to the right. Approach velocity twenty-two!" There were six of us, and he really got to us—only Jan, the group leader, kept trying to convince us that we should forgive others their little faults. In principle we did not disagree, but did not want to forgive him just the same. We all considered the flight to be a joke, and no one got excited when the ship suddenly went into a spin with fourth-degree overload. We scrambled into the control room where the member of the commission pretended to be dead from the overload; we brought the ship out of the spin. Then the commission member opened one eye and said, "Good work, interplanetaries," and we immediately forgave him his faults, because until then no one had called us interplanetaries in all seriousness, apart from mothers and girlfriends. But they had always said, "My dear interplanetary," and they always looked petrified when they said it. . . .

The *Takhmasib* suddenly shook so violently that Zhilin was thrown to the floor and hit the back of his head against the shelves.

"Damn!" Yurkovsky said. "This is indeed hardly trivial; if the ship keeps on yawing, we won't be able to work."

"Right," Dauge said. He held his hand over his right eye. "What kind of work can you expect?"

Apparently, bigger and bigger meteorites were appearing in the ship's path, and the frantic commands of the antimeteorite locators to the cybernavigator threw the ship from side to side more and more frequently.

"Is it a swarm?" Yurkovsky asked, holding tight to the periscope. "Poor Varya, she doesn't hold up well when the ship shakes."

"She should have stayed home," Dauge said testily. His right eye was swelling fast. He felt it with his fingers and muttered indistinctly in Latvian. He was no longer squatting but half lying on the floor, his legs spread for greater stability.

Zhilin held on tight, his hands squeezing the shelves. The floor suddenly fell out from under his feet, then leaped up and hit his heels painfully. Dauge groaned, and Zhilin's legs gave way. Bykov's hoarse bass roared over the loudspeaker: "Flight engineer Zhilin to the control room! Passengers in the shock seats!"

In a rocking trot Zhilin raced to the door. Behind him Dauge asked, "So it's the shock seats?"

"To hell with it!" Yurkovsky responded.

Something rolled across the floor with a metallic clatter. Zhilin jumped out into the corridor. The adventure was beginning.

The ship bobbed continuously, like a chip of wood in the waves. Zhilin ran down the corridor and thought: That one's past. And that one's past. And that one's past too, and they're all past. . . . Behind him he heard a *pkk-pshshsh*. . . . He flattened against the wall and turned around. In the empty corridor, about ten paces from him, a dense cloud of white steam was floating, just like when a tank of liquid helium breaks. The hissing quickly died down. An icy cold spread through the corridor.

"It broke, the bastard," Zhilin said and tore himself from the wall. The white cloud crept along behind him, slowly settling.

It was very cold in the control room. Zhilin saw a shining rainbow of frost on the walls and floor. Mikhail was sitting at the computer and pulled a printout toward himself. Bykov was not to be seen. He was behind the reactor casing.

"It happened again?" the navigator shouted in a high voice.

"Where is that flight engineer?" Bykov boomed from behind the casing.

"Here I am," Zhilin answered.

He ran across the control room, slipping on the frost. Bykov leaped out to meet him, his red hair standing on end.

"Take control of the reflector," he said.

"Yessir," Zhilin responded.

"Navigator, is there an opening?"

"No, Alexei. Equal density in every direction."

"Turn off the reflector. We'll get on emergency power."

Mikhail hurriedly turned in his revolving chair toward the control panel behind him. He put his hand on the keyboard and said, "Maybe if. . . ."

He stopped. His face twisted in horror. The keyboard panel bent, straightened out again, then slid silently to the floor. Zhilin heard Mikhail's wail and in confusion jumped out from behind the casing. On the wall, clasping the soft padding, sat Varya, the five-foot-long Martian lizard, Yurkovsky's favorite. An exact copy of the control keyboard on its back was already fading, but on its fearsome nose an image of the red stop signal was still flashing slowly. Mikhail stared at the checkered Varya, sobbed, and held his heart.

"Scat!" Zhilin yelled.

Varya scooted away and vanished.

"I'll kill them!" Bykov roared. "Zhilin, to your post, damn it!"

Zhilin turned around, and at that moment the *Takhmasib* really got hit.

AMALTEIA, J-STATION

Water carriers chat about famine, and the gastronomic engineer is ashamed of his cuisine.

After supper Uncle Valnoga came into the recreation room and without looking at anyone said, "I need water. Any volunteers?"

"Yes," Kozlov said.

Potapov raised his head from the chessboard and also volunteered.

"Of course," said Konstantin Stetsenko.

"Can I come?" Zoya Ivanova asked.

"You can," Valnoga said, staring at the ceiling. "Come on along."

"How much do you need?" Kozlov asked. "Not much," Uncle Valnoga answered. "Just ten tons."

"Sure thing," Kozlov said. "Right away."

Uncle Valnoga left.

"I'll go along," Gregor said.

"You'd be better off sitting here and thinking about your next move," Potapov advised. "It's your move, and you always spend a half hour on each move."

"It's okay," Gregor said. "I'll still have time to think."

"Galya, come with us," Stetsenko called out.

Galya was curled up in an easy chair in front of the magnetovideophone. She answered lazily, "Sure."

She stood up and stretched sensuously. She was twenty-eight, tall, dark-skinned, and very, very beautiful. The most beautiful woman on the station. Half the men on the station were in love with her. She ran the astrometric observatory.

"Let's go," Kozlov said. He strapped on his magnetic boots and headed for the door.

They set off for the storeroom and got fur coats, electrosaws, and a self-propelled platform.

"Eisgrotte"—that was the name of the place where the station got water for technical and hygienic purposes and for consumption. Amalteia, a flattened sphere one hundred and thirty kilometers in diameter, was made of solid ice. It was ordinary water ice, just like on Earth. Only on the surface was the ice sprinkled slightly with meteorite dust and chunks of stone and metal. No one could say for sure what the origin of the icy body was. Some—who knew little of cosmogony—considered that Jupiter long ago sucked off the water from a planet that carelessly passed too near. Others were inclined to view the formation of the fifth satellite as the result of the condensation of ice crystals. Still others maintained that Amalteia did not originally belong to the solar system, that is came from interstellar space and was seized by Jupiter. But however it may be, an inexhaustible supply of water beneath their feet was a great convenience.

The platform went down a corridor on the lowest level of the station and stopped in front of the broad gates to the Eisgrotte. Gregor jumped off the platform, walked up to the gates, looked at them nearsightedly, and searched for the handle to the lock.

"Lower, lower," Potapov called out. "You blind owl."

Gregor found the handle and the gates swung open. The platform entered the Eisgrotte. The Eisgrotte was indeed just that—a cave of ice, a tunnel cut out of solid ice. Three gas-illuminated pipes lit the tunnel, but the light was reflected from the ice walls and ceiling, was broken up into sparkles by uneven places, so it seemed that the Eisgrotte was illuminated by many light fixtures.

There was no magnetic field here, and they had to walk cautiously. And it was unusually cold.

"Ice," Galya said, looking around. "Just like on Earth."

Zoya hunched over, shivering, wrapping herself in her fur coat.

"Like in Antarctica," she muttered.

"I was in Antarctica," Gregor announced.

"Where is it you haven't been!" Potapov said. "You've been everywhere!"

"To work, guys," Kozlov commanded.

The men took the electrosaws, walked over to the far wall, and began cutting out chunks of ice. The saws went through the ice like hot knives through butter. Ice dust sparkled in the air. Zoya and Galya came closer.

"Let me," Zoya asked, looking at Kozlov's bent back.

"I won't," Kozlov said without turning around. "You'll hurt your eyes."

"Just like snow on Earth," Galya noted, holding her palm out under a stream of ice crystals.

"Well, there's no lack of this stuff anywhere," Potapov said. "For example, on Ganymede there's all the snow you want."

"I was on Ganymede," Gregor announced.

"Enough to drive you crazy," Potapov said. He turned off his saw and pushed a huge ice cube away from the wall. "Here's the way to do it."

"Cut it into pieces," Stetsenko advised.

"Don't," Kozlov said. He also turned off his saw and punched a chunk of ice away from the wall. "Just the opposite"—with effort he shoved the chunk and it slowly floated toward the tunnel exit—"it's easier for Valnoga when the blocks are larger."

"Ice," Galya said. "Just like on Earth. I'm going to come here after work."

"Are you that homesick for Earth?" Zoya asked timidly. Zoya was ten years younger than Galya, worked as a lab assistant in the astrometric observatory, and was shy in front of her boss.

"Very much," Galya said. "For everything on Earth. I want to sit on the grass, go to the park in the evening, go dancing. . . . Not our air dances, but an ordinary waltz. And to drink out of ordinary glasses, and not out of these stupid pears. And to wear dresses instead of pants. I really miss my ordinary skirts."

"Me too," Potapov said.

"I agree about the skirts," Kozlov said.

"Big mouths," Galya objected. "Wise guys."

She picked up a piece of ice and hurled it at Potapov. Potapov jumped up, hit his back against the ceiling, and collided with Stetsenko.

"Easy does it," Stetsenko said angrily. "You'll end up under the saw."

"Well, that's probably enough," Kozlov said. He pushed a third block away from the wall. "Load up, my friends."

They loaded the ice onto the platform, then Potapov unexpectedly grabbed Galya with one hand and Zoya with the other and tossed them both onto the stack of ice. Zoya shrieked in fear and grabbed onto Galya. Galya laughed.

"Let's go!" Potapov shouted. "Now Valnoga will give you a prize—a dish of chlorella soup each."

"I wouldn't refuse," Kozlov mumbled.

"You never have," Stetsenko noted. "But now, when we have a famine. . . ."

The platform went out of the Eisgrotte, and Gregor closed the gates.

"Is this really a famine?" Zoya asked from the top of the ice. "I read a book not long ago about the war with the Fascists—they really had a famine. In Leningrad, during the blockade."

"I was in Leningrad," Gregor announced.

"We eat chocolate," Zoya continued, "but there people got one hundred fifty grams of bread a day. And what bread! Half sawdust!"

"Sawdust?" Stetsenko said with doubt.

"Imagine, sawdust, really."

"The chocolate is all well and good," Kozlov said, "but things will be very tight if the *Takhmasib* doesn't get here."

He was carrying his saw over his shoulder, like a gun.

"They'll get here," Galya said confidently. She jumped down from the platform, and Stetsenko hurried to catch her. "Thanks, Konstantin. They have to get here."

"All the same I think we should suggest to the director a cut in the daily portions," Kozlov said. "Even if only for the men."

"What nonsense," Zoya said. "I read that women hold up under famine much better than men."

They walked down the corridor after the slowly moving platform.

"Women and children," Potapov said.

"Leaden wit," Zoya said. "Or cast iron."

"No, really," Kozlov said. "If Bykov doesn't get here tomorrow, we'll have to get everyone together and ask for agreement to restrictions."

"Well," Stetsenko agreed. "I don't think anyone will object."

"I won't," Gregor said.

"That's great," Potapov said. "I was about to think you were going to object."

"Greeting to the water boys," the astrophysicist Nikolsky shouted as he walked past.

Galya noted with annoyance, "I don't understand how you can worry so bluntly about your bellies, as though the *Takhmasib* was automatic and there weren't any people on board."

Even Potapov turned red and could not find anything to say. The rest of the way to the galley they were silent. In the galley Uncle Valnoga was sitting, dejected, next to a huge ion-exchange device for the purification of water. The platform stopped by the entrance to the galley.

"Unload it," Uncle Valnoga said, staring at the floor. It was uncharacteristically quiet, cool, and odorless in the galley. Uncle Valnoga was overwhelmed by the devastation.

The blocks of ice were unloaded in silence and placed in the gaping maw of the water purifier.

"Thanks," Uncle Valnoga said, his head still lowered.

"You're welcome, Uncle Valnoga," Kozlov said. "Let's go, guys."

They set off in silence toward the storeroom, then returned in silence to the recreation room. Galya took a book and curled up in her easy chair. Stetsenko hovered indecisively around her, looked at Kozlov and Zoya, who sat down at the table to study (Zoya was studying by correspondence at the Institute of Energy and Kozlov was tutoring her), sighed, and wandered off to his room. Potapov said to Gregor, "Go on, it's your move."

2. OVER THE ABYSS

1. *The captain announces unpleasant news, and the flight engineer fears not.*

Apparently a large meteorite had hit the reflector and the symmetrical distribution of force over the surface of the paraboloid was destroyed for an instant, and the *Takhmasib* was spun like a wheel. In the control room only Captain Bykov did not lose consciousness. True, his head hit something, and then his side, and for a moment he could not breathe, but

24   Arkady Strugatsky and Boris Strugatsky

with both arms and legs he managed to hold onto the seat into which the first jolt had thrown him, and he held on, stretched out, and twisted until he somehow reached the control panel. Everything around him was spinning with unusual speed. From somewhere above Zhilin floated by, his arms and legs akimbo. It seemed to Bykov that no life was left in him. He pressed his head against the panel and aiming carefully, pushed the necessary button with his finger.

The cybernavigator turned on the emergency hydrogen engines, and Bykov felt a jolt, like an emergency stop on a train, only much stronger. Bykov expected it and pressed his legs against the side on the control panel with all his might. He did not go flying out of his seat. His head spun, and his mouth felt dry. The *Takhmasib* righted itself. Then Bykov took the ship straight through the cloud of stone-and-iron particles. On the screen of the monitoring system blue lights splashed. There were many of them, very many, but the ship did not tilt anymore—the antimeteorite equipment had been shut off and did not affect the cybernavigator. Through the noise in his ears Bykov heard a piercing *pkk-pshshsh* several times and each time he was struck by a freezing mist and curled over toward the panel. Once something burst and flew into pieces, behind his back. Then the signals on the screen were fewer, and finally completely disappeared. The meteorite attack was over.

Then Bykov looked at the coursograph. The *Takhmasib* was falling. The *Takhmasib* was passing through Jupiter's exosphere, and its velocity was much less than orbital, and it was falling in a narrowing spiral. It had lost speed during the meteorite attack. During meteorite attacks ships always lose speed, since they depart from their course. That is what happens in the asteroid belt during the ordinary Mars-Jupiter or Earth-Jupiter flights. But there it is not dangerous. Here, over Jupe, the loss of speed would mean certain death. The ship would burn up when it hit the leviathan planet's dense layers of atmosphere—that had happened ten years before with Paul Darget. And if it did not burn up, it would fall into an abyss of hydrogen from which there was no return—that had happened, most likely, with Sergei Petryshevsky at the beginning of the year.

The only way to tear loose was with photon drive. Completely automatically Bykov pushed the fluted starter button. But not one light blinked on on the entire control panel. The reflector had been damaged, and the emergency system blocked the impossible command. It's all over now, Bykov thought. He neatly swung the ship around and put the emergency engine on full power. The five-g acceleration pressed him back into his chair. It was the only thing he could do—reduce the speed of fall to a minimum to keep the ship from burning up in the atmosphere. For thirty seconds he sat motionless, staring at his hands, which swelled quickly from the overload. Then he decreased the fuel supply to the engine, and the overload fell off. The emergency engine would gradually slow their fall—while their fuel held out. And there was not that much. Emergency rockets had never yet saved anyone over Jupiter. Over Mars, over Mercury, over Earth—perhaps. But never over the giant planet.

Bykov got up stiffly and looked around. On the floor, amid fragments of plastic, Mikhail Krutikov was lying belly up.

"Mikhail," Bykov called out, speaking for some reason in a whisper. "Are you alive, Mikhail?"

He heard a scratching noise, and Zhilin came crawling out from behind the reactor casing on all fours. Zhilin also looked bad. He looked thoughtfully at the captain, at the navigator, at the ceiling, and sat down, folding his legs.

Bykov made his way over to the navigator and squatted down, bending his legs with difficulty. He touched the navigator on the shoulder and called out once again, "Are you alive, Mikhail?"

Mikhail squinted, and without opening his eyes, licked his lips.

"Alexei," he said in a weak voice.

"Does it hurt anywhere?" Bykov asked and began to check for broken bones.

"Ouch!" the navigator said, and opened his eyes wide.

"What about here?"

"Ugh!" the navigator said in a pained voice.

"And here?"

"Ouch, don't!" the navigator said and sat up, pushed his hands against the floor. His head was tilted toward one shoulder. "Where's Ivan?" he asked.

Bykov looked around. Zhilin wasn't there.

"Ivan," Bykov called out softly.

"Here," Zhilin answered from behind the casing. They heard him drop something and whisper a curse.

"Ivan is alive," Bykov informed the navigator.

"Well, thank God," Mikhail said and grabbing the captain's shoulder, struggled to his feet.

"How are you, Mikhail?" Bykov asked. "Fit to work?"

"Fit enough," the navigator said without any great confidence. "I guess I can handle it."

He looked at Bykov with eyes wide with amazement and said, "How hardy we humans are, Alexei. . . . How hardy!"

"Mmm-yes," Bykov said vaguely. "Hardy. Listen, Mikhail. . . ." He fell silent. "Things are bad. We're falling. If you're fit, sit down and calculate what's happening. The computer is intact, I believe." He glanced at the computer. "However, see for yourself."

Mikhail's eyes became as round as saucers.

"We're falling?" he asked. "Oh, so that's it! We're falling. Onto Jupiter?"

Bykov just nodded.

"Ay-yay-yay, That's all we need! Okay, then. I'll get right to work."

He stood a moment, grimacing and craning his neck, then let go of the captain, and holding onto the edge of the control panel, wobbled over to his seat.

"I'll calculate it right away. Right away."

Bykov watched him, holding his side, plop down in his seat and make himself comfortable. The chair tilted noticeably. Having settled himself, Mikhail suddenly looked at Bykov with an expression of fear and asked, "You have braked, haven't you, Alexei?"

Bykov nodded and walked over to Zhilin, crunched the fragments on the floor. On the ceiling he saw a small black spot and another on the wall itself. They were meteor holes, sealed by a resin plastic. Around the holes large drops of condensed moisture quivered.

Zhilin was sitting cross-legged in front of the reflector controls. The casing was split in half. The sight of the system's insides were not comforting.

"How are things with you?" Bykov said. He could see for himself.

Zhilin raised his puffy face.

"I don't know the details yet," he answered. "But it's obviously been smashed."

Bykov squatted down beside him.

"One meteorite hit," Zhilin said. "And I hit it twice myself." He pointed to the place but it was obvious anyway. "Once at the very beginning with my feet and then at the very end with my head."

"Yes," Bykov said. "No mechanism will take that. Hook up the spare. And I should tell you: We're falling.

"I heard, Captain Bykov," Zhilin said.

"But really," Bykov said thoughtfully, "what's the sense of the control system if the reflector is shattered?"

"But maybe it isn't," Zhilin said.

Bykov looked at him and grinned.

"Our merry-go-round ride," he said, "can be explained by only two causes. Either-or. Either for some reason the plasma ignition point jumped out of focus, or a large piece of the reflector was knocked off. I think the reflector was shattered, because there is no God who could shift the ignition point. But go ahead and try. Hook up the spare."

He stood up and, leaning his head back, inspected the ceiling.

"We still have to cover the holes good and tight. Down there the pressure is great. The resin plastic will be squeezed out. I can do it myself."

He turned to go but stopped and asked softly, "Are you afraid, kid?"

At school the "kids" had been the freshmen—or younger still.

"No," Zhilin said.

"Good. Get to work," Bykov said. "I'll go inspect the ship. I have to go let the passengers out of the shock seats."

Zhilin did not answer. He accompanied the broad, bent back of the captain with his eyes and suddenly saw Varya right alongside. Varya was standing up on her back legs and slowly blinking her protruding eyes. She was all dark blue with white polka dots, and the spines on her muzzle bristled fearfully. That meant that Varya was terribly upset and felt out of sorts. Zhilin had seen her like that once before. It had been a month before, at the Mirza-Charle spaceport, when Yurkovsky spoke at length on the remarkable adaptability of Martian lizards and as proof tossed Varya into a bathtub of steaming water.

Varya convulsively opened her huge gray mouth, then closed it.

"Well, then?" Zhilin asked softly. A large drop fell from the ceiling and—tock!—into the control system. Zhilin looked at the ceiling. Down there the pressure was great. Yes, he thought, down there the pressure is in the tens and hundreds of thousands of atmospheres. The resin plastic corks, of course, would be squeezed out.

Varya squirmed and opened her mouth again. Zhilin groped in his pocket, found a candy, and threw it into her gaping jaws. Varya swallowed slowly and fixed her glassy eyes on him. Zhilin sighed.

"You poor creature!" he whispered.

2. The planetologists are silent, and the radio optician sings a song about swallows.

When the *Takhmasib* stopped somersaulting, Dauge tore himself loose from the breech ring and dragged the unconscious Yurkovsky out from under pieces of equipment. He did not have time to notice what had been broken and what was intact; he noticed only that much had been broken, the shelves with the clips tilted, and the clips spilled out onto the radiotelescope instrument panel. In the observatory compartment it was hot, and there was a strong smell of burning.

Dauge had gotten off relatively lightly. He had immediately latched onto the breach ring, and his only problem was a headache. Yurkovsky was pale, and his eyelids purple. Dauge blew on his face, shook him by the shoulders, slapped his cheeks. Yurkovsky's head wobbled loosely, and he did not regain consciousness. Then Dauge dragged him to the medical compartment. In the corridor it was terribly cold, and frost glittered on the walls. Dauge rested Yurkovsky's head on his knees, scraped some frost off the wall, placed his wet cold fingers against Yurkovsky's temples. At that moment he was caught by the overload—when Bykov began to brake the ship. Dauge lay down on his back, but he felt so bad that he turned over on his stomach and began rubbing his face against the frosted floor. When the overload stopped, Dauge lay for a while, then got to his feet and, holding Yurkovsky under his arm, staggering, went on. But he understood immediately that he would not make it to the med station, so he dragged Yurkovsky into the lounge, dropped him onto the couch, and sat beside him, gasping and trying to catch his breath. Yurkovsky was breathing terribly roughly.

Having rested, Dauge got up and went to the buffet. He took a decanter of water and started drinking straight from the neck. The water ran down his chin, his throat, under his collar, and it was very pleasant. He returned to Yurkovsky and spattered water on his face. Then he set the decanter on the floor and unbuttoned Yurkovsky's jacket. He saw a strange branched design on his skin, running across the chest from shoulder to shoulder. The design was like the silhouette of some fantastic algae—dark purple against tanned skin. For a while Dauge stared blankly at the strange design, then suddenly realized that it was the mark of a strong electrical shock. Apparently Yurkovsky had fallen on an exposed contact with high voltage. All the planetologists' instrumentation operated under high voltage. Dauge ran to the med station.

He had to give Yurkovsky four injections before he would open his eyes. His eyes were dull and blank, but Dauge was very relieved.

"Damn it all anyway, Vladimir," he said, "I thought that things were really bad. How are you? Can you stand up?"

Yurkovsky moved his lips, opened his mouth, and gasped. His eyes focused, and his face assumed a normal expression.

"All right, all right, lie there," Dauge said. "You should lie still a while."

He looked around and saw Charles Mollart in the doorway. He was standing there holding onto the jamb and rocking slightly. His face was red, puffy, and he was all wet and covered with little white icicles. Dauge even thought he saw steam coming from him. Mollart was silent for several minutes, shifting a melancholy glance from Dauge to Yurkovsky and back again, and the planetologists looked at him with concern. Yurkovsky stopped gasping. Then Mollart pitched forward, into the room, and taking short, quick steps, made his way to the nearest chair. He looked wet and unhappy, and when he sat down, the room was filled with the delicious smell of cooked beef. Dauge sniffed.

"The soup?" he inquired.

"*Oui, monsieur*," Mollart said sadly. "*Vermicelle*."

"And how was the soup?" Dauge asked. "Good?"

"Very good," Mollart said and began to pick vermicelli off his clothes.

"I love soup," Dauge clarified. "And am always interested in how."

Mollart sighed and smiled.

"There is no more soup," he said. "It was very hot soup. But it was not boil."

"My God!" Dauge said but still laughed. Mollart laughed, too.

"Yes," he said. "It was very funny but not comfortable, and the soup is gone all."

Yurkovsky wheezed. His face shuddered and turned red. Dauge returned him with alarm.

"Voldemar hurt bad?" Mollart asked. Craning his neck, he looked at Yurkovsky with a wary glance.

"Voldemar received a shock," Dauge said. He was not smiling any more.

"But what happened?" Mollart asked. "It was so uncomfortable. . . ."

Yurkovsky stopped wheezing, sat up, and grinning terribly, began groping in the chest pocket of his jacket.

"What is it?" Dauge asked in confusion.

"Voldemar cannot talk," Mollart said quietly.

Yurkovsky nodded hastily, pulled out a pen and pad, and began writing, his head twitching.

"Calm down, Vladimir," Dauge mumbled. "It will go away soon."

"It will go away," Mollart confirmed. "With me, too, was like it. Was very large current, then everything passed."

Yurkovsky gave the pad to Dauge, lay back, and closed his eyes.

" 'I can't talk,' " Dauge made out with difficulty. Yurkovsky's face twitched impatiently. "Okay, right away. 'How are Alexei and the pilots? How is the ship?' I don't know," Dauge said, dismayed, and looked at the hatch to the control room. "Damn, I forgot about everything."

Yurkovsky shook his head and also looked at the hatch.

"I will find out," Mollart said. "I will learn all right away."

He stood up from his chair, but the hatch burst open and Captain Bykov strode into the lounge, huge, tousled, with an abnormally purple nose and a black-and-blue mark over his right eye. He cast a furious glance at all of them, walked over to the table, spread his feet, leaned his fists on the table and said, "Why aren't you in the shock seats?"

He said it softly, but in such a way that Charles Mollart immediately stopped smiling joyously. A short awkward silence followed, and Dauge grinned uncomfortably and looked away, and Yurkovsky closed his eyes again. Things are bad, Yurkovsky thought. He knew Bykov well.

"When are we going to have discipline on this ship?" Bykov asked.

The passengers did not answer.

"Wise guys," Bykov said with disgust and sat down. "Bedlam. What's the matter with you, Monsieur Mollart?" he asked wearily.

"It is soup," Mollart answered readily. "I will go clean myself."

"Wait, Monsieur Mollart," Bykov said.

"Wh-where are we?" Yurkovsky wheezed.

"Falling," Bykov snapped.

Yurkovsky shuddered and sat up.

"Where to?" he asked. He had been expecting the answer but still shuddered.

"Into Jupiter," Bykov said. He did not look at the planetologists. He looked at Mollart. He felt very sorry for Mollart. Mollart was on his very first spaceflight, and he was eagerly awaited on Amalteia. Mollart was an outstanding radio optician.

"Oh," Mollart said, "to Jupiter?"

"Yes," Bykov said, then fell silent, rubbing the bruise on his forehead. "The reflector is broken. The reflector control is broken. There are eighteen holes in the ship."

"Are we going to burn up?" Dauge asked quickly.

"I still don't know. Mikhail is calculating. Perhaps we won't."

Silence reigned. Then Mollart said, "I will go clean myself."

"Wait, Charles," Bykov said. "Comrades, did you understand what I said? We're falling into Jupiter."

"We understand," Dauge said.

"Now we will fall to Jupiter all our life," Mollart said. Bykov looked at him out of the corner of his eye.

"Well said," Yurkovsky commented.

"*C'est le mot,*" Mollart translated. He smiled. "May I . . . may I now go clean myself?"

"Yes, go ahead," Bykov said slowly.

Mollart turned and left the lounge. The others all watched him leave. They heard him singing in the corridor, in a weak but pleasant voice.

"What's he singing?" Bykov asked. Mollart had never sung before.

Dauge listened closely and began translating: " 'Two swallows kiss outside my starship window. In the vacu-u-u-m. They love each other very much and leaped out there to admire the stars. Tra-la-la. And what business is it of yours?' Something like that."

"Tra-la-la," Bykov said pensively. "That's great."

"Y-you t-translate l-like LIANTO," Yurkovsky said. "A m-masterpiece."

Bykov looked at him in amazement.

"What's the matter, Vladimir?" he asked.

"A p-permanent s-s-stammer," Yurkovsky answered with a grin.

"He received an electrical shock," Dauge said.

Bykov bit his lips.

"It'll be okay," he said. "You're not the first. It's been worse."

He knew that it had never been worse. Not for him, not for the planetologists. From the half-opened hatch Mikhail's voice rang out. "Alexei, it's ready!"

"Come in here," Bykov said.

Mikhail, fat and scratched, burst into the lounge. He was not wearing a shirt and his skin was glistening with perspiration.

"Uh, it's cold in here!" he said, putting his short pudgy arms across his fat chest. "In the control room it's terribly hot."

"Let's have it, Mikhail," Bykov said impatiently.

"But what's the matter with Vladimir?" the navigator asked.

"Come on, come on," Bykov commanded. "He got an electrical shock."

"And where's Charles?" the navigator asked, taking a seat.

"Charles is alive and well," Bykov answered, restraining himself. "Everyone is alive and well. Begin."

"Well thank God for that," the navigator said. "So here it is: I have done a few calculations, and the picture is that the *Takhmasib* is falling, and there is not enough fuel to blast out."

"You don't need calculations to know that," Yurkovsky said, almost smoothly.

"There's not enough. We can blast out only with the photoreactor, but it seems the reflector is broken. But we do have enough fuel to brake. I figured out a program. If the generally accepted theory of Jupiter's composition is correct, we will not burn up."

Dauge wanted to say that there was no generally accepted theory of Jupiter's composition but held his tongue.

"We are braking quite nicely," Mikhail continued. "So I believe we will descend successfully. And there's nothing more we can do, my friends." Mikhail smiled guiltily. "Unless of course, we fix the reflector."

"On Jupiter there are no repair stations. That follows from every theory on Jupiter." Bykov wanted to make sure they understood. Fully. He still felt that they were missing the point.

"What theory do you consider generally accepted?" Dauge asked.

"Kangren's." Bykov stared at the planetologists, biding his time.

"Well," Dauge said. "Kangren's is okay."

Yurkovsky was silent, and stared at the ceiling.

"You planetologists"—Bykov could no longer resist—"are experts—what will it be like down there? Can you tell us?"

"Yes, of course," Dauge said. "We'll tell you very soon."

"When?" Bykov came to life.

"When we get there, down below," Dauge said. He laughed.

"You planetologists," Bykov said, "are real ex-perts."

"We have to calculate," Yurkovsky said, staring at the ceiling. He spoke slowly and smoothly. "Let Mikhail calculate the depth at which the ship will stop falling and start hanging suspended."

"Yes," Dauge said. "What will the pressure be? Maybe we'll just be crushed."

"It's not that simple," Bykov muttered. "Two hundred thousand atmospheres we can take. And the photon reactor and the rockets' hulls much more."

Yurkovsky sat up and crossed his legs.

"Kangren's theory is no worse than the others," he said. "It will give the order of magnitude." He looked at the navigator. "We could calculate it ourselves, but you have the computer."

"Of course," Mikhail said. "Not worth mentioning."

Bykov asked, "Mikhail, give me the program. I'll look it over. Then enter it. Into the cybernavigator."

"I already did, Alexei," the navigator answered guiltily.

"Ah," Bykov said. "Well, okay then." He stood up. "So then. Now everything is clear. We won't be crunched, but we can't go back—let's say so up front. Well, we aren't the first. We've lived well, and we'll die well. I'll try something with Zhilin to get the reflector working, but that is . . ." He grimaced and rubbed his swollen nose. "What do you plan on doing?"

"Observing," Yurkovsky said in a hard voice.

Dauge nodded.

"Very good." Bykov glanced at them furtively. "I have a request. Keep an eye out for Mollart."

"Yes," Mikhail agreed.

"He's new to this, and . . . when bad things happen . . . you know how it is."

"Okay, Alexei," Dauge said, smiling in a chipper way. "Put your mind at ease."

"Mikhail," Bykov said, "go into the control room and do the calculations, and I'll go to the med station and get my side massaged. I really hit it hard."

As he left he heard Dauge talking to Yurkovsky: "In a certain sense, we've been lucky, Vladimir. We'll see things no one has ever seen. Let's go fix the equipment."

"Let's go," Yurkovsky repeated.

You can't fool me, Bykov thought. You still haven't understood. You still hope. You think: Alexei got us out of the Black Sands of Golkonda, Alexei got us out of the rotting swamps, so Alexei will get us out of this hydrogen grave. Dauge undoubtedly believes it. And will Alexei get you out? Could it be that Alexei actually will get you out?

In the med station Mollart, wincing from the pain, was applying an ointment. His face and his hands were red and shiny. Seeing Bykov, he smiled politely and broke out singing about the swallows: He had almost calmed down. If he had started singing, Bykov would have thought that he had calmed down for real. But Mollart sang loudly and carefully, hissing from pain from time to time.

3. *The flight engineer indulges in memories, and the navigator counsels him against doing so.*

Zhilin was repairing the reflector control system. In the control room it was very hot and stuffy—the air-conditioning had apparently been thrown out of whack, but there was no time to worry about it. At first Zhilin took off his jacket, then his jumpsuit, working in just his shorts and undershirt. Varya curled up on his clothes and soon disappeared—only her shadow remained; from time to time her large protruding eyes would appear, then disappear.

One by one Zhilin took the printed circuits out of the system, saved the good ones and put the bad ones aside, replacing them spares. He worked methodically, unhurriedly, as during a final examination, because there was no need to rush, and the whole thing was apparently pointless. He tried not to think about anything and just be happy that he remembered the circuits very well, that he hardly had to look at the manual, that he had not been hurt too badly, and the cuts on his head had stopped bleeding and did not hurt at all. On the other side of the photoreactor the computer was humming. Mikhail rustled papers and hummed something unmusical under his breath. Mikhail always did that when he was working.

I wonder what he's working on, Zhilin thought. Perhaps he's just trying to distract himself. That is very good—to be able to distract yourself at such a time. The planetologists were most likely working too, tossing out the bomb probes. And I've never had a chance to see so many things. For example, they say that Jupiter is very beautiful from Amalteia. And I always wanted to take part in an interstellar expedition or in one of the Pathfinders' missions—the scientists who search for traces of the Visitors on other worlds. . . . Then, they say that on J-Station there are great girls, and it would be nice to get to know them, and then tell Pierre Hunt about it— he was assigned to lunar runs and was glad about it, the nut. It's funny, Mikhail is hypocritical. He has a wife and two, no, three, children, and the oldest daughter is sixteen—he kept promising to introduce us and would wink knowingly, but now it will never happen. There's a lot that will never happen. Father will be very upset—oh, that's very bad. How mixed up the whole thing is! During my first real flight. It's a good thing I quarreled with her, Zhilin suddenly thought. Now it's simpler, but it might have been very complicated. Mikhail is worse off than I am. And so is the captain. The captain has a wife—a very beautiful woman, happy, and very intelligent. She saw him off, never suspecting a thing—or maybe she did, but you couldn't tell. Most likely she wasn't worried because she was used to it. A person can get used to anything. I, for example, got used to overloads, even though at first they made me sick, and I even thought I would be transferred to the automatic control division. At the school that was called "being sent to the little girls": There were a lot of girls in that department, and things were always fun with them, but being transferred was still a disgrace. Completely incomprehensible why. The girls went to work on different Sats and on stations and bases on various planets and did not do worse work than the men. Sometimes even better. All the same, Zhilin thought, it's a good thing we quarreled. What would she feel like now?

He stared blankly at the cracked surface of the printed circuit he was holding in his hand.

. . . We kissed in Bolshoi Park and then on the quai under the white statues, and I walked her home, and we kissed for a long time in the entryway, and people kept going in and out, although it was late. And she was afraid that her mother would come up and ask, "What are you doing, Valya, and who is this young man?" It was in the summer, during the white nights. And then I came home for winter vacation, and we met again, and it was just like before, only snow lay in the park and the bare branches waved against the gray sky. A wind starting blowing, whirling the new-fallen snow, and we were frozen and went to warm up in the café on Interplanetary Street. We were very happy when there was no one there, sat by the window and watched the cars passing by. I argued with her, said that I knew all the different makes of cars—and was wrong. This great, low-built car came by, and I didn't know what it was. I ran out and someone told me it was a Golden Dragon, a new Chinese atomcar. We argued to beat the band. Then it seemed that it was the most important thing, that it always be—winter and summer, and on the quai under the white statues, and in Bolshoi Park, and in the theater where she was so beautiful in her black dress with the white collar and kept poking me in the side to stop me from laughing so loud. But once she didn't come when we had a date, and I talked to her on the videophone, and she didn't come again and stopped writing me letters when I went back to school. I still didn't believe it and kept writing long letters, stupid letters, very stupid, although I didn't know it then. And a year later I saw her again. She was with a girlfriend and didn't recognize me. I thought then I was over it, but it lasted until my final year in school, and I don't even know why I'm thinking about it now. Probably because it doesn't matter anymore. I could not think about it, but since it doesn't matter. . . .

The hatch slammed. Bykov's voice said, "Well, Mikhail?"

"We're finishing the first circuit, Alexei. We fell five hundred kilometers."

"So. . . ." They could hear plastic fragments snapping underfoot. "So that's the story. There isn't any radio contact with Amalteia, of course."

"The receiver is silent," Mikhail said with a sigh. "The transmitter is working, but the radio storms here are. . . ."

"How are your calculations coming?"

"Almost finished, Alexei. It looks like we will fall about six or seven megameters and then hang. We will float, as Vladimir says. The pressure is enormous, but we won't be crushed, that's clear. Only it's going to be hard—the force of gravity is going to be two and one-half g's."

"Oof," Bykov said. He was silent a while, then said, "Do you have any ideas?"

"What?"

"I said, do you have any ideas? About getting out of here?"

"Come on, Alexei," the navigator said affectionately, almost ingratiatingly. "What kind of ideas could I have? This is Jupiter. I've never heard of anyone . . . getting out."

A long silence set in. Zhilin once again set to work, quickly and noiselessly. Then Mikhail said suddenly, "Don't reminisce about her, Alexei. It's better not to, you'll just feel lousy—"

"I wasn't reminiscing," Bykov said in an unpleasant tone. "And I wouldn't if I were you, either. . . ." Then he yelled, "Ivan!"

"Yes?" Zhilin answered, hurrying.

"Are you still messing around?"

"I'll finish in a minute."

Zhilin could hear the captain kicking the plastic fragments as he walked over.

"Garbage," he muttered. "A pigsty. A madhouse."

He walked around the casing and squatted down next to Zhilin.

"I'll be finished in a minute," Zhilin repeated.

"Don't rush, Flight Engineer Zhilin," Bykov said angrily.

Bykov breathed heavily and began to pull spare parts out of the box. Zhilin edged over to make room for him. They were both broad, huge, and it was a tight fit in front of the system. They worked in silence and quickly, and they could hear Mikhail turn on the computer again and hum.

When the repair was finished, Bykov called out, "Mikhail, come here." He straightened up and wiped the sweat from his forehead. Then he pushed away a pile of broken circuit boards with his foot and turned on the general control system. On the screen a three-dimensional plan of the reflection could be seen. The picture turned slowly.

"Oy-yoy-yoy," Mikhail groaned.

A blue printout tape crawled out of the output.

"But there aren't many micropunctures," Zhilin said softly.

"To hell with the micropunctures," Bykov said and bent over the screen. "There's the real son of a bitch!"

The plan of the reflector was drawn in a dark blue color. White spots designated tears, places where the mesomatter layers had been pierced or where the control cells had been destroyed. There were many white spots, and on one edge of the reflector they fused into a large white smudge that covered no less than an eighth of the paraboloid's surface.

Mikhail threw up his hands and returned to the computer.

Zhilin reached out for his jumpsuit, shook Varya out of it and began to dress: The control room was cold again. Bykov was still standing there staring at the screen and biting his nails. Then he picked up the printout tape and glanced through it.

"Zhilin," he said suddenly. "Take two sigma testers. Check the power supply, and go into the caisson. "I'll wait for you there. Mikhail, drop everything and work on reinforcing the holes. Drop everything, I said."

"Where are you going, Alexei?" Mikhail asked in amazement.

"Outside," Bykov snapped, and walked out.

"Why?" Mikhail asked, turning to Zhilin.

Zhilin shrugged his shoulders. He did not know why. Repairing a mirror in space, while in flight, without expert mesochemists, without huge crystallizators, without reactor furnaces was simply unthinkable. Just as unthinkable as, for example, pulling the moon toward the Earth with your bare hands. And as it was, in this condition, with the broken edge, the reflector could give the *Takhmasib* only rotational motion. Like during the accident.

"It's crazy," Zhilin said indecisively.

He looked at Mikhail, and Mikhail looked at him. They said nothing, and then they both started to rush like mad. Mikhail gathered all his papers in a burst and said hurriedly, "Well, go on. Go on, Ivan, get a move on."

In the caisson Bykov and Zhilin climbed into spacesuits and with some difficulty squeezed into the elevator. The elevator box plunged down along the photoreactor pipe, on which all of the ship's components were strung— from the living gondola to the parabolic reflector.

"Good," Bykov said.

"What's good?" Zhilin asked.

The elevator stopped.

"It's good that the elevator is working," Bykov answered.

"Ah," Zhilin sighed in disappointment.

"It might not have," Bykov said sternly. "Just try crawling two hundred meters there and back."

They went out of the elevator shaft and stopped on the top platform of the paraboloid. Beneath them the reflector's black ribbed cupola sloped away gently. The reflector was enormous—seven hundred fifty meters wide and five hundred across. Its edges were not visible from where they were standing. Above their heads hung the huge silvery disk of the freight section. Along its sides, held out far from the surface by supports, were the hydrogen rockets, whose apertures were fluttering with a soundless blue flame. And all around a strange and threatening world glittered.

A wall of brown fog extended on the left. Far below, at an unimaginable depth, the fog separated into thick, taut layers of clouds with black clear bands between them. Even farther and even deeper these clouds fused into a solid dark brown smoothness. On the right stood a solid pink haze, and Zhilin suddenly saw the sun—a blinding bright-pink tiny disk.

"Let's get going," Bykov said. He handed Zhilin a coil of thin rope. "Fasten it to the shaft," he said.

On the other end of the rope he tied a loop and tightened it around his waist. Then he hung both testers around his neck and dangled one leg over the railing.

"Let it out little by little," he said. "I'm off."

Zhilin stood next to the railing, holding onto the rope with both hands, and watched the fat clumsy figure in the shining suit crawl slowly over the surface of the cupola. The suit reflected a pinkish light, and motionless pink reflections also lay on the black cupola.

"Let it out faster," Bykov's angry voice said in the helmet phone.

The figure in the suit disappeared, and on the ribbed surface only the shining taut thread of the rope remained. Zhilin began to look at the sun. Sometimes the pink disk was overcast—then it became even sharper in outline and completely red. Zhilin looked down beneath his feet and saw his dim pinkish shadow on the platform.

"Look, Ivan," Bykov's voice said. "Look below!"

Zhilin looked. Far below, a gigantic whitish mound floated out of the smooth brown surface; it resembled a puffball. It slowly spread out to the sides, and Zhilin could make out a streaming, twisting pattern, like a tangle of snakes.

"An exosphere protuberance," Bykov said. "Very rare, it seems. Damn it anyway, the guys should see this."

He meant the planetologists. The mound suddenly shone from the inside with a trembling lilac light.

"Ooh," Zhilin said involuntarily.

"Let it out," Bykov said.

Zhilin let out some more rope, keeping his eyes on the protuberance. At first it seemed to him that the *Takhmasib* was flying straight into it, but after a minute he realized that the ship would pass it by on the left. The protuberance tore loose from the smooth brown surface and floated into the pinkish haze, dragging behind it a sticky tail of yellow translucent threads. In the threads a violet glow flared up, then died out. The protuberance dissolved into the pink light.

Bykov worked for a long time. Several times he came back up to the platform, rested a while, and then went back down, each time choosing a different direction. When he climbed up the third time he had only one tester. "Dropped it," he said. Zhilin patiently let out rope, braced his leg against the railing. In that position he felt very stable and could look from side to side. But nothing changed on the sides. Only when the captain came up for the sixth time and barked, "Enough, let's go," did Zhilin suddenly realize that the brown foggy wall on the left—the cloudy surface of Jupiter—was now noticeably closer.

The control room was clean. Mikhail had swept up the fragments and was now sitting in his usual place, in a fur jacket over his jumpsuit. Steam was coming from his mouth—the room was cold. Bykov sat down in a chair, rested his hands on his knees, and looked intently first at the navigator, then at Zhilin. The navigator and Zhilin both waited.

"Did you reinforce the holes?" Bykov asked Mikhail.

Mikhail nodded several times.

"There's a chance," Bykov said and cleared his throat. "Sixteen percent of the reflector is out of order. The question then is, can we get the other eighty-four percent to work? Even less than eighty-four percent, because ten percent can't be controlled—the system of control cells was destroyed."

The navigator and Zhilin were silent, craning their necks.

"We might," Bykov said. "In any case, we can try. We have to shift the plasma ignition point so that it compensates for the asymmetry of the damage reflector."

"That's clear," Zhilin said in a quavering voice.

Bykov looked at him.

"It's our only chance. Ivan and I will work on the reorientation of the magnetic traps. Ivan is fully capable of the work. You, Mikhail, will compute the new position of the ignition point in accordance with the plan of the damage. You'll get the plan right away. It's a crazy job, but it is our only chance."

He looked at the navigator, and Mikhail raised his head and crossed glances with him. They understood each other immediately and completely. That they might not make it in time. That down below, under enormous pressure, corrosion would eat away at the hull and the ship could dissolve before they finished the work. That it was impossible to compensate for the asymmetry totally. That no one had ever tried to save a ship with similar compensation, with an engine that was weakened at least by half.

"It's our only chance," Bykov said loudly.

"I'll do it, Alexei," Mikhail said. "It's not that difficult—to compute a new ignition point. I'll do it."

"I'll give you a plan of the dead sections right away," Bykov repeated. "And we have to rush like hell. Soon overload will begin, and it will be very hard to work. And if we fall too deep, it will be dangerous to turn on the engine, because a chain reaction in the condensed hydrogen is possible." He paused, then added, "And we would be gassified."

"It's clear," Zhilin said. He wanted to begin that very minute.

Mikhail reached out with his short arms and said in a high-pitched voice, "The plan, Alexei, the plan."

Three red lights blinked on the emergency control panel.

"Well," Mikhail said. "The emergency rockets are running out of fuel."

"To hell with them," Bykov said and stood up.

3. IN THE ABYSS

1. *The planetologists find diversion, and the navigator is convicted of smuggling.*

"Load," Yurkovsky said.

He was hanging by the periscope, poking his face against the chamois lens frame. He was hanging horizontally, his stomach down, his elbows and legs spread wide, and alongside him a thick observation journal and a pen floated in air. Mollart exuberantly threw open the breech cover, pulled a clip of bomb probes from the shelves, and nudging it from the top and the bottom, with difficulty got it into the rectangular opening of the firing chamber. The clip slid slowly and soundlessly into place. Mollard closed the cover, clicked the lock, and said, "Ready, Voldemar."

Mollart held up well under weightlessness. True, he sometimes made careless movements and ended up on the ceiling, and then he would have to be pulled back down, and sometimes he felt nauseous, but for a newcomer to space he held up very well.

"Ready," Dauge said from the exosphere spectrograph.

"Fire," Yurkovsky commanded.

Dauge pushed the button. *Du-du-du-du*, came a muffled rumbling from the bomb release. And that was followed immediately by the *tk-tk-tk* of the spectrograph shutter. Through the periscope Yurkovsky saw white clumps of flame flash one after the other, then flew upward in the orange mist that the *Takhmasib* was now passing through. Twenty flashes, twenty burst bomb probes carrying meson irradiators.

"Great," Yurkovsky said softly.

The pressure outside was growing. The bomb probes exploded closer and closer. They slowed down all too soon.

Dauge spoke loudly into the dictaphone, glancing from time to time at the spectroanalyzer dials: "Molecular hydrogen—eighty-one and thirty-five, helium—seven and eleven, methane—four and sixteen, ammonia—one zero one. . . . The nonidentified line is increasing. . . . I told them: Put in an automatic counter, it's very inconvenient this way."

"We're falling," Yurkovsky said. "We're really falling. . . . The methane reading is only four."

Dauge, turning dexterously, took readings from the equipment.

"So far Kangren is right," he said. "Look, the bathymeter has already stopped working. The pressure is three hundred atmospheres. We're not going to be able to measure the pressure anymore."

"Okay," Yurkovsky said. "Load."

"Is it worth it?" Dauge asked. "The bathymeter isn't working. The synchronization will be destroyed."

"Let's try," Yurkovsky said. "Load."

He glanced at Mollart. Mollart was gently rocking back and forth along the ceiling, smiling sadly.

"Pull him down, Grigory," Yurkovsky said.

Dauge got to his knees, grabbed Mollart by the feet and pulled him down.

"Charles," he said patiently. "Don't make sudden movements. Plant your feet here and be careful."

Mollart sighed painfully and opened the cover. The empty clip floated out of the chamber, struck him in the chest, and flew slowly to Yurkovsky. Yurkovsky dodged it.

"Oh, again," Mollart said guiltily. "Forgive me, Voldemar. Oh, this weightlessness!"

"Load, load," Yurkovsky said.

"The sun," Dauge said suddenly.

Yurkovsky pressed himself against the periscope. In the orange cloud a dim disk appeared for several seconds.

"That's the last time," Dauge said.

"You said already three times 'last time,' " Mollart said, closing the cover. He bent over, checking the lock. "Farewell, sun, as Captain Nemo said. But that was not the last time. I am ready, Voldemar."

"So am I," Dauge said. "But maybe we should quit?"

Bykov entered the observatory compartment, scraping the floor with his magnetic soles.

"Finish your work," he said gloomily.

"Why?" Yurkovsky asked, turning around.

"Enormous pressure outside. Another half hour, and your bombs will be blowing up right here."

"Fire," Yurkovsky said hurriedly. Dauge hesitated a moment but still pressed the button. Bykov waited until the *du-du-du-du* was over, then said, "That's enough. Fasten down all the testers. This thing"—he pointed to the bomb release—"has to be blocked up. And do it right."

"Are periscope observations still permitted?" Yurkovsky asked.

"The periscope is fine," Bykov said. "Enjoy your diversion."

He turned and walked out. Dauge said, "Well, it's like I said—we got nothing. No synchronization."

He turned off the apparatus and began taking the reel out of the dictaphone.

"Dauge," Yurkovsky said. "I think Alexei has come up with something—what do you think?"

"I don't know," Dauge said and looked at him. "Why do you think so?"

"He has this special look," Yurkovsky said. "I know him."

For a moment everyone was silent. Only Mollart inhaled deeply—he was feeling nauseous. Then Dauge said, "I'm hungry. Where's the soup, Charles? You spilled the soup, and we are hungry. Whose turn is it today, Charles?"

"It's me," Mollart said. The mention of food made him even more nauseous. But he said, "I will go and prepare a new soup."

"The sun!" Yurkovsky said.

Dauge pressed his blackened eye to the videosearch eyepiece. "Sun again."

"It's not the sun," Dauge said.

"Right," Yurkovsky said. "I can't think it's the sun."

A distant patch of light in the light-brown murk became pale and, swelling, broke up into gray spots, then disappeared. Yurkovsky watched, his teeth clenched. Farewell, sun, he thought. Farewell.

"I'm hungry," Dauge said angrily. "Let's go to the galley, Charles."

He agilely pushed himself away from the wall, floated to the door, and opened it. Mollart also pushed off but hit his head against the doorway. Dauge caught him by the arm and pulled him out into the corridor. Yurkovsky heard Dauge ask, "How's life, *bon*?" Mollart answered, "Very good, but uncomfortable." "It's okay," Dauge said in a cheerful voice. "You'll get used to it soon."

It's okay, Yurkovsky thought, soon it will all be over. He glanced through the periscope. He could see that above, from where the ship was falling, the brown fog was getting denser, but below, out of the unimaginable depths, out of the bottomless depths of the hydrogen abyss, a strange pink light was sputtering. Then Yurkovsky closed his eyes. To live, he thought. To live long. To live forever. He pressed both hands against the side of his head and narrowed his eyes. To be deaf, to be blind, to be numb—

but to live. To feel the sun and wind on your skin, and have a friend near you. Pain, weakness, pity. Like now. He pulled his hair hard. Just like now, only forever. Suddenly he heard himself breathing noisily and came to. The sensation of an unbearable, insane horror and desperation had disappeared. That's the way it had been before—twelve years ago on Mars, and ten years ago on Golkonda, and the year before last on Mars again. An attack of a desire to live, a dark and ancient desire, as old as protoplasm itself. Like a brief fainting spell. But it was passing. It had to be endured, like pain. And you had to get busy with something. Alexei had ordered them to fasten down the testers. He took his hands away from his face, opened his eyes, and saw that he was sitting on the floor. The fall of the *Takhmasib* had been halted, and things had acquired weight.

Yurkovsky reached out to the small control panel and pushed the button to fasten down the testers. Then he carefully blocked up the bomb release, gathered the discarded clips from the bomb probes and put them neatly in the shelving. He glanced through the periscope and it seemed to him— and undoubtedly was the case—that the darkness above had become thicker, and the pink glow below, stronger. He thought about the fact that no person had ever been so deep into Jupiter before, except, perhaps, for Sergei Petryshevsky—may his memory be blessed—but he probably exploded before this. His reflector was also broken.

He walked out into the corridor and headed for the lounge, glancing on the way into all the cabins. The *Takhmasib* was still falling, but with every minute more slowly, and Yurkovsky started tiptoeing, as though he were under water, maintaining his balance with his arms and from time to time taking involuntary hops.

In the deserted corridor Mollart's muffled shriek suddenly resounded, similar to a war cry: "How is life, Grégoire? Good?" Apparently Dauge had succeeded in restoring the radio optician's usual mood. Yurkovsky could not make out Dauge's reply. "*Bon*," he muttered. And he did feel good.

He looked in Mikhail's cabin. It was dark and there was a strange spicy aroma. Yurkovsky went in and turned on the light. In the middle of the cabin lay a smashed suitcase. Yurkovsky had never seen a suitcase in such a sorry state. A suitcase would look like that if a bomb probe had gone off inside. The dull-colored ceiling and walls were smeared with a brown slippery-looking substance. The smudges gave off an appetizing, spicy aroma. Spiced midia, Yurkovsky immediately determined. He was very fond of spiced midia, but it was strictly forbidden for all interplanetaries. He looked around and saw over the door a shining black spot—a meteorite hole. All the sections in the living gondola were hermetic. In case of a meteorite attack the air supply was automatically cut off until the resin plastic—a gooey and strong layer on the hull—had closed up the hole. That required one, at most two, seconds, but during that time the pressure in the section could fall drastically. It was not dangerous to humans but fatal to smuggled canned goods, which simply exploded. Especially expensive canned goods. Smuggled goods, Yurkovsky thought. The old glutton. Well, you're going to get it from the captain. Bykov could not tolerate smugglers.

Yurkovsky looked the cabin over one more time and noticed that the black hole had a slight tinge of silver. Aha, he thought. Someone has already metalized the hole. True, at these pressures the plastic stopper would have been blown out otherwise. He turned off the light and returned to the corridor. And then he felt weariness, a leaden weight in all his body. Oh, damn, how soft I've gotten! he thought, and suddenly felt the microphone cord cutting into his neck. He realized what was happening. The flight was coming to an end. Within a few minutes there would be double gravity, and there would be ten thousand kilometers of condensed hydrogen overhead, while below there would be sixty thousand kilometers of very dense liquid hydrogen. Each kilogram of your body would weigh two kilograms, and even a little more. Poor Charles, Yurkovsky thought. Poor Mikhail.

"Voldemar," Mollart called to him from behind. "Voldemar, help us take the soup. A very heavy soup."

Yurkovsky glanced around. Dauge and Mollart, red and sweaty, were pushing an unwieldy, wobbling table on wheels out the galley door. On the table were three barely steaming pots. Yurkovsky went toward them and suddenly felt that he had become heavy. Mollart groaned softly and sat on the floor. The *Takhmasib* came to a halt. The *Takhmasib*, its crew, its passengers, and its freight, had reached its last stop.

2. *The planetologists torment the navigator, and the radio optician torments the planetologists.*

"Who cooked this meal?" Bykov asked.

He looked around at everyone and then fixed his eyes on the pots again. Mikhail was breathing with difficulty, whistling, resting his chest against the table. His face was scarlet, puffy.

"I did," Mollart said, not very boldly.

"What's the matter with it?" Dauge asked.

All their voices were hoarse. They all spoke with difficulty, barely squeezing the words out. Mollart smiled awkwardly and lay face up on the couch.

He felt terrible. The ship was not falling anymore, and the gravity had become unbearable. Bykov looked at Mollart.

"This meal will kill you," he said. "Eat this meal and you will never get up again. It will crush you, do you understand?"

"Oh, damn," Dauge said with annoyance. "I forgot about the gravity."

Mollart was lying with closed eyes and was breathing heavily. His jaw was sagging.

"Let's eat the bouillon," Bykov said. "And that's all. Not a bite more." He looked at Mikhail and bared his teeth in a glum grin. "Not a bite," he repeated.

Yurkovsky took the ladle and began dishing out the bouillon.

"A heavy meal," he said.

"It smells good," Mikhail said. "Could you dish me just a little more, Vladimir?"

"Enough," Bykov said firmly. He slowly sipped the bouillon, his spoon in his fist like a small child.

They began eating. Mollart raised himself with difficulty, then lay back down.

"I can't," he said. "Forgive me, I can't."

Bykov put down his spoon and stood up.

"I suggest that all passengers remain in the shock seats," he said. Dauge shook his head no. "As you wish. But be sure to put Mollart in one."

"All right," Yurkovsky said.

Dauge took a dish, sat down on the couch next to Mollart, and began to feed him with the spoon, like an invalid. Mollart swallowed noisily, without opening his eyes.

"And where's Ivan?" Yurkovsky asked.

"On watch," Bykov answered. He took the pot with the leftover soup and went toward the hatch, walking heavily on stiff legs. Yurkovsky, biting his lips, looked at his bent back.

"That's all, my friends," Mikhail said in a pitiful voice. "I'm beginning to lose weight. But I won't make it. Right now I weigh over two hundred kilograms. And it will get worse. We are still falling slightly."

He leaned back in his chair and put his puffy hands on his stomach. Then he turned slightly, put his hands on the arm of the chair, and almost immediately went to sleep.

"He's sleeping, the fat man," Dauge said. "The ship is going down, and the navigator is sleeping. Come on, Charles. Another spoonful. For Papa. That's the way. And now one for Mama."

"I can't, forgive me," Mollart babbled. "I can't. I will lie." He stretched out and began to mutter indistinctly in French.

Dauge put the spoon down on the table.

"Mikhail," he called out softly. "Mikhail."

Mikhail responded with a thunderous snore.

"I'll wake him," Yurkovsky said. "Mikhail," he said furtively. "Midia. Spiced midia."

Mikhail shuddered and woke up.

"What?" he asked. "What?"

"A guilty conscience," Yurkovsky said.

Dauge fixed his eyes on the navigator.

"What have you been doing in your cabin?" he asked.

Mikhail blinked his red eyes, then fidgeted in his chair. He said barely audibly, "Ah, I completely forgot," and tried to stand up.

"Sit," Dauge said.

"So what have you been doing there?" Yurkovsky asked.

"Nothing unusual," Mikhail said and glanced at the hatch to the control room. "Really, nothing, guys. It was just—"

"Mikhail," Yurkovsky said. "Come clean."

"Talk, fat man," Dauge said truculently.

The navigator once again tried to get up.

"Sit," Yurkovsky said pitilessly. "Midia. Spiced midia. Talk."

Mikhail turned lobster red.

"We're not children anymore," Dauge said. "We faced death before. Why in hell the big secret?"

"There's a chance," the navigator mumbled.

"There's always a chance," Dauge objected. "More specifically?"

"An infinitesimal chance," Mikhail said. "Really, it's time for me to go, guys."

"What are they doing?" Dauge asked. "What are they up to, Alexei and Ivan?"

Mikhail looked at the hatch with anguish.

"He doesn't want to say anything to you," he whispered. "He doesn't want to give you false hopes. Alexei hopes to blast out. They're retuning the magnetic trap system. . . . Leave me alone, please!" he shouted in a high, piercing voice, somehow got to his feet, and wobbled into the control room.

"*Mon Dieu*, Mollart said softly and turned face down.

"Ah, it's all nonsense, just busywork," Dauge said. "Of course, Bykov is incapable of sitting around doing nothing when the evil one has us in his power. Let's go. Come on, Charles, we'll put you in the shock seat. Captain's orders."

They took Mollart by the arms, lifted him up, and led him out into the corridor. His head wobbled.

"*Mon Dieu*," he mumbled. "Forgive me. I am very terrible interplanetary. I am only *radio-optique*."

It was very hard for them to walk themselves and support Mollart, but they managed to get him to his cabin and tuck him away in his shock seat. He lay there in a much too large box, small, pitiable, gasping, with a bluish face.

"You'll feel better soon, Charles," Dauge said.

Yurkovsky nodded and then winced from pain in his back.

"Lie there and rest," he said.

"*Bon*," Mollart said. "Thank you, comrades."

Dauge pulled down the cover and knocked. Mollart knocked in response.

"Well, okay," Dauge said. "We should get into our overload costumes ourselves."

Yurkovsky went to the exit. The ship had only three overload suits—for the crew. The passengers were supposed to get into their shock seats.

They went through all the cabins and gathered all the blankets and pillows. In the observatory they set themselves up by the periscope, spreading soft things on all sides, and then lay down and rested in silence. It was hard to breathe. A huge barbell seemed to be resting on their chests.

"I remember them giving us heavy overloads back in school," Yurkovsky said. "You had to lose weight."

"Yes," Dauge said. "I had forgotten. What was that nonsense about spiced midia?"

"A very tasty treat, isn't it?" Yurkovsky said. "Our navigator snuck several jars on board behind the captain's back, and they exploded in his suitcase."

"So?" Dauge said. "Again? What a treat? What a smuggler! He's lucky Bykov doesn't have time for that now."

"I don't think Bykov knows yet," Yurkovsky said.

And never would, he thought. They were silent, then Dauge took the observation journal and began going through it. They calculated for a while, then argued about the meteorite attack. Dauge said that it was a random swarm. Yurkovsky declared that it was a ring. "A ring around Jupiter?" Dauge said condescendingly. "Yes," Yurkovsky said. "I've suspected it for a long time." "No," Dauge said. "It still wouldn't be a ring. A semiring, perhaps." "Well, a semiring then," Yurkovsky agreed. "Kangren's work is great," Dauge said. "His calculations are remarkably accurate." "Not entirely," Yurkovsky said. "Why is that?" Dauge inquired. "Because the temperature increases noticeably more slowly," Yurkovsky explained. "It's internal luminescence of a nonclassical variety," Dauge objected. "Yes, nonclassical," Yurkovsky said. "Kangren could not take that into account," Dauge said. "You have to take it into account," Yurkovsky said. "They've been arguing about it for a hundred years—you can't ignore it." "You're just ashamed," Dauge said. "You had a real brawl with Kangren in Dublin, and now you're ashamed." "Blockhead!" Yurkovsky said. "I took the nonclassical effects into consideration." "I know," Dauge said. "So if you know," Yurkovsky said, "don't talk nonsense." "Don't yell at me," Dauge said. "It's not nonsense. You took nonclassical effects into consideration, but look at the price you paid." "What price do you mean?" Yurkovsky exploded. "You still haven't read my last article!" "Okay," Dauge said, "don't get mad. My back feels numb." "So does mine," Yurkovsky said. He turned over onto his stomach and climbed up on all fours. It was not easy. He made it to the periscope and looked out.

"Take a look," he said.

They began looking through the periscope. The *Takhmasib* was floating in an emptiness filled with pink light. Not a single object was visible, no motion, nothing your gaze could settle on. Only an even pink light. You seemed to be staring at a phosphorescent screen. After a long silence Yurkovsky said, "It's boring."

He fluffed up the pillows and lay down on his back again.

"No one has ever seen it before," Dauge said. "It's the luminescence of metallic hydrogen."

"Observations like that," Yurkovsky said, "aren't worth a plugged nickel. Maybe we should hook up the spectrograph to the periscope?"

"That's foolish," Dauge said, barely able to move his lips. He crawled onto the pillows and lay down on his back. "It's a shame," he said. "After all, no one has ever seen it before."

"What a rotten thing it is to do nothing," Yurkovsky said with sadness. Dauge suddenly propped himself up on his elbow and tilted his head, listening. "What's up?" Yurkovsky asked.

"Quiet," Dauge said. "Listen."

Yurkovsky listened. A low roar reached them from somewhere, growing in waves and then dying down, like the buzz of a giant bee. The roar turned into a drone, became higher, then stopped.

"What is it?" Dauge asked.

"I don't know," Yurkovsky answered. He sat up. "Could it be the engine?"

"No, it's from that direction," Dauge said, waving his hand at the periscope. "Well now. . . ." He listened, and once again the increasing drone could be heard.

"We'll have to look," Dauge said. The giant bee was silent but started in again a moment later. Dauge got to his knees and stuck his face against the periscope. "Look!" he shouted.

Yurkovsky crawled to the periscope.

"Look how beautiful!" Dauge shouted.

Enormous rainbow spheres rose up out of the yellow-pink abyss. They resembled soap bubbles and shone green, blue, red. It was very beautiful and totally incomprehensible. The spheres rose out of the chasm with a low but increasing roar, raced by quickly, and disappeared from view. They all varied in size, and Dauge frantically reached for the rangefinder. One sphere, especially huge and fluttering, passed by quite close. For several instants the observatory was filled by an unbearably low, nagging drone, and the ship rocked slightly.

"Hello, observatory," Bykov's voice came over the loudspeaker. "What is that out there?"

"Phenomena," Yurkovsky said, leaning his head to the microphone.

"What?" Bykov asked.

"Some kind of bubbles," Yurkovsky explained.

"I can see that for myself," Bykov roared.

"It's not metallic hydrogen," Yurkovsky said.

The bubbles disappeared.

"So then," Dauge said. "Diameters of five hundred, nine hundred, and three thousand three hundred meters. Unless of course the perspective here is distorted. That's all I managed. What could it be?"

Two more bubbles flashed by in the pink emptiness. A low bass sound intensified, then ceased.

"The planet seems to be in working order," Yurkovsky said. "And we will never find out what is going on."

"Bubbles in gas," Dauge said. "Although, some gas! Its density is more like benzine."

He turned around. Mollart was sitting in the doorway, leaning his head against the jamb. The skin on his face drooped toward his chin because of the gravity. His forehead was white and his neck cherry red.

"Here is I," Mollart said.

He rolled over onto his stomach and crawled to his place by the bomb release. The planetologists watched in silence, then Dauge stood up, took two pillows—for himself and Yurkovsky—and helped Mollart get comfortable. They were all silent.

"Very miserable," Mollart finally said. "I can't alone. I want to talk."

"We're glad to see you, Charles," Dauge said sincerely. "We, too, are miserable, and we talk all the time."

Mollart tried to sit up but thought better of it and remained lying, staring at the ceiling."

"How's life, Charles?" Yurkovsky said with curiosity.

"Life is *bon*," Mollart said, smiling palely. "Only too little."

Dauge lay down and also stared at the ceiling. Too little, he thought, much less than you would like. He cursed under his breath in Latvian.

"What?" Mollart asked.

"He's cursing," Yurkovsky explained.

Mollart said suddenly in a high voice: "My friends!" and the planetologists both turned toward him.

"My friends! What should I do? You are experience interplanetaries. You are great people and heroes. Yes, heroes. *Mon Dieu!* You look into eyes of death more than I look into the eyes of the *mademoiselles*." He shook his head sadly. "But I am not experience. I am terrified, and I want to talk much now, but now the end is close, and I not know how. Yes, yes, what should say now?"

He looked at Dauge and Yurkovsky with glistening eyes. Dauge mumbled awkwardly, "Oh, damn it!" and looked at Yurkovsky. Yurkovsky was lying with his hands behind his head and looking at Mollart out of the corner of his eye.

"Oh, damn!" Dauge said. "I've already forgotten."

"I could tell you how they wanted to amputate my leg once," Yurkovsky said.

"That's right!" Dauge said happily. "And then you, Charles, can also tell us something amusing."

"Oh, you still joke me," Mollart said.

"Or we could sing," Dauge said. "I read that somewhere. Will you sing to us, Charles?"

"Oh," Mollart said, "I've gone to pieces."

"Not at all," Dauge said. "You're holding up very well, Charles. And that is the most important thing. It's true that Charles is holding up very well, isn't it?"

"Of course," Yurkovsky said. "Remarkable well."

"But the captain isn't sleeping," Dauge continued cheerfully. "Have you noticed, Charles? He's thought up something, our captain."

"Yes," Mollart said. "Yes, our captain. He is the great hope."

"And how," Dauge said. "You don't even know how big a hope."

"Six foot one," Yurkovsky said.

Mollart broke out laughing.

"You still joke," he said.

"We will go on chatting and observing," Dauge said. "Do you want to look through the periscope, Charles? It's very beautiful. No one has ever seen it before." He got up and leaned against the periscope. Yurkovsky saw his back suddenly bend. Dauge held on with both hands. "My God!" he said. "A spaceship!"

A spaceship was hanging in the pink emptiness. It was distinctly visible in full detail and was about three kilometers away. It was a first-class photon freighter with a parabolic reflector that resembled a skirt, with a round living gondola and a disk-shaped freight section, with cigarlike emergency rockets on long supports. It was hanging vertically and completely motionlessly. And it was gray, as though it were part of a black-and-white movie.

"Who is it?" Dauge muttered. "Could it be Petryshevsky?"

"Look at the reflector," Yurkovsky said.

The reflector on the gray spaceship was broken off at the edge.

"Those guys had bad luck, too," Dauge said.

"Oh," Mollart said. "Another one."

A second spaceship—exactly the same—was suspended beyond the first.

"And that one has a broken reflector, too," Dauge said.

"I know," Yurkovsky said. "It's our *Takhmasib*. It's a mirage."

It was a double mirage. Several rainbow bubbles rose rapidly from the depths, and the phantom ships were distorted, trembled, and melted. And to the right and higher, three more phantom ships appeared.

"What beautiful bubbles," Mollart said. "They sing."

He lay down on his back again. His nose was bleeding, and he blew his nose and frowned and kept looking at the planetologists to see if they noticed. They, of course, did not.

"So," Dauge said, "you say that things are dull."

"I don't say so now," Yurkovsky said.

"But you did," Dauge said. "You were grumbling about it being boring."

Both of them tried to avoid looking at Mollart. It was impossible to stop the bleeding. It would have to clot by itself. The radio optician should have been taken to the shock seat, but. . . . Well, it would stop. Mollart blew his nose quietly.

"There's another mirage," Dauge said. "But that is not a ship."

Yurkovsky looked through the periscope. It can't be, he thought. It just couldn't be. Not here, not on Jupiter. Underneath the *Takhmasib* the peak of a huge gray mountain floated slowly by. Its base was lost in the pink haze. Alongside was another cliff—bare, steep, jagged, with deep straight fissures. And beyond that was a whole series of similarly steep peaks. And the silence in the observatory changed to scraps, rustles, a low roar, similar to the echoes of distant avalanches.

"That's not a mirage," Yurkovsky said. "It looks like a core."

"Nonsense," Dauge said.

"Still, Jupiter might have a core."

"Nonsense, nonsense," Dauge said impatiently.

The mountain chain stretched out beneath the *Takhmasib*, and there was no end to it.

"Look at that!" Dauge said.

Above the jagged peaks a dark shapeless silhouette appeared, grew, turned into an eroded chunk of black rock, and disappeared again. After it came another, then a third, and in the distance, barely distinguishable, a gray mass shone in a gray patch. The mountain range below gradually got lower and disappeared from view. Yurkovsky, not leaving the periscope, brought the microphone to his lips. His joints cracked under the stress.

"Bykov," he called, "Alexei."

"Alexei isn't here, Vladimir," the navigator's voice answered. The voice was hoarse and gasping. "He's in the machine."

"Mikhail, we're flying over mountains," Yurkovsky said.

"What mountains?" Mikhail exclaimed, with fear in his voice.

In the distance there was a remarkably smooth, seemingly polished surface—an enormous plain, framed by a low ridge of hills. It passed beneath and drowned in the pink glow.

"We still don't understand everything," Yurkovsky said.

"I'll take a look right now, Vladimir," Mikhail said.

Still another mountainous land floated past. It floated high up in the sky, and its peaks were upside down. It was a wild, fantastic sight, and Yurkovsky at first thought that it was another mirage, but it was not. Then he understood and said, "It's not a core, Dauge. It's a cemetery." Dauge did not understand. "It's a cemetery for lost worlds," Yurkovsky said. "Jupe swallowed them up."

Dauge was silent for a long time, then muttered, "What discoveries! A ring . . . pink luminescence, a cemetery of worlds . . . it's a shame . . . a real shame."

He called out to Mollart. Mollart did not answer. He was lying face down.

They dragged Mollart to the shock seat, woke him up, and he, exhausted, swollen, went to sleep immediately, as though he had fainted. Then they returned to the observatory and hung onto the periscope. Under the *Takhmasib* and alongside the *Takhmasib*, and even at times above the *Takhmasib*, chunks of increate worlds floated slowly by in the streams of condensed hydrogen—mountains, cliffs, monstrous cracked blocks of rock, and transparent gray clouds of dust. Then the *Takhmasib* was carried to the side, and in the periscope was only the empty, even, pink light.

"I'm dog-tired," Dauge said. He turned on his side, and his joints cracked. "Hear that?" "I did," Yurkovsky answered. "Let's see." "Go ahead," Dauge said. "I thought it was a core," Yurkovsky said. "It can't be," Dauge said. Yurkovsky began to rub his face with his hands. "Take a look," he said.

They saw and heard much more, or at least they thought they saw and heard much more, because they were both very tired, and their vision blurred, and then the walls vanished and there was only the even, pink light. They saw broad motionless zigzags of lightning, running from the darkness above to the pink abyss below, and heard the lilac discharges pulsing with an iron thunder. They saw some sort of fluttering films that flew close by with a high-pitched whistle. They studied weird shadows in the darkness, which twisted and turned, and Dauge maintained that they were three-dimensional shadows, but Yurkovsky argued that Dauge was hallucinating. And they heard wails, and squeaks, and bangs, and strange voicelike sounds, and Dauge suggested recording them on the dictaphone, but noticed that Yurkovsky was asleep, lying on his stomach. Then he turned Yurkovsky over on his back and went back to the periscope.

Varya, blue with white polka dots, came crawling through the open door, her belly flat against the floor. She nestled on Yurkovsky, curling up on his knees. Dauge was about to chase her away but did not have the energy. He could no longer hold his head up. And Varya breathed deeply and blinked slowly. The spines on her snout were bristling, and her half-dead tail whipped around in time to her breathing.

3. *Time comes to say farewell, but the radio optician does not know how.*

It was hard, unimaginably hard, to work in such conditions. Zhilin lost consciousness several times. His heart seemed to stop, and everything was clouded over in a red murk. And the taste of blood was constantly in his mouth. Zhilin was ashamed, because Bykov continued working indefatigably, smoothly, and accurately, like a machine. Bykov was wet with sweat, and it was unimaginably hard for him too, but he, apparently, knew how to force himself to keep from losing consciousness. After two hours Zhilin had lost any sense of why he was working; he had no more hope, no love of life, but every time he came to he continued where he left off, because alongside him was Bykov. Once he came to and did not find Bykov. Then he broke out crying. But Bykov soon returned, set down a pot with soup in it, and said, "Eat." He ate and set to work again. Bykov's face was white and his sagging neck was scarlet. He breathed heavily and frequently. And he was silent. Zhilin thought: If we get out of this, I'm not going on any interstellar expedition, I'm not going to Pluto, I'm not going anywhere until I become like Bykov. So ordinary and even boring, during ordinary times. So sullen and even a little funny. So hard to know that it is difficult to believe, looking at him, in the legend of Golkonda, in the legend of Callisto, and in all the other legends. Zhilin remembered how the young interplanetaries furtively made fun of the Redheaded Anchorite—incidentally, where did that nickname come from?—but he had never seen even one pilot or scientist of the older generation speak of Bykov in derogatory terms. If I get out, I must become like Bykov. If I don't, I must die like Bykov. When Zhilin lost consciousness, Bykov took over his work in silence. When Zhilin came to, Bykov returned to his own work, also in silence.

Then Bykov said, "Let's go," and they climbed into the chamber of the magnetic system. Everything seemed to float before Zhilin's eyes, and he wanted to lie down, stick his face in something soft, and lie there until he was carried away. He climbed out second and got stuck and still lay there on the cold floor, but quickly regained consciousness and then he saw Bykov's shoe right in front of his face. The shoe was stamping impatiently. Zhilin strained and crawled out of the hatch. He squatted to fasten the hatch properly. The lock did not do what he wanted, and Zhilin tore at it with his scratched hands. Bykov towered above him, like a radio antenna, and looked without blinking from top to bottom.

"Right away," Zhilin said hurriedly. "Right away. . . ."

The lock, finally, fell into the right place.

"It's ready," Zhilin said and straightened up. His legs shook at the knees.

"Let's go," Bykov said.

They returned to the control room. Mikhail was sleeping in his chair by the computer. He was snoring loudly. The computer was on. Bykov leaned over the navigator, took the microphone, and said, "All passengers meet in the lounge."

"What?" Mikhail asked, awaking with a shudder. "What, already?"

"Already," Bykov said. "Let's go into the lounge."

But he did not leave immediately—he stood there and watched Mikhail, blinking abnormally and groaning, climb out of his chair. Then he seemed to awaken and said, "Let's go."

They went into the lounge. Mikhail headed straight for the couch and sat down, his hands folded on his stomach. Zhilin also sat down, so his legs would not shake, and started staring at the table. On the table there was still a pile of dirty dishes. Then the door to the corridor opened and the passengers tumbled in. The planetologists dragged Mollart with them; Mollart was hanging, limp-legged, his arms around the planetologists' shoulders. In his hand he was squeezing a handkerchief covered with dark spots.

Dauge and Yurkovsky put Mollart on the couch and sat down on either side of him. Zhilin studied them. So that's what it's like, he thought. Does my face look like that? He stealthily felt his face. His cheeks seemed lean and his chin very fat, like Mikhail's. He felt pins and needles in his legs. Not from sitting too much, he thought.

"So then," Bykov said. He was sitting on a chair in the corner and then stood up, walked over to the table, and leaned heavily against it. Mollart unexpectedly winked at Zhilin and covered his face with the spotted handkerchief. Bykov looked at him coldly. Then he began staring at the wall.

"So then," he repeated. "We were busy with the re-out-fit-ting of the *Takhmasib*. We have finished the re-out-fit-ting." The word *reoutfitting* gave him trouble, but he stubbornly repeated it a second time. "We can now use the photon engine, and I have decided to do so. But first I want to inform you of the possible outcomes. I warn you that the decision has been made, and I do not intend to discuss it with you or ask for your opinion."

"Make it quick, Alexei," Dauge said.

"The decision has been made," Bykov said. "But I believe that you are entitled to know what might happen. First, the ignition of the photoreactor might produce an explosion in the condensed hydrogen around us. Then the *Takhmasib* will be totally destroyed. Second, the first explosion of plasma might destroy the reflector—possibly the outer layer of the mirror has been worn away by corrosion. Then we will remain here and. . . . Well, you know. Third, and last, the *Takhmasib* might successfully clear Jupiter and—"

"Got you," Dauge said.

"And the supplies will be delivered to Amalteia," Bykov said.

"The supplies will be eternally grateful to Bykov," Yurkovsky said. Mikhail smiled timidly. He did not find it funny. Bykov stared at the wall.

"I intend to take off immediately," he said. "I suggest that passengers take their places in the shock seats. All of them. And none of your tricks." He looked at the planetologists. "Acceleration will be eight g's at the minimum. I ask you to obey the order. Flight Engineer Zhilin, check that the order is carried out and report to me."

He looked at them all, turned, and went into the control room on stiff legs.

"*Mon Dieu*," Mollart said. "That is the life."

He was bleeding from the nose again, and he began to blow softly. Dauge said, "We need a lucky devil. Anyone here on good terms with Lady Luck? We could use her help."

Zhilin stood up.

"It's time, comrades," he said. He wanted it to be over as soon as possible. He wanted to have it behind him. Everyone remained sitting. "It's time, comrades," he repeated absentmindedly.

"The probability of a successful outcome is point one," Yurkovsky said, and began massaging his cheeks. Mikhail, his joints cracking, climbed out of the couch.

"Friends," he said. "We have to say good-bye. Just in case, you know. . . . Anything can happen." He smiled pitifully.

"So then, let's say good-bye," Dauge said.

"And I again not know how," Mollart said.

Yurkovsky stood up.

"Well, this is it," he said. "Let's go to the shock seats. Otherwise Bykov will come out, and then. . . . I'd rather burn up. The man has a heavy hand, I still remember. After ten years."

"Yes," Mikhail hastened to agree. "Let's go, guys. Let's shake hands." They all shook hands solemnly.

"Where will you be, Mikhail?" Dauge asked.

"In the shock seat, like everyone else."

"And you? Ivan?"

"Me, too." He supported Mollart by the arm.

"And the captain?"

They went out into the corridor, and once again they all stopped. There were only a few steps left.

"Alexei says that he does not trust the automatic guidance on Jupiter," Zhilin said. "He will fly the ship himself."

"That's Bykov," Yurkovsky said, smiling awkwardly. "Carrying the weak on his broad shoulders."

Mikhail, sobbing, went into his cabin.

"I'll help you, Monsieur Mollart," Zhilin said.

"Yes," Mollart agreed and obediently put his arm around Zhilin's shoulders.

"Success and good plasma," Yurkovsky said.

Dauge nodded, and they each went to their cabin. Zhilin led Mollart into his cabin and put him in the shock seat.

"How is life, Ivan?" Mollart asked sadly. *"Bon?"*

"Bon, Monsieur Mollart."

"And how are the girls?"

"Very good," Zhilin said. "On Amalteia the girls are marvelous."

He smiled politely, closed the cover, and immediately stopped smiling. If only it were over, he thought.

He walked down the corridor, and the corridor seemed very empty. He knocked on the cover of each shock seat and heard the answering rap. Then he returned to the control room.

Bykov was sitting in the senior pilot's seat. He was wearing an overload suit. The suit resembled a silkworm cocoon, and Bykov's tousled red hair stuck out of it. Bykov seemed totally ordinary, only very angry and tired.

"Everything is ready, Captain Bykov," Zhilin said.

"Good," Bykov said. He looked at Zhilin out of the corner of his eye. "Afraid, young man?"

"No." Zhilin said.

He was not afraid. He just wanted it to be over. And then suddenly he wanted to see his father, when he climbed out of a stratoplane, bulky, mustached, his hat in his hand. And to introduce his father to Bykov.

"Get moving, Ivan," Bykov said. "You have ten minutes."

"Good plasma, Captain Bykov," Zhilin said.

"Thank you," Bykov said. "Now get moving."

I have to hold up, Zhilin thought. Damn, why won't I hold up? He walked to the door of his cabin and suddenly saw Varya. Varya was crawling stiffly, pressing herself against the wall, dragging her tail behind her. Seeing Zhilin, she raised her triangular snout and slowly blinked.

"Oh, you poor thing," Zhilin said. He took Varya by her loose skin and dragged her into his cabin, pulled up the cover on the shock seat, and looked at his watch. Then he threw Varya into the shock seat—she was very heavy and quivered clumsily in his hands. Then he climbed in himself. He lay in total darkness, listened to the noise the shock-absorbing mixture made, and his body felt light and lighter. It was very, very pleasant, only Varya kept digging him in the side and sticking his arm with her spines. I have to hold up, Zhilin thought.

In the control room Captain Alexei Bykov pressed the large fluted starter button.

EPILOGUE: AMALTEIA, J-STATION

The director of J-Station does not watch the setting of Jupiter, and Varya gets pulled by the tail.

The setting of Jupiter is also very beautiful. The yellow-green glow of the exosphere slowly dies out, and one after another the stars come on, like diamond needles against black velvet.

But the director of J-Station did not see the stars, nor the yellow-green tints over the nearby cliffs. He was watching the icy field of the spaceport. The gigantic tower of the *Takhmasib* was descending, slowly, barely noticeable to the eye, onto the field. The *Takhmasib* was a monster—a first-class photon freighter. It was so huge that there was nothing on that world to compare it to, on the blue-green plain dotted with round black spots. From the spectrolite dome it seemed that the *Takhmasib* was falling by itself. In reality it was being laid down. In the shadows of the cliffs and on the other side of the plain powerful cranes pulled on cables, and the brilliant threads sometimes flashed in the rays of the sun. The sun illuminated the ship blindingly, and it was entirely visible, from the huge cup-shaped reflector to the spherical living gondola.

Such a mutilated spaceship had never landed on Amalteia before. The edge of the reflector had been broken off, and a heavy broken shadow lay in the huge cup. The two-hundred-meter photoreactor pipe looked spotted and corroded. The emergency rockets on crumpled supports jutted out every which way. The freight section was tilted, and one compartment crushed. The freight section disk resembled a flat, round jar, on which someone in lead boots had stepped. Part of the food supplies, of course, would be lost, the director thought. What nonsense creeps into your mind. What did it matter? Yes, the *Takhmasib* was not about to leave soon.

"Our chicken soup cost a lot," Uncle Valnoga said.

"Yes," the director mumbled. "Chicken soup. Knock it off, Valnoga. Don't even think it. What does chicken soup have to do with it?"

"A lot," Valnoga said. "The kids need real food."

The spaceship was lowered to the plain and sank into darkness. Now only a weak greenish glimmer on the titanium sides was visible, then lights flashed and small black figures darted about. Jupiter's shaggy hump went behind the cliffs,, and the cliffs turned black and stood higher, and for an instant a fissure burned brightly, and the mesh construction of the antenna was visible.

In the director's pocket a radiophone sang out. The director pulled out the smooth box and pushed the receive button.

"Yes?" he said.

The dispatcher's tenor, very happy and without the slightest deference, said rapidly, "Comrade Director, Captain Bykov and the crew and passengers have arrived in the station and are waiting for you in your office."

"Coming," the director said.

Together with Uncle Valnoga he went down in the elevator and headed for his office. The door was open wide. His office was full of people, and they were all talking and laughing loudly. Still in the corridor, the director heard a joyous shriek: "How is life—*bon*? How are the guys—*bon*?"

The director did not go in immediately, but stood outside a moment, searching for the new arrivals. Valnoga breathed noisily behind him. They saw Mollart with his hair wet from a swim. Mollart was gesticulating and chuckling madly. Around him stood the women—Zoya, Galya, Nadya, Jane, Yuriko, and the women on Amalteia—and they were all laughing, too. Mollart always managed to collect all the women around him. Then the director saw Yurkovsky, or more exactly, the back of his head, sticking up above the others, and the nightmarish monster on his shoulder. The monster made circles with its snout and yawned horribly every once in a while. People tugged on Varya's tail. Dauge was not to be seen, but made himself heard as well as Mollart. Dauge shouted, "Let me through, my friends, let me through!" To the side stood a huge unfamiliar young man, very handsome, but too pale amid all the suntanned people. Several local planet fliers were talking with him with great animation. Mikhail Krutikov was sitting in a chair by the director's desk. He was telling a story, waving his short arms, and raising a crumpled handkerchief to his eyes.

Bykov was the last person the director recognized. He was so pale he almost seemed blue, and his hair seemed copperish; under his eyes were dark blue bags, the usual result of strong and prolonged overloads. His eyes were red. He spoke so softly that the director could not make out his words and could only see that he was speaking slowly, moving his lips with difficulty. Near Bykov were the division directors and the head of the spaceport. It was the quietest group in the room. Then Bykov raised his eyes and saw the director. He stood up, and a whisper ran through the room, and everyone suddenly stopped talking.

They walked toward each other, their magnetic soles clinking against the floor, and met in the middle of the room. They shook hands and stood motionless for a moment. Then Bykov drew back his hand and said, "Comrade Kangren, the spaceship *Takhmasib* has arrived with its cargo."

A Part of the World

SEVER GANSOVSKY

They were standing on the landing. The elevator was coming from far below—the fifty-fifth floor. Or the hundred and fifty-fifth.

Rona said, "Find out what he thinks about it. After all, a man like him should know his way around. You and I are the ones who live in ignorance. But Kisch might take one look and figure out what exactly is hidden between the lines. In my opinion there's nothing wrong with your going to see him. He's always issuing invitations. And at the same time we might learn who he really is."

"He does it out of politeness."

"Out of politeness he would write one letter. Or just send a postcard at the holidays. But since he writes long letters, that's not it. Tell me, during the last few years, how many long letters have you written?"

"Well . . . let's see. . . ."

"None."

"You're right."

"So don't be so lackadaisical. If that's the way you handle it, you'll either forget to ask him or forget the most important things he says."

"No, I won't. I'll be okay."

"Pull yourself together, Lek. Let's take another look at it. Before the elevator comes."

"Give it to me."

"You have it!"

Out of his pocket Lek pulled a flexible yellow sheet, made of some mysterious material. The letters and lines leaped out into your eyes, distinct, gaudy.

Without loss of self, without harm to health
THE CAUSE OF YOUR PROBLEMS is that
your desires do not coincide with your opportunities.
WE WILL REMOVE THIS DISPROPORTION:
(1) WITHOUT WORRY

(2) THE FULFILLMENT OF ANY DREAM!!!

In strict accordance with the cost, you are guaranteed stable satisfaction until the end of your days. WE THINK, DECIDE FOR YOU.

You still will have things to talk about with your friends and neighbors. NOT A SECOND of BOREDOM!!!

PERFECTLY LEGAL, GOVERNMENT-APPROVED.

Confidence, Inc.

"I'm glad to see there'll still be things to talk about." Rona took the sheet out of Lek's hands. "Ever since the kids left, you and I just have one topic of conversation—how bad the TV programs are. And that's only in the evening, so we keep quiet all day long. If we had something to talk about, we wouldn't have a problem."

"Yes . . . but look, it's all contradictory. On one hand, 'the fulfillment of any dream,' but right afterward, 'in strict accordance with the cost.' The way I understand it, they'll take your money, your hard-earned money, everything you have, and according to the result reduce your desires by means of a brain operation or psychotherapy. That's the only possible way. But at the same time they write: "without loss of self." But self is just that: desires, dreams, and all that. Right? They probably had trouble with electrodes, so they came up with something else, more radical. . . . These handouts, by the way, are all over the place: newspaper stands, in the post offices, even in the subways."

"Who are 'they'?"

"The people on top. . . . And then, the question of money. Stocks will fall, money will be worth less, because of inflation—actually not 'because of,' that's what inflation is. But here they say 'Stable satisfaction.' "

"We could certainly use some stability. How much have we lost because of the exchange rate? The paper we hold is constantly falling in value. But as soon as we sell, it shoots up. It seems to be a law of economics: What we sell will increase in value; what we hold onto will gradually fall."

"There's no such law. It's just that they buy the papers that will go up— the smart people."

"All right, if you say so. All I know is that if it keeps on going this way, we're going to lose everything."

"Yes. But how is the company going to guarantee stability if money and stocks constantly change in value?"

"That's what you should be asking Kisch about."

"Maybe we should give their agent a call first?"

"No." Rona shook her head. "You know very well that he'd talk us into it right away. We can't handle those agents, they go to special schools.

For every objection they have a smart answer. They put you in a position where you end up agreeing to anything out of embarrassment. . . . Once the agent gets a foot in the door, it's all over. That's why I think that we should get Kisch's advice first, see what he thinks. And while we're at it, find out who he really is. Or else he'll sign his name Setera Kisch, as though that was the way it had always been."

The elevator on the fifteenth line clanked by and floated upward. The elevator on nine stopped, but at the very moment a man jumped out of nowhere, leaped inside, slammed the door, and raced away. Elevator cages flashed by behind the grating. A popular tune reached out from behind the door opposite the elevators, and from the side came the rattle of machinery. An airway trained roared outside, and from the sky a sound wave from a jet boomed; the pneumomail tossed a package of newspapers and a whole heap of yellow fliers into the transparent box on the landing.

"Press the button again. And let's go out on the balcony."

A dim sun was just rising. The street canyon was clouded over with a reddish-gray sooty haze.

"How strange!" Lek leaned against the parapet. "Once in a while you spot some little corner in the distance, and you think that the people there must lead interesting lives, there's something mysterious, intimate. But if you go there, it's the same old trains, stores, walls. And no mystery, although there may be secrecy."

"It's all right, Lek, don't be sad. Confidence, Inc., will help us. It's better than a poorhouse. And what kind of a poorhouse could it be, with you forty-seven and me two years younger?"

"You know, I just realized what the difference is between Confidence and the other systems." Lek turned to Rona. "When, for example, a person is on a leash, he pays a fixed amount one time, and he is guaranteed only cheerfulness. How you spend your remaining money or earn more is something they don't care about. They don't want to know what you do for a living. Whether you work in an office with a computer or in an alleyway with a revolver. You can even be an extreme leftist and fasten bombs to doorknobs. But Confidence is different in principle. You give them your every last cent, and for that you get satisfaction, but in the way they want, as they see fit. 'Until the end of your days.' Those are the essential words. So that if we sign up, nothing will belong to us, that's for sure. No independence."

"But what has independence ever gotten us? You feel like a human being only when you deal with other people, develop relationships. But at home there's the TV, self-service in the department stores, computers in the clinics, a computer directs your work, and your work is for computers. There are people around, but it's hard to get through to them; they all seem to be just passing through. You stand in front of a crowd as though it were a blank wall. When you went away to visit the kids, for two weeks I didn't open my mouth. If there is something human within me, there's no one to show it too." Rona twirled the yellow flier in her hand. "To make it short, we have to do something soon. Or else we spend our last cent and have nothing to take to Confidence. . . . Look here, I just noticed—when I stretch the flier the letters remain the same and the lines don't bend. How did they manage that? Here, see for yourself."

"Yes, that's remarkable. But here's my elevator."

Like a bullet the road pierced it straight through, the little town of five thousand.

To reach it Lek turned off the eight-lane government highway onto a four-lane one—at the transfer he had to sit in the driver's seat and take over the steering wheel himself. And from there onto a worn concrete road without a dividing line. And even this road did not lead straight to town but left it on the side. The pavement did not flow into it and dissolve but raced on ahead, cracked and jagged.

Despite all this, and perhaps even because of it, Lek, as he drove, looked around at the scenery with enjoyment. Along with the eight-lane highway, the hateful and invariable industrial-technological landscape disappeared: the many-leveled overpasses, the steel masts and flues reaching to the horizon, the solid stone walls for miles on end concealing who knew what, the gigantic mouths of ventilating shafts, the totally windowless automated factories, the incredibly huge bowllike gas tanks, concrete fields bristling with antennas for directional communication.

The four-lane highway rejoiced the eye with a view where civilization was not yet fully established but just gathering its forces. Here much had been begun, but not everything was finished. Steel pipes, red with mossy rust, and ferroconcrete plates with the steel rods jutting out had not yet been placed in precise constructions, and amid the brick wasteland grew clumps of—Lek searched for the word—thistle. And the sky, even though pale gray, was free from the whine of jets.

And on the concrete road there were miracles. Patches of blue chicory on the side of the road, a harvest of blackberries and gooseberries alternating with plain grass, a tree in the distance. Silence. Every five miles or so the sky seemed clearer, brighter, bluer. Imperceptibly the inside of the car was filled with the scent of flowers and leaves. A summer smell. In the city you just didn't notice the months, the seasons, except when the TV and radio started in about fall hats or spring ties. Here it was clear even without advertising that June or maybe July was freely and leisurely floating over a grove, a lake that glittered in the distance. Lek even had a twinge in his heart when he thought of building a house here and dispatching technology along with science to the netherworld.

Ahhhh!

He remembered a song from his childhood, born on asphalt, next to brick and concrete walls. A stupid song, but Lek knew that it had his deepest dream—forest, fields, a garden, his own house, enough necessities for several years, independence. Everything is clear, and you are not afraid of accidents because you know that you are capable of overcoming any danger. By day you work, by night you savor quiet joys with your family, and no fall in the stock market threatens you. You handle everything, and extraneous and incomprehensible forces like inflation have little effect on you.

But he knew that even Confidence, Inc. could not achieve that. The most it could do was make his apartment on the two hundred eightieth floor more to his liking. . . .

Even the people in this area were different. At the railroad stop, a modest shelter, Lek sat on a bench next to a woman who was knitting. An electroloco of primeval manufacture hauled behind it a long string of freightcars and rumbled into the distance. The rails just lay there, calm, empty, as though they existed only for themselves, a branch line that came from nowhere and led nowhere. There was even a cat. The rare animal jumped up on the bench next to Lek, demandingly shoved its forehead under his hand, and let out a low rumbling sound. Cautiously, afraid of being rude, Lek asked the woman whether she was bored here. She looked at him good-humoredly. "Bored—what's that?"

Then, after a pause, she explained. "I don't have a TV. It's like this. Sister writes to me from town: Every evening she hopes there's something good on, and every evening she's disappointed. But when you don't have anything, you don't feel bored."

Along the embankment flowers had been planted. The black cat climbed onto the woman's lap, rubbing its head against her hand. These people had the life!

All the same, on the wall of the shelter was a poster:

EVEN IF

your family perished in an accident

EVEN IF

you lost your job

    EVEN IF

you come down with an incurable disease

    STILL

YOU CAN BE

    COMPLETELY HAPPY!

See us TODAY!

Lek read it and laughed bitterly. When you lost your job, it would probably be too late to see them. With nothing in hand. . . .

After another hour's travel he stopped his car to check the mile signs to make sure he was headed in the right direction. He took Setera Kisch's last letter out of his pocket and unfolded it. The world around him was flooded with grandeur. Grasshoppers chirped, variegated flowers, free for the taking, gleamed amid thick grass, and a grove of maples contributed a scent without requiring recompense. And the whole countryside was the way it might have been in 1870.

Only a strangely tilted tower on the horizon, at the very limit of vision, spoiled somewhat the idyllic scene, as though a gigantic gray finger were pointing from earth to the sky—you could spend your whole life without finding out what that tower was. But here too, he soon discovered, was a billboard with a provocative puzzle:

ARE YOU ASHAMED?

The next billboard was even larger. Against a pink background were the words:

AN UNHAPPY MOOD

IS AS ABSURD AS

A TOOTHACHE

The series was capped by a gaudy Day-Glo wail of advertising, right as you entered town:

The difference between UNHAPPINESS

and a TOOTHACHE:

UNHAPPINESS can be CURED

IMMEDIATELY

PAINLESSLY

FOREVER

See our local representative TODAY!

After Lek had turned onto local streets and made his third turn, he felt that he knew this town backward and forward from the old books he had read. In towns like this, for want of anything else, people took pride in their past, and usually had an impressive one. Either a minor battle was fought nearby, or a century ago there had been a boom connected with coal, gold, oil, or gambling resorts. The usual accoutrements, as established in old novels, for such inhabited areas included a genuine graybeard, a statue of a general (no one remembers whom he fought), a "historic street," where every house is at least twenty years old and the one with the restaurant inside is eighty, a mass of greenery, and clean air. In these areas—again, according to old novels—young people tried to run away and old people frequently returned to live out their days.

Lek rolled along, and the town seemed intent on demonstrating just such a literary reputation. Memorial tablets with inscriptions adorned the houses; an ancient cannon, lying inside a ring of a cast-iron fence, rested peacefully; and the square around it was paved with cobblestones; the stones waved under the sensitive wheels just like the aching teeth that were harder to cure than unhappiness.

There were almost no pedestrians on the sidewalks (although there were sidewalks), but ever since Lek left the concrete road he had not met a single one. Amazement set in; he just could not believe that in the prosperous, smoke-clouded world there could remain such a backward, un-muddled little town.

Sitting in a restful armchair on his front porch, a graybeard raised his arm and nodded in greeting to the newcomer. Lek stopped his car. It had occurred to him that Kisch might be put in an embarrassing situation by his unexpected arrival.

The old man stood up with alacrity. It was immediately evident that sclerosis had worked its will on the venerable townsman.

"You say you'd like something to eat? Here any . . . any . . . Damn, I've forgotten what the word is!"

"Any day?"

"No, that's not it."

"Any time?"

"No. Any fool. . . . The old man waved in his hand in a sign of helplessness. "No, that's not it either."

"Idiot?" Lek was trying to help.

"Any one-who-wants—that's the word! Anyone who wants to eat his fill can go to the restaurant. Right over there."

"You're kidding! You mean you have an Eat 'n' Run out here?"

"No, who the hell needs all those. . . ."

"Pills?"

"No."

"Capsules?"

"Of course not. Teeth! Who needs teeth if all you're going to do is swallow concentrate?"

The old guy had a healthy mouthful of teeth, and judging by their yellow color, they were his own. He took it upon himself to show Lek the way and in answer to the sympathetic remark that forgetfulness can be cured, stopped short and craned his neck.

"But I don't have any complaints about . . . about my. . . ."

"Memory, fate, life?"

"No complaints about my wife. She almost died fifteen years ago from those chemical treatments. Not a single capsule since then. . . . And as far as my memory goes—it's excellent. For example, I never forget . . . what is it?"

"Words?"

"Not words, those. . . . The ones that run, jump, and read. They do everything."

"You don't forget people?"

"Verbs! I remember verbs, every last single one. It's just nouns that slip away sometimes. But to hell with 'em."

The lack of mobiles and the presence of the irrepressible graybeard harmonized with the appearance of the restaurant. The establishment was suitable for archaeological interest, as proclaimed by a brass plate on the wall: "In existence since 1009."

Massive chairs, pleasing in their lack of comfortableness, with high straight backs, walls covered with dark wood, an electric coffee grinder—a contemporary of Napoleon, no doubt—the unhurried, hospitable (to say nothing of courteous) waiter. The inexpensive lunch was amazingly delicious. It was strange to eat a boiled potato that had not been processed, totally unimproved; a cucumber that was not limp; when you chewed, the part in your mouth underwent a chemical change, electrons jumped to new orbitals, molecules were formed; growth processes and cell formation took place according to the unimaginably complex genetic program, according to the laws of open biosystems.

Having eaten his fill, Lek sat for a while, savoring the quiet. There was no point in hurrying—Setera Kisch was not waiting, did not even have the slightest notion that an old acquaintance was going to descend upon him within a quarter of an hour.

The correspondence had started a dozen years before. Long ago they had gone to school together and had shared their first cigarette. By the time they reached adolescence they had gone their separate ways, forgotten about each other as usually happens with classmates. And then, two decades after they shared a school desk, a letter from Kisch found its way to Lek. Although a somewhat dull kid, Kisch had blossomed into an important specialist in electronics and had worked all these years in the same scientific organization. Now he regularly sent photographs and tapes, let them know what was happening with his family, his trips abroad, how they spent their holidays—a boat on a lake, a helicopter for their summer house. And every letter ended with an invitation to come and visit.

. . . A pink street, Shade Street. Just looking at the houses, two or more stories high, was a pleasure in itself. Especially since they all had windows with flowerpots. And especially since each had a little garden.

Almost a resort, guaranteed to double your life span.

Lek came to a crossroads. Here Shade Street met the one he was looking for, Lilac Lane. Number thirty-seven was on the corner, so number forty would be on the other side.

He crossed a small square, and marked time. There was no house number forty. The numbers were already in the fifties. Lek went on, and Lilac came to an end, hitting Elm Avenue. Without any hope, he looked at the opposite side; they were all odd-numbered.

Beginning to get concerned, he returned to his starting place, took the letter out of his pocket, and reread the return address. Yes, the continent, country, city, and street all matched.

He looked around.

The grass growing sparsely between the pavement was motionless, and a light cloud hung fixed against the sky.

The whole street was very old, without any traces of construction.

At house number fifty a man was sitting on his heels; he was wearing an old hat and a soiled, faded jumpsuit. He put his hands on his knees, staring blankly into space, looking as though he had not changed position for several years.

Lek went over to him. The man's mouth was so big that the ends of it reached back to his jaw.

"If it wouldn't be too much trouble, could you tell me where number forty is?"

The question traveled for an entire minute to reach its destinatee's brain, and finally hit the region where consciousness is located. The man in the hat unhurriedly raised his head, shifted his black heavily smoked pipe from one corner of his mouth to the other. It was a long trip.

"There is no forty. Burned down."

"What do you mean, burned down? When?"

"About ten years ago."

"How could that be—ten years! I have a letter from my friend, from Setera Kisch." Lek in his excitement pulled the letter out of his pocket again. "Maybe you know him? Setera Kisch, a physicist. It was mailed this month, and he wrote down the address."

"You have a letter from Kisch?"

"Yes."

The man took the pipe out of his mouth, stood up. His face became set and firm.

"Hm, let's see it. . . . Yes, it's his writing." He flipped the envelope. "And there's the return address."

He looked Lek over from head to feet.

"Are you alone?"

"I am. . . . What about it?"

"No police?"

"Police? With me?"

"Okay, come this way."

Following the man in the hat, Lek stepped up on the porch of house number fifty. The man opened a rickety squeaking wooden door. Behind it was another, metal, polished, shining. Inside, in a square room without windows a man was sitting; he was wearing a uniform that resembled an army uniform but wasn't quite exactly like one: The insignia were made up of X's and O's. He was reading a pamphlet.

The man in the hat said, "He has a letter from Kisch. Personal. An invitation to come."

The man in the uniform finished reading his page, took the letter, and began examining it. The pamphlet was entitled "Why Aren't You a Millionaire?"

"Do you have your documents? With the seals?"

Lek took out his identifier.

The man in the uniform lazily got to his feet, led Lek over to the wall. He gave it a kick, and at eye level a small dark window opened.

"Well, be quick about it."

He grabbed Lek's hand and shoved it into the window. Something tickled Lek's fingers, and he tried to jerk his hand free. The man in the uniform, holding it in, guffawed.

"Why are you squirming about? The first time, eh?"

The tickling stopped. Lek went back. The man in the uniform picked up the telephone receiver.

"Twelve. . . . Hi, it's me. Is this twelve? Went out to fix a lighter? He's never there when he should be. Listen, there's a guy here with a letter from Kisch. . . . Yes, from him himself. He invited the guy to come. . . . And the guy checks out. . . . Wait? How long are we supposed to wait—until he fixes his lighter and then goes out for dinner? . . . Okay, okay. . . . Got it."

He hung up, turned to Lek. He thought a moment, rummaged around with something under his chair. A door suddenly opened in the middle of the wall. And there was an elevator.

"Level five. Room five hundred forty or forty-one. You'll have to ask."

All of this overwhelmed Lek, and he automatically pushed the button, descended, and only when he came out into a spacious people-filled room with a glowing blue ceiling did he come to himself and, perplexed, set about cursing. "God damn it to hell! Let them be smashed, squashed, and flattened."

And so it turned out that the old houses with the flowerpots, the cannon with the fence, the restaurant with the real cucumbers were all an illusion, a lie. Camouflage concealing an ordinary work complex, the same old military-industrial power. Lek's heart ached—there was nowhere to go, nowhere—but a half-minute later he cheered up. This is the way it has to be, you have to accept the world for what it is.

"Okay, then . . . to hell with the bastards!"

"To hell with who?"

He had spoken out loud and now looked straight ahead at a girl in aluminized pants and a bright blouse who just happened to be passing. She thought that he was addressing her.

"No, not you, I was just letting off steam. Could you tell me where the five hundred forties are?"

The girl pointed to one of the corridors that led away radially from the blue central room. He wandered along, glancing at the numbers. He really wouldn't have been able to say exactly who he wanted to smash, squash, and flatten. Somebody in charge of planning all this to persecute Lek, but who really was in charge? It was not just Lek who was affected, of course, but everyone. The people who start with little concessions to injustice, evil and gradually climb the ladder of the social hierarchy, ending who knows where.

Five hundred thirty-five, thirty-eight. Finally, here was forty.

He knocked gently. No answer. He opened the door himself. It was something like a lobby, furnished with expensive Indian furniture. Two doors on the inside. He knocked on one at random.

Inside someone shouted, "Come in!"

It was the voice of Kisch, which Lek recognized from the tapes he had sent.

In a tall easy chair sat Setera Kisch. He was writing something.

He had two heads.

For an instant they looked at each other, both shaken. Lek with his two eyes, Kisch with his four. Then Kisch jumped up with a quiet shout, and flipped a switch on his desk. For a minute some sort of racket resounded out of the darkness. Kisch's voice, with a catch in it, quavering, asked, "Who are you? And what's going on?"

Lek cleared his throat, feeling his mouth suddenly gone dry.

"Lek."

"Lek who?"

"Your wrote to me. Your school friend."

"Oh, my school friend! Aahh!"

Once again the switch clicked. Kisch stood in the middle of the room, pale, his lips shaking. He straightened his hair. The second head, the extra one, which had looked a little younger, had disappeared. True, the light in the room was unreal—all over there were mirrors reflecting each other.

"Who let you in?"

"Me?"

"Of course!"

"I had your letter on me. They looked at the signature. They checked my fingerprints."

"And how did you manage to find this town?"

"But you invited me! More than once. You really insisted."

"Oh, Lord!" Kisch sighed. "What a crazy deal. I never imagined that you would really come. Never even crossed my mind."

"Then why did you invite me so often?"

"If someone says to you, after they've just been introduced, 'Pleased to meet you,' you don't take it literally. You don't really think that a person who's never heard of you before is in ecstasy now."

"Of course not." Lek now understood that his mission was in vain. "I made a mistake."

"The question you should ask is why I started the correspondence in the first place. If you were cooped up underground for almost fifteen years without getting out, you'd remember more than old school friends."

"But you wrote that you were always going to colloquiums, to conventions."

"I wrote a lot of things. Where I am going to go looking like this?"

"Looking like what? . . . Oh, so you mean . . ." Lek was embarrassed to say the words. "So you don't have just one head?"

"Not just one. Right now you can't see it because of a special lighting effect—reverse holography. But they don't let people leave here, it's all top secret. It was an accident that you got in."

"My God!" Lek was overwhelmed by fear. So this was it, the latest in scientific advances. "You have to understand, I had no idea that you were sitting out here underground. Of course, it was naive of me to just up and come, without writing first."

"It's all right. It's done."

"Please forgive me."

"It's okay. Have a seat."

They sat down. Lek looked around. The room was large and crammed with furniture. In addition to the countless mirrors there were cabinets, couches, a Swedish room divider, a horizontal bar for gymnastics. There was also a piano, a green school blackboard on rollers, a shelf of minibooks, a television set, a lathe, an easel with a palette and brushes. You got the feeling that Kisch spent most, or even all, of his time here.

Kisch drummed his fingers on the table. "So here's the homestead. Beyond that door is a summer house with a swimming pool. This is my whole life. But how are you?"

"Like everyone. . . ." Lek stumbled. "In general, the way I said in my letters. It's getting really tight with money. We get by. We don't get a new mobile every year, but we still have all the necessities."

"How about Rona? Is she bored now that the kids are away at school?"

"She's gotten used to it."

They fell silent, and the silence was immediately awkward. The yellow flier from Confidence, Inc. appeared before Lek's mind's eye. What was the point, if a man like Kisch had become a prisoner, of thinking about independence?

Feeling that he should say something, he cleared his throat. "What happened with the heads? Was it your own idea?"

"It happened during an experiment on the regeneration of organs. I myself am not in biology but in electronics, but I had to work with bioplasma. I was working on an electronic scalpel and somehow I cut myself—and pandemonium broke loose with all different kinds of irradiation. To make a long story short, an extra head grew. At first it was treated as an experiment, and things might have turned out different. But then all of a sudden it was too late."

"Why?"

Kisch did not answer

"And when you want to think," Lek said, "or when you do think—is it in both heads? At the same time? Like playing a piano with two hands? Or, more likely, with four?"

"Why in both—" Kisch suddenly broke off. His hand flew up to the wall switch, then he lowered it awkwardly with an effort that was visible on his face. "Stop it! Come on now, stop it!" The hand once again rose, then descended. "Excuse me, Lek, that wasn't meant for you. So what were we talking about? Oh yes—I am not in two heads, of course. Each is on its own."

"What do you mean, each?" Lek felt a sudden chill. "After all, it is your head, isn't it?"

"Not entirely. A head, strictly speaking, cannot be 'my' head or 'your' head. Only 'its own.' "

"But I, for example, have my head."

"No. There is no 'you' who would exist separately from that head. Therefore it is incorrect to speak of it from the side, so to speak—to say, 'This one is mine.' "

"I don't understand."

"It's not that complicated—outside of the head there is no person. On the other hand, inside the head, in the brain is where consciousness is found. . . . Do you have any idea at all of what your own 'I,' your person, is?"

"The brain." Lek felt like asking for an explanation of 'person.' "The brain, because the body can be changed, if necessary."

"Not completely exact. The brain is only the storehouse for the 'I.' If it is empty there is no person. But its contents are contemporaneity—a condensation of symbols of the outer world. At first, at birth, the brain is a tabula rasa—what we both learned in school. A clean blackboard ready to be written upon, a yet-to-be-filled structure. Then, through the sense organs, information about the world begins to fall into it. Not the outside

environment itself, but information in the form of signals on the electro-
chemical level. Ones that leave signs in nerve cells. The signs gradually
arrange themselves in concepts, and they in turn form images, associations,
thoughts. In other words the 'I' is what the sense organs have seen, heard,
and felt, which is processed in the brain in a way that is unique for
everyone."

"And that's all?"

"What more do you want?"

"No mystery? No divine spark that has to be preserved? So the result is
that every person, who walks, talks, acts, is nothing more than a condensation of the same reality? But only in symbols?"

"The mystery is in the mechanism of life itself, in the essence of thought.
I don't know how divine it is. But there's no getting around it—a person
is the outside world processed into images. True, in each person this occurs
according to a unique genetic pattern. Hereditarily. Therefore Roland says,
'Man does not have a nature, he has a history.' That is, he implies that
the 'I' is a condensation of images that develops gradually, historically,
day by day."

"Who is this Roland?"

"Gugliemo Roland, the Peruvian philosopher."

"And now you're fooling around with philosophy?" Lek suddenly felt
animosity toward Kisch. He sits there with it made, couldn't care less about
inflation. "Damn it, but you've become clever. And I'm still the same old
blockhead I was in school. I can't even fathom how it is you've become
such a genius. Do you get special food?"

"The food has nothing to do with it."

"But what is the 'it' in 'with it'? You always dragged along behind in
your schoolwork. And then with your first company you barely hung on."

Kisch stood up, paced the room, his reflection showing in all the mirrors.
For an instant the other head appeared, but it vanished almost immediately.

"You know, if you want the truth, I am really not me. Not the same
Setera Kisch you went to school with."

"Then who are you?"

"Pmois."

"Pmois?!" Lek leaned back in surprise and almost fell over backward—
he was sitting on a stool, not a chair. "Very clever! A brain transplant."

"Mmm. I can't recall whether you ever met him, that is, me, Pmois.
. . . I think you did, at Lynne Lacombe's. I—I was still Pmois, was
demonstrating the materialization of Beethoven for them. I was working
for Art the Easy Way, Inc."

"I remember," Lek said. "How young we were then! We believed in everything! At least I did. It seems a thousand years ago." He sighed. "Chison and I came for the materialization. Pmois was, as I remember it—a hefty guy, self-contained. So it's him I'm talking to? But in Kisch's body?"

"Close. . . . Setera Kisch just barely managed to become a physicist. The first four years he passed with good grades, even brilliant grades. But after that he went downhill. He became a scientist but a mediocre one, without any flights of the imagination. He drudged along, but nobody in the company was wild about him, and he himself was discontented. His parents, of course, were to blame. You remember, in those days if you didn't have a B.A. you were a flop. But Kisch still had the honesty to admit to himself that he wasn't in the right place. And then we met each other. I'd been pushed in the tailor business and was working a shop. And lo and behold Setera Kisch pops in to order a suit. I take his measurements, and he joins in, gives me advice. Everything seemed to come natural to him—a born tailor. I could see the man come to life whenever he picked up a pair of scissors or some pins. And that he was sorry to have to go to his lab. And I, on the other hand, was in love with electronics. I read books, collected schematics. But I had only finished high school."

"So," Lek said. "Please continue."

"I forget exactly how, but the two of us tried to come up with a plan. For him to quit physics to become a tailor was embarrassing. What would his relatives say, his friends? And among tailors he would stick out like a sore thumb. At the same time, no one would accept me in a research institute without a degree, even if I had Faraday's ability. Finally we decided to switch brains. He told me everything about himself, I gave him a complete description of my life. And then it was to the operating tables. I've really done well in electronics: a couple of dozen patents, and soon I picked up a doctorate. Only then came the accident and the two heads. And Setera Kisch in the shape of Pmois, my old form, made it big. As a designer. Prizes in Paris, a gold medal in Sydney. His own business."

Lek nodded. He stood up and started pacing the floor nervously.

"Listen, as long as we're being honest with each other, I'm not Lek."

"Really? Then who are you?"

"Skrunt. Lynne Lacombe's husband. . . . It's a long story. A question of feelings, you see. Lek, that is, me . . . that is, no, him really. . . . Well anyway, Lek was head over heels in love with my Lynne Lacombe. And me, that is, Skrunt, she had pushed to the edge of a heart attack. Remember what an airhead she was? She always wanted to make me perfect, just nagged me to death. Take up archery, or drawing, or study chemistry. And even though I was very much taken by her at first, later

I had a rough time and realized that I would be pushing up daisies very soon unless a change was made. But all the same I knew that a divorce would have been a terrible blow to her. And then Lek turns up, and he can't take his eyes off her. Once I had a chance to talk to him alone. He didn't think twice, got all excited as soon as he caught on. We were in the conservatory, and he grabbed a palm so hard he pulled it out by the roots. But there was one slight complication: Lek didn't have a cent to his name. We agreed that as soon as he became me, Skrunt, he would sign over eighty percent of his resources to his old self."

"So what then?" the host asked. He had listened with an intense interest. "He deceived you, and that is why you live so modestly now."

"Not at all. Lek is a decent person. It's just that when I changed to Lek from Skrunt, even with the money nothing turned out right. Success is more in connections than in capital itself."

"Very interesting." The man who had called himself Setera Kisch strolled over the thick carpet between rooms, then he stood still, looking his visitor straight in the eye. "Are you really Skrunt? Tell me the whole truth, from beginning to end."

"What do you mean?" The visitor turned red.

"That when Pmois changed with Setera Kisch, he himself was already a changeling. He had changed with Skrunt . . . The doctors probably warned your Lek that it wasn't Skrunt's first operation."

"Yes, that's true." The visitor plopped down on his stool. "But if we only knew who the original Skrunt was, then we'd be able to straighten the whole thing out."

"In the former Pmois? If there weren't further changes."

"Damn!" The guest grabbed the head. "After all this I just don't understand anything anymore. Then who are you, after all?"

"Who knows. And you?"

"Let's straighten things out. It all depends on the time. If Pmois in actuality—"

"Hold on!" The man who called himself Lek stared at the ceiling. "Don't start from there. In actuality, originally I was Setera Kisch, to be completely honest. That was my original condition. So you were talking about me: the tailor shop, needles and threads. Then my consciousness went over into the body of Pmois. . . ."

"Now don't get the bodies mixed up—who is in which body? Or we'll never get things straightened out. Talk about the brains."

"That's what I've been doing. So then, I, Setera Kisch, became Skrunt, who, having already been changed, moved into you. . . . No, that's not right."

"I told you to follow the brain line, not the body line. The body line can throw us off. The brain in you is Setera Kisch's, right? You began life as Kisch?"

"Damn right!" The man who had arrived as Lek shrugged his shoulders. "I've never had any doubt about it."

"Excellent. So then—"

"To tell the whole truth, that was the purpose of my trip—to find out who had my old body. And since Setera Kisch was writing letters, my wife and I read them and wondered who he was."

"So then," the host repeated, "in your former body is Lek."

"Very clever! It turns out that you are me. In the sense of our bodies, at least."

"And you are me. Incidentally, I started the correspondence to determine who it was buried under the old me. So how are you making out in my body—is it a good fit?"

"It's okay, thanks. I've gotten used to it." The visitor fell into thought, shaking his head. "Damn it all anyway, but how low we've sunk! You get to the point where you just don't know who you really are. I mean, I've moved five times—into Pmois, into Skrunt, into you, after you had already left, then a couple of others. Every time you have to get used to things all over again, remake yourself, deceive everyone around you. You keep searching for somebody just a little better. You jump without really knowing where you'll land, like a flea, and nothing sacred is left, nothing human, no dreams, no ideals. . . . I've reached the point where I've had it. I'm not setting foot out of your body."

They were silent a while. A low roar broke through the walls. The trapeze hanging from the ceiling in the gym swayed.

"They're dynamiting somewhere," the host said. "Expanding the underground territory. They have an agreement with the town—they can spread out below but they can't show themselves on top."

The guest raised his eyes to the ceiling.

"And that town up there—a genuine antiquity? Or just a model, something they built for show?"

"An authentic antique. The houses don't even have TVs or record players. Instead, they get together in the evenings and sing and dance. During the day it's empty—one person is working for the railroad, another for the mill, but late in the day there are a lot of people on the streets. They're all conservationists. They restrict new technology and protect nature."

"Yes," said the guest. He looked around again. "It's convenient here, comfortable. But tell me, how did you manage to hang on all these years without going crazy? On a leash, too?"

"On a leash?"

"Yes, connected, you know. Connected with a computer. To prevent bad moods."

"You mean stimceivers, two-way radio devices?"

"Of course. Absolutely essential for protection against bad moods. You can get one hooked up to stop smoking or drinking. A microtransceiver is introduced into a specific location in the brain. Whenever you feel like a drink, neuron activity in the location increases, and a signal is sent to the computer in a clinic or wherever. From there an irritant signal is transmitted to a different brain location and just the sight of a glass of vodka makes you feel nauseous. Or take a case like this: A husband gets interested in another woman, and the wife runs out and hires an under-world doctor. There's a regular organization. They kidnap the husband, put him to sleep. The electrodes are implanted, and he is kept until the scars heal and given hypnosis so he doesn't remember a thing. And he's all set!"

"All set for what?"

"For anything. He'll be interested only in his wife. . . . Or for example, gangsters, the Mafia. They've all gone into surgery. Pay them what they ask, and they'll take care of anybody you name, hook him up to a computer program profitable to you. With one guy it even turned out that he had made an agreement with a gang but they captured him, used narcotics and hypnosis and a program, and then he transferred all his money to them."

"Rumors."

"Why so?" The guest stood up. "Why look any further—I'm your man. Four three-channel stimceivers. It's rare to meet a person these days without them. Some are stuffed with them to the point where you can't tell whether there's more brain tissue or more wires. The computer controls every step."

"It doesn't matter how many there are. A person still receives information from the external world through his sense organs. The person is formed by the surrounding reality, and not by anything else."

"Reality, you say! Is it really natural today?" The guest started pacing the room. "Television, newspapers, radio, hit films—that's what we get our tanks filled with. What you see and understand in life on your own is only a tiny fraction of the sum of daily impressions. Out of your apartment, hello to your neighbor, and a token in the turnstile. With all that in mind, how can you say that a sense of person still exists, that it is sovereign? A bit of society's consciousness, like two drops of water between each other, similar to all the other bits. Eh, somebody must want it this way! Everyone's struggling for a profit, for power. They ought to have electrodes implanted and a special program to calm them down. Only it wouldn't work." The guest laughed. "They live behind steel walls and deal with others only through bullet-proof glass. Or by video hookups—a friend told me that he went to a reception. When he got there there was a chair in the middle of an empty room. He sat down and waited, and a screen came on on the wall. It showed faces, closeups—go ahead and chat. . . . When you side inside your mobile, how many blank stone fences do you see along the highway? What's behind them? Either the computer blocks that hold people on a leash or the courtyards of the rich."

The guest fell silent, then, blushing, stroked his chin.

"I don't know why I'm talking so much all of a sudden. Just like a TV announcer. . . . Well, then, so long. You know, on my way here I was thinking that at least one of our old schoolmates was living like a human being—I suspected that it was one of my old classmates who was living in my body. At home we talk about you—that is, Setera Kisch—very frequently, how lucky you are, with an interesting job, trips, a life that is free and thriving. We held you up to the kids as an example. But you, it turns out, have spent fifteen years trapped in a basement. And if you are like this, there's no sense Rona and I thinking about good luck. There's only one thing to do—get the last of our money together and give ourselves up to Confidence."

The guest pulled the yellow flier out of his pocket and handed it to the host.

"Take a look."

"I know." The host glanced at the flier cursorily and pushed it aside. "But knock it off, don't get depressed. I think that very soon there will be big changes for us."

"Where are these changes supposed to come from? For us, you say? You know, now instead of the survival of the fittest, according to Darwin, it's the fitting in of the survivors. Before it was the fight to exist, in which the fittest species survived. But today, those who have survived, who have hung on to the present day, like us, for example, are struggling to fit in with a world of technology. Last year I was visiting a friend, Chison. His apartment was on the fifteenth floor right next to an airport. Right there the gravitationals were picking up speed, and the roar was murderous. It drove me up a wall, but he didn't even notice. And afterward it turned out that all the local residents had had an operation—they lowered the threshold of hearing, that is, on the contrary, they raise it. You can see what that means. Man does not have technology for himself, he exists for technology. And you can't do a damned thing! There is such a force guarding it that you can't shoot your way in with a cannon."

"Come on now, don't exaggerate." The host stood up, too. "It's hard to explain to you exactly, but I do have the feeling that there will be big changes. You, for example, are discontented with life, right? Do you like all this?"

"What's to like or dislike?"

"But your consciousness is really a part of something that is dissatisfied with bourgeois society. Even though advertising, television, the newspapers drone away that we have entered a golden age. They drone on, but it doesn't affect you. Or your mood. You're in a bad one now, aren't you?"

"And is there any reason for it to be good?" The guest bit his lips, looked to the side. "My soul aches. Even if it is a condensation of symbols."

"See? But you maintain that you're on a leash and your mood can't be bad. So why is it?" The host slapped the guest on the back. "I think you and I will meet again in more favorable circumstances. Hold on, old man!"

"Has something happened to you?"

Setera Kisch, the original Setera Kisch, raised his head. The fog was dispersing—Kisch hadn't even noticed when all that murk floated in around him. He stood in the corridor not far from the large hall, and the girl he had spoken to before, the one in the aluminized pants, was holding him up by the arm. She had black eyebrows and blue eyes.

"If you ask me, you're very disturbed. You saw Kisch, right?" The girl looked at him searchingly. "You've been standing here like this for five minutes already. Can I get you anything?"

"N-no, don't bother."

"But you're very pale. Is your heart all right?"

"It's okay." He inhaled and slowly let the air out. "Nothing like that happens to me. I'm fundamentally a healthy person."

People were scurrying past. The roar of voices reached them from the hall.

"You need something to bring you around. Let's go have a cup of coffee."

But when the hall was well behind them and they were going up a narrow staircase, the girl suddenly stopped and turned around abruptly.

"Hey, wait, listen, I almost forgot. You wouldn't happen to be a dog, would you?"

"A dog?"

"A tumor?"

"What's the idea!"

"You know, a higher-up, a big wheel, somebody who's finally come around to get things going his way. Although, to be honest, you don't look like one."

"No. I'm just an ordinary person."

"But why did you go to see Kisch?"

"We went to school together. I took it into my head to pop in unexpected. I wasn't expecting anything like that. I feel overwhelmed."

"Then everything is normal. Because otherwise I'd be making a mistake to talk so much. . . . Through here! We're going to a different ring where entry is prohibited to me. For the bosses. But the dining room will be empty now. And the coffee is better."

Corridors, passageways. In the comfortable dining room, its wall covered with real wood, there was no one else except the waiter who was clicking away on a calculator behind the counter. He smiled at the girl.

"Welcome." The girl nodded. "Two cups of your special blend. And two pieces of cake."

They found a table and sat down. The girl took a compact out of her purse and refreshed her lipstick. Then stretching forward toward the visitor, she took off the top crosspiece on the back of his chair. From one end a fine wire hung down. The girl raised the crosspiece to her lips and flicked it with her tongue.

"Eavesdropper. There is equipment for eavesdropping and monitoring everywhere."

A voice out of the microphone said, "Who's there? Niole, is that you?"

"It's me. Hi, Sang. Would the genius up there happen to be around?"

"He's in his office writing a report. Everything's safe."

"Come to gymnastics today. I'll be there."

"Okay. Who's that with you?"

"A school friend of Setera Kisch. I brought him over for coffee."

The girl put the crosspiece back.

"They have this boss who's a terrible blockhead. He takes all these rituals seriously. But the people who sit there listening, they are people too, like you and me. That's why the system is so ridiculous." She stood up to go get the coffee from the counter. "Incidentally, you're not the first person who's felt sick after seeing that."

"After seeing what?"

"Why, Kisch's two heads. Or more exactly, Kisch and Arth in one body. That's the way it usually happens: at first no sign of trouble, then a heart attack or depression. There was a kid here, Pruz, the son of the Pruz with Water Furniture. He came out of Arth's and just keeled over."

Setera Kisch took a sip of coffee—it really was good. His heart seemed to calm down, he could not get his mind off the yellow flier. To hold up his end of the conversation, he asked, "The son of Pruz himself? The tall, lanky kid? Does he work here, too?"

"He doesn't work anywhere. He's a dropout. Left his father, wanders around with his guitar. . . . Just imagine, how it is on the top with all that competition, the tension, with everybody trying to stab each other in the back. So they're always afraid for their hides. Either they can't take it and leave it all, or their kids renounce them."

"But about the kid. The father could keep him on a leash—computerize him against bad moods."

"First of all, not every father will want to stuff his child's head with metal. And second, the kid warned them that if he ever found something in his brain or if a period of time mysteriously disappeared from his life, he'd throw himself off the twentieth floor. It happens very often—the older generation crawls up, sparing no one, and the younger generation doesn't need it, so the sacrifice is in vain."

The girl exuded confidence and efficiency despite the fact that at the moment she was not doing anything. Her complexion was unbelievable and almost certainly her own.

"Why did he come here, the young Pruz?"

"To see Arth. The kid needs friends his own age. So they try to bring in some other kids. Now he knows all the latest songs."

Kisch took another sip of coffee. Because of the presence of the girl, the world seemed better—calmer and not as gloomy.

"Who is this Arth? You've mentioned him twice. And what do you mean by 'Kisch and Arth in one body'?"

"What do I mean? You did see a second head on Kisch's shoulders, didn't you?"

"Yes, I did. In all those mirrors."

"So that's Arth."

"Arth! . . . Hold on. You mean, it's not Kisch's head? I thought that the reason he was so successful these last few years was that he was working in two heads."

"Oh, come on now!" The girl threw up her hands. "If that's the way it was, it'd be much simpler. But the combination 'two heads, one body' cannot be treated as simply a body with two heads. More correctly, it is two heads with a common body."

"But the person is the same, isn't he? Especially if a person is result of the environment. The environment of both is the same. . . . Although I just don't understand anymore."

"What do you mean, the environment was the same for both? Kisch was born, like everyone else, as one person. His childhood was normal—you should know, you went to school together. But Arth! His consciousness came into being here, underground. In laboratory surroundings. He and Kisch have entirely different experiences. . . . I see that you are still missing the main point. Or that your conversation didn't touch on it. The problem is that two quite dissimilar persons are in the same body and take turns using it, in shifts. One is in control, and the other switches off—sleeps or thinks his own thoughts. Sometimes, of course, they can read the same book together. But even then each one is by himself. And perceiving in his own way."

"It just seems to get harder and harder! You're right, I didn't understand the main point. So, another independent consciousness?"

"And one that's developing. Growing. The baby was named Arth because he came into being through arthenogenesis. And now he's an adolescent. Fourteen years old."

"Is he taking a normal form? In the mental sense, of course."

"More or less. At first Kisch had a terrible time because Arth kept taking over his arms and legs. You know how active kids are, always squirming around. But then the mind grew, and he realized that he and his father had only one body between them."

"His father?"

"Kisch has ended up being something like a father to him. He tries to give as much as he can—films, books, television. In the beginning he told fairy tales. But now the kid paints pictures, knows two languages, takes part in sports—did you notice the equipment? Kisch, I think, survived the experience because of all those efforts."

"You mentioned sports?"

"Yes. If the body is under his control at a given time, why not? Actually, I was the one who got him started on gymnastics. My concern was for his social well-being. And now he's a whiz on the horizontal bar, his dismounts are according to the Olympic program—a special trainer goes to help him."

"But that means that Kisch is swinging around at the same time? Since the body is shared?"

"At the age of fifty?" The girl stopped and blushed slightly, glancing at the visitor. "That is, I meant to say that he's not as young as he used to be, right? And in gymnastics everything depends on brain's automatic movements, which lose something with time. It's not the muscles. Of course, Kisch enjoys the flexibility that Arth has developed. But he doesn't have the control that Arth does. Generally speaking, the situation is nightmarish for the two of them, but as an experiment it has revealed a whole lot of information. For example, Arth and I work out at gymnastics. He works for several hours on the parallel bars and the horizontal bars. He's perspiring profusely. But meanwhile Kisch is catching up on his sleep. Then Arth switches off, and the body belongs to his father. And it's like new."

"Can't be," the visitor said. "There've been changes. Acids accumulate in the muscles."

"But they disappear in an instant, as soon as a fresh brain is connected. That's the really strange thing, but the concept of fatigue itself is related only to consciousness. The body can go on for a year without stopping. Like an internal combustion engine—give it fuel, oil, and drive it hard for months at a time. Or take the piano. A friend of mine is their teacher, and I've been at their lessons several times. Kisch and Arth began at the same time. The boy is now a decent pianist, while Kisch can't play "Chopsticks." But the hands are the same. Imagine this—the teacher showed them an exercise. Arth takes control and repeats it effortlessly. He turns off, and Kisch tries to do the same, but gets nowhere. By the way, do you understand what 'turning off' means? It's as simple as sitting in a comfortable easy chair or lying down. Let yourself go limp, and giving yourself over to other thoughts. But if they wanted different things, like one hand here and the other one there, then it would depend on whose impulse was stronger. They often play tricks on each other. At first, of course, Kisch would win easily, but now Arth puts up a good fight. A good kid. Everybody in the institute likes him. But you know what's interesting, he has no talent in mathematics. In that regard he does not take after his father."

"What's going to happen to them later? After all, one of them could be transplanted."

"At the end of this year they are going to be split. Any sooner and it would have been too much of a shock for Arth. A developing consciousness needs stability. Otherwise it's like a child whose parents drag him from one country to another—there is no cultural background for him to build a personality. . . By the way, you probably didn't see them right away. When a new person shows up, they use a special system to make sure the newcomer isn't dumbfounded. When it's turned on, it gives you an unusual feeling, as though the body belongs first to this person, then to that one. If you are talking to Arth or listening to him, the arms, legs, and trunk are his. And Kisch's head seems extra. In the way. But as soon as Kisch says something, the situation reverses immediately. They ended up hopping back and forth before your eyes, like a visual illusion where you see alternately an old woman and a young woman. But never the two at once."

The waiter brought them more coffee. Kisch thoughtfully lit up a cigarette. There was something hopeful in the fact that his old acquaintance had taken the situation in hand and not been a passive victim of circumstance. There was even a heroic quality to it—to love such a strange child, to raise him. In any case, it all shed new light on Lek.

"Tell me, the other kid, the one with the guitar. How did he get in to Arth? Isn't it all top secret?"

"And who let you in?"

"It was an accident. I had a letter on me from Kisch. And some higher-up at the checkpoint wasn't around. Went out to fix his lighter."

"Sure thing. And the lieutenant on duty, was he reading a pamphlet about millionaires?"

"Yes. . . . So he was a lieutenant? A strange uniform."

"Internal security. The company has a whole army of them. To protect secrets. A huge armed contingent, complete with ranks—sergeants, lieutenants, colonels. But most of them are regular guys. That lieutenant always keeps that pamphlet alongside him, so that outsiders will feel he's not thinking about anything else. And that business about the lighter is code. When he mentions the lighter, it means that the visitor, in the lieutenant's opinion, is okay. They usually let in anyone they like. But if some inspectors or managers show up, they dawdle for two, three hours, pick at every detail. I work in that department. You wouldn't be able to begin to guess my job. I'm called the 'going-out girl.' "

It occurred to Kisch that the job fit her. She certainly was outgoing, not at all secretive. The girl had a figure like a gymnastics champion: thin body, strong thighs, strong arms.

"It's my job to go out from time to time, dressed in a white apron, into a little garden on the surface to take care of the flowers. Wearing a dress, not pants. I smell the roses, raise my eyes to the heavens, sigh, and turn around in embarrassment if someone is looking from the street. The house where our station is cannot differ in any way from the others. But everybody in town knows me by now. So the whole act is performed just for the benefit of the Directors Council, which is so well informed about the underground." The girl ate some cake with gusto. "Of course, I love to take care of flowers, but then who doesn't?"

She glanced at her watch, and her face changed expression.

"Did you come here without any papers at all?"

"I have my identifier."

"And a pass?"

"No."

The girl's eyes showed worry.

"Damn! We were just wanted—we're having an unscheduled inspection. Management goes into convulsions like that. First a bell, then they let the dogs loose. During that time everyone has to clear out of the corridors and take a seat in his workplace. What should we do?"

She reached over and took the crosspiece again.

"Sang, we have a problem. . . ."

"I heard everything," a voice said. "There are also some bunglers in the first station. Say, Niole, can your friend run?"

The girl looked at Kisch.

"I think so."

"Take off right now for Passage Four. I'll inform the guys to hold up the screen for a minute. They might let dogs loose on the other side, of course. Then go into the Computer Room, a little door on the left after the intersection. Now run! Only take it easy in the Computer Room, don't foul up!"

The girl stood up.

"Let's run. Follow me!"

She was already by the door, when Kisch began unsteadily to get to his feet. He didn't care about running—he didn't care about anything anymore.

The girl turned around angrily.

"What's the matter, do you want to end up in the Circuit? It's your life, you know."

A piercing quavering whine seized the building. It seemed that the walls were ringing, objects, even human bodies. A growing sense of alarm, physical anguish. Solid reality crumbled, and a volcano eruption, an earthquake, possibly even a war was about to break loose. Kisch's heart beat fast, and the world around seemed about to disappear in a fog. Overcoming his weakness, he rushed toward the girl. They leaped out of the dining room.

Niole raced down some stairs. Then they were in a large corridor filled with people—the bell had found very few at their workplaces. The girl pushed her way forward, and Kisch followed her, spewing out apologies as he went.

The ringing became louder and louder, setting nerves on edge, and sending out waves of fear. Gradually there were fewer and fewer people, doors slammed shut with metallic clangs. Niole dove into a narrow corridor, up a stairway into another large corridor, then into another narrow one. Up, down, right, left, forward, back. Kisch could hardly keep up. He went past the place where the girl had turned and was forced to go back. Niole kept picking up the tempo.

"Faster! Faster!"

The soles of his shoes slipped on the smooth metal floor, and he had to redouble his efforts, work with his whole body. He had a pain in his side, and a burning sensation spread upward from his stomach to his chest.

The ringing was so strong that no other sounds could be heard. The girl turned around, opened her mouth, screamed, but then had to gesture to keep Kisch from lagging. The sound intensified in a new wave, and it seemed as though there was nothing else in the whole world except that all-consuming, murderous ringing.

It intensified, then broke off! A deafening silence.

"Even faster!"

He raced after Niole through an oval arch. The girl slowed to a walk, then stopped, coming up against a transparent wall, on the other side of which was a stairway.

"Look!"

Kisch turned around. Behind his back in the arch a ribbed polished barrier descended noiselessly.

"Whew, we made it!" Niole was breathing heavily. "It's been a long time since I ran like that." She looked at Kisch with admiration. "You did very well. Running second is much harder when you don't know where you're going."

Between his gasps for air he asked, "Was it really necessary? Suppose they did find me. So what?"

"They'd send you to the Circuit. And not just you. The lieutenant who let you in. Setera Kisch, since he talked with you. You know, the company presents things as though you were infringing on interests of the state if you infringe on its own interests."

They were now walking down a corridor that, straight as a taut wire, stretched to infinity.

"The Circuit is a mechanism," the girl said. "Every process elicits the next according to its own logic, which can be established only post factum. It's impossible to foresee anything, but once it's done it seems that it couldn't have been any other way. Every organization has its own thought structure, and Surveillance, for example, believes that every person is guilty of something."

She suddenly froze in her tracks.

"Uh-oh, what was that?"

Through the transparent right wall they could see three men in rigid clumsy worksuits and masks on their faces running up the stairs two at a time. A pair of enormous long-haired dogs ran alongside them, tugging at their leashes, and a third, already turned loose, was already headed toward the flight of stairs that led to their corridor.

"They're letting them loose on this side too!" Niole looked back in desperation. "There's the door!"

They raced back to where a small door stood right before the arch. Kisch pulled on the knob. The door did not open.

"It's locked!"

"Push! The other way!"

The door slammed open. The room was occupied by a gigantic construction of jumbled, interwoven pipes, fat, medium, and air ducts. And that was all. Just these pipes and ducts; their irregular network extended up, down, and out, getting lost in the dim light.

Stepping out onto a small metal platform by the door, Kisch and Niole felt as though they were on a ledge over an abyss.

Kisch slammed the door shut. There was no lock.

"Maybe I could just hold it from the inside?"

"No way!" The girl grabbed him by the hand. "The guards will follow the dogs."

In all of this there was a tinge of unreality. Niole rushed down the metal staircase that seemed to be hanging in air. Kisch, after pausing for a second, hurried after her.

Once again, up, down, left, right. Behind them a dog was barking resonantly. The aluminized sparkling pants and the white blouse flashed a few steps in front of him. An evenly modulating whispering sound arose and became stronger as the two descended into the depths of the structure.

Steps, crossways, railings. The hand holds, the feet move. Kisch and the girl were now in the thick of complexly intersecting pipes. In some places they had to climb across, in other places crawl on all fours, or even jump. The noise increased.

"Hey, listen!"

Kisch stopped. The girl was near but on a different crossway. They were about five yards apart.

"Come here! I'll wait for you!" she shouted, using her hands as a megaphone.

Kisch nodded and strode across his crossway. But the stairs took him down and away from Niole. It was clear that earlier, in his haste, he had jumped onto the wrong path. He would have to go back.

"Somewhere we got separated! Let's try going back!"

He motioned to her with his hand, and the girl signaled that she understood. Kisch went out on a platform, from which there were two staircases.

The right one seemed to lead him closer to Niole. He started to climb it, but not far away the girl was now going down. Soon he saw her below his feet. They continued walking and in two minutes had changed levels. They were still three yards apart but in such a way that you would need wings to cross the distance. They set off again. Kisch entered a gallery covered on the top and sides with mesh wiring. The white spot of the blouse was ahead of him. Finally! He hurried up, and the girl started running. In a moment they were next to each other.

But separated by the wire mesh. Fine but strong.

Niole shoved her fingers into the mesh.

"Maybe it would be better to stay here. The inspection will be over, and the guys will find us. Unless. . . ."

Following her arrested glance, Kisch turned his head. A black-and-white dog, agilely mounting the stairs, was headed toward his side. He raced ahead, came out on some kind of platform, and became confused. There were stairways up and down, but the dog would be able to use them.

He heard a snarl behind him.

Without thinking any longer, he leaped from the landing onto the nearest pipe; embracing it with his arms, he crawled two yards to a fork. He climbed onto a square beam, then jumped onto something, and then climbed over something else.

And the dog jumped, too. Its compact body flashed through the air and crashed into the pipe. It was able to hang on and howled with rage.

In a panic Kisch rushed inside the tangle of pipes. Bending over when necessary, stretching out when required, he went farther and farther from the wire mesh area. The dog lagged behind. He heard its piteous yelps somewhere below.

Several leaps and bounds more and Kisch climbed through a thick tangle of pipes and found himself in a more open area. He sat down, straddling a beam, his legs dangling, gathering strength. It seemed that he was inside a gigantic cage. Pipes, ribbed and smooth, vertical, horizontal, and slant, surrounded him on all sides. In some directions they were situated tightly packed, in others more open. Carelessly applied stripes of chemiluminescent scantily lit the innumerable junctures. It was hard to believe that anyone could understand the system, to make their way around this thicket of pipes, much less to build it in the first place.

Where to now? He could not determine where the platform he had jumped from was.

Call out to the girl?

He gathered air in his lungs, opened his mouth, and then closed it. A steady droning noise embraced everything around him. One that could swallow up any other sound before it could travel more than two or three yards.

He now felt very unsure of himself. On all sides his glance hit pipes—close by or a little more distant. His view was limited. No way of telling where he would end up if he decided to move on—into the depths of the system or out to its edge. And what were those depths like?

"To hell with it. Anything but sitting."

Rising to his feet, Kisch walked along a thick pipe while steadying himself by holding onto a thin one. He ran into a group of pipes so tightly interwoven that he couldn't climb through, so he came back. He walked in the other direction and saw that the thick pipe ended, joining a vertical one. He turned to the right, hopping from pipe to pipe. The artificial grove did not let him go, but held him like a portable cage. It was amazing how fast he had forgotten how he had ended up here.

The pipes began to thin out. Kisch, overjoyed, quickened his pace. He hurriedly jumped over a five-foot gap, grabbed a slant pipe, and—letting out a scream—jumped back. The pipe was boiling hot. For a second he struggled desperately to maintain his balance, waving his arms. He managed to do a 180-degree turn and jumped down. On a thick pipe now, he felt the steam even through the soles of his shoes. He grabbed a thin pipe again, but it was hot as well. He found himself on a pipe alongside, he went down—he was turned around, and hit against something with his chest. He managed to grab a thick pipe that was just warm, fortunately, and descended to a juncture.

And below him was an abyss—dark, like the depths of outer space, very rarely crossed by a pipe.

Kisch was trembling all over from fear, pain, and nerves and almost broke out crying.

"God damn it, somebody's taunting me! I'm a human being, the father of a family!"

Then the memory of Rona and the kids gave him courage. He gritted his teeth and looked around carefully.

The same thicket of metal and kigon. Now he was quite far below the landing he had started from and had totally lost his sense of direction. To go in a horizontal directon did not make any sense. His goal was to find the end of this building, a wall, which would lead him back to the very first landing. But the thicket of pipes provided no hint of direction, and he could not tell whether he was headed in the right direction or going around in circles. To move in a straight line was possible in only two directions: straight up and straight down. To climb up would have been too difficult, so that left one path, to the bottom, no matter how far it might be.

But even this path was not easy. Descending a thin pipe that was by itself, Kisch reached a place where it joined another, also vertical but so thick he could not hold on. Only with great effort did he manage to climb back up. Another time he barely escaped from a cluster of hot pipes, and then later hit a group that was so cold that his fingers went numb, and refused to obey. When he finally reached a warm and thick horizontal pipe, he sat down on it, weak and exhausted. His first thought was that a person could wander around for weeks or months without ever meeting anyone.

"But you wouldn't last a week. Civilization's jungle, that's what this is."

He was suddenly overwhelmed by anger at Niole and her friends. He could end up dying in the effort to save them. After all, they did let him in without concerning themselves overmuch with security. But then he thought better of his anger. No one was guilty. After all Kisch himself had wanted to see his old friend and ask for advice.

A brilliant light flashed in the distance. Kisch's heart beat faster, and he headed in that direction, climbing from pipe to pipe with the help of all four extremities. The light came nearer. It was coming from a glowing fluorescent wire that was wrapped around a pipe leading down into the depths.

His mood improved. Kisch descended to the next tier, then to the next. His arms ached, his hands were weak and felt as though they were filled with cotton. The glowing wire branched. More effort, a little more, and finally Kisch felt a hard kigon floor under his feet.

It was over!

He walked at random between large catafalquelike chests. The entire surface here was covered with slightly oily metal filings. But he was still worried about whether he was really on the bottom or not. The pipes here did not bend for some reason, did not come to an end, but went straight into the kigon floor. As though there were something else below.

A rectangular structure loomed ahead, with a steel door. Kisch went over, examined the door. As he opened it, it creaked loudly. Inside it was dark. But maybe it was the place to seek an exit back to human beings.

He looked around. He went over to the fluorescent wire, and twisting and bending, broke off a piece at one end, then the other. Holding it as far as possible from his eyes, he entered the building. He took several steps and felt a strange sense of relief. As though a weight had been removed from his shoulders. He stopped and asked himself what was happening— and then he realized. The constant noise was getting weaker. He kept walking forward and reached a low room filled with machinery. Huge gears, levers, connecting rods—it was all motionless. The darkness gave way timidly, inaudibly before his light, the shadows tossed in fright, intersecting in complex patterns.

Stairs led down, and Kisch followed them; a hatch, and Kisch walked around it; a system of gears, he bore to the right; a steel basin, he turned left. With each step his hopes grew that he would reach the final wall and open the door onto a bright human corridor, clean, without the metallic dust.

He passed a palisade fence of steel columns, climbed up on a platform of some kind, and then noticed that the piece of wire in his hand was growing dim.

Damn it all! It happened to be one of the old fluorescents that needed a constant source of power. Frowning, Kisch looked at the wire, then realized that there was no time for lamentations. He rushed back. The shadows hopped up and down. When he looked back, everything seemed different from what it was coming forward. He collided with a pillar, almost fell into the hatchway, tripped on the stairs. The darkness grew thicker, the cold wire in his hand was glowing a dull red, hardly casting any light at all. The stairs came to an end. Kisch hit his head against something, caught his jacket pocket on something. Complete darkness. Trying not to give in to panic, he took one step, then another, then a third, in what he thought was the direction of the exit. Darkness, terrible moments of terror. Another step, and he could see the door.

Stepping out of the building, he slumped against the wall to catch his breath. There was an experiment only an idiot would have tried. With shaking hands he took out a cigarette, and struck a match against the wall. He lit up. It looked like he would have to follow the wall around on the outside. Possibly he could find the main wall for the whole building? He stamped out the butt, and set off, going around a structure made of large kigon bricks. True, he did not really believe that he was standing on the very bottom floor.

The building came to an end, as though it had been clipped, and the platform came to an end as well. Beyond a low railing was a gap. Both near and far pipes descended, into the unknown, like vines in a tropical forest. Kisch could not see where they ended.

The piece of wire, now only a dull red, had caught on Kisch's pocket. Leaning over the railing, Kisch dropped it into the abyss. It flew downward, diminishing rapidly until it seemed to dissolve into the bottomlessness.

Kisch bit his lips, trying to suppress tears. After all his work he was still only in the middle of the diabolical system. Or more accurately, he did not even know what part of it he was in. He had only climbed down to a kigon island floating in space. And that was the difference between natural and technological jungles. In a natural, real forest you can wander around on only one level, on the ground. But here there could be any number of levels at all. And even if they came looking for him, would they be able to find him?

He returned to the entrance to the building, and looked for the shining wire where he had torn the piece off. Hadn't it, too, become dimmer?

Indeed it had: The two loose ends were now dull red.

Kisch waved his hand, as though driving away a terrible thought. After all, it was impossible for him to destroy the whole lighting system by breaking it in just one place.

He exhaled deeply, climbed over the barrier, and grabbing the nearest pipe began a new descent. Now he was a little more familiar with the system; he had discovered that only the brass pipes were hot, that it was easier using the kigon because your soles didn't slip. The scene kept changing—at times he came up against such dense intersections that it took him a long time to find a way down, and at other times he dangled in almost complete emptiness. It was hard to believe that somewhere there was human life, a sky, wind, billowing fields of grain. Twice he saw kigon islands off to the side, but he did not even make an attempt to get close, just kept sliding, crawling, jumping downward. An hour passed, or maybe it was three or even four. Finally he saw beneath him some sort of tanks, the outline of some incomprehensible constructions. Kisch descended a thin, sticky pipe, squeezing it between his legs. Finally he stood on the top of a tank, filthy, his clothes ripped. His chest, his pants, his hands, even his face were grease-stained; his jacket was torn, rumpled, his face wet with sweat, his hair fallen in his eyes—an entirely different man than the one who not too long before was sitting in the restaurant in an antique chair.

He climbed down a metal ladder, and tested the floor. Stone, real, natural stone, not kigon. Solid ground at last.

The bottom. The real bottom.

He took several steps, then sat down. An immense space extended upward; alongside, something gurgled softly in the tanks. Stuffiness, intense heat, a heavy, dense air saturated with tiny droplets of oil, an oil mist.

Not a living soul.

Kisch raised his hand to his face. His watch was missing—torn off somewhere up above. His throat was dry, and hunger gnawed at his stomach. The thought came to him that in a real forest, not this technological jungle, he would be able to find some seeds, some fruit, he would come across a stream, or at worst lick dew from leaves.

But just try licking a pipe!

He got to his feet and started wandering without knowing where he was heading. The tanks ended, replaced by concrete cubes. What was inside them? Perhaps computers, perhaps even one of the systems that was holding him on a leash? Whatever it was that was connected to the electrodes in his brain. The doors to the cubes were fastened tight. But no handle, no sign of an outside lock, not even a keyhole. As though the whole cube had been molded in one solid piece.

A ceiling appeared overhead, and Kisch found himself in a corridor. He heard a new sound unlike the previous ones—a metallic din, caused by something moving. Kisch stood still at an intersection to get his bearings. He set off, hurrying, and soon stepped out into open space again.

From an opening in the wall a cable bridge ascended on a slant, disappearing in the darkness. Thick steel wires trembled in the air. A string of carts floated out of the wall, illuminated briefly by luminescent wire, then leisurely climbed upward. Another string slid down and darted into the wall.

But not a sign of a human being. Once created, once sown here in the ground, technology reigned supreme and grew more and more powerful, oblivious to any need for its creator.

It was astounding that the crazy situation he was in had come about quite naturally. After all, it was a quite sensible thing to want to see the present Setera Kisch. And it was easy to understand, from a human point of view, why the lieutenant had let him in despite the prohibition. And it was natural, too, for him and the girl to try to avoid the inspection. And very natural for him to flee the huge vicious dog by jumping onto a different pipe. Everything was very logical—Kisch could not blame himself for having acted stupidly even once. But somehow all those natural actions had led him into a horrifying, gigantic nightmare. Why?

The corridors branched, forming now and then small rooms at their intersections. At times the corridors were blocked by kigon beams, and Kisch had to climb over them. He tried to keep on in one direction, remembering each turn, but he kept being led farther and farther away from the course he had established in his mind when he started. And thirst was tormenting him.

He stopped, leaned his head back, and stared at the light-giving wires on the ceiling. Now there was no doubt that they had become dimmer.

Noticeably so. When he had descended he could see thirty yards ahead. Now everything beyond ten yards merged into a gray murk.

Suddenly his body ached and he felt like tearing at his flesh. He pressed his hands against his temples. Lord, it was a dream, a dream! He would scream, let out a cry of desperation, and the hallucination would collapse.

But he did not scream. He took his hands away, and the gray walls stared at him reproachfully, sarcastically. The wire on the turns was now a dull red. Two hours, or maybe even only one, until total darkness.

He started to run but slowed down to a walk. Another quarter of an hour found him in a narrow corridor, hitting against the wall on one side, then on the other. He heard a kind of snuffling sound and rushed toward it.

A steel door, and once again no knob, no sign of a lock. He knocked— no answer. He pushed with all his strength, but it was like trying to move a cliff. He pounded on it with his fists until they ached and screamed.

The snuffling inside gave way to a knocking. A tiny bell rang, something buzzed, clicked, strummed, and then snuffled again. Behind the door machines were talking in their machine language, not hearing him, not having the ability to sense his presence in any way. Even if the steel door had been open.

With a groan he slid to the floor. It occurred to him that the right thing to have done was to stay where he had torn off the wire. He would have been able to hope that someone would come to repair the damage and tumble over him. (By this time he was no longer worried about the guards or about the Circuit he might end up in—he wanted to get out at any price!) But on the other hand, there was no way of knowing how long he would have had to wait down there in the darkness by the abyss. It was quite possible that light was needed only during repairs, and that no humans ever came that way. And there was no way to climb the hundreds and hundreds of yards up to the original kigon island.

"Maybe it's all for the best," he said aloud. "Our civilization is dying."

He sighed. That was it! Sometime in the middle of the century humanity had reached its peak. But now there was only emptiness ahead, an emptiness that roared metallically. He was just sorry for the kids. They would have a lot to figure out if they tried acting like human beings and collided with a hostile world. And they too would finally rest beneath some machine.

He suddenly realized that he really did not feel like seeing other people anymore. In any case, if they were security agents, salesmen, judges, or executioners, or Mafia gangsters. They were all the same. It was better to die and eventually be found there, not having betrayed himself.

Right beside him was something soft, yielding. Kisch picked it up.

Without understanding why, he felt an invigorating cool wave pass over his body.

In his hand was Niole's white blouse. Made of a wrinkleproof, soilproof fabric, it was even now glowing as though straight from the store.

So that meant the girl was here!

He jumped to his feet, leaving all his gloomy thoughts behind.

"Hello-o-o! Hello-o-o!"

The sound rushed away but collided in the darkness against a wall and fell back at his feet.

"Hello-o-o!"

He ran forward.

A dead end.

He turned around and rushed to an intersection. For some reason he felt that Niole had to be somewhere near but was momentarily about to leave.

He listened carefully, holding the blouse against his chest as a proof to fate that he had the right to expect an answer.

Nothing.

He ran down a corridor but once again hit a wall, then raced back. Turns flashed by, all identical. He had not the slightest idea of the direction.

An hour later, hoarse, sore all over, he sat down on a beam that crossed the narrow corridor. The wire on the ceiling glowed dully. A soft layer of dust on the beam showed that no one had been here in years. His throat was raw from thirst and screaming, his dry tongue felt like a piece of wood.

It occurred to him that he should compose his last words—perhaps in a year, or ten, they would be passed on to his wife and children. He shoved his hands in his pockets and found the flier for Confidence. He was racked by a convulsive anger.

"You bastards! I'm going to keep on until I keel over!"

He tried tearing the flier but could not. He threw it on the floor, spat at it, stamped on it. His legs were giving way, but he stubbornly set off, his shoulder brushing the wall. In the darkness he did not see but somehow sensed the presence of a hole at knee level. He bent over, his bones cracking, then squatted, but the opening was too small, and the passage behind it tilted downward. He got down on all fours and felt that the air was fresher. He started in and soon the passage narrowed, he had to lie flat and crawl—and it was clear that there was no going back. But there was no hope in that "back" anyway.

Thanks to the slope, crawling was a snap. He broke out laughing.

"I've turned into a worm, a termite."

A breeze now touched his face. Something glimmered in the darkness ahead.

A half-turn. A half-open grate.

Kisch pushed it open and looked out. Then he climbed out into some kind of recess and stood up.

To the right and left stretched a brightly lit wide tunnel with greenish walls. And a yard-wide rail ran down the center.

A magnetic road. And he was in one of the repair recesses.

On the right he heard a quickly increasing whistle. Something flashed in front of his eyes, and the wind tugged at him so hard he had to grab the grating. Vague spots danced around, the wind roared. Then it was all over. Silence.

"So. That's just fine. The cars have passed. . . ."

He carefully inspected the surroundings, with a determined efficiency that was a surprise to him. His strength seemed to have returned—even in areas he never before knew. From here he would be able to find his way out, even if it took days. The road must have recesses at regular intervals, so all he had to do was determine how far apart they were. And not be caught by a train as it whizzed by at 150 miles an hour.

Kisch started to tick off the seconds in his mind. He had counted to fifty three times when he heard a whistle and stepped back in his recess.

It all happened just as it had before. And then once more—the trains flew by every three and one-half minutes.

"Good. That means I can run for a minute and a half, and if I don't see a recess ahead, I can run back."

He waited out just one more train, noticing that the cars came right up to the tunnel wall. He jumped out and sprinted along the central rail. Ten seconds, twenty. . . . He felt winded. Then he realized that he had gone past the limit of a minute and a half. The greenish polished walls shone evenly. Kisch picked up the pace. On his right he saw a dark shadow in the wall. He ran to it, squeezed into the recess, and at that very moment a sharp whistle blasted and the wind tugged at him with a soft but unrelenting force. The cars were flying by in their automated course.

When everything had settled down he shook his head, puffing madly.

"That was too close a shave."

He realized that he could get rid of his shoes and ran the next stretch barefoot. It was better—he finished with thirty seconds to spare. He took off his jacket, putting his identifier in his pants pocket. Running was even easier, and things started looking brighter. Another two intervals and he had the knack of it, taking only one train to catch his breath. He even began wondering how many passengers there were in each train, whether they could see him, and if so, what they thought of him.

In the seventh interval he felt a little tired but caught himself in time to run for all he was worth. He made it to the recess just as the whistle sounded.

Someone's hand grabbed him by the belt, and pulled him back forcefully. He flailed out in a panic, trying to tear loose. The hand did not let go, and the cars flashed by in his peripheral vision.

The wind ceased. The person holding Kisch relaxed his or her grip. Kisch stepped back. Niole was standing in the recess.

For a second they just stared at each other.

"Very good," she said. "You know, I thought we would meet. Pretty neat, isn't it?"

"You've got quite a grip." Kisch felt his face dissolving into the most idiotic of grins. He looked the girl over. Niole was smeared all over with grease and almost naked, wearing only panties and a bra. Kisch felt like grabbing her and kissing her.

In response to his stares she shrugged her shoulders.

"I left everything behind as a signal for you. Earrings, shoes, pants, stockings. Did you find anything?"

"The blouse. How did you get down?"

"I climbed down to find you. I got lost and decided that you would descend all the way to the bottom."

It sounded so simple the way she said it—"I climbed down to find you." As though indifference, cowardice, and betrayal no longer existed on the earth.

"A terrible place, isn't it?"

He nodded.

"You probably don't know where this tunnel leads. . . . Nowhere. They started building a suburb in this area, then the appropriations ran out, right in the middle of the construction cycle, when the foundations, water lines, had already been installed. What happened to the money is a mystery. The answer is in the computers, somewhere in a memory block—but all the companies are keeping quiet, holding onto their secrets. They didn't even know where to find the plans. And this railroad keeps on running. By itself."

Kisch cleared his throat. He wanted to ask Niole something quite different but instead he said, "So who does travel here?"

"No one—not ever. Down here on the railroad and underground in general there is not a single person. But the energy is still supplied, so all the automated machines still work. In fact, new lines are even being constructed. Oh yes! Your watch! I found it down below."

She raised her hand with the watch.

"You're remarkable," Kisch said. "To tell you the truth, I have already pushed myself to the point of collapse. But you really are incredible."

The girl looked at him, then reached out and embraced him, pulled him against her.

At that very second the whistle struck both their ears, the cars roared behind Kisch's back, the hurricane wind pulled at his shirt, at the cuffs of his pants, attempting to pull them off, to pull him from Niole's embrace. Kisch finally grabbed the grating.

The train was gone, and they stepped apart.

Niole, inhaling deeply, said "These cubicles aren't meant for two. How many sections have you run? I did three. If you have come farther, let's head in your direction."

A station appeared after the fifteenth section. In the smooth wall there appeared a platform ledge. Kisch managed to run up and duck under it just as the dark dot materialized; the train instantaneously grew as it approached, then stopped.

Up on top of the platform lights were shining on glistening white artificial marble, and gleams dotted the floor's geometrical patterns. Silence, not a single human voice, no sound of steps. Deserted. The center of the spacious platform was occupied by the escalator.

But it was motionless, frozen still.

Kisch walked over to it. The escalator ascended as far as he could see, the up and down sides met in the distance. All his tired muscles ached when he thought of climbing on foot what looked like at least thirty stories.

The girl was standing next to the escalator. She motioned with her head to begin the climb.

"Can you imagine how high it is? I guess it's more than a kilometer."

"A kilometer?"

"Yes. And up stairs. . . . Let's go on to the next station, there's nothing to lose. Let's have a look."

The next train, a transparent one made entirely of glass, pulled in quietly. Rustling in unison, the doors of the empty cars opened. Beginning to feel like carefree tourists, Kisch and the girl hopped in happily, and fell onto the soft seats, stretching out their legs with great relief. The train gained speed rapidly, pulling them both to the side—the only sign that they were moving.

"Oh, to sleep," Niole said dreamily. "Do you know how long we've been traveling? Six hours. We met in the corridor at eleven, and now it's five. Oh, those pipes! Never again—I'm afraid of them now. . . . I wonder whether we're headed toward our town or away from it?"

Kisch felt as though months, not hours, had passed since he had met Niole. It was the first time in his life that he had seen the hostile, soulless face of technology. And then there was Lek with his two heads. And. . . .

"Strange," he said. "A railroad no one needs. It exists for itself. When our civilization finally bursts, this tunnel will remain a monument to purposeless work, And it's also a form of enslavement for human beings—tremendous, pointless work. Like the pyramids at Cheops. If no one undertook such things, life would be much sweeter. What a strange paradox—each element in our economic system is rational, brings a profit, but taken all together it creates a mass of things no one needs.

"But no human beings have ever worked here," Niole said. "That is, human work lies behind it, but the underground area itself was planned and constructed without human involvement. Now it grows by itself, moving where it wants, avoiding obstacles. No one knows what its energy sources are. Before, some people knew, of course, but they died, or transferred to a different company. So now it seems that it is cheaper to let the system have its way than to determine what is really happening—you know how expensive investigations like that are, ones that require experts."

"But suppose you just destroyed it? Just go and blow up a length of track. Or a depot. Otherwise it will sap the ground beneath cities."

"You can't destroy it. After all, it's private property. Of course, we don't know exactly whose, since the whole thing is terribly complicated. And if you destroy only part, it will repair itself. And finally, who's going to bother? You're not going to come down here with a bomb, nor am I. So it's simpler to forget about it or think of it as a natural phenomenon. . . . It's really been lost from sight. Only a few people know that it exists. When I tell the people in my department that I've been here, their mouths will drop."

The train slowed down, the doors opened. Kisch and the girl got out, and both were immediately overjoyed to hear a low rumble. The empty station, like the previous one, was sparkling clean. On the right side the escalator went up, on the left it came down. The two of them stepped onto the flexible stepped ribbon and were carried away. There was no handrail, no bannister. Just a round tunnel with polished walls, where the bottom was a quickly moving staircase. At first Niole and Kisch stood, then they sat on the steps.

"So you were talking about blowing it up." The girl returned to the subject of their conversation. "That could even be dangerous. Where will the enormous quantity of energy go if it's not consumed by the railroad? You blow something up here, and in Megapolis there's an equipment failure or something totally unexpected, like a financial crisis. A friend of mine says that we just can't touch technology—it has its own ecological chains and cycles."

"The moral is," Kisch said, "that technology should develop only to the point where it can still be controlled. No further."

"True. But take the example of specialists. Most of them work without having the slightest idea of what they're doing. A person is hired by a company and told what the immediate responsibilities of the position are. But to explain why he should do this or that would take too long and involve too many secrets. A muddle, in other words. Somehow it's all got to come to an end, because everyone is sick of it."

Ahead and back the escalator tunnel diminished to a dot. They had been traveling for about ten minutes, and the sense of going up disappeared as soon as they lost sight of the station. Only by touching the wall could they be sure that the rumbling staircase was still moving. And by feeling the slight tremor of the steps.

"My stomach is howling for food," the girl said. "I wouldn't mind the restaurant about now. By the way, we really should introduce ourselves. My name is Niole."

"I know." Kisch blushed. "That's what your friend called you. And I am Lek—or actually, Setera Kisch."

"What? Setera is—"

"If you want the truth. You see, the fact is that—"

"You and he had an exchange, right? And you were born Setera Kisch?"

"Right. However, it's better if you call me Lek. I'm more used to it."

"If that's what you want. Pleased to meet you. You know, when I first saw you, for some reason you reminded me of Hagenauer."

"Who's Hagenauer?"

"A friend of Mozart's. A kind, modest man. He was always lending Mozart money. He never got it back but kept on giving—I just finished a novel about Mozart. I keep hearing the theme from the Thirty-Eighth— do you know it?"

The name of Mozart sounded totally out of place.

"You, it seems, can't stay mad long," the girl remarked.

"Perhaps. But do you think that that's a bad trait?"

"On the contrary, it's great. I'm the same way. You get mad at someone and then think, 'Oh to hell with it.'"

Finally the ceiling of the entryway appeared at the top of the escalator. Lek and Niole stood up. The mouth of the tunnel broadened as they approached. The steps flattened and disappeared under the comb of the top step.

The two of them took several steps in the large round hall that was covered with red marble. Then they looked at each other.

There was no way out.

There were no doors on the opposite side; the lobby ended in a wall of yellow rock.

A trap. A continuation of the nightmare.

The girl frowned.

"Tough luck." She turned around and looked at the stairs running up the tunnel. "It looks like it's going to be tough getting down."

And indeed the escalator was turned against them now. They had come up with its help, but now they would have to overcome its inhuman strength to get back down. To race madly down the stairs knowing that the slightest delay, even several seconds' rest, would mean the loss of all you had gained.

For an instant Lek had the vision of dusty corridors and a tangle of pipes. As long as he didn't have to go back! In addition, he had already destroyed the lighting system.

"No way!" He rushed over to where the yellow rock came up from the floor and bent over.

"Look! It's sand! Dry and light. We can dig. There are probably doors here, an exit."

He climbed up, casting down little avalanches with every movement. Under the top layer of sand it was wet. Lek began throwing the sand aside with his hands. After a minute of this, a wall became visible, then the edge of a lintel. Lek dug with the fury of a dog searching for the bone it buried. Finally, a little hole formed. Fresh air flowed in. The opening widened. Daylight flooded in.

"Come here! Hurry!"

Helping each other, they climbed out underneath the lintel and found themselves at the bottom of a sand crater. Above them was the bright sky, still blue despite the dusk.

"Let's go! Hurrah!" Niole embraced Lek, then, flailing with her arms, fell over on her back and slid down twenty yards, back into the dark lobby.

Five minutes later they had climbed to the edge of the crater. As far as the eye could see there were only piles of rubble, ditches, cranes that had fallen over, stacks of concrete slabs, pipes sticking up out of the ground— the primeval chaos of an abandoned construction site. The scene stretched out to the horizon without a sign of a bush or tree or any living being.

"Majestic!" Niole said.

Lek turned his head and even stepped back in amazement, almost falling back into the crater. Only one hundred yards away the sky's delicate blue was cut by a tall tower. The same one he had seen early in the morning from the road.

Every window was lit brightly.

"It's a hotel." Niole shifted her weight from foot to foot. "Honest. I was told that even though there is no town, there is a hotel, and it's open."

A young man was standing off to the side of the hotel's majestic entrance. He watched the approaching Lek and Niole without a smile. His face, tanned, seemed cut out of dark stone and drew attention with the immobile certainty of its features. Individuality, some kind of stubbornness, fanaticism, came to the surface distinctly, as in Renaissance portraits.

"Hi," Niole said. "We've run away to keep from ending up in the Circuit. Can we rest here?"

"Of course." The man glanced at Niole, not without a certain delight, then modestly looked away. He was strangely dressed. Something like a shirt made of coarse, stiff material, pants in the same style, clumsy, formless shoes. "The hotel is at your service. I'm the manager . . . and the owner, for all practical purposes. Where've you come from?"

"From the underground."

"The underground? Is it close?"

"Of course. There's a hole right up there."

From close up it was evident that the man was not the picture of health. Distinct black circles gaped under his eyes—a sign of nervous disorder or chronic lack of sleep.

"Too bad," he said. "An expedition just set out into the desert in search of it."

"What desert?"

"This one." The man pointed toward the horizon. "Three days they spent swarming around there with their equipment but missed that spot. Well, let's go in. I'll give you some food, you can wash up, change your clothes." Once again he looked away from Niole in embarrassment.

The lobby was huge, like a Gothic cathedral or the hangar for a Martian rocket. The walls were faced with aluminum sheets the color of old gold, columns of relief-ornamented kigon, sofas and armchairs with legs curved in the old style. All the horizontal and vertical lines had shifted by fifteen degrees. They had to walk with one leg bent, as on a slanted roof.

"The hotel was built flat," the clerk explained. "They started to put it up but hadn't quite finished when work stopped. But everything works."

They entered the tilted elevator. The man pushed a button.

"It's best if I put you on the third floor. That's the only place I have the candles out."

"Candles?"

"Something's haywire in the electric wiring. During the day it's on and the lights work. But when it gets dark, it shuts off." As he explained he was careful not to look at Niole. "I tried straightening it out, but it didn't work. The system is automatic."

"Do you have to take care of things all by yourself?"

"I have for eight years already. But it's not that much work. The cleaning is automated, the bedding, towels, and the dishes are all disposable." He suddenly looked at Lek and the girl with an unexpected suspicion. "Both in the same room, or separate rooms?"

"Separate," Niole said. "But you have to understand, we just don't have any money. Everything happened by accident."

"It doesn't matter. I was saying, all the services work even when no one is living here. Food supplies and so on. Goods regularly are delivered from the department store. Half my time is spent piling the stuff up and burning it. The hotel is part of a different system than the construction and functions normally, except for the fact that there are no guests. You are the first real guests."

In the hall the walls were decorated with complicated white designs depicting fish and algae against a blue background.

"The annual inspection by NAHRC is coming to an end. You can have supper with them. But after that it's canned food. But if you really want fresh vegetables and meat, I can prepare it for you." The clerk now looked at Niole. "If you wait an hour, I'll do it. No more than an hour."

The girl sighed.

"As quick as possible."

"Then eat with the commission. I'll set two more places in the Beach Room and ask them to wait. It's right here, on this floor."

The room the man gave Lek was a double. From the window there was a wide view of the wasteland. Along the opposite wall, separated by a night table, were two beds—Lek realized that the clerk had placed them so that the slope was lengthwise rather than sideways. On the table was a crudely made candlestick holder with a candle. Above it was an aquarium built in the wall, where some red fish slid sadly from side to side. Finding some bath towels in the bathroom, Lek let out a roar of pleasure. Unfortunately, because of the slope he couldn't fill the tub all the way, but it was still a delight.

Scrubbed and softened, he went out into his bedroom and found a blue sizeless suit with matching shoes. Just then the clerk knocked on the door.

"How is it? Will it do? I let the girl into the department store so she could choose for herself. What's her name?"

"Niole."

"A fine girl. My name is Grogor."

"Lek. Pleased to meet you."

They shook hands, and Lek felt that his fingers were being held very carefully in a steel vise. They went out into the blue hall. The setting sun shaded the tritons and sharks on the wall with yellow-pink tints. The floor was devoted to the theme of the sea.

They strolled along. Because of the slanting floor, Lek bumped into his companion every now and then. The clerk said, "If you always walked in the same direction, your spine would be bent. But wherever you go, you have to come back."

"Is it lonely here without other people?"

"Without other people?" The clerk suddenly stopped, leaned against the wall, pressing his forehead against the protruding head of the white triton, and closed his eyes. Then after a second he lifted up his head. "What were you saying?"

"I was asking if you were bored here all alone. Are you sick?"

"Why do you ask? I just fell asleep." Grogor shook his unevenly cut blond hair. "No, I'm not bored. I have things to keep me busy. But the most important thing is the freedom. There's no one over me."

"Do you go into town often?"

"Not once since I've been here."

"But there is a road? What about transportation to town?"

"There used to be a road. They had just started widening it when work stopped. Now it can't be used—all dug up. So the company switched to supplying the hotel by air. And so it will be until the computer program ends. But when that will happen is anybody's guess. A helicopter is supposed to pick up the commission—they came for three days."

Niole appeared in a red, shimmering dress. With her arrived a cloud of perfume. Her eyes were shining.

"Like in a fairy tale. I've never had such a choice in all my life. Do you really destroy it all?"

"What am I supposed to do with it?" The clerk shrugged his shoulders. "I have to make room for new deliveries. The wild tribes come in from the desert for food. But they don't take any goods."

"Wild tribes?"

"There are three of them, I think. Two nomadic and one settled. The settled people eat tremendous amounts. There are more of them. They call themselves the Canons. I'm not really interested in them."

The Beach Room did indeed resemble a beach. The floor was made of glued-down pebbles and stones, a long table had a sandlike surface, and the ceiling featured a sun composed of light-carrying fibers. In the center of the room deep-blue water gushed from a fountain, forming a pool that flowed along a wall.

Nursing their glutamine cocktails, the four members of the commission sat around the table. When Niole walked in, they all rose. A plump man, bowing, presented the group: "We're from NAHRC—the National Association of Hotel and Restaurant Construction."

"Inspectors from TSK," Niole responded perkily. "Actually, from TSK and ZPT. I'm not at liberty to say any more."

The plump man nodded knowingly.

The appetizer was a petroleum-based caviar, quite zesty. Grogor took all the dishes out of a window in the wall: synthetic chops, bacterial vegetables, all sorts of side dishes. All the food came on dissolvable plates; the knives and forks were also dissolvable. The caretaker, who sat at the head of the table, was the only one who did not take part in the repast. Lek was struck by the fact that he would rest his head in his hands and nod off for three or four seconds. (The black circles under his eyes had become more prominent as the day grew later.) Everyone threw their dishes into the deep-blue water, where they immediately melted away without leaving a trace. Because of the slant everyone had to sit stiffly, bending their bodies and bracing themselves with their legs.

Once they had assuaged their hunger, they began to converse.

The plump man passed Lek a bowl with artificial boiled potatoes.

"Have you noticed the decoration in the hall? They create the impression of solidity but are really polyphotographic lifeprints. Thinner than cigarette paper. The whole wall is done with one roll that weighs a little more than a pound."

"My pride and joy," another man joined in, "is the boiler system. Grown-in pipe without a single seam, can you imagine?"

"Yes," Lek began, "but then there's those—"

Niole, her mouth full, had a choking fit and gave Lek a strange look before she managed to swallow successfully.

"—those excellent pipes," she said. "I haven't seen them, but I'm sure they are."

"A leak is totally impossible." The man who was so proud of the boiler system caught a glass just as it was about to slide over the edge of the table.

"As the representative for architectural inspection," a third man said, "I can say that the unobtrusive repair work has been documented superlatively."

Out in the hall Niole lit into Lek. "What were you trying to accomplish in there? Start a public meeting on the fate of civilization?"

"But the whole thing is crazy—talking about pipes and decorations in a situation like this!"

"Why? They're just doing their jobs, and they don't really know us—so of course they come out looking like fools. But get to know them in other circumstances, and each of them could turn out to be highly intelligent and interesting. It's just that they have to go along with the ritual. If they refuse and get fired, you're not about to pay their salaries."

"Well. . . ."

"Besides, the fat man probably built the wall himself. He invented the material, was inspired, put himself through hell to get it right. He really needs to hear a word of praise, especially since his creation has ended up in a place where no one sees it." Niole touched the fin of one of the fish. "Look, they really aren't three-dimensional."

Lek tried to grab the fin, but his fingers slipped over the smooth surface. He looked up and down—the illusion of solidity returned. He put his cheek against the wall, and only then did the white relief retreat into flatness.

"Well, I'll be!"

"Very nice." Niole suppressed a yawn. "Let's get to sleep, okay? It looks like the only way back is on foot through the desert. I talked with our host. He thinks it's about twenty-five miles to town. We'll have to leave at dawn. Unfortunately he doesn't have a compass. But I think we'll be all right if we just head toward the sun. In any case, it's better than going back underground."

"You can say that again."

"So then, good night."

No sooner had Lek stretched out blissfully and fallen into oblivion than he felt someone shaking him by the shoulder. Grogor was standing next to the bed.

"Excuse me."

"Ugh."

"I knocked but you didn't answer."

"I was asleep, but what is it?"

"Wouldn't you like to see the hotel? I can show you."

Lek stood up, swaying and still not understanding what Grogor wanted. He looked regretfully at the depression in the bed made and warmed by his body.

"Okay, let's go. I mean, it would be a pleasure."

The caretaker stopped by the elevator. "Suppose we invite Niole?"

"Let's."

"Could you knock on her door and ask?"

"Why don't you do it yourself?"

Grogor's sharp face turned crimson. He dropped his eyes.

"I'm embarrassed. I never meet women. And especially with a girl like her. . . ."

"Well, all right."

Niole had not yet gone to bed and to Lek's surprise accepted the invitation without complaint.

The sun was at the horizon when the three of them went out through the hotel's magnificent entrance. The building's enormous shadow was broken by the piles of trash. The evening breeze picked up an old blueprint, twirled it around, and threw it high in the air.

Following the caretaker, Lek and Niole went around the hotel. Grogor strode over the heaps of kigon fragments like a mountaineer used to steep paths since childhood. They passed a group of half-destroyed brick columns, made their way through a crowd of bulldozers whose rotting drive belts squirmed like snakes beneath their feet.

They climbed to the top of a dune of crushed stone.

Here Lek and Niole came to a sudden and enchanted stop. Lek gave out a low whistle. "Now that's more like it!"

A square hollow about five hundred yards on each side was drowned in greenery all the way to the other side. At first the carpet of vegetation seemed monotonous, but the eye soon distinguished a grove here, a meadow there, a freely growing thicket of bushes in one place, a neatly planted garden in another. Approximately in the middle of the plot, a thin pipe supported by braces reached up toward the sky. Alongside, the red tile roof of a small house stood out against the surrounding green. An exact duplicate of a peasant farm of two hundred years before. Even the pipe did not spoil the effect because of its light cream color.

"An oasis in the middle of the desert," Niole gasped.

"Look at me," Grogor said rapidly, taking advantage of the effect the sight had produced. He pulled out the collar of his clumsy shirt. "Look at this. It's all my work! I grew the cotton, I spun the thread, I weaved the cloth. And my shoes. Do you know what they're made of? Leather!"

"Oh, leather." Niole looked at the strange shape of the clumsy shoes in bafflement. "Valsamite, apparently. Or maybe some carbon-based compound."

"The whole point is that they're not chemical. Just plain leather!"

"I see that they're made of leather. But what's leather made of?"

"From a pig. I read in an old book how to tan the hide, and I did it. I'm not wearing anything artificial. On principle."

"You mean, you killed a pig?" Niole frowned.

"First I put it to sleep with an injection. You have to kill them—they multiply very fast. Here, come down this path."

They entered the green kingdom. The air was saturated with the pungent odor of caraway, lime trees, pines, which struck Lek and Niole all the more powerfully after their underground travels. A large, heavy bee took off from a flower and flew away buzzing—a yellow-and-black clump suspended in air by the miracle of living nature. Then it disappeared against the background of the leaves. Beneath the trunk of a small pine a prickly reddish-brown pile jutted up, covered with quick little dots.

"An anthill," Grogor explained. "There's one here, and another over that way. There are a lot of insects here—even if I do say so myself. Even pests. Cabbage moths, plant lice. . . . They're hard to find, pests. I wanted to raise Colorado beetles in the potato patch. But you just can't find them. Destroyed everywhere in the world. Only a few specimens left in military laboratories. Very rare."

"Why would you want Colorado beetles?"

"For naturalness. . . . Look at this field of millet. It's rich black earth, by the way. But do you know how I made it? With my own two hands. In this area there was no topsoil left. Whatever had been here before had been mixed with crushed rock, cement, brick. So first I covered the area with a mixture of vermiculite, sand, and clay. I planted alfalfa and Sakhalin bamboo, in turn, and watered it with a solution of phosphorous, potassium, and nitrogen. Three years running I mowed it, then plowed it under. Only then did I begin to plant bushes and other stuff. Now I have five inches of humus. True, that's with manure, which I add all the time. In the grove everything underground is all tangled with roots. Some of the trees are so solid that you can't even shake them."

They went into the fruit orchard. The cherry trees were heavy with fruit, and the limbs of the apples were bent to the ground, the ground was littered with fallen fruit.

"Do you like it?" Grogor asked Niole. "Please, eat something. You can see that it's all going to waste, just rotting."

"Thanks." Niole handed Lek an apple, then picked another.

"You, too, please eat. You know, when a person plants an orchard, he at least can be sure that the plants he grows will return the oxygen to the atmosphere to compensate for what he uses in breathing. But that's not all. The most important thing is that I'm completely safe. If the computer suddenly stops bringing supplies and servicing the hotel, if all your technological civilization splits apart, I'll manage quite nicely with food, clothing, and fuel."

"So you think everything's going to fall to pieces?" Lek asked.

"I don't think anything. I just want to be independent. Just think: Before, people used to be much less dependent on technology than we are now dependent on nature. If one thing doesn't work, we just go ahead and try another. Take for example the Neolithic Age, ten thousand years ago. If someone's crops failed, he could feed himself by hunting. When there was no game, they could gather wild fruit, beetles, mushrooms, frogs. All around them were living things, edible things. But today? In the city try stopping just one service for a short time—the water supply or garbage pickup. Within a few months millions would die. I'm not saying anything like that could happen—there are all sorts of backup systems. But still, it's disgusting to think that your existence depends on the water pipes or the garbage truck. . . . there's a stream here, and I dug a cistern."

"Oh, look!" Niole pointed. "Mickey Mouse."

Between clumps of grass the tiny animal, stretching itself high, sniffed the air with his keen nose, then ran off.

"The place is full of mice." The caretaker grinned with satisfaction. "One time I even raised rats. But I caught a disease from them, barely pulled through. So what were we talking about?—oh, yes, independence."

He led Lek and Niole to the pipe, which extended about fifty feet into the air. The foundation was a block of kigon, and a cable went into the ground.

"First of all, energy. Because of the difference in temperature above and below, there is a constant flow of air in the pipe. I have hooked up a generator. I can pump water, run a tractor—whatever you want. And the thing works in any weather. The brushes wear down, but I have a whole boxful in reserve. The bearings may wear out, but I'll find a replacement. Now about food. Flour, vegetables, fruit—I have ten times what I need. And then there's the hothouse and the pond stocked with carp. In the cellar I have a mushroom cave. I already told you about the pigs. To that, add six cows and two dozen sheep. And you know where all this leads? To a complete ecology, a closed cycle. If you sealed me in with a huge dome, I could survive forever."

Grogor looked triumphantly at Niole and Lek.

"Let the whole world go to hell—I'm going to survive. Just like in a well-balanced aquarium."

"Would you like to be covered with a dome?"

The caretaker frowned.

"I'm not sure. . . . But let's go inside."

The house turned out to have two floors and be quite spacious. Grogor told them how he made the fire-resistant brick, how he had built the walls all by himself. He was bustling about, running ahead of Niole and Lek, then returning. He was carried away, his immobile face had come to life, his eyes shone sharply.

The inspection began with the cellar. "This is synthetic milk. Two-hundred-pound boxes. At first I dragged over supplies from the hotel; now I am replacing them with what I grow myself. But I've kept the boxes for the time being—enough milk for three years, drinking it like crazy. Down here is the soy protein. But those hams over in the corner are mine—I mean, they're real. The food is still in artificial packaging, but I intend to replace it with my own work. You see, the goal is to master every aspect of production. After all, it is the division of labor that has robbed man of his independence. A person knows how to do only one little thing and depends on others for everything else. That's not my way. If I need wire or a file, I learn how to make it. I try to start from nothing. I've already learned pottery—you see that jug of olive oil over there?"

Lek and Niole looked at the lopsided clay jug. In that corner of the building there was a heavy, suffocating odor.

"That's the tallow. In this vat I heat the tallow to make candles." Grogor was talking faster and faster. "Behind the vat is a spinning wheel, and behind it a loom."

The caretaker was jumping around so fast that it was hard to follow his movements. He opened a door in the brick wall; behind it was a dark corridor.

"An underground passage."

"Where to?" Lek and Niole asked simultaneously.

"Outside, beyond the crushed rock. It's still not finished. I plan to build a wall around my land, and the passageway will go beyond it."

"What for?"

"Anything can happen. It's always nice to know that you can leave without being seen. Isn't that right?"

"And the wall? Is that so the tribes can't enter?"

"No! They're weak, can't really do anything. Some of the Canons snuck into the garden once. In the beginning. But I warned them that I would stop giving them canned food. Then they stopped. Canned food is more convenient—easier to cook."

From the cellar they went right up to the second floor. There, too, the rooms were jammed with supplies—for the most part produce from the garden and hothouse. Mounds of beans, dried apples, raisins. Everything was covered with dust, filthy, and much was spoiled. An enormous rat jumped out from a pile of apples, and ran past Lek's feet. The caretaker with an animal quickness darted after, bent over, and caught it by the tail. He knocked its head against the wall, then threw it out the window. All this took just seconds, and soon he was standing in front of a window pointing at a large meadow in one part of which cows were grazing, and in another, sheep.

"I used to milk the cows and separate the milk. I stopped—I just don't have time. Now the calves nurse for a year or more."

Almost a third of the first floor was taken up by the kitchen, which had an enormous brick stove with a metal top. On it, however, was a modern microwave with programmable settings.

"For the time being I'm cooking with electricity. When there's more kindling I'll try the stove. However, this trough here is natural—I made it out of a huge log that the artists left here when the energy stopped. It's just like the old days, and when I get the soapmaking down, the mistress of the house will be able to wash clothes by hand. . . . The rags for scrubbing the floor are authentic, real cotton, just like in the nineteenth century. I cast the frying pans myself, out of iron. They came out pretty heavy."

He looked at Niole with anxiety.

"How do you like the kitchen?"

"It's okay." Niole maintained a neutral expression. "I've never tried washing clothes by hand. It might even be amusing."

The caretaker beamed.

At the beginning of the excursion Lek was simply fascinated by Grogor's little world. But he gradually began to feel something strained in the caretaker's personality, even something evil. He had the feeling that Grogor was waiting for a catastrophe just so that his ideas and actions would be justified. Lek was not sure, however, which came first: whether the refuge had shaped Grogor's character or whether he had stamped his own consciousness on his private kingdom.

The caretaker, however, did not notice his guests' mood. He led them to the bedroom and the nursery.

"See, everything is ready. A cradle for the youngest, little beds for when they get bigger. And here are the medicines." He opened a cabinet. "Take your pick. One for every sickness."

"But where are the children?" Lek asked. "Do you have a family?"

"Well . . ." Grogor stumbled. "Not really. I haven't had time yet. But there has to be a family. It's in the plans."

It was strange to see him, so strong and hardy, suddenly blush like a schoolboy. He snuck a glance at Niole.

"I think that any woman would find this to her liking. I haven't spared any effort. There has to be a family, with a lot of kids. Otherwise what am I supposed to do with all of this by myself?"

In the next room, where the walls were hidden behind bookshelves, stood a huge television set, a stereo, a desk, and several easy chairs.

"I bought all of these on time—that's what I use my pay for. When new goods come in to the hotel, I burn them or give them away. The things I have are paid for, I have receipts."

He walked along the book shelves.

"World culture. Literature, music, art. . . . If the world were destroyed, its culture would remain. In this row are the classics: Aristotle, Dumas, Dostoevsky, Shakespeare, Byron over there, Seton-Thompson. And so on. The books are all real paper—I won't accept minis. This section is for art books. Painting, sculpture, architecture—the main trends in every country are represented. And over here are the videocassettes. Five hundred fifty films. Put a cassette in the player and take a look. Charlie Chaplin, if you want. I have it all. Comedies, historical films. You work hard in the gardens all day, at night you can listen to music, watch the great films. And you don't need anybody. Take this for example." He took out a cassette, then looked in confusion past Lek. "But where's Niole?"

Lek looked back. Niole was no longer behind him.

The caretaker asked, "Maybe she stayed behind in the nursery? Let's see."

He left the room, then his footsteps resounded up and down the stairs.

"She's not in the house. Or the garden."

"She probably went back to go to sleep." Lek shrugged. "We've had a rough day."

"Really?" Grogor looked around in dismay. His animation had deserted him. He even seemed to shrivel up. His eyes seemed dull, and the circles under his eyes even blacker. "So she didn't like it here. Why? What do you think?"

"Well. . . . I think it's—"

"You try and you try, but nothing works." Grogor sat on the table with a cassette in his hand.

"Nothing works?"

"I need to have a family. Or else I'll end up like a hermit crab here."

"So go ahead and raise a family! What's the problem?"

"How can I if she doesn't like it here?"

"She?"

"The girl, Niole. She just walked away."

"Listen!" Lek was dumbfounded. "Before today you didn't even know her. Didn't know that a person like her existed on the earth."

"So now we've met."

"But you—you haven't known her long enough. And besides, is the problem that there are never any women here? You said that people come from the Canons."

"They do." Gregor nodded despondently. "Only they're dirty. The tribe has group marriages, free love. They take drugs, and not one of them wants to work. They traipse around naked through the desert, and all they want to do is eat and. . . . But I liked Niole right away." The caretaker walked over to a shelf. "It's really amazing. There's everything a person could desire. Here are the mysteries, over there the travel books. And all the classics."

"Have you read them?"

"What, the classics?"

"Any of the books."

The caretaker looked at Lek in perplexity.

"Are you making fun of me? Where would I get the energy? Or the time. What kind of reading can I do when I've only been getting three hours' sleep for the past few years? To create a farm like this! Look at my hands." Grogor tossed the cassette on the table, and held up his hands, covered with amber calluses, like a turtle shell. "I'm the only one around here. It's not the city, where you sit out your two hundred minutes at your desk and then go out looking for fun. Here you're lucky if you remember the alphabet. The farm takes everything. You set aside enough for a year and then start thinking that maybe you need enough for ten. You try doing something else, but the idea eats away at you. Take water, for example. The cistern out there holds ten thousand gallons. First I prepared the spot with a bulldozer and backhoe, then found the cistern itself out in the desert and hauled it back behind the tractor, through all that chaos. It was a real job. From lack of sleep your head aches, and you walk around like a zombie. And you tell me to read! I haven't even seen the films, or even opened one of the art books. I walk over every once in a while and touch the binding very carefully so I don't dirty it with my hands."

"Well, thanks for the tour. I think I better be going, too."

"Don't you want to see the cow barn? I'm just finishing installing the automation."

"I'm exhausted. I can hardly stand up."

The valley was already plunged in shadow. Moisture and dampness rose from the ground. Grogor stopped near a field.

"Tell me. . . ."

"Yes?"

"But be honest."

"Well . . . of course."

"Have I gone crazy? What do you think?"

"What are you talking about?" Lek was taken aback. "Of course not."

"I have here a Noah's ark. The more you save, the more you find has to be added. There's no end to it."

On the other side of the hill of crushed rock the innumerable windows of the hotel were shining brightly against the dark sky. Then they all went out simultaneously.

In the lobby the caretaker lit a candle—the small yellow flame hung in the gloom of the huge room as in the emptiness of space. Next to the broad staircase, Grogor handed Lek the candle, shuffling his feet.

"Well, I guess I'll still go back to my place. I have to finish up in the barn. Just too much work. And the sheep have to be fed. If you should need anything, push the button next to the door in your room. The signal will be sent out to the farm; I have a bell I can hear from anywhere."

Once again Lek collapsed onto his bed. But sleep was not to be. At twelve he was awakened by a dog's bark in the corridor.

Barking, growling, steps—and it all came nearer. Alarmed, Lek sat up in bed.

The door opened. The caretaker and a tall man with sideburns stood on the threshold. The man held a white mask and was wearing a stiff jumpsuit with collar tabs with ones and zeros as insignia.

"I have to bring you another guest." Grogor lit the candle on the night table with the one he was carrying. "He got lost in the underground and just got out. And there aren't any candles for the other rooms."

A huge black-and-white dog—an exact copy of the one that made him jump onto the pipes—squeezed through the stranger's legs and began sniffing Lek's knees. Its head was larger than a human's. Having finished, it raised its attentive, searching eyes at Lek. Lek was petrified.

"She's okay," the man said. "She only bites while protecting territory. Lie down, Bianca. . . . I hope you forgive the intrusion."

The dog turned a few times trying to catch its tail, then lay down, its head on its front paws, its gaze fixed on Lek.

"Not at all." Lek could hear his own voice tremble. "No problem."

The caretaker did not leave.

"Excuse me. Could I talk to you for a minute?"

"Me?" Lek got up. The dog also stood up. "Just let me get dressed."

"You don't have to. There's no one in the hall."

Lek went out in his shorts. The dog made an attempt to follow, but the man pulled it back.

Grogor led Lek a few steps away from the door.

"Please excuse me once again."

"Well?"

The caretaker rested his hand against a pseudorelief on the wall.

"Tell me, is she married?"

"Who, Niole?"

"Yes."

"I don't know. I don't think so. But I really haven't the slightest idea."

"Has she said anything about me? That I'm not really all there?"

"We haven't talked about you at all."

"You didn't stop and see her tonight?"

"No."

"Did she stop here?"

"No. I think she's been asleep for a long time."

"A fine girl. Where does she work?"

"In town. For some kind of company."

Grogor struck his forehead with his fist.

"Damn it! What do you think, maybe I should forget everything? Ecology and all that?"

"Well. . . . You know. . . ."

"Okay." Grogor suddenly stuck out his iron hand. "Thanks for the advice. Maybe I'll take it."

When Lek went back to his room, the man was already undressed and sitting on his bed.

"My name is Tutot. I'm from Security."

"Lek."

"Where do you work?"

"ITD," Lek said, immediately terrified by his own stupidity. But despite all his efforts, it was the only thing he could think to say. "ITD. Inspection."

However, Tutot just sighed as he got under the covers.

"You never can tell about people. . . . I have a friend who answers questions about what he does, who he is, by saying that he's with OAF. And he's serious—there is an Office of Accounting and Finance. . . . But how did you get into this Godforsaken place?"

"On f—by helicopter."

"Me too. I had to call in a helicopter by radio. There doesn't seem to be any other way. If you want, I'll give you a lift tomorrow. Only to town, but it's better than nothing."

"Thanks. But I'm with a coworker. And there's more work to be done."

"Have a cigarette?"

"No thanks—on second thought, yes."

They lit up. Tutot stretched out in bed, staring at the ceiling. His cigarette was pressed tight between his lips.

"Ah, this is great—to have your legs raised. I'm wiped out. We were chasing violators, and I ended up in the underground technology. And the lights gradually went out. Imagine, I was in total darkness. If Bianca here hadn't led me out to the magnetic railroad, I don't know what would have happened. Two of our guys got lost down there last year—not right here but farther to the west, near the old concrete highway. Still no sign of them. Have you ever been on the magnetic?"

"Yes. I mean, no. Never."

The man looked at Lek attentively.

"Who are you here with?"

"A coworker. A woman."

"Is she young?"

"Sort of. No older than forty. The girl is . . . well, it's hard to tell these days. Perhaps she's only in her early twenties." Lek felt that he had really blundered. "Excuse me, but let's get some sleep."

He stretched out and turned toward the wall. His heart was throbbing loud enough, he thought, to be heard out in the hall. He could hear Tutot put out the candle, then toss in his bed.

Lek waited about an hour, then trying not to make a single sound, sat up in bed. He pulled on the pants Gregor had given him, groped with his foot and found a shoe. His plan was to wake Niole and immediately, in the middle of the night, set off into the desert. His brain seethed with anger at the caretaker—what a roommate he had found for Lek, that poor melancholy Grogor.

He bent over for his second shoe, and his cheek touched against something wet. He raised his hand, felt in the darkness a huge furry muzzle, and realized that the wet object was the dog's nose.

At that very moment a cigarette lighter flashed on. The candle was lit.

The dog stood next to Lek, and Tutot was sitting on the edge of his bed.

"Can't sleep?" the security officer asked sympathetically. "Neither can I. When you get overtired, it always happens. But I always have trouble with insomnia. You want to chat a while?"

He stood up and paced the room. From the door to the window he went downhill, then uphill on the way back.

"You know what I do at night when I'm away from home like this? I get mad. I lie with my eyes open and give endless interior monologues. In my mind I curse my bosses, in my mind I rescue the people I chase during the daytime. . . . At night I reject my days. Do you know what I'm talking about? Maybe you don't know it, but our security service can chase violators only within the limits of the company's jurisdiction. In any other territory there is a presumption of innocence, the principle 'if he isn't caught, he isn't a thief.' Even if I were to meet a violator right now and recognize his face"—Tutot stopped in the middle of the room and fixed Lek with his glance—"any attempt on my part to seize him would be prohibited. I do not even have the right to follow him or make any accusations. . . . But all this is neither here nor there: As I said, at night I turn into a completely different person."

Once again he began to pace back and forth. The dog sat down on the carpet next to Lek, resting its strong and unexpectedly heavy body at his feet.

"Yes, the night. . . . An interesting time. You have probably noticed that it is during the night that people try to make sense of their daytime life and of the world we live in. During the day we have no time. However, making sense of our life is impossible. You know why? Because it does not form a consistent and harmonious whole. Because ninety percent of the effects are the result of ten percent of the causes. What we—both you and I—do and say has no effect on the world. The only decisions that count are the ones made in big houses behind high walls. And everything there is secret, while we meet a chaos of conflicting appearances that are falsified by advertising and the personal interests of the big shots and their battles with each other. You see what I mean?"

"M-m-m . . . eh, if we only think and don't share our thoughts with anyone else, of course we can't have any influence on the world."

"True. In other words, our world of appearances is joyless, incomprehensible, and my only consolation is collecting old postcards."

He turned toward Lek.

"Haven't you ever gotten interested in old postcards?"

"Postcards?"

"At home I have an excellent collection—not of the very oldest ones, since they are fantastically expensive, but of contemporary copies. Kittens with ribbons. Santa Claus with Christmas gifts, flower gardens and birds, that kind of thing. In addition, I have one original. It's a German congratulatory postcard, Munich, 1822, which is a copy of an old German leaflet from the beginning of Protestantism. There's a quite complex symbolic system. Two lions—one with a tail split in two, the other with two heads. Because of the postcard's great value, I always carry it with me. Here, take a look."

Bending over his jumpsuit that was draped over the footboard of his bed, Tutot took a dark case out of an inside pocket, opened it to reveal an uneven cardboard rectangle with torn edges. He carefully set it near the candle.

"Look close. By the way, it's lucky we have a candle—these old postcards always look better in candlelight."

Lek stared blankly at the postcard. He could see nothing on the dark surface.

Tutot lit up a cigarette with a match, shook it out, then started pacing again.

"I hope I'm not boring you. If I am, please tell me. Let me explain my interpretation of the symbols. Both lions are sitting on a rostrum and joined by a chain. On the head of one is the papal tiara. . . ."

Lek pressed his hands against his temples. For a moment the floor and ceiling seemed to change places, and the security man was pacing upside down, like a fly. It had been a long topsy-turvy day, even without leonine postcards to top it all off. He shoved the dog away with one foot, and just as he was, in his pants and wearing one shoe, fell onto the bed. He set the alarm for four-thirty and closed his eyes.

He heard a muffled voice, as though he had cotton in his ears: "The pope lion has a tail that is split at the end, signifying. . . . On the other decorated rostrum. . . . The second lion is two-headed. The first is wearing the Elector's crown, the second a cap, which denotes. . . ."

Half asleep, Lek murmured, "That lion cannot be considered a single two-headed one. Only as two sociable lions."

And then lapsed into deep sleep.

The sky outside the window was greenish mother-of-pearl when he awoke. Tutot lay on his back, snoring loudly. In the light of early morning his sharp-featured face looked younger than it had at night. He had left the postcard on the table.

Lek washed and dressed. The dog kept his eyes peeled on him. Lek picked up the cardboard quadrangle and studied it, then put it back. He could not make out a single thing on the dark surface.

He went out into the hall. The dog went with him. Lek scratched it on the head, then went back in the room. The dog also went back. He tried to jump out quickly. But the dog was even quicker than he was.

He had to do something. He shook Tutot by the shoulder.

"Hey, wake up. Your dog—"

Tutot, without opening his eyes, picked up the postcard and put it in the case. He tucked it away in the pocket of his jumpsuit. He mumbled something in his sleep, and covered his head with the edge of the sheet.

The dog stood alongside Lek, tall, broad-chested. Half of its muzzle was black, half white.

"What do you want?"

The dog wagged its tail.

"Damn it! If you insist, let's go."

In her room Niole was looking at herself in a new dress in the mirror. Her eyes opened wide when she saw the dog. Lek told her about Tutot.

"Exactly," she nodded. "Yesterday I forgot to let you know you didn't have to worry anymore. Grogor knows the ropes, so he brought the guy to us." She turned to the dog. "What's her name?"

"Hmm . . . Bianca."

"Here, Bianca."

The dog looked at Lek as though asking permission, shifted her eyes to Niole, and wagged her tail.

Outside it was cool, even cold, as they stepped onto the stone path that lead through the caretaker's garden. There was no sight of Grogor, and the whole hotel seemed deserted.

Something about the garden had changed since the night before, but Lek could not figure out what. They passed the fields. Then Lek saw the fallen pipe and realized what he had missed. Grogor had destroyed his energy plant, cutting through the braces that held the pipe in a vertical position. The cable system was lying in a jumble, and an ax had been left on the ground.

Without saying a word to each other, Lek and Niole continued on their way. The greenery was left behind, and from the top of the hill they beheld an unearthly landscape. Lifeless asphalt, craters of sand, concrete canyons—everything was drenched in a gloomy purple color of the cloudy sunrise. Rusting cranes towered here and there as dark silhouettes, like trees on an alien planet. From the nearest one a bird took off, spiritlessly waving its wings, and flew toward the east, where there still seemed to be a hint of forests and meadows.

But the sun rose quickly. One minute after its glowing sphere had made its appearance, the sky started to turn blue, the desert lost its gloominess, taking on shades of yellow, red-brown, and deep blue. It immediately became warmer.

"Maybe we should stock up on water?" Lek asked. "Only there's nothing to take it in."

But Niole was against the idea.

"I don't feel like wasting time. I think there must be wells . . . or outlets of the water lines. Most likely those wild tribes travel from one well to another."

They strode off enthusiastically. The dog ran ahead, disappearing behind piles of broken kigon, then returning.

The path turned to the left, away from its previous eastern direction, and Lek stopped.

"Better stay on the path, I think. If we just walk straight, we'll lose our bearings. Even rhinos in game preserves follow paths, I remember reading."

"It's not worth the trouble. We'll get there faster if we go straight. I have to be at work this evening—watering the flowers in the garden."

Midday found them worn out amid endless heaps of crushed rock that blocked their path. Lek and Niole, by their own calculation, had covered twenty miles, and at first they had gone quite easily. Twice they had come upon stretches of road—clay over sand—that may have been the beginnings of a highway or a street; the last one moved them ahead four miles. Walking was interesting, because the area constantly changed. Now a valley divided by kigon foundations, now enormous white stacks of some kind of slabs, now almost impenetrable thickets of rusted wire fencing, now sand or gravel dunes. Sometimes, descending to the bottom of the next hollow, Lek felt himself in a primeval world. There they were, the two of them, a man and a woman, a couple to once again begin the human race amid the wilds of construction wasteland. And they even had a dog with them— a domesticated animal. But they could believe that on the basis of technology—the new nature—they would be able to create artificial plant life.

However, later on he was suffering too much to have such ideas. For an hour they wandered through a plain with crushed-rock hillocks, where the monotony of the surroundings was occasionally interrupted by a huge shapeless chunk of concrete, the lifeless corpse of a small compressor or the huge carcass of a mighty bulldozer, half-drifted over with sand, as though it had perished at the very moment it was about to push a pile of rock fragments. It was terribly hot, and the contours of the hillocks seemed to waver, disturbed by the hot air rushing upward. Lek tried to spit, just to see if he could, but the thick saliva he gathered could not be forced out of his dry mouth.

The ground seemed to descend, and the leaning tower disappeared behind the horizon.

"I can't take any more," Niole said hoarsely. "Let's rest."

She sat down on the casing of a compressor but immediately leaped to her feet. "Ow! It's like a frying pan." She looked around. "There's nothing to sit on. We'll just have to stand. Are you sure we're headed in the right direction?"

"I hope so. We're still headed toward the sun."

Niole fell into thought, then raised her worried eyes at Lek.

"Listen, I have a terrible thought. Doesn't the sun move, too?"

"Well, so what?"

"It only rises in the east. By noon it must be in the south. Where are we headed?"

Lek looked toward the sun, perplexed.

"Yes, I guess we've been turning the whole time, going in an arc. That's why we can't see the town. Why didn't we realize sooner?"

"Of course. If we keep following the sun, by nighttime we'll be back at the hotel. Now we should travel so that the sun is over our right shoulder."

Lek, very upset, nodded. His thickened blood pounded in his temples, and he was afraid of passing out.

"You can also determine the direction by the azimuth. I think the azimuth is the angle between something and something else."

Niole grinned.

"That's what I think, too. You're not mad that we didn't bring water?"

"No, not at all."

"Even if we never get out, you won't be mad? It looks like a person could get lost forever in here."

"We'll get out."

The dog, breathing frequently and shallowly, sat down next to Lek. In her fur she was hottest of all. She stuck out her moist tongue—Lek never would have thought that a dog could have such a long tongue. Whenever he spoke, the dog began staring him in the face. As though she were on the brink of crossing over the threshold where human speech would be intelligible to her.

Above they heard a distant roar. A light blue airplane, almost invisible against the cupola of the sky, was headed toward the south. It seemed absurd that the passengers could be sitting up there in comfort, without the slightest suspicion that the two of them down in the desert were following the plane's flight with a melancholy gaze.

Niole sighed and looked at the dog.

"I have an idea! Let her look for it! Maybe she can smell water."

"Seek, Bianca, seek!"

The dog began to rush around, whimpering.

"Seek water! Seek people!"

The dog stopped dead, then raced away full speed. Her saillike tail flashed in the distance several times, then disappeared behind a hill. A minute passed, then another . . . five, ten. The heat became totally unbearable. Niole and Lek tried to avoid looking at each other—it would have been terrifying to hear or to say that Bianca was still not back.

But then in the distance they heard a howl, and it came closer. Lek and Niole beamed.

The dog flew out from behind a mound. The two of them hastened toward her. Beyond that mound the crushed rock came to an end, finally. Even the heat seemed less after they left the gray monotony behind. They went down into a little valley. The dog would run, look around, stop, and wait. Then she put her nose to the ground and kept it there.

"A human footprint!"

They hurried behind the dog down the valley. But the path was blocked by a gigantic trash heap of empty tin cans that ascended on their left to the horizon. It was torture walking through them—with each step their feet sank in, cans crunched and slipped from beneath them, and rust ascended in columns in the motionless air. Lek and Niole each slipped and fell several times, then held hands for support. The dog hopped forward, its nose raised, sniffing—apparently it had picked up a scent. Talking was impossible because of the constant racket.

They got past the tin cans—their main mountain range extended to the east. Next came milk containers. Resilient, they also shot out from underfoot, but falling was not so painful. Then Lek and Niole found themselves in a narrow passage between uncompleted buildings that were also heaped with containers.

They were both rapidly running out of energy and stopped to rest.

"Hey!"

Niole and Lek turned around in a split second.

On a kigon wall there was a man wearing a bright green jumpsuit.

A half hour later, having eaten and drunk their fill, they were blissfully resting on a canvas mat in the tent of the director of the expedition. It was the group searching for the underground railroad. Learning that they could enter right near the hotel, the green-clad director gave his colleagues instructions to wrap things up; he himself, overjoyed, garrulous, kept filling his guests' glasses with iced seltzer.

"Drink, drink. To honor a guest is the law of the desert. For our group it is a great stroke of luck that you happened upon us. This is the fourth week we've been looking—a government assignment. Somewhere in some computer's memory there is full information about it, of course, but try and find it. It just can't go on like this. Complex technology requires a centralized and unified control. You just can't have a situation where one person is looking for firewood, the second is in the forest, and the third knows but won't tell because there's no profit in it."

"How have you been looking?"

"The usual way—we drill. Do you think it's easy? First, it's very, very deep. And then the ground is honeycombed—pipes, cables, tanks, storage areas. We have to keep changing the bits, because we keep hitting metal. The desert itself is poorly understood. There are no maps. Plans were made for topographic studies, but it never got past the talking stage. One adventurer from the Geographic Society took it upon himself to study the Great Tin Can Dump that begins right around here. He circled it in several weeks' travel, but couldn't get inside—wore himself out trying to walk through. No vehicle will get through. He asked for camels from the Zoological Society, but they turned him down. . . . I, for example, know that in the northwest there are lakes of oil and not far away mountains of computer cards. I flew around them in a helicopter, but from up there you can't determine their structure, their real nature. In one of the largest lakes, the oil is waste, but in others it isn't. The devil knows where they came from."

Since the desert had almost finished them off, Lek and Niole were eager to learn more about it. They kept the subject alive.

"But there are the local tribes. Couldn't they help?"

"They're wild—what good can they be? They wander from water supply to water supply. The settled tribe, the Canons, aren't that far away, it's true. But you were lucky you didn't run into them."

"Why so?"

"They'd take you captive, and you'd never get away. That's their religion. They believe that the end of the world is here, and in civilization's final hour, everyone must turn away from everything human. Some woman hypnotist is in charge. Anyone they catch is stuffed full of drugs."

"But what do they eat?" Lek asked. "I thought that they lived near the hotel. And used food from there."

"They drive there. They tame vehicles and drive them."

"What do you mean, tame vehicles."

"They switch them to manual control. They catch an electrocart—one of the automatic ones that runs on the narrow-gauged track. They convert them. Generally speaking, they're terrifying. They dance wildly, howl their lungs out, and dance some more. They have orgies—you can't tell which are the men and which are the women. They're perverted and think that the whole world ought to be the same way."

"Brrr," Niole shrugged her shoulders with feigned horror. "What about the nomadic tribes?"

"They seem harmless enough. For the most part they're literary scholars, theater critics. A skinny bunch, made of wire. Their leader is an art historian who's gone wild. They eat practically nothing, just argue all the time. Once I wandered across a band, spent a night in their camp. I lay down exhausted in one of their tents but couldn't shut my eyes all night long: The air was filled with "deconstruction," "cultural revolution," "semiotic structure," "subject/object," "dialectical *Aufhebung*," "alienation"—enough to drive a person up the wall. In that tribe the severest punishment is enforced silence. One man found a can of food and ate it without sharing. He was sentenced to a week of silence. They gagged him—removing the gag once a day to let him eat. And do you know, the man died, suffocated by the objections he had to the others' discourse. But generally speaking, they're okay. Sometimes they come into town to look for a temporary job. They're hard workers, and honest. But they just don't know how to do anything, that's the problem. There's one working here on the drill site now. He just can't be given any serious work—he'll try and try but get nowhere. Although it's hard finding good people these days." This was apparently a sore spot with the director, because he winced as he mentioned it. "For instance, we're going down into the underground railroad, but how are we going to manage without an electronics expert? We need one desperately. But just try to find one for work like this. All the good people are taken by the big companies. Of course, they can offer more money and better benefits than the government. Our budget is constantly being cut.

"Of course, all this damned technology has gotten out of hand since the specialists in the private sector all work against each other. To speak seriously, under these conditions it's all-out war—either the industrial-technological system will enslave humanity once and for all, or humanity will succeed in making technology its partner. I'm not so much worried about myself. But our children, and grandchildren—what kind of world will they live in?"

He paced the cramped tent, brushing against protruding parts of various equipment with his elbows and shoulders.

"You wouldn't happen to know an electronics specialist, would you? Who'd volunteer to work for peanuts? Otherwise when we go down into the underground, we won't know where to begin."

The drilling derrick was taken down, the camp packed away, and after a sumptuous meal the director led his guests down a well-worn path.

*   *   *

. . . Rose Street. Elm Street. On Elm things became unexpectedly lively. A dozen young people in elegant, practically identical suits and with practically identical faces, had gathered in a crowd and were talking in low voices: They followed Lek and Niole, all tattered and sunburned, with their eyes. One of them whistled to the dog, and she growled. Lek and his friend could barely drag their feet, but on Lilac they and the dog had to fight their way through a crowd of mobiles and people. Only near number fifty was there room. A heavy-set man, dressed like a mannequin in the window of the most expensive and fashionable shop and with a face better cared for and more commanding than any Lek had ever seen before, was trying to prove something to the guard with the old hat and huge mouth.

"But I have a permission!"

"It doesn't matter."

"And an admission. My secretary just didn't know that I needed a promission, too."

"Ignorance of the law is no excuse." The man in the old hat casually spat to the side. "Especially since we have an unusual situation."

Someone tapped Lek on the shoulder.

"Hello. I see Bianca is with you."

Tutot was standing there. The security officer took a collar and a muzzle out of his pocket and with the dexterity of a magician put them on the dog and then hooked on her leash.

"Good to see you again. We had a great conversation last night, didn't we? How'd you get here? I came by helicopter." He took Lek by the arm. "Incidentally, inside the garden fence is company jurisdiction. I'm telling you just as a piece of information. If I, let us say, were to see the person I was pursuing through the pipes yesterday inside the garden, I would be required to perform my official duties. On the other hand, out here on the street, where we are standing now, that person would have nothing to fear."

The cross fire near the entrance continued.

"But why wasn't I given a demission, if a demission, as you maintain, is really required?"

"How am I supposed to know?"

"Call your superior."

Tutot gave Lek his card.

"Stop by sometime. You can see my collection."

Niole looked around, perplexed.

"Something has happened here. There've never been this many people. Let's say good-bye, Lek."

The large-mouthed man saw Niole, and his mouth in some miraculous way returned to normal. He walked over, leaving the lieutenant behind, and said in a whisper, "Where did you disappear to?" He nodded at Lek. "The guys created an accident, turned off the Field." At this point Tutot discreetly walked off, pulling the reluctant dog. "Hurry in and tell them that you're here."

Niole turned to Lek.

"Get away from here and go around to the little garden from the other side. I'll be right there."

Lek began to push his way out.

On the narrow street everything was quiet. Lek leaned against the wooden fence. The small garden had grown luxuriantly—Niole had not wasted her time in vain.

Niole stepped out on the back porch. She had already changed into the long skirt with a blouse and a white apron. She had a watering can in her hand.

She ran over to Lek.

"Well then . . . I told the guys. They all said to say hello."

Lek nodded. They looked at each other.

"We'll never forget each other, will we? It's remarkable that we met at all."

"It is, isn't it?" It was so good to look at her, graceful, beautiful. And those blue eyes beneath the dark brows.

"You'll write to Kisch, so include a page for me. I'll write. We'll always be friends."

Niole embraced Lek over the low fence. She gave him a peck on the cheek and then Lek walked to the intersection where he had left his mobile. The town seemed deserted.

He walked up to his mobile, rested his hand on the hood.

"Ee-eeh."

He had had some two days, that was for sure.

He was surrounded by the smell of his mobile: the usual tobacco; the gas he used to start up, the old-fashioned way; Rona's faded umbrella. It all moved him toward home, presaging the end of the journey. If not physically, then psychologically.

He lit a cigarette. He had to come to a decision—at home his wife was waiting for an answer. He lifted his hand to his chest pocket to take out the yellow flier from Confidence, then remembered that it had been left behind in the underground.

"Okay."

He already knew what he was going to do.

He sat down behind the wheel. But as soon as he had started the engine, he saw Niole, with Bianca, running down the street. The white apron and the dog's white tail did not move in time with each other.

He opened the door and got out.

"It's a good thing you didn't leave yet. What happened is that Bianca refuses to go underground. Maybe she's afraid, or maybe she just doesn't like the work anymore. They had to drag her, but that didn't work. Tutot wanted to know if you'd take her."

"Me? For good?"

"Yes, she's a good dog."

"Well, I guess so."

He opened the back door. The dog, as though she had long since decided what she was doing, hopped right on the seat. She lay down, filling the seat entirely, her head on her paws, making herself comfortable. She raised her head, stretched her long body, then put her head back down.

"Just be sure not to change your mind. Or else what would happen to her? However, you won't refuse to take care of her."

"I won't. She is a good dog. My wife will like her. And the kids, too."

"Won't it be hard with her in the city?"

"No. We won't be in the city long. Soon it'll be a tent."

"A tent?" Niole stared at him in confusion, then started to blush. She understood. She stepped up to him, kissed him on the cheek. "If that's the way it is, I may be seeing you sooner than expected. Be sure to read the book about Mozart—that's where it tells about Hagenauer. You'll like the book. . . . How should I write to you—will you be Lek or are you going back to your original name?"

"I think I'll be Kisch again."

. . . The restaurant in the hundred-year-old house, the ancient cannon inside the iron fence, the rocking cobblestones of the main square, the editorial offices, the houses on the outskirts of town.

The wide-open spaces of the fields were in front of him. Setera Kisch shifted to fourth, and the car started to bounce along the potholes more quickly.

The setting sun stood straight above the end of the highway. Kisch was driving straight at the sunset.

It was still not all that bad on this earth.

A billboard suspended high on two pillars slowly floated toward him. From this direction the message was backward.

AREN'T YOU ASHAMED?

That was about bad moods. And what kind of mood was he in now?

He felt a shiver run up his back, and somewhere deep inside his consciousness a triumphant rhythm arose and broke loose.

A vague mood. But that was not the point. What was important was the fact that yesterday his mood had not just once, not just twice, been terrible, desperate and hopeless. Even though he was on a leash and the company guaranteed that such things could not happen.

Maybe they could not, but they did! Had he really broken free from the computer's control?

That's the way it seemed. Even though the electrodes were where they had been. Take yesterday as an example. Wasn't it a cause for joy that he had felt really bad when he saw Lek with two heads? Was it really bad that he felt terrible out in the hall? After all, previously nothing like that had happened; he couldn't even think because of those stimceivers. As soon as he started thinking something over, stroking his chin, frowning, immediately a signal would be transmitted and another received, and he would be flooded with a simpleminded joy in existence. Only with a metallic taste in his mouth. He would feel like running, jumping. He and Rona would read a stock market report and get upset, but immediately they'd be smiling at each other, everything would be forgotten, and they'd be gamboling like lambs in a meadow. But over the last few years it was not quite the same. He and his wife had been more in control of themselves—they could get excited or upset. But yesterday, when he got lost in the technological jungles, no forcible joy affected him. He was master of himself—he understood that he could die, and found a way out.

But why had everything changed? Where did his brain get the ability to oppose what the computer imposed? It must be that the brain still knew enough to survive, to protect itself. It mobilized the unimaginable complexity, evolved over millions of years, against the monotonous electrical commands, created a structure, connections, that permitted it to avoid the computer's influence. And it was victorious. . . . But that was natural in a way: After all, the computer did not invent the brain—quite the reverse.

However, if that was the case, it was still remarkable. It meant that the leash was not that strong.

But then there was another question—why did the brain need those capabilities? Wouldn't it be more fun to have fun, without any break, more pleasurable to enjoy pleasures? Perhaps it was the case that the brain reserved its right to independence because it was the creation of society and as such took care not only of the individual but of all people. From the point of view of a single individual, what could be better than to lie there in bliss. But from the point of view of *Homo sapiens*. . . . It's possible that the mind of today's human being is not a separate entity limited to this day and this play but a sphere containing the experience and dreams of many countries and many centuries. Despite everything most of his contemporaries had an idea of true humanity.

Niole, for example, remembers Hagenauer. In his out-of-the-way Salzburg he didn't give what he was doing much thought, but the good he did was not lost and will survive century after century.

The workday had come to an end, and people were thronging the roadside—all those condensations of images. The town's residents, who would gather later in the wood-paneled restaurant, or in some garden, would spend their free time making music, dancing, conversing—one condensation of symbols talking with another, one system of images in love with another.

Kisch lit a cigarette.

He was a little sad that another lace curtain had been drawn shut, another "divine spark" had gone out. But to tell the truth, even before he had known that there was no divine spark. It was simply a case of the spark being his last refuge, since it seemed that the idea of money had conquered everything. He grasped at the spark like a drowning man at a straw—they can do anything to us they want, but they can't touch the spark. But now it was clear that the civilization built on profit was crumbling—huge fragments were already falling away. And he could admit that human beings were temporary matter/energy structures, born at birth, dying at death. But beyond that, they left to others what they had lived through. Adding to the enormous potential of knowledge, understanding that accumulates and under the right circumstances allows each new generation to live better, more generously, more beautifully. And this was the purpose of humanity, a purpose that had been forgotten during the last decades. What a secret! Let's take him as an example, Setera Kisch. He loves Rona and the kids, is worried about them. But do his worry and his love take a material form? If not, what form do they take? There is an appeal in the incomprehensible reality of thought that spreads over the planet with such rapidity. It's a puzzle how such a tiny mind can hold so much—from molecule to galaxy. It makes everything fruitful by expending itself. It is a component of the world, yet it does not obey a single law that solid or liquid, plasma or gaseous matter cannot escape. It is magnificent, once you think about it, to be called to expand the infinite sphere of thought that exists is some other dimension, to lose nothing from the previous gains, to grow forward. . . .

AN UNHAPPY MOOD
   IS AS ABSURD AS
   A TOOTHACHE

Another billboard.

You can all go to hell! Only dissatisfaction moves people. Otherwise they'd still be sitting in caves.

A black cat on the bench near the railroad intersection was licking its fur. Something moved suddenly behind Kisch, and his heart beat fast from the surprise. Bianca barked so resoundingly that she sounded as though she were in a barrel. The cat seemed to have been pulled away by some invisible force, and Kisch, regaining his composure, glanced respectfully at Bianca. Even though she had probably never seen a cat before, she still was aware of her duties.

Kisch leaned back, with just one hand lightly on the wheel. There was a lot to think about. Would the green-clad expedition director accept such an out-of-date specialist? He probably would, both him and Rona, but out of desperation, because there were no good people. But Kisch would show him he could handle things. In school he had been considered very bright. Only later he lost interest in the subject. In any case, first things first—buy a bunch of books and stick with them for a month or two.

The sky was becoming murky, and the fields gave way to brick wastelands and concrete squares. The mobile raced past the rubble.

Hold on a minute! That was the desert! Kisch braked and pulled over. He climbed out and waited for this eyes to adjust to the no-longer-moving world.

Bianca jumped out after him and vigorously shook her whole body.

It was indeed the desert. And the leaning tower made a tiny silhouette on the horizon.

Ten steps from the concrete ribbon . . . another ten steps. How ordinary and safe it was here—when you knew that the highway was right at your back.

A fat steel pipe with a slant opening peered out of the ground. Kisch shuddered—it was just that kind of pipe he had spent all those hours climbing, even loosing his human form.

Feeling the necessity of rehabilitating himself, he marched decisively over to the pipe.

"At ease! No talking!"

The dog expressed agreement, barking behind him. She too had had her fill of the pipes.

The pipe maintained a prudent silence.

"There!"

He and the dog went closer. Kisch sat down on the edge of the pipe. He looked around. He took a cigarette out of the pack, opened his lips to hold it, but his hand dropped of its own will.

Ten yards to the left there was an opening to the underground, framed by a low parapet. The entrance gaped, pitch-black.

Could he overcome his fear?

He walked over. Kigon steps slanted downward, into the darkness.

He went down. A small quivering yellow flame tore a hole in the darkness, revealing the rail of a metal staircase. So far so good. Here the whole earth must be crammed with technology.

He looked back. The dog, a dark contour at the top of the steps, whimpered softly.

Did he have enough willpower to go down?

Ten steps, then another ten.

From a low-ceilinged room three halls led in different directions. The one on the right was blocked by a board with a plate on which were drawn stars between wavy lines—the international symbol of high radiation. In the hall to the left a reddish light glimmered in the distance. It was quite possible that the two men Tutot said were lost had started right here.

He stepped into the central, totally dark hall. Reaching out with the tip of his shoe, like a ballet dancer, he felt the floor in front of him, and took ten careful steps. He stopped.

Alongside him he heard panting. The dog pressed her trembling body against his leg. He petted her large head.

"It's okay, you'll get used to it. We'll travel together, maybe for weeks. We'll take a supply of water, food, light. And tools. There's a lot of work."

He made a sharp 180-degree turn. And an inertial compass, of course. Even a compass belt, one that squeezes on the left or right whenever you go off course. The kind spelunkers use, or geologists in jungles.

On the surface it was unexpectedly cool after the stale stuffiness of the underground. The mobile by the road seemed quite tiny amid all the desolation.

"How about it, shall we go?"

The dog jumped onto the driver's seat. She curled up, making space behind the wheel.

"You want to sit next to me?"

The motor droned. Once again the crumpled case of a compressor, kigon slabs, coils of wire, and sand dunes raced backward.

The last billboard flashed by in a second.

The difference between UNHAPPINESS
and a TOOTHACHE:
UNHAPPINESS can be cured
  IMMEDIATELY
  PAINLESSLY
  FOREVER
See our local representative TODAY!

See whom! Let them find somebody else. We have to get to work. Do something real. And then we'll have the right kind of mood.

He felt as though a boil had burst. For many long years he had lived repressed. All the monkeying around with body transfers and electrodes in his brain was an attempt to avoid responsibility, to run away from himself. An admission that his environment had overcome him. But now it was clear that the gigantic apparatus of profit was not omnipotent, despite the power of its computers, the cleverness of its labs, the heavy steel tread of its mechanized armies, and the scientific sophistication of its security forces.

There was hope, hope in people like Niole and her friends, like the director of the expedition, like Lek, who had managed to love so strange a child. Right here, even in this environment, a new world could be born and resist the rituals of profit that were forced down from above.

At the transfer to the state highway Kisch stopped the mobile and climbed into the back seat. He selected the program.

The mobile snorted and began to change space into time. Every thirty miles in three minutes. More than Kisch and Niole had covered, struggling on foot from dawn to noon. The furrows in the kigon surface melted into solid lines, everything to the sides into an even, gray blur. Only far ahead in the distance did the gas reservoir tanks stand in a blue line.

Now there was real technology! Could anyone think of refusing it and breaking up the world into little pedestrian closed spaces, smashing the wings on airplanes and the tracks of the magnetic railroads? To cut off radio waves, television, and in the silenced houses to light torches? Grogor's example showed what it meant to rely on yourself alone, to turn away from what the human mind had developed, from the arts of humanity— terrible purple-black rings under the eyes, bone-hard callused hands, years without books, years without bathing the heart in music. No, you might even change bodies, if there were a sound reason. And electrodes in the brain were fine when they cured a real illness.

On the right, near the highway, the tall stone fence flashed by, like a train headed in the other direction. It's all right—we will win eventually.

The precipitous movement, the impulses of strength and will. My God, what inspiration lies behind each and every discovery in science! What a happy flame warms the breast when the inventor finally finds it, finally understands. And we hurl accusations at technology, incite anger against it!

A melody seemed about to take form in his mind, to rise to the surface and fall in waves. Something half-forgotten, a melody from the days when Kisch was young, daring, and confident. The melody was pressing to reach the surface of consciousness, calling out to him to remember.

Bianca, on the front seat, sat up and sighed, just like a human being. Kisch petted her.

The route bent in a vicious arc. All the mobiles slowed slightly. To the side Kisch could see the megapolis of a million rectangular peaks, between which there were a million abysses.

His heart beat faster, and—finally the melody broke out. The beginning of the Thirty-Eighth Symphony. It flowed in pearly, sparkling waves. From where? From the distant past, from the green hills around old Salzburg. From its narrow winding streets, from the well-worn fountain in front of the university. From the love with which the modest Leopold cared for his son, from the help friends provided for the poor musician's family, and from the jealousy, torment, and hope of Wolfgang Amadeus Mozart himself.

But would they ever meet—the genius of art that bore the ideal, and the stern, powerful genius of technology that incarnates the ideal in real life? He would do what he could, and he and his friends would see.

Another's Memory

KIR BULYCHEV

1

Over the years Sergei Andreyevich Rzhevsky had grown used to not noticing the institute and the buildings that surrounded it. But on that Monday the institute car did not show up. He had to get to work by bus and noticed that they had begun to tear down the barracks village that stretched from the bus stop to the institute itself.

The village was about fifty years old; it had been built in the thirties, slightly before the institute itself. Tall poplars had grown between the two-story yellow barracks. Sergei realized that the barracks were being demolished when he saw a gap between the trees, like a frame from which the picture had been removed, and vacant land extending to the horizon, to the jagged white outline of the new part of town.

Near the next building was a crane with a huge cast-iron ball dangling from a cable. The barracks had been emptied, the windows removed, the iron sheets from the roof were lying on their sides in uneven piles of a dull green color.

Rzhevsky stopped by the third building without at first realizing why. Yes, he had lived there for six months when he was just getting started at the institute. He had rented a room on the second floor.

The barracks were deserted, the front door ajar, but Sergei did not go in, suppressed the sudden desire to be in the room, and go over to the window facing the street, to stand there and wait as he had done many years before.

Rzhevsky looked at his watch, as though seeking a reason to leave. The watch said nine-ten. Sergei walked on another hundred yards and saw his institute—a gray four-story building with big square windows and a disproportionately small door. When the institute had been built, Moscow did not yet reach out this far into the countryside, and everyone had to come on foot from the suburban station. And then the city engulfed it with its buildings, and the institute became part of Moscow, but along with the barracks village a creek remained, surrounded by tall banks of new buildings.

We should make repairs, Rzhevsky thought, looking at the crumbling stucco on the second story. They've been promising us a new building for five years now and might go on promising for another ten. I'll complain to Alevich and ask him why we have to stay in such a hovel. Isn't he ashamed himself? At least he could get the facade repaired.

2

The hall was empty: Everyone had already gone to their departments and laboratories. In half an hour they'd be out for a smoke. The tiny sauna in front of his office was also empty. On the desk was his secretary's message: "SR! I'm at the local committee. We're discussing the Pioneer camp. Lena."

Alongside were several official-looking envelopes. A new English journal. An abstract, from Leningrad.

Sergei was in a rotten mood. He looked for the reason but did not want to admit that it was the fault of the barracks. What was it he was going to do? Call up Alevich? No, first he had to read the mail.

He heard a rustling sound in his office, then a soft creak. Someone was opening the middle drawer of his desk. That's all he needed!

Rzhevsky was about to walk over to his office.

He stopped. He was afraid.

The fear was irrational. The director of an institute afraid to go into his own office. Rzhevsky stood there and listened. He wanted Lena to walk out of the office and say, "I straightened up your desk." But the office was dark, the blinds lowered. The first thing Lena would do would be to open them.

"Who's there?" Rzhevsky asked from the doorway. His voice cracked. He had to clear his throat.

Whoever it was that was hiding in the semidarkness did not want to answer.

He had to go in and turn on the light. But it was hard to turn on the light—you had to take two steps to the right to get to the switch. You couldn't reach it from the doorway. Why were the blinds so heavy? Were they planning on showing films?

The room was not totally dark. He could make out the table, the bookshelves against the wall. . . . Rzhevsky strode into the room and, his back pressed against the wall, edged toward the switch.

And as he reached out toward the switch he saw a dark figure seated at his desk. He realized that the figure did not have a face. That is, the face was dark, like his body, like his arms. . . . His dark head moved, following Rzhevsky, and small eyes glistened in the light that came in through the door.

Rzhevsky realized, in the pit of his stomach, that he should run to the door, slam it shut, and call for help. But he kept moving away from the safety of the door toward the switch.

And then a huge dark folder, as though hurled by a catapult, flew through the air and hit Rzhevsky.

He did not realize it—everything happened too quickly—but the dark body was headed toward the door. Where he himself was headed.

And he reached it at the same instant as the dark figure. He bounced to the side, hit the table, and everything seemed to spin, to fall into an abyss—for several seconds he lost consciousness. He revived from the pain in his back and leg.

And from the horrible scream in the hall.

From the clatter of footsteps. From the shouts.

He realized that he was sitting on the floor, leaning against his secretary's desk.

3

Alevich was the first to run in. He helped the director to his feet and wanted to call an ambulance, but Rzhevsky told him to help him into his office.

Alevich opened the blinds, picked up the overturned chair.

He shook his head sorrowfully and kept repeating, "That's the limit! Just think!"

Sergei was silent.

He sat down at his desk, glanced at the half-open middle drawer, picked up a crumpled red piece of paper, flattened it, and set it on the desk. Then he suddenly smiled. The smile was sheepishly stupid.

"Why didn't I realize?" he said.

"The cage was left open, very carelessly," Alevich explained, squatting on the floor and picking up papers that had flown off the desk. "Maybe the lock was defective. Gurina swears that she locked the cage yesterday."

"Was she in the vivarium this morning?" Rzhevsky folded the red paper in two, then in quarters, ran his fingernail down the fold, and tossed it in the air. It descended in a gentle arc onto his desk.

"This morning? I'll call right now."

"Don't bother," Rzhevsky said to his assistant director. "I'll go down there myself."

"Should I call a doctor?"

"Nothing really happened," Rzhevsky said. "I was shaken up a little, that's all. I should have guessed. I was afraid."

"It happens—even to directors."

He walked to the door two steps behind Rzhevsky. In the doorway he turned around and estimated the distance from the desk. Shaking his head, he said, "What a jump! A frightening animal."

"It's my own fault," Rzhevsky repeated as he unfolded the red candy wrapper.

4

Both chimps lived on the first floor, in a large room divided in two by a thick mesh partition—away from the dogs, who were housed in the basement and sometimes staged loud concerts, as though they lamented their experimental fates.

Gurina was already there.

"I did lock the cage," she said. "I checked it, then checked it again before I left."

The two chimps resembled each other closely, although Jon, the adult male, had lost the look of slyness and mischievous liveliness. He was calmly scratching his belly, his eyes slightly closed. He nodded authoritatively at Rzhevsky and did not start asking for anything—he knew that it was pointless with the director. If Rezhevsky felt like it, he would give the chimp a treat. Lev was more lively. Lev wrinkled his face, extraordinarily like his father's—chimps have unique faces, just like humans, and once you get to know them, there's no confusing them. Lev stuck his lips out. Lev was pleased with himself.

"What's the idea, you almost killed the director," Alevich said to him reproachfully.

"Whose cage is this?" Rzhevsky asked.

"What do you mean?" Alevich reponded.

"Is Lev in his own cage?"

"Of course he is," Gurina said.

"Not quite right," Alevich corrected her. "We moved him here just last week. We exchanged cages."

"Right," Rzhevsky said. "Then it all makes sense."

"What?" Gurina asked. She was very pretty, fragile, with a pink beauty straight from a German Christmas card. Even though her eyes were still damp with tears. She had been very frightened when she was told that Lev had broken loose and almost killed the director.

Rzhevsky walked over to the cage and stuck his hand in. Lev reached out his paw and touched Rzhevsky's hand with his index finger.

"Careful," Gurina whispered.

"Don't worry, Svetlana," Rzhevsky answered. "We're old friends. Five years already."

Gurina did not argue. She did not dare. Lev had just arrived in the vivarium three weeks before. Before that he could not have seen Rzhevsky. But it was pointless to disagree—the director knew what he was saying. Unless he was suffering from a concussion.

"Show us, Lev," Rzhevsky commanded, "how you open the lock."

Jon became excited in his cage, muttering discontentedly.

"Come on, now," Rzhevsky insisted. "We know your little secret."

Lev tilted his head sideways. He understood everything. Then with the familiar, Jon-derived motion he scratched his belly.

"You already ate it," Rzhevsky said. "It's not fair to get your reward twice. You ate it without permission."

He took the red wrapper out of his pocket, showed it to Lev; Jon went into a rage. He shook the partition, tried to grab his son to punish his unauthorized act.

Lev lazily reached out, and with his long fingers played with the lock. The lock clicked and opened.

"That's the secret," Rzhevsky said. "Thanks for the demonstration, Lev."

"I didn't know, I really didn't," Gurina said.

"That's right, you didn't. Only Jon and I knew. But Jon did not use his knowledge—he's a very responsible person."

The responsible person was still angry at his son. He had yellow, terrifying fangs, and in his rage he rolled his eyes so that only the whites were visible.

"We'll change the lock," Alevich reassured Rzhevsky. "I'll call the handyman right now. But what a stinker! To find his way to your office. What a bright fellow!"

"Thank you, Lev." Rzhevsky said. "Thanks, and good work!"

Lev and Jon started taunting each other. They growled, made faces at each other, bared their teeth, all in almost identical style.

5

Rzhevsky walked over to his office window. Outside he could see a broad swathe of trees, interrupted periodically by identical dark green roofs. At the end of the trees, near the highway, there was a gap instead of the last roof.

Back then it had been tight with money, or more exactly they hadn't any. And Elsa's neighbor went away somewhere, Saransk, was it? and sold her things. She sold them a sofa for a hundred rubles, in the old money. It was cheap. They dragged the sofa halfway across the city. Viktor stopped more and more often to rest, sitting on the sofa right there on the sidewalk; people walked past, stared, some even joked. Viktor enjoyed that. Liza was embarrassed, and stepped away, Elsa kept after Viktor to get going, to push himself—but Viktor couldn't take it, he smiled gently, threw up his hands, wiped the sweat from his forehead, delaying the inevitability of the difficult ordeal. He always tired fast, physically and mentally. "A minute more," he'd say. "One more cigarette, and we're off!" The sofa did not have legs, but they found bricks in the dump next to the barracks and propped it up. Liza was happy. She saw the sofa as a symbol of her future home, of everlasting happiness. The sofa had been thrown away. Who needed it—breeding grounds for vicious and ineradicable fleas?

Elsa's steps resounded nervously and even indignantly through the little room to his office. They stopped. Rzhevsky did not turn around.

"Sergei, what does this mean?"

"Nothing."

He walked away toward his desk. Elsa looked remarkably young. Her black hair lay flat against her head, with a straight part, and not a single gray hair. He, on the other hand, was graying. At first glance she could be taken for a young girl. If only she didn't hop around so much at parties, rush to the piano to play Chopin enthusiastically and amateurishly, and then switch from Chopin to some pop tune, if only she didn't try so hard to look young.

"Seryozha, tell me honestly, were you hurt bad? Is it true they tried to kill you?"

Good God, thought Rzhevsky, I'm still her personal property. She divides the whole world into what's hers and what's others'. And for her things life is hard. The demands on them are greater. You have to live up to expectations. And don't dare step out of line and break Elsa's laws of love. Then you might as well belong to others. Rzhevsky recalled with anguish the years when they had become alien to each other. Elsa came from the past Rzhevsky preferred not to remember, which he had almost forgotten. And now she had to seek him out, after all these years. To ask for something. As an old friend. For the sake of the old days.

"Thanks for your concern, Elsa," Rzhevsky said. "Everything's fine."

"How can it be fine if wild animals are running around loose in the institute? What are you hiding from me?"

"Nothing happened," Rzhevsky insisted. He walked over to his desk and leaned over, inspecting the drawer. No scratches. The chimp knew how to open the desk. "By the way, do you remember which barracks we lived in, the third or the fourth?"

"Barracks?"

"You know, twenty-five years ago. Remember, we rented a room there. They're tearing them down now. Didn't you notice?"

"I don't remember," Elsa answered quickly. "It was a long time ago. Should I call a doctor?"

"And you always bragged about your photographic memory," Rzhevsky said. "If I had your memory, I'd be in the Academy of Sciences by now."

"You'll get there anyway," Elsa said confidently. "If a tiger doesn't eat you next time. But tell me how it all happened."

Somehow Rzhevsky did not feel like telling her about all the confusion. Besides, the head of the institute's library didn't really need to know.

"How are things at home?" he asked. "How's Viktor?"

Elsa just shrugged.

"And how's Mom? And Nina?"

"Oh yes, I was going to stop by yesterday about her. Ninochka should get into the institute. You know that."

"Yes, I know," Rzhevsky answered. In the summer Nina had entered the bio department but had failed. Neither Elsa's irresistible force nor Rzhevsky's help—she had him call the top man—did any good. Now Nina was waiting out the year, working in the library with her mother.

"I wanted to ask you to transfer her to some laboratory. It will be easier for her to get admitted that way. You did promise, as soon as there was an opening. And I was told that we're hiring lab assistants."

"Okay," Rzhevsky said, pulling a folder with mail toward him. Maybe Elsa would take the hint and leave?

Elsa walked over to the window.

"Are they really tearing down the barracks?" she asked. "I didn't notice. How fast time flies. You're getting quite gray. You ought to take it easier."

Rzhevsky raised his head, and their eyes met. Her look and her tone demanded a warm response. But he had none—what could he do?

6

Elsa opened the scratched brown door and stepped into the semidarkness of the foyer. The bulb had been out for a long time, and she had almost bought one the week before, but her shopping bag was heavy and she put it off. The parquet floor squeaked familiarly as Elsa hung up her coat. Viktor, of course, was not home—he'd come home tipsy later—and to-morrow was Saturday, so she would have to prepare dinner. And then there was Sergei with his monkeys.

Elsa went into the kitchen, put the bag of groceries down next to the dishes left from breakfast—Viktor had promised to wash them. Of course, no one had thought to straighten up. The bread was dried out, the sugar was spilled. So they're tearing down the barracks, and good riddance it is. Why should she worry about the barracks? Elsa lit the stove, poured water in a pot, and put in some vermicelli.

"Puss," a voice sounded from behind. "I'm starving."

"You're home?" Elsa did not turn around. "I thought you went to the soccer match."

"I bought bread. Two loaves. I ate one, Puss."

Over the years Viktor had unraveled, gotten soft. Elsa had the impression that chairs began to squeak a second before he sat down on them.

"A monkey attacked Sergei," Elsa said.

"They're running through our institute?" Viktor asked, holding the refrigerator door open as he searched for something to eat. It was like a sickness. "Aren't you afraid for Nina?"

"A young chimpanzee got out of his cage, managed to find Sergei's office, and rummaged through his desk."

"That can't be!" Viktor found a piece of sausage and quickly shoved it in his mouth before Elsa could take it away. Like a child, a fat, spoiled little child, Elsa thought.

"The monkey was only two weeks old," Elsa said. "You've forgotten everything."

"Oh, those experiments of his. . . . I was starved to death all day today. There was practically nothing to eat in the cafeteria. Say, Puss, could you give me half a ruble more? A ruble just isn't enough."

Elsa ignored the request. Viktor could eat them out of house and home—no matter how much she gave him, it wouldn't be enough. Now Sergei won't have any doubts, she thought. He'll start with humans next. Very dangerous and even repulsive.

"There's no stopping him now," Elsa said. "He's going to move on to humans."

She remembered that she had forgotten to put salt in with the vermicelli and reached for the saltshaker.

"Do you really want to stop him?" Viktor asked.

"He's changed for the worse," Elsa said. "To satisfy his vanity he won't stop at anything."

"You're exaggerating, Puss," Viktor sighed. "Is there anything to drink?"

"All gone. Humanity just isn't ready for such a step."

"Not ready?" Viktor repeated. "Then you should write to the proper authorities. Tell them, and they'll stop him."

"No," Elsa said, "people have already written. He's charmed everyone. Have you forgotten what a charmer he is?"

"You just have to write more," Viktor said confidently. "At least they'd send a commission."

The door slammed, and Nina ran in. She was always running, as though she had never learned to walk in all her eighteen years.

"I'm not hungry," she said from the kitchen doorway, without saying hello.

Nina did not like to eat at home. She tried to eat as little as possible, so she wouldn't get fat.

"Nina," Elsa said. "I have it all set up. On Monday you'll be transferred to a laboratory."

7

Rzhevsky finished speaking and sat down.

They were looking at him. Fifteen, no, sixteen persons who had the right to say yes. Or to refuse him the money. Ostapenko was convinced that everything would be fine. The office had an excellent view. The Moscow River, the ski jump on Lenin Hills, and the stadium. The evening sun gilded the bald heads of the academicians and highlighted the silvery fluff over their ears. Why were they quiet?

Ostapenko tapped on the table with his pencil.

"Any questions?" he asked.

"What are our colleagues doing?" asked a strong, broad man in a bright tie—the tie was so bright in fact that it pushed everything else into the background. "What are they doing in the States?"

Rzhevsky stood up again. The question was useful.

"We believe," he said, "that the Japanese are already close to success. With the Americans, the picture is a little more complicated. Last year there was an article claiming success with dogs."

"Jackson?" Semansky asked from the other end of the table.

"Jackson and Hedges," Rzhevsky answered. "Since then there has been silence."

"Well, that's clear," the man in the bright tie said. "So they're on the threshold?"

"It's hard to maintain that an entire trend in biology could be the monopoly of a single country. We are all riding on parallel rails."

"Well, my friend," a voice piped up from beside him. Rzhevsky turned but could not make out the speaker—the sun was in his eyes. The voice was squeaky, ancient. "So you intend to take the place of the Lord God?"

Aha! that was Chelovekov, the former director of the IGK. A major consultant and famous toastmaster at doctoral banquets.

"If the funds are granted, we will try to act as a collective deity."

Those were not the questions he was afraid of.

"Remarkable," Chelovekov said. "And how much is this homunculus of yours going to set us back?"

"Rzhevsky has already acquainted us with the figures," Opanasenko said. "Although, of course, there may be more needed."

"Do you think the Pentagon has made it top secret?" the man in the bright tie asked.

"I don't know," Rzhevsky said. "Although I am convinced that it is cheaper to create humans in the orthodox manner."

Someone laughed.

"The prospects are attractive," the secretary of the division said. "Although it's just prospects. Someday we will learn to do it on a mass scale."

"I don't think that will happen in the near future," Rzhevsky said.

"The first atomic bomb was very expensive, too," Sidorov said. Sidorov was opposed to Rzhevsky's methods. His outfit was working on closely related problems, but as far as Sergei knew, they were at a dead end. "I am concerned by something else—the unjustified risk. Someone here mentioned the word *homunculus*. But even though literary analogies may seem superficial, I'd use the word *Frankenstein*. Where's the guarantee that you're not going to create a monster?"

"The methodology has been perfected," Rzhevsky said.

"Between experiments on animals and experiments on humans there lies a chasm, as each of us knows very well."

"What do you propose?" Opanasenko asked.

"To form a commission, an authoritative one, to study the results of the institute's work."

"I'm already heading a commission in January," Semansky said.

"At that time the question of experiments on humans had not been raised."

"They had been. It was to be the final goal."

"Consider me a skeptic."

"But suppose the Americans do it?" the man in the bright tie added.

"Well, God be with them," Sidorov responded. "Are you afraid that over there there are also . . . shortsighted people who want to throw away several hundred million dollars on a poor imitation of a human being?"

It's begun, Rzhevsky thought.

"I understood," Airapetyan interrupted, spitting out his words as though each were wrapped in paper, "Professor Rzhevsky in a different way. I thought that the most interesting aspect of his work lay elsewhere."

Ostapenko nodded. Rzhevsky remembered that he and Airapetyan had discussed the matter before.

"Cloning is no secret anymore," Airapetyan said. "Experiments have been conducted and continue to be conducted."

"But to grow an adult in vitro, quickly. . . ," Chelovekov said.

"Even that is nothing new," Sidorov said.

"It's not new," Airapetyan agreed. "They've succeeded. But with one drawback. The person grown in vitro was a Mowgli."

Ostapenko nodded once again.

"A Mowgli?" the man in the bright tie asked.

"In the history of humanity," Airapetyan said measuredly, like a teacher, "there have been cases where children have been raised by animals. If the child was found, it would not return to being human. It would remain incomplete. We are social animals. An adult person, grown in vitro, is a baby. His brain is empty. And it is too late to teach him."

"That's precisely it," Sidorov said. "And there's no proof—"

"Excuse me," Airapetyan said. "Let me finish. The achievement of Sergei Rzhevsky and his colleagues is that they can give the clone the memory of the genetic parent. That is why we're here."

They've heard it all already, Rzhevsky thought. But there are blinds in the intellect that are keeping out the most important thing.

"Would you confirm this, Sergei?" Airapetyan asked.

Rzhevsky rose. The river was golden. A pink riverboat slid over its surface.

"In experiments with animals we have demonstrated," Rzhevsky said, "that the new individual inherits not only the physical characteristics of the donor but his memory, his experience as well. In all its aspects."

"Until what moment?" Chelovekov asked.

"Up to the time the cell is extracted from the donor's organism."

"More specifically?" Opanasenko asked.

"We grow the individual up to the completion of physical development. For a human, about twenty years of age. If the donor, let us say, is fifty at the time, then all his knowledge, all his experience, everything he has acquired during those years, is inherited by his 'son.' I thought that all this was clear from my reports."

"It is clear," Semansky said. "Clear, but incredible."

"It's not incredible," Airapetyan objected.

"Every single one of the animals we cloned by our method," Rzhevsky said, "inherited the donor's memory. Incidentally, three days ago, a chimpanzee got loose and came into my office—the chimp was just two weeks old. But he not only knew how to open his cage but even remembered the way through the institute to my office, and where I kept candy in my desk. He had never learned this, but his genetic father had."

"Did he break anything?" Sidorov asked.

He must have a spy in my institute, Rzhevsky thought. My shame has been revealed.

"Nothing," he answered. "I did get very frightened. I walked into my office and wondered who it was sitting at my desk."

Ostapenko tapped his pencil against the table, trying to calm the laughter.

"If your homunculus decides to take a stroll through the institute, the results might not be so amusing," Sidorov said.

"I think we'll be able to talk our problems over," Rzhevsky said.

"There's no guarantee," Sidorov insisted, "that the intelligence of the homunculus will be human. Normal and human."

"So far with animals, everything has been normal."

"But wait a moment!" Chelovekov suddenly shouted. His sharp Adam's apple stood out under his ancient skin. "You are proposing a new step in human evolution, and we are arguing about trivia. Don't you realize that if the experiment is a success, human beings will be immortal? We can all be immortal—me and you, and anyone at all. The death of the individual, the death of the body, will cease to be the death of the soul, the death of ideas, the death of personality. If I have to, Rzhevsky, I'll give you my pension. I'm not joking, so don't smile."

Rzhevsky had known Chelovekov for a long time, even though not that well. And he knew his two sons—Chelovekov had set them up in institutes and rescued the middle-aged dimwits whenever the sword of Damocles was about to fall.

"Thank you," Rzhevsky said, without a smile.

"All my life I've been accumulating knowledge; like the covetous knight I have stuffed my skull with facts and theories, observations and questionable hypotheses. My whole life I have hastened to work, because I knew that I would die, and life flies by so quickly that I could not use a tenth of what I had acquired. And I knew that with my death all that treasure would be swept away." Chelovekov tapped his forehead with a bent finger. "And now a man has come—and he doesn't seem to be a charlatan—and says that the key to my treasurehouse can be given to someone else, who will go on further after I have stopped. You aren't a charlatan, are you, Rzhevsky?"

"No one has accused me of being one yet," Rzhevsky said. He noticed that Sidorov's lips began to move—but Sidorov remained silent. Sidorov did not believe him but saw that the elder people gathered in the room would agree to give Rzhevsky his money.

But maybe I am a charlatan, Rzhevsky thought. Suppose what happened with the dogs and the chimpanzees doesn't happen with human beings? Well, if it doesn't work for me, it will work for someone else, in the future.

"I am not offering my cells," Chelovekov said. "Especially now, when so much depends on the first experiment, on the first *Homo futurus*. My brain is already damaged by sclerosis. Too bad I didn't hear you even ten years ago. I would have insisted that you make me a son. We would have worked so well together."

"By the way," Semansky said, when Chelovekov wearily sank back in his chair. "Have you thought about the first donor?"

"Yes," Rzhevsky said. "I will take the cell from myself."

"Why?" the man in the bright necktie exclaimed. "What's your reasoning? The question should be decided at a higher level."

"You don't have to decide," Airapetyan said. "In my opinion, it's all clear. Who can make better observations of himself than the experimenter himself—as he was at twenty?"

8

Beginning on Monday Nina was in the laboratory but not in the role for which she prepared herself. She ran errands. Every day she traveled somewhere, either with papers or without. With Alevich or without, by car or by bus. She picked up, signed papers, and hauled things back to the institute. As though Rzhevsky was preparing for a siege and stocking up on everything that might be useful.

The director's laboratory occupied half the first floor and overlooked a park. The trees were still green, but leaves were already falling. A pair of tame squirrels lived there.

Nina had been in the lab's inside rooms, behind the heavy metal door with the windowpane, only once, on a volunteer Sunday, when they had scrubbed the walls and floor that had been clean to begin with, even though cluttered with equipment. Even Grisha the electrician entered wearing a white coat. There was nothing interesting in there, the first room with equipment, the second, to the right of the first, with the tubs with biological solution—the incubator. One tub was smaller—in that one the chimpanzee Lev was being cloned; the second one was new and had not been set up yet. There was a third room, which Rzhevsky had moved into.

Rzhevsky was cared for by two doctors: his own, Volkov, a redhead with thick lips who was always smiling and eating chocolates, and a stranger from Tsinkelman's institute.

A kind of nervous field surrounded the institute. Even the technicians, who sat behind the bushes in the park and smoked for hours, and sometimes even had a few drinks, stopped grumbling under his window. They put on serious expressions, walked around businesslike.

Twice Nina's mother ran down to see how she was doing, although there was no need. Actually, she stared at the metal door and spoke in a loud whisper, and Nina felt awkward in front of the other lab assistants. Her mother was out of place here, and her presence immediately set Nina apart from the others and turned her into a child who had been given a job through nepotism.

At home in the evening there were endless discussions about Rzhevsky and his work. They went around in circles, with few variations, and Nina knew in advance what would be said. She hid in her room and tried to study. But she could not help hearing.

The refrigerator door slammed—her father was getting a snack.

"What are you doing?" her mother objected. "We're eating in half an hour."

"I'll eat again," her father answered. "So you're going to stop Rzhevsky?"

"If he succeeds, he's certain to nail down the state prize in biology. Almost guaranteed. Alevich said so."

"It would have been better if he had married you and put an end to it all," her father responded.

"I didn't want to."

"Right, Puss, I was always your ideal."

"Oh, stop being silly."

At this point Nina got up from the couch, closed her math text, and went closer to the door. She did not know exactly what had happened, many years ago. Something that had joined all of them together until this very day. She knew that Rzhevsky had betrayed Mama and killed poor Liza. For years Nina had been used to hearing of Rzhevsky as a traitor and an ingrate. Before it had never mattered to her. Rzhevsky had never visited them. At the same time the acquaintance with him allowed her to say to her friends, not without pride, "Seryozha Rzhevsky, our old friend. . . ." And then Mama got her the job in the library, and she saw Rzhevsky, who did not seem like a traitor—her image of a traitor had been formed by television, and traitors were always played by identical actors. Rzhevsky was dry, smart, well built, with a red face, blue eyes, and graying, poorly barbered hair. On his round chin was a white scar, and his hands were small. Rzhevsky always greeted her absentmindedly, as though each time was an effort to remember where he had met her. Then he smiled, almost timidly, probably remembering how many bad things Nina undoubtedly knew about him. Nina was ready to fall in love with him, the villain, who carried his secret within. True, Rzhevsky was very old. More than forty.

From behind the door she heard her parents' voices.

"You know, they're tearing down the barracks," her mother said.

"What barracks?"

"Where he and Liza lived."

9

Rzhevsky led the latest of the commissions out of the laboratory. They sat for a while in his office. Lena brought coffee and cookies. They talked about some minor details—Strumilov pointed out that there were no bars over the windows on the first floor. Alevich took advantage of the opportunity and asked for money for repairs. The facade was hopeless and the parquet floors were literally falling apart. Suppose there were foreign delegations? "Don't be in such a hurry about foreign delegations," Opanasenko said. Khrutsky asked about the congress in Brno; whom should he send? Rzhevsky drank coffee, chatted with the higher-ups, pretending that he belonged to that category of people, but in his mind he was picturing how the first cells divided. It was as though he could see them move under a microscope. The main thing was to prepare the transfer in time. . . .

Then Rzhevsky sat up until the wee hours in the special lab. Downstairs the dogs were barking, then a God-awful racket resounded. Rzhevsky realized that the apes were bored and calling for someone to come—hitting their cups against the bars of their cages.

In the special lab, everything was surgically bright. The assistant, Kolya Milenkov, pretended to read an English mystery so as not to bother the director. He considered the director a genius and was therefore happy.

Rzhevsky walked home. He stopped near the barracks; the door was open. Rzhevsky walked in. It smelled of dust and of long years of human habitation. There was no light, it had long since been turned off. Rzhevsky was about to light a match when he realized that it wasn't necessary—he remembered very clearly how many steps were in the flight. He climbed the stairs to the second floor and had the strange feeling that he was climbing not into the emptiness of a deserted building but to his home, where, on the other side of the door, Liza would be standing, listening to his footsteps. He would open the door—and Liza was waiting, watching silently. He would wearily hand her the bag of groceries or his briefcase— she would put it on the table in the little foyer, and he would say to her: "Don't be mad, Liz, I was studying in the library and missed the train." Katya was sleeping on the trestle bed he himself had made, not very prettily but soundly, would groan in her sleep and Liza would say with a guilty smile, "The cutlets are stiff—I warmed them up twice already."

The door was not locked. The moon was hanging in the sky outside the window, and old newspapers littered the floor. That was all. Not a single thing from the past. Even the wallpaper was different.

Rzhevsky walked over to the window and realized how much everything outside had changed. Because whenever he couldn't sleep he would climb out of bed and go to the window, open it, and smoke a cigarette, looking at the vacant land. Out there where there were now the white buildings of the new district, everything was dark greenery. A village was hidden in it—Liza would run over for milk when Katya caught cold. He suddenly pricked up his ears. He realized that Liza would wake up—she always did when he got up at night. "What's the matter? Are you sick?" "Just can't sleep." "That's not like you. Are you upset?" "No, I'm fine. I'm thinking." He was rude to her, he was tired of her worrying, her outbursts of jealousy, and her gentle, almost timid touches. "Do you want an aspirin?" "That's all I need!"

A step on the stairway squeaked. Then a thud. Noise. As though the person climbing the stairs was groping along the wall with his hand and had run into the corner.

I should be frightened, Rzhevsky said to himself. Who could be climbing the stairs of a deserted building at midnight? The door began to open slowly, as though the person was not sure that this was the right door. Rzhevsky stepped aside so he could not be seen against the window.

10

The man who entered the room hesitated in the doorway; Rzhevsky's eyes had already grown accustomed to the dark. In addition, the moon shone into the room, so he could see the man grope to the right along the wall. He realized that there must be a light switch there—how many times had he reached out and turned on the light? A click resounded.

"Oh, damn!" the man whispered.

"You know, the lights have been turned off," Rzhevsky said. "Everyone has moved out—did you forget?"

The man froze, pressing himself against the wall. He did not recognize Rzhevsky's voice, and he was so frightened that his tubby body seemed to spread over the wall.

"Afraid?" Rzhevsky walked over to Viktor, hit a pile of newspapers with his foot and almost fell. "It's me, Sergei."

"You? What are you doing here?" Viktor asked hoarsely. "I was afraid. I never expected meeting anyone here."

They were silent. It was awkward.

"Want a cigarette?" Rzhevsky asked.

"Yes, let's have a smoke."

Rzhevsky took out his cigarettes. When Viktor lit up, he bent over, and Rzhevsky saw his bald spot, covered by sparse hair combed over the top.

"I haven't seen you for a long time," Rzhevsky said.

"Well, I guess I'll be going," Viktor said.

Rzhevsky nodded. He, too, felt like leaving but did not want to walk down the night street with Viktor. Viktor's shoes thudded heavily on the stairs. The staircase groaned. Then everything was still.

Elsa must have told him the barracks were being torn down, Rzhevsky thought. Although maybe Viktor had come here before? The past drew Rzhevsky like a murderer who returns to the scene of the crime. And then he is caught. Had Viktor caught him? No. He had come himself. Rzhevsky closed his eyes and tried to picture the room the way it was then. He forced himself to put out the furniture and even mentally put his books on the table. He even remembered that the table lamp was covered with an old handkerchief, so that the light would not wake Katya up. And Liza lay in the semidarkness and stared at his back. He knew she was staring at his

back, trying not to cough or toss. But her stare still prevented him from
working. And he would say softly, "Go to sleep, you have to get up early
tomorrow." "Okay," Liza would answer, "of course. I'll go to sleep right
away."

But on the last morning, when they had gotten to sleep at five in the
morning after talking all night long, he had opened his eyes and as in
the continuation of a nightmare saw her standing in the door, holding the
warmly dressed Katya in one arm and a suitcase in the other. He still did
not realize that Liza was leaving forever, but the fact that she was going
was a relief, a way out of the dead end, a solution. And he fell asleep
again. . . .

Rzhevsky opened his eyes. A brisk night breeze blew in the window and
rustled the paper on the floor.

Rzhevsky threw his cigarette out the window and went downstairs. He
was overwhelmed by such a mortal, deep, hopeless sadness that when he
saw Viktor standing not far away and waiting for him, he stopped short
before stepping outside; then, waiting until Viktor lit a match to light
another cigarette, he jumped out the entrance and slid along the wall,
around the corner, and into the bushes.

11

Nina wanted to look at the special lab very much: It had been the center
of the institute's life for six weeks already. But she could not manage. Only
five or six persons had access, in addition to Rzhevsky and Ostapenko from
the presidium. True, a few times friends of Rzhevsky came, gray, respectable. Kolya Milenkov knew them all, of course—academician so-and-so,
academician such-and-such. Rzhevsky himself took them inside, and they
spent a long time there.

"You know, Milenkov," Nina said (she had gotten used to Kolya and
was no longer intimidated). "For me it's like the door to Bluebeard's castle.
Do you remember?"

"Yes. You want to finish your youth without fame. You know that
Bluebeard would kick us both out of the institute immediately. And I have
my eye on a doctorate."

Nina did not dare ask Rzhevsky himself, even though she saw him every
day and he had gotten used to considering her his colleague—not Elsa's
daughter—and even raised his voice at her. He was short-tempered, har-
assed, attacked people without cause, but no one took offense; instead,
they sympathized—after all, right here in their institute, not in distant

Switzerland, the first artificial human being was growing in a biobath. Finally Nina did manage to get into the laboratory.

It was evening, already dark and somehow heavy. The trees outside were almost bare; a single maple leaf clung to the glass and that was beautiful. Kolya came out of the special lab, saw Nina, who was sitting at her desk with a book, and asked, "Why are you still here?"

"I'm taking Yura's place. I just don't feel like going home. I'm studying."

"I'm going to run over to the store before it closes. The one on the corner. I need some mineral water. Sit here, watch the control panel. Nothing should happen."

Nina nodded. The outside control panel took up an entire wall. Rzhevsky had made all the assistants learn about the dials and scales. Just in case.

"The main thing," he said, "is the temperature of the broth, and of course. . . ."

"I know," Nina said and felt herself blush. She had very white skin and blushed easily.

"I'm not closing up," Kolya said. "but don't go in."

He hurried to the door and as he opened it said, "Bluebeard's eighth wife."

He laughed and went out the door.

Nina stood up and walked over to the control panel. Inside nothing was happening. If something did happen, what an alarm would be sounded through the whole institute! That had happened last week when the acidity had risen. Fortunately, Rzhevsky had not been in the institute, and by the time he arrived everything was in order.

Nina paced the room. The institute was very quiet. The yellow leaf on the window was quivering and apparently planning to fly away.

"If it flies away," Nina said, "I'll peek. Very quickly."

The edge of the leaf tore loose from the glass, and Nina stiffened, afraid that it would fly off. Then she would have to look. But raindrops beat the leaf back against the glass. It was motionless.

Then Nina thought that Kolya would be back soon. She went over to the door and pushed it gently. Maybe it wouldn't open.

The door opened. Easily, silently.

The small changing room was brightly lit, the door to the right, the one to the incubator, was ajar. Nina's heels pounded quickly against the floor. White coats were hanging in the closet. Water was dripping from the sink. Nina froze by the door, listening intently. It was quiet. Even too quiet.

Only a few instruments were humming.

A soft light shone from behind the door.

Nina opened the door slightly and slipped inside.

For some reason, first she saw the soft black couch, an open book on it, and half an apple. That's where Kolya Milenkov must sit. An ordinary table lamp stood on a small table next to the couch. There were two tubs. One was empty. The large one, just like an Egyptian sarcophagus on display. Or like a submarine. The mystery was occurring in the second bath, slightly smaller, sunken in the floor, and unfortunately opaque. That is, the top was transparent, but inside was a yellowish thick liquid, and the body was not to be seen. Nina bent over the bath, but still could not see anything. Then she touched its smooth glass side. The side was warm. Her touch produced a reaction by the instruments: They blinked, a buzzing increased, as though a bumblebee had flown closer, right next to her ear. Nina pulled her hand back, and right then the door opened and Rzhevsky walked in. Nina thought that it was Kolya and as the door opened had time to say, "Kolya, don't be mad."

She fell silent, pressed her hand against her chest, as though a sign that she had touched the bath had been imprinted on it.

"What are you doing here?" At first Rzhevsky did not seem surprised, walked over to the instruments, turned toward Nina, and she started for the door, realizing how stupid it was.

"Kolya asked me to stay while he went for mineral water," Nina said.

"Asked you? To stay?"

Rzhevsky turned around abruptly.

"How could he dare! To leave everything in the hands of a girl! What did you touch?"

Nina thought he was going to kill her on the spot.

"I didn't touch anything."

"Why are you smiling?"

"I'm not smiling, baron."

"Who?"

"Bluebeard. Or was he a count?"

Rzhevsky listened to the buzzing of the bumblebee, then hit a button and the buzzing decreased.

He apparently realized what had happened and smiled.

"I was very curious," Nina said. "Excuse me, Doctor Rzhevsky. I understand the problem, but it's hard to take, sitting there every day without being able to come in."

"It's not a question of whims," Rzhevsky said. "Like with a child. . . . Bluebeard. What nonsense!"

"It is nonsense," Nina agreed quickly. "It looks like a sarcophagus. Only the pharaoh isn't visible."

"Even if you did see him, you wouldn't understand anything," Rzhevsky said. "The process of body construction is different than in nature. Completely different. It's a lot nicer seeing a baby than what is lying inside here. The day after tomorrow will be the big move." Rzhevsky rapped his knuckles against the big, empty sarcophagus. "But please don't sneak in here anymore. You came in in your ordinary lab coat—a hotbed of bacteria."

No, he was not angry. What a stroke of luck!

"But everything here is sealed hermetically, that I know," Nina said.

"But I can't take any chances. I've been working twenty years for this. A failure would never be forgiven."

"You're on good terms with the presidium."

"You've picked up some of the institute gossip, I see. The presidium is on good terms with winners. Ostapenko is taking a chance, too, by supporting us. You know what is the accepted wisdom? Try another five years with rats . . . well, if you must, with apes—remarkable experiments . . . a great step forward! But dangerous! Risky! A triumph of genetic engineering—they created a homunculus! But suppose it's the Soviet Frankenstein? You know about Frankenstein, I suppose?"

Rzhevsky sat on Kolya's couch, picked up the book, leafed through it lazily.

"Yes, I've heard of him," Nina said with the tone of a student answering her teacher. "He was sewn together out of corpses, and then attacked women. But you are growing yours according to biological laws—"

"Against the laws." Rzhevsky put the book aside. "Against all laws. Didn't you know that? Even if this fails, science will still move on. Despite any prohibition. Most often failures serve as catalysts. But my funding will be cut off. . . ."

Rzhevsky stood up from the couch, lightly, as though he had been pushed.

"And you come in here with unwashed hands."

"I won't anymore."

Nina understood that she should leave—who could say what would happen in another two minutes? But she would be sorry to leave. And sorry for Rzhevsky: He had turned pale, seemed to shrivel up, as though the incident had cost him greatly.

"You don't have children," Nina said without thinking, surprised at her own words. "Now you will."

"You mean him?"

"Of course. It would be better if you already had children of your own, but this is all right for a start."

"It's crazy," Rzhevsky was amazed. "So then, just march right out of here!"

In the changing room Nina bumped into Kolya, who was carrying five bottles in his arms.

"Where are you coming from?" he asked in surprise.

"There," she said. "With him."

"Who?"

"Rzhevsky."

"Oh God, what bad luck!" Kolya was dumbfounded. "I leave for five minutes, the first time in two months. And he would have to. . . . I thought he had gone home."

"I came back," Rzhevsky's threatening voice resounded from the special lab. "Come here."

12

Ivan was born November 21 at 6:00 P.M.

No one left the institute—even though the end of the experiment was not announced. They waited. Rzhevsky did not leave the special lab for three days—literally, and Nina took turns with the other women buying and cooking for whoever was inside. They ran out for several minutes to the women, grabbed up whatever was available, and disappeared again behind the metal door.

Beginning on the morning of that day some new faces appeared at the institute—doctors. Then Ostapenko came twice, and one of the old academicians. In the director's office the telephone was ringing constantly, but Lena had firm instructions from Rzhevsky not to call him, not to send him messages, even if an earthquake broke loose.

Nina herself did not go out to eat. Her thoughts were inside, behind the door. The boy, the homunculus, the Frankenstein. . . . he turns, he tries to open his eyes, and a weak, hoarse groan breaks from his blue lips. Or suddenly his breathing stops—Rzhevsky starts to massage his heart. . . . She did not know enough about the instruments to be able to read the dials on the panel. Biologists from other labs were crowded around them and acted as though they were watching a soccer match.

At several minutes after six o'clock one of the budding geniuses who filled the institute looked at the green curve on a screen and said, "It's okay" and clapped his hands. They all started talking, arguing, and began looking at the door. For some reason Nina felt that Rzhevsky was about to walk out with him.

Rzhevsky did not come out for a long time, and when he did, one of the doctors was accompanying him. And that was all. Nina could not get

a good look at Rzhevsky from behind the backs of the budding geniuses—
and he was swept away by the crowd and only once did his tired voice rise
above the others: "Does somebody have cigarettes without filters?" Nina
felt that she was completely exhausted but could not resist looking at the
door to the special lab, because he could come out all by himself, forgotten
and uncontrolled. And when Kolya Milenkov came out for a break, she
could not refrain and asked him, quietly, so that no one could hear and
make fun of her: "Can he walk? Can he talk?"

"He'll walk," Kolya said with great self-satisfaction.

Then Rzhevsky returned and asked Faleyeva for the work schedule for
the assistants. He was sitting at the desk. Nina walked over, and she felt
touched that the hair on the top of his head was thinning—she felt like
stroking it.

"In the coming weeks," Rzhevsky said to Faleyeva loud enough for
everyone to hear, "attendants will sit up with him. I talked to Tsinkelman,
but they're having a hard time with junior personnel. There will be nurses,
but we'll have to call on some of our people to help out. Are there any
volunteers?"

Rzhevsky looked around.

"Of course there are," Faleyeva said. But no one spoke up, because
they were all frightened.

Even Yura turned timid, the lab assistant who was into pumping iron.
And Nina was more frightened than any of the others. So therefore she
said in a weak voice, "Could I?"

"Of course," Rzhevsky said. He was apparently not worried about Nina's
fate. "Anyone else?"

Then Yura and Faleyeva herself volunteered.

13

All around was darkness and deafness, darkness and deafness, but the
darkness was not endless—you could crawl out of it and know where to
crawl through it, but no one could say where you should crawl, and if
you crawled the wrong way you could fall in a well, this was not a well,
but a concept for which there are no words, a place you fall into, fall,
fall, and your body becomes heavy and it keeps growing, bigger than the
sides of the well but it doesn't touch the sides, they move away faster to
let him into the abyss.

And he did not know what it meant, although he should, otherwise he
could not climb out of the darkness. . . .

14

Nina came home at nine.

It was quiet in the kitchen. So quiet that Nina decided that no one was home. But they both were sitting there.

Her father was reading *Soviet Sport* and her mother was chopping cabbage.

"Why so late?" her father asked peaceably, as though relieved.

"We got so tired. . . ." and Nina fell silent. On her way home she couldn't decide whether she should run in with a shout—"He was born!"—or just go straight to bed.

"Of course you're tired," her father said, rocking slightly. "Every day you don't come home until the middle of the night. Now at least you will stay home for a while."

"No," Nina said. "Now there's going to be even more work. I've been assigned to watch him."

"Who?" her mother asked. Her knife stopped in midair.

"Ivan. His name is Ivan, remember?"

"I don't remember," her mother said. "I left before that. Ivan—that's his kid?"

The word *kid* made him sound like a newborn. A bad sign.

"I'm going to watch him."

"My God," her mother said. "You're going to watch that monster? By yourself?"

"He's not a monster. He's Rzhevsky's son. Do you understand, biologically he's Rzhevsky's son, he was grown from his cell."

Her mother threw down her knife, and it bounced off the table and fell on the floor. No one picked it up.

"He's a murderer!" her mother screamed. "He killed Liza! He kills everything he touches. He's gone ahead with this whole business because of a pathological desire to prove to me that he can have a child."

Nina was about to leave, as she always did during such scenes, but now everything connected to Rzhevsky interested her so much that her feet refused to move.

"What Liza?" Nina asked.

Her mother picked up the knife and said, as though she had not heard the question, "I am categorically opposed to Nina's going near that mongrel. If I have to, I'll take it to the very top. I'll leave no stone unturned."

And then Nina ran out of the house. It was dark and freezing. She had Rzhevsky's home phone number and had written down his address out of the phone book. She found a phone booth, still not believing that she was going to call him—it was just that the well-lighted booth was a warm and protected spot to take refuge in. And then she dialed Rzhevsky's number.

She could tell from the sound of his voice that she had woken him up. She was about to hang up but did not.

He asked sternly, "Who's there?"

And she did not dare to ignore him.

"Excuse me, I didn't want to wake you up. This is Nina Gulinskaya."

"Has something happened? Are you calling from the institute?"

"No, I went home, but then I had a fight with Mama, not really a fight, but I left them."

"Then don't cry," Rzhevsky said. "Nothing that bad has happened."

"She won't let me, but I want to. I'll leave them, if she doesn't let me—"

"Are you calling from a pay phone?"

"Yes."

"Then come see me. Do you remember my address?"

"I have it. I copied it a long time ago. . . . But it's late, and you have to sleep."

"If you don't come here, where will you go?"

"I don't know."

"Dry your tears and come." She heard a touch of irony in Rzhevsky's voice, so she said drily, "No, no thank you."

She was not out for pity.

Then she walked two or three blocks, called her friend Sima, announced that she would spend the night there, and then went to see Rzhevsky.

15

Rzhevsky's apartment fascinated Nina. She often imagined how he lived, all alone, and she thought his world was a pile of books, a mountain of manuscript on the table, of course a large black leather chair, a picture by Levitan on the wall—the disorderly refuge of a great man. But the apartment turned out to be small—three rooms, neat, and boring.

"I was going to have some coffee," Rzhevsky said. He was wearing jeans and a sweater. "Would you like some?"

"Please."

He went into the kitchen, and Nina remained standing next to the neat desk. She looked around and saw a wide couch and thought, He probably brings women here. They come, and he makes them coffee and then gets a drink from the bar over by the wall, a cognac. Suppose he started treating her like a woman?

"Should I cook up some sausages?" he asked from the kitchen.

Nina walked over to the kitchen door and looked in. The kitchen was appropriately clean and not overstocked with china.

"Thanks, but I'm not hungry. Does anyone help you with the cleaning?"

"I have someone from the Dawn firm to wash the windows. Here, take the cookies. Put them on the coffee table."

He really doesn't see me as a woman, Nina realized. It was insulting. She did not change her mind even when Rzhevsky got the bottle of cognac and two little glasses from the bar. The coffee was very aromatic and strong—the kind only men know how to make.

"Let's drink together to the first step," Rzhevsky said.

He poured cognac into the glasses, and Nina made herself comfortable on the couch. She realized that she was his colleague and that they were discussing the experiment. In addition, the families knew each other. Mama should see her now, drinking cognac with the director of the institute. What would the expression on Faleyeva's face be like? Of course the director's reputation would ruin her for good. Nina wanted to ask Rzhevsky not to say anything about her visit, but he cut her off.

"Tell me what happened at home."

"They made a big fuss. My mother won't let me work with Ivan. She says he's a mongrel. Please don't be offended."

"I've known your mother for many years, and I know what she's like when she gets mad."

"She'll settle down, you know how she is, she'll settle down very soon."

"Not exactly. She'll calm down on the outside, but without a Canossa you won't get her forgiveness."

"Without a Canossa?"

"My dear, don't they teach you anything in school these days?"

Nina noticed that a pair of skis was standing in the corner, very expensive foreign skis; they didn't belong in the room, but who was going to tell Rzhevsky what he could put in his living room and what he couldn't?

Nina nodded, agreeing that she had been poorly educated by her school.

"What should we do now. Transfer you to a different lab?"

"No way!" Nina exclaimed. "Am I such a bad worker?"

"I have no complaints. But perhaps you're a little afraid of him yourself?"

Nina shook her head no. To say that she wasn't afraid was not quite true.

Rzhevsky stood up, walked to the window, and opened it slightly; the intermittent roar of a busy street rushed into the room.

"Are you cold?"

"No. Don't think I'm afraid. But it is the first . . . the first person like that."

"But not the last," Rzhevsky said. "Your mother is expressing the opinion of a significant fraction of mankind. . . . There are some things that a human being is meant to do, and others that he isn't. For example, he is meant to create his image and likeness in the orthodox manner."

Why is he talking to me like a little girl, Nina wondered. As though the secrets of life were hidden from me behind locked doors.

She took the bottle of cognac, poured herself some, then some for Rzhevsky.

He looked at her attentively, smiled at the corners of his mouth, took the bottle, and returned it to the bar. He closed the bar and said, "So let us have our drink."

Nina tossed down the little glass. The cognac was hot and soft. But why had she bothered to come?

Nina noticed that Rzhevsky was missing a button on his shirt. Never in her contact with people her own age would Nina have thought of looking at their buttons. She knew how to sew on buttons very well. But she couldn't tell him—I want to sew on your button, Uncle Sergei.

Rzhevsky suddenly fell silent and Nina realized that he had remembered Liza, the one he had killed. Twenty-five years ago. They had been friends, her mother, father, and Rzhevsky. Rzhevsky had wanted to marry her mother, but she preferred her father—Nina had known that for a long time, from the noisy scenes in the kitchen, when her mother shouted at her father, "If I had married Rzhevsky, we wouldn't be vegetating now."

Rzhevsky frowned, as though he remembered only with difficulty where he had stopped.

"Isn't it time for you to go home?"

"No, they're used to my running away. They think I'm spending the night at Sima Miloslavskaya's."

"Perhaps you should call?"

Nina shook her head no.

"Twenty-five years. Do you think that's a lot? Well, I still remember the steps and I remember the words that were spoken. As though it were yesterday. And my memory is anything but photographic. It's just that it all happened not that long ago. . . . Twenty-five years ago I was cutting planaria, staring in a microscope, and reading. And they said that I had promise, they said it without envy since I was a dreamer. Even when the Americans started working in the field. Most likely inside both my friends and enemies was the command "render unto God"—even though they were convinced atheists. And now cloning is an everyday affair. The first healthy babies have been born, whose entire genetic material is derived artificially from the father. The oldest one, in Japan, is—"

"Three years old."

"Thanks. Three years old. And he does not suspect that he is a monster. He grows, he drinks milk, says his first words. Never trust clichés. We have created the most ordinary human being. An ordinary human being by an extraordinary method. But in contrast to the baby, we have gone a step further and created an adult. And spared Ivan the long and unproductive years of childhood. Some more coffee?"

"No thanks."

"I'm going to make myself some."

Rzhevsky went into the kitchen and put up the coffee. Nina stood up from the couch, went over to the window—it had rained, and the wet black asphalt reflected the automobile lights.

"Why don't you object?" Rzhevsky asked loudly from the kitchen. "Everyone seems to object."

"Do you think it's a good thing for him not to have a childhood?"

"What's so good about childhood? Study, study. . . . you're ordered around, prohibited from what you want. Would you want to relive your childhood?"

"I don't know. Probably not. But I have already lived through it."

Rzhevsky savored his coffee, taking tiny sips, and Nina was silent. There was something incorrect about that, in connection with Ivan. But she could not formulate her doubts.

"Are you sure?" she asked.

"About what?"

"That he will understand you."

"If he argues with me, I'll welcome it. Do you know why?"

"No."

"Because I always argue with myself. There are no greater opponents than the people close to you. And he is not only close to me, he is a continuation of me, my replacement. I have reached my peak and now, whether I wish it or not, it is time to descend. I will try to do it as slowly as possible, but it is impossible to stop the process. Impossible? But now it is possible! It is possible—do you understand that, my girl?"

"Why did you choose yourself as the father?"

"I have the feeling that this is another topic discussed in your mother's kitchen—the center of the universe. And I was condemned for that, too."

Nina did not answer.

"Whom would you suggest in my place? Alevich? Opanasenko? An anonymous donor? Well?"

"No, I understand. . . ." Nina said guiltily, as though she and not her mother had condemned Rzhevsky.

"You don't understand a damned thing. You think that it was because I consider myself more intelligent and talented than they are? No, it was because I know more about the experiment than the others. So it is in the general interest for our son, like me, to be aware of what was involved in the experiment. Why the devil should I waste time understanding the artificial son of Comrade Opanasenko and Comrade Opanasenko himself? And if I don't understand them both, then I might overlook something that could be important to the experiment."

"And you understand yourself?" Nina dared to ask. She suddenly realized that Rzhevsky had been justifying his decision to himself as well as to her.

"I?" Rzhevsky suddenly broke out laughing. "I got carried away. Please forgive me. What time is it? Twelve? Let's get going. I'll go with you. I could stand a breath of fresh air."

16

I feel a solitude in which my body is coming to life.

I have arms, they are growing on my shoulders, they are long and on the end of them are slender growths that grow out of the air, but what the growths are called we don't know yet. I have legs, they also have growths on the ends. Liza called them—but I don't know who Liza is. If I only knew how to forget things . . . they can forget but we cannot. And once again falling into the well, although now there is meaning in it—meaning in the consciousness that the growths are called fingers. But it is so hard to breathe, and through the wall instead of showing me the way out they are talking about adrenaline levels . . . the giant adrenaline will come when my mama bathes me in the tub. . . . What is mama? It is warmth and quiet. . . .

17

Outside in the street it was cool and pleasant. Rzhevsky supported Nina by the arm when they crossed the street, and Nina resisted the temptation to squeeze his hand with her arm. She just barely resisted. He would have laughed. And that would have been unbearable.

They stopped at the bus stop—Nina refused to take money for a cab. The bus was a long time in coming. Rzhevsky lit up a cigarette and started talking again, avoiding looking at Nina.

"What is death? It is not only the cessation of the body's functioning. Human beings have always, in every religion, reconciled themselves to the perishing of the body. But they have been unable to reconcile themselves to the fact that with each person, a world of thoughts, memories, and feelings also dies. Therefore some people dreamed up the idea of the immortality of the soul. Others dreamed of reincarnation, the rebirth of the essence, the weave of thoughts and memories, in another being. In time, I will die. But in that young man who is slowly coming to life, my thoughts will be continued. And thirty years will pass, and he, Ivan, will create his son, in the same way, his spiritual descendant, and give him not only his but also my thoughts. The product of almost a century. Can you imagine, in two or three hundred years there will be several hundred thousand geniuses on Earth who have collected the experience and thoughts of many generations—people with five, six, ten souls. . . ."

"That's frightening," Nina said. "The soul will be the same."

"It's not frightening to me," Rzhevsky said matter-of-factly. And tossed away his cigarette. It flew like a red star to a puddle on the sidewalk, hissed, and was gone.

"What about feelings?" Nina asked. "The feelings of several generations?"

Rzhevsky did not answer. He saw a free taxi and raised his arm.

"Nina, suppose we stop by the institute for five minutes? See how things are going? Then I'll take you to your friend's place."

"Fine," Nina said, and tensed up, as though she was unexpectedly and ahead of time told to go see a dentist.

Rzhevsky sat far away from her in the taxi, and she suddenly realized why—he was embarrassed in front of the driver. He did not want the driver to think, "Such an old man with such a young lover." They drove for five minutes in silence. Then Rzhevsky said, "I'm grateful to you for coming. I had to talk to someone. Someone who is closer to me than just a colleague."

"I'm glad you did," Nina said and began to wonder why he felt differently about her. Because of his old friendship with her parents? Or because of her herself?

The taxi pulled into the road that led from the highway to the institute. The trees were practically bare. The usual row of barracks.

"I lived in one of them," Rzhevsky said suddenly.

Only two windows in the institute's facade were lit—the duty room. The laboratory windows looked out over the garden. The guard was slow to open the door, but even when he did he expressed no surprise—just started mumbling about everyone going bananas, turning day into night, and it all doing nobody any good.

They walked down a dimly lit corridor to the laboratory. Yura the lab assistant was sitting in the outside room twirling the dial on a radio.

"Not so loud," Rzhevsky said to him.

"You can't hear in there," Yura said, but turned the music down so that it was practically inaudible. He looked at Nina. Why had she come here at night?

Rzhevsky nudged Nina into the prep room. There he made her wash her hands with a foul-smelling substance, helped her put on a lab coat, and handed her a mask. He did it quickly, nervously, as though he were rushing.

Then he rang at the door to the special lab. An eye in the middle of the door changed color, then the door opened.

Inside everything had changed. The sarcophagi were gone. Nina had somehow not noticed them being disassembled and taken out. However, a bed had been brought in. An almost ordinary bed. Hospital-style. Near it stood a small control panel. The man in the bed was sleeping. Nina was fascinated by his face. It was smooth and pale. Flaxen hair had grown in a short stubble. His hands lay will-lessly at his side on the sheet. The man on duty at the control panel stood up and began whispering to Rzhevsky. Rzhevsky listened to him attentively but studied Ivan. The nurse, who was sitting on the black couch that had been there before there was an Ivan, looked up, half asleep.

Nina searched the young man's face for a resemblance to Rzhevsky. Of course, there was one. The same nose, the same chin. . . . She wondered about his eyes.

It was as though the young man read her thoughts.

His hands moved. He slowly opened his eyes. Rzhevsky's eyes. He looked at Nina, but somehow lazily, sluggishly, as though he didn't want to. He did not recognize her.

18

One of the first, if not the very first, real memories of Ivan was the following.

He woke up at night. After a very long sleep, and the sleep had not gone away, he had just let go of it for an instant. . . . And he saw a thin, big-eyed girl with luxuriant dark hair leaning over his bed in the semi-darkness and staring at him fearfully, as though she was having a nightmare. The girl's face was familiar but it was very hard to concentrate and remember where he had known her—then the girl stepped away and at that very moment he realized that Nina had come, Ninochka, Elsa's daughter, although he hadn't the slightest idea of what those sounds, El-sa, really meant.

Then Ivan woke again, it was morning, and through a crack in the blinds the sun shone in, just as it was when he and Liza and Katya were living near Kaunas, in the country, and he did not have to wake up early, he waited for Liza to hop out of bed and run to the window, slapping her bare soles against the shining floorboards, and throwing open the shutters with one abrupt gesture, as though she were tearing them apart, and the hot cube of sunlight filled with the lacy shadows of leaves would tumble into the room. . . .

Nina was in the laboratory. She was sitting in the corner and copying some papers, her head bent over, sometimes sticking out her pink tongue—rapidly, like a snake—to moisten her lips. It was strange that he had never really noticed her. She had been in the institute for half a year already but practically never saw him—but then why would she? If he had transferred her to the lab, it was only because of Elsa's request, which she found unpleasant to make but had to since mothers had to worry about their children and suffer for them. But why was Nina here?

Immediately after that came the awareness that he was sick. He did not know how long or with what—but it was serious, otherwise he would not be in this hospital room. At this point a new memory arose—memories developed like pictures on photographic printing paper in the developing tray; in the dull red light you cannot tell what picture will appear next on the white sheet.

The memory was unpleasant and upsetting—he had to come to terms with it, understand it, but understanding it was impossible, since he, Sergei Rzhevsky, lying here in his own special lab, was not Sergei Rzhevsky at all, but someone else, someone who still did not have a name, and therefore an anomalous, nonexistent person, who could be terminated as easily as he had been initiated, and the impossibility of comprehending all this lay in the fact that he, Sergei Rzhevsky, had started the whole thing, he himself, who now existed outside him. . . .

Here his thoughts broke off—he heard excited voices, and a plump woman in a white coat whom he did not know started talking about stress;

a young man with a familiar face—he works here as a technician—started to do something with the equipment. Then came a needle, a sharp pain, and a sliding into oblivion.

Voices from the outside penetrated the oblivion. And he learned that they referred to him as Ivan, and all the time, without indignation, with anxiety, dully and calmly, he wanted to correct them and say that they were in error—he was Sergei Rzhevsky, although he knew himself that he had no right to call himself Sergei Rzhevsky, since the real Sergei Rzhevsky designed him and made him.

And when he woke, the next morning, he was aware of, and suffered from, his separation from Rzhevsky, his uniqueness, and was not at all surprised when Sergei Rzhevsky, sitting at his bed and following the instruments up to the moment of his awakening, said, "Good morning, Ivan. I'd like to talk with you."

He shut his eyes, then opened them to indicate that he was willing to listen.

19

"Hello, Ivan," Nina said as she ran into the lab in her usual fashion, and as always it seemed to Ivan that a fresh breeze had blown her in. "Have you already eaten? I didn't have time—I went into the cafeteria but there was a horrendous line, can you imagine?"

Ivan nodded. He remembered immediately the lines in the cafeteria and felt like calling Alevich and reminding him that the old man had already promised three times to expand the cafeteria into an adjoining room.

Ivan shook his head, as always when he was chasing away superfluous, alien ideas—a gesture his father did not have.

"You eat the chicken," he said. "I don't want it anyway."

Maria Stepanovna, the nurse, sighed reproachfully. She could not tolerate familiarity between patients and staff, and Nina was staff, Ivan a patient. There was no getting away from it—that was what created order, the only thing you could hold onto in this madhouse.

"True," Nina said. "Are you really full?"

"They feed me as though I were a member of the Olympic weight-lifting team," Ivan said.

Nina started the chicken. Ivan looked out the window. This year snow had fallen early—perhaps it would melt. Ivan thought about how long it had been since he had been skiing, then shook his head to get rid of the thought. Nina, noticing the gesture, said, "I know what you're thinking about. You're thinking how good it would be to go skiing."

"How did you guess?"

"I'm telepathic. And I thought the same thing myself—so why shouldn't you? Do you know how to ski?"

"I did," Ivan said.

"I'm stepping out," Maria Stepanovna said. "I'll be back in half an hour."

"Why don't you just go home?" Ivan said. "Why must you watch over me? I'm as healthy as an ox."

"Many people seem healthy. They give that impression." Maria Stepanovna's voice contained a reproach, a denunciation of the patient's pitiful attempt at deceit.

Ivan looked at his hands. Quite ordinary hands. A strong resemblance to the hands of Sergei Rzhevsky. Only his fingers had thickened in the joints, became squatter, and the back of his hand was freckled.

Ivan stared at his hands as though they were a stranger's. Nina neatly gnawed on a chicken leg and out of the corner of her eyes peeked at Ivan. She was always trying to guess his thoughts and often succeeded. During these few days Nina realized that Ivan was trying to see the world with his own eyes, his own feelings, that he was trying to distance himself from the old Rzhevsky, separate the entire mass of experience and memory of his father from his own microscopic experience limited to the four walls of the special lab. He waits for me so eagerly and loves to talk with me so much, Nina thought, because I provide a tiny piece of independent experience. She would definitely argue with Sergei. Imagine what I would say to Mama if I found out she had been going to school for me.

A buzzer sounded briefly. The technician turned a switch.

Rzhevsky asked for Nina Gulinskaya to stop by his office.

"Right away," Nina said, wiping her lips. "I'll be right there."

Ivan watched her leave. With jealousy? How funny.

Nina ran along the corridor and tried to figure out why she was no longer shy in front of Sergei Rzhevsky. Such a difference in age and in everything else. A chasm. Alevich himself was intimidated by Rzhevsky. Even Opanasenko sometimes. When did her shyness disappear? After their conversation in his apartment? And in the institute Nina was no longer an insignificant lab assistant—she was part of the experiment, and she caught a reflection of the mystery and grandeur of what had happened. For there was mystery and grandeur in it.

Her mother was standing in the corridor, having a cigarette with an unfamiliar man and laughing with restraint but nervously. Her mother liked it when men paid attention to her and would always say that men were far more interesting than women, but she had no real admirers—perhaps because she really did not need them, perhaps because the men were afraid of her all-consuming sense of possession. Nina sometimes felt sorry that she was her mother's daughter. Her mother lived in a whirlwind of guests, in a vain striving for constant although not extravagant amusement—to visit someone at his dacha and see so-and-so there, and later say that she knew him and his wife, who disappointed her; to buy something; to express loudly her sympathy for another's problem—in this whirlwind her mother would forget about Nina for a long time—send her to her paternal grandmother, who had died several years ago. But then it was as though the dam burst with her mother—and for two weeks she would receive infinite love, until she was suffocated in it. It would have been better to have a mother like the other children's . . . without all that emotion.

As soon as her mother saw her, she abandoned her companion and squinted nearsightedly.

"Nina, what are you doing here?"

Nina guessed immediately that her mother had been lying in wait for her, and that was why she had chosen this spot on the first floor.

"Sergei Rzhevsky called me to his office," Nina said. "And you?"

"Me. I'm having a smoke."

"Don't you usually take your cigarette breaks in the third-floor corridor?"

"I don't have to ask you where I can take my breaks. You've really gotten out of hand. Why does Seryozha want you?"

Aha, with that nickname her mother was taking Rzhevsky away from her. But we just won't give him up. . . .

"Mama, try to understand," Nina tried to be tender, no worse than her mother. "Rzhevsky and I are working on the same experiment. It's natural that we have a lot to talk about."

"Ah," her mother said with irony and emitted a cloud of smoke. Smoking was for her a form of social activity. "A child without a college degree is now the irreplaceable assistant of the great Rzhevsky. Are you having an affair with him?"

"Mama!" Nina blushed furiously. She was in love with Sergei, although he didn't notice, and she was beginning to be in love with Ivan Rzhevsky, although she hadn't yet noticed. So she was doubly guilty, caught in the act, exposed, and therefore terribly angry.

She set off running down the corridor, her mother's quiet laughter following her.

Then Elsa threw her unfinished cigarette away. She had not wanted to quarrel with her daughter; she had intended to invite herself into the lab to get a look at that Ivan. Ivan was according to the rumor the exact copy of Rzhevsky in his youth. But no one except Elsa could be sure of that—she was the only person in the institute to have known him when he was young.

All was not yet lost. Elsa looked around. The corridor was empty.

She walked toward the wooden door: "Laboratory 1" a modest black sign read. Nothing to be afraid of—everyone knew that her daughter worked in there. Elsa just might have something important to say to her daughter.

Elsa walked up to the door, stopped to gather courage so she could open the door with a simple and confident movement, like a person who has come on business. She pushed the door. Nina, it seemed, was not in the large room.

Faleyeva raised her head and said, "Hello, Elsa Aleksandrovna. Nina's run over to the director's. Can I give her a message?"

"No thanks, that's not necessary," Elsa said. She had to leave. But her eyes held her back, fixed on the white door in the far wall.

"Will your patient be walking soon?" Elsa asked, coming in and closing the door behind her.

"He's already standing," Faleyeva said. "But Dr. Rzhevsky has not given him permission to come out."

"Quite right," Elsa said. "It's not a zoo. But aren't you afraid of him?"

"Of whom?" Faleyeva was surprised. "Of Ivan?"

How stupid, Elsa thought. To name an artificial man Ivan, like a tame bear.

The white door opened abruptly from the inside. Rzhevsky walked out quickly. Behind him followed a plump woman in a white coat.

"You're crazy!" she shouted at Sergei. "What am I going to tell Rzhevsky?"

Elsa suddenly felt nauseous and a lump formed in her throat. From fear. And indeed she was the only person in the institute who would recognize the young Rzhevsky. And he looked at her, greeted her with a nod, as though he had seen her only yesterday. There was something not right about him. Only when Rzhevsky had walked past, into the hall with the nurse after him, did Elsa realize what it was: Sergei's hair was cut wrong—he had never had a crew cut.

20

"I'd like to know your impressions," Rzhevsky said. "They might be, in view of your closeness in age, unique."

"I'm older than he is," Nina said. "By eighteen years."

"Of course, of course," Rzhevsky grinned, but only with his mouth—his eyes did not smile. "But he is also a half-century older than you are."

"Of course. Older. And he really doesn't understand about himself."

"Is he trying to understand?"

"He is. For him there are two worlds," Nina said. "One is in his room. In it there are me and the nurse, Maria—a tiny world. And your world is oppressive."

"To what degree is my world real to him? With me he seems on guard."

"I don't know. He still isn't fully awake." Nina frowned, she wanted to be up to the occasion.

"Do you sense me in him?"

"Oh, I don't know. Today he gave me some chicken."

"What?"

"I was hungry, and he gave me his chicken."

"I would have done the same. Thirty years ago. Of course, in those days chicken was harder to come by."

Rzhevsky opened a packet on his desk; in it were some photographs.

The photographs were old, amateurish.

"You see, on the right, that's me, in the tenth grade. You see a resemblance?"

"To whom?" Nina asked.

"I guess you didn't. . . . Aha, here I am in the institute."

"Yes, that's him," Nina said as though she were answering a detective who asked her to identify the criminal. She took another photo. In it were four people. Her young father and mother, Ivan and another girl. The girl had a thick braid that lay over her chest. But most of all Nina was surprised by the fact that her mother was holding a little girl, about three years old, in her arms.

Rzhevsky guessed Nina's surprise and said, "That's her daughter." He pointed to the round-faced girl with the braid.

Rzhevsky took the photo and tried to hide it, then glanced at it again and asked, "Did you recognize your mother right away?"

"She hasn't changed much," Nina said. "She always liked to hold other people's children. If she was sure she'd be able to give them back soon."

"Quite a tongue you have," Rzhevsky remarked.

The telephone on the table burst out in a squeal—it was a green, inside line. Rzhevsky grabbed the receiver.

"Why didn't you tell me immediately? I'm coming."

He threw down the receiver, furious, his lips compressed.

"Ivan has left," he said. "They didn't guard him."

"Where did he go?"

"Who knows! Maria ran after him. Well, what can you do? I talked to him about it. You can't keep him locked up!"

21

They found Ivan in the vivarium. He was standing in front of the cage with Lev. Lev carefully inspected his visitor, as though he had met him before. Jon, who was not the object of anyone's attention, fussed around in his cage, grumbling, and Maria Stepanovna stopped in the doorway.

"It's a little too soon for you to go out," Rzhevsky said from the threshold.

"Hello," Ivan said.

"Why didn't you warn me?"

"I know the institute inside out," Ivan said. "Just as well as you do."

Nina was standing a step behind Rzhevsky, and looked back and forth to study the difference between them. For example, Ivan's somewhat higher and piercing voice.

"Wait now," Rzhevsky said suddenly, "give me your hand, I have to take your pulse."

Ivan stretched out his arm. Lev, seeing this, stretched his arm out of the cage; he too wanted someone to check his pulse.

"Why such a high pulse?" Sergei asked.

"You're right," Ivan said. "Let's go back. My head is spinning. You made me out of inferior raw materials. Who knows what you put in!"

"The same stuff that's in everyone else," Sergei answered. "According to Mother Nature's recipe."

They met several workers in the hallway. Few people had seen Ivan yet, so people stopped and turned around to watch him. Someone shouted, as he opened a door, "Semenikhin, come here, quick!"

Nina suddenly felt how much Ivan disliked attention. He had already started walking faster and taken his hand out of his father's.

22

He had a long dream. In the dream he was little, very little. He was walking through a glade, and flowers as tall as he was were swaying, and between the flowers the sun was blinding. Alongside his mother was walking, he didn't see her, he saw only her hand that he held so tight because he was afraid that a bumblebee would swoop down and take him away. He knew that this was happening in Tarusa and he was four years old, that it was one of his first memories, but at the same time it was a dream because the memory itself had already wafted out of Sergei Rzhevsky's memory, it was family folklore—how Seryozha was afraid of bumblebees. But somehow in his mind there was no picture of a bumblebee but only a sound image—*bzzzbeee*. The uncertainty of the threat made him expect it from everywhere, it might even change into his mother's hand—and he tried to pull his hand away but his mother held it tight, he raised his eyes and saw that it wasn't his mother but Liza, who was crying because she knew that soon the bumblebee was going to swoop down and carry him off. . . .

He awoke and lay there without opening his eyes. He was being sneaky. He knew that people would stop talking about ordinary things in front of him—as though he were forbidden to know. He understood that his dissembling would soon be exposed—the instruments always betrayed him.

This time no one was watching the instruments; perhaps they did not expect him to wake up. They were whispering. Maria and another, unfamiliar nurse.

"His eyes are dead, old," Maria Stepanovna was whispering. "I have had a lot of patients in my time—millions—but I've never seen eyes like that."

"How come he knows everything? Is it true that he's a copy?"

"I can't say," Maria Stepanovna said. "When they sent me here, he was already ready."

"Does he think?"

"He does. Sometimes he talks, of course. For the first while he thought he was the director."

Ivan slowly opened his eyes just slightly—only the table lamp was lit, the technician was dozing in his chair, and the two nurses were sitting on the couch. It was quiet, peaceful, and the conversation seemed as though it did not concern him.

"But aren't you afraid of him?" the unfamiliar nurse asked.

"Oh, no, he's kind, I can sense aggressiveness in people, from my postoperative experience. No aggressiveness in him. But the eyes are bad. I'm afraid he's not long for this world."

That's me who's not long for the world? Is there really something unreal in me, unfinished, vessels that are too fragile, or malformed erythrocytes?

Ivan automatically listened to his heart thumping. His heart survived. . . . At least the nerves are working.

23

Once again Ivan awoke before dawn. Something wasn't right. . . . Snow was lashing the closed windows, the wind was so strong the panes were shaking. Somehow it seemed that Liza was lying beside him and sleeping silently, in order not to disturb him, even in her sleep she was afraid of disturbing him. . . . He reached out to touch her shoulder, which fit so perfectly the arch of his bent hand. And he understood that it was not his memory! He shook his head, fluffed up the pillow. Maria, stretched out on the couch, turned in her sleep, mumbled, but did not wake up.

Wide awake, Ivan began to listen to the sounds of the institute at night, in which there was something that was not right. He just could not lie there any longer.

Carefully putting his bare foot on the floor, in his pajamas, he walked to the door. He turned the handle slowly. The lock clicked almost inaudibly.

It was dark in the prep room. He shut the door behind him, searched for the light switch in the outside room. The lights flashed on, and he closed his eyes for a second. It was quiet here, too—only a noise coming through several walls reached him, dull and indistinguishable. Ivan ran down the hall. The soles of his feet slapped against the floor. Behind one of the doors—the chimpanzees lived there—he could hear grumbling, knocking. He turned the doorknob. It was locked. Ivan bent over, peeked through the keyhole. He could see part of a cage dimly lit by an overhead bulb. Jon was clambering around his cage, shaking the bars; then he realized that someone was at the door and began to cry out, to chirp, as thought he just could not remember the right words.

"What's the matter?" Ivan asked quietly. "What happened?"

Jon heard him, and began to bang the floor with his hands, jerking them back as though they had been burned.

"Downstairs?" Ivan asked.

Jon jumped up and down and roared.

Ivan bent over and touched the floor with his palms. Perhaps it only seemed that way, but the floor felt hotter.

And then he heard the dogs barking. The dogs often howled at night, but now their cries were entirely different, hysterical. . . .

Ivan ran forward several steps, then went down the stairs; he felt the air grow hotter, as though someone had opened a door to a laundry.

The door to the vivarium was not locked; Ivan pulled it toward him, and when it opened, a hot thick steam struck him in the face. There were another five steps leading down, and the lowest was covered with water.

The ceiling lights barely glimmered through the cottony air. The pitiful howling covered the hissing and bubbling of hot water—apparently the dogs realized that someone had come.

Ivan stepped down, into the water, which was hot. He felt himself get wet all over, breathing became difficult in the hot steam. In the middle of the long basement that had cages along its walls, the steam was thicker. Not far from the floor a pipe had burst and hot water was gushing out.

He had to turn off the water. But how could he get to the pipe, and how could he close it? Run upstairs and call for help? He almost turned for the door, but the dogs' howling intensified—they were crying, whining, afraid that Ivan would leave. Ivan understood that he first had to let out the animals—that could be done quickly, in several minutes. By the time an emergency squad came, the dogs could be dead.

He went down another step, then another. . . . He was up to his knees in water, and it was hot.

Two steps away, fighting his way through the water as though it were the ocean and he had to resist its pull, he reached the first cage. The dog was standing on its hind legs—it was a huge dog, and the water here was not so hot. Ivan opened the lock, tore open the door; the dog almost knocked him over and raced to the door. It tried to run but couldn't and had to swim to the steps. Ivan went on to the next cage.

There were many cages. He tried to count them. He could not hurry, and the water was getting hotter and hotter and his feet began to turn numb from pain. At each cage he had to stop for two seconds to open the lock and pull the door toward him, overcoming the water's resistance. Nothing came out of the fifth cage—there was a little dog who could barely keep its head above water. He had to reach out into the cage and pull the dog out, losing valuable seconds. The dog, maddened by pain and fear, tried to bite him, and succeeded. He threw it toward the door and hurried on. He felt that the skin must have already peeled off his legs and that he would never get out, but he kept on wading, like in a slow-motion film, from cage to cage, afraid to let go of the screening and get lost in the steam, bending over, opening the locks, pulling out the dogs. And only when he saw that the next cage was empty did he turn around, holding onto the hot bars of the cages, worried that beyond the empty cage was still another one he did not reach, but even his stubbornness was not enough to make him turn back. . . .

He managed to notice that one of the dogs had not left the cage—it was swimming on the surface, but he went by, stepping carefully to keep from falling, and then right near the door, he saw a little dog struggling and picked it up and carried it out, stepping over the body of a dog as it climbed out of the water and got stuck on the stairs. On the landing lay another two dogs; a third was already in the corridor, licking its burned paws.

Ivan stopped for a second, breathing in the cold air. He had to call the emergency number. Or go up to Maria, so she could treat his burns? He climbed up the stairs, to Rzhevsky's office, although the janitor's was closer. His legs obeyed him, but they started to hurt—and for some reason his hands, too, but he did not have nerve enough to look at his hands. He went around Lena's desk, the office was locked, he knocked in the door with his shoulder, trying not to hurt the half-dead dog he was still carrying.

He went to Rzhevsky's desk, set the dog down on the desk, pushed the button on the desk lamp, and with difficulty pulled the lamp toward himself. Only then did he see his hand, red and swollen. But he did not know how to call for emergency help. Whom should he call? Rzhevsky? No. He would not help. Someone had to be in charge of such things. . . . Ivan dialed Alevich's number. The phone rang and rang.

Something moved in the open doorway. Ivan felt nauseous. He could not concentrate his vision, then realized that a wet dog, the one he had released first, was standing in the doorway.

The dog was not severely burned—he had been closest to the door. He sat down and shook himself, spattering the carpet.

"Hello?" Alevich said sleepily.

"Dimitri," Ivan said. "Excuse me for waking you. It's Rzhevsky."

Alevich immediately realized that something had happened. The director's voice sounded strained. And it was four in the morning.

"I'm listening. What happened? Something with Ivan?"

"Could you call emergency service? A pipe of hot water burst . . . and flooded the vivarium."

"Good God," Alevich sighed with relief. "And I thought. . . ."

"Hold on," Ivan said. "I've forgotten the number. And call for medical help."

"Veterinarian?" Alevich still could not conceal his relief.

"No, for me," Ivan said, and dropped the phone.

Water from the dog lying on the desk had formed a puddle.

In the corridor steps resounded—Maria was rushing around looking for her patient.

24

"Now you differ even more from Sergei Rzhevsky," Nina said. "And my blood is inside you."

"Thank you," Ivan said. They were sitting on a bench in the institute's winter garden. "Even though I sometimes wish that no one had saved me."

"Was it that painful?"

"No."

They were silent. Ivan adjusted his crutches so they wouldn't fall off the bench, then took out his cigarettes.

"Why does he allow you to smoke?"

"Probably because he does himself," Ivan answered.

"You still haven't had time to adjust to it."

"I have the memory of smoking inside me, his memory, and there's nothing I can do about it."

"All right, go ahead and smoke," Nina said condescendingly. "So you have inherited his bad habits?"

"Of course."

A crow carefully landed on a snowdrift.

"And what did they say at home?" Ivan asked suddenly.

"My mother said that she never would have expected it from you. That you were always careful with yourself."

"Not true," Ivan felt insulted on Rzhevsky's behalf. "And she knows it isn't."

"Ivan, why did you do it? That is, I can understand even though I wouldn't have had the courage, but everyone says that it would have been smarter to call in the emergency service."

"Of course it would have been smarter. But I too am an experimental animal. You have to look out for your own."

"That's silly," Nina said. "Now no one looks at you like that. Especially the ones who have given you blood."

"And then. . . . It's Sergei's fault. I had the feeling that it was my institute, my dogs . . . without him I would never have found the way down to the basement."

"It's remarkable," Nina said. "You got scalded for his sake, while he calmly sleeps at home."

A sharp and freezing wind started up and the crow took off, into the wind, to keep from being blown away.

25

Ivan put down his *Scientific American*—on his night table were a pile of journals. His father brought them every morning, as though the father would receive part of the information if Ivan read them. It was a curious thing to observe how Rzhevsky kept running off—gradually a sense of separateness was taking hold, and with it, curiosity. Concerning himself, from a distance. Curiosity concerning his father, the way he moved his hands. Immediately a desire would arise to do things otherwise. His father, when he picked up a pen, would hold out his little finger—so under no circumstances would Ivan hold out his little finger, he had to remember not to. His father, when thinking, would scratch his temple. Ivan also felt like scratching his temple—but he had to refrain. . . .

The magazine slipped to the floor. They took off the bandages from his hands—they had pink spots. And he was glad—his father didn't. His father had never done what he had—it was his own, personal deed.

His organism was weaker than predicted—no one admitted it in his presence, but phrases slipped out—"for a normal person this burn would not require further treatment." So he was abnormal?

His dreams, long and detailed nightmares, were more in the form of memories. Another's memory had carefully selected past moments of stress, things that had seared Sergei Rzhevsky's brain. Ivan supposed that he had received two sets of memories—sober, everyday ones and uncontrollable nightmare ones. Sergei, like all human beings, had concealed the stressful recollections deep in his mind, so that they tormented his memory. Ivan's brain perceived these recollections as though they were another person's. And when daytime control melted away, his dreams, freeing his subconscious, released upon Ivan's brain detailed pictures of another's past, in which each detail was brightly illuminated and protruded outside—there was no escaping, not by closing one's eyes, not by thinking of other things.

Waiting for the nurse to come and give him a painkilling shot, Ivan rolled the film of the past—Sergei had no idea he was doing this. He restored, putting everything in chronological order, what remained in his memory from another's childhood. Before the war he had been seven years old, and his father went to the front. His family left Kursk on a special train; the train took a long time, a whole month. All this lived in Sergei's memory as the collection of facts that were comprehended in a formal statement in his biography: "Before the war we lived in Kursk, but then we were evacuated and spent a year near Kazan." In Ivan's brain there were only fragmentary pictures, and there was no guarantee that they fell in the same order as in his father's. Ivan forced himself to dig in his father's memory, learning about himself and as far as he could, creating himself. Ivan tried to remember: How was it when we left Kursk? It was summer.

Summer? Yes, and was the car a passenger car or a *teplushka*? Of course, a *teplushka*, because his memory showed him a picture: A long line of *teplushkas* was standing in the steppe, and he, with his mother and another girl, had gone far from the track, picking flowers. The train had been standing for a long time and was supposed to stand even longer, but suddenly the cars, which looked so small from the distance, began to move and the locomotive's terrifying whistle carried up to them through the thick hot air. And then they ran for the train, but the train was already far away, and it seemed they would never reach it. . . . Then someone ran to them from the train. . . . Then they were in the train. And that was all Ivan could remember.

At night—Ivan was already used to it, as he was used to the inevitability of needles and changes of bandages—this memory too, so cherished during the daytime, would return in the form of a nightmare, filled with details of things that had once happened and then been forgotten. Once again he would run toward the little train that stretched along the horizon, but this time he would see Mama pick up the strange little girl in her arms, because she was crying and falling behind. He, too, Sergei, became terrified that he would fall behind, and he would pull at the edge of the girl's dress, floating behind, so that his mother would drop her—she was his mother and she should save him—and he ran behind his mother and shouted, "Drop her, drop her!" but his mother did not turn around, she was wearing a blue dress, and the girl was quiet, because she was terrified too, and the run to the train, so short in reality, in his nightmare turned into an eternity, so that he could study his mother, remember her short hair, cut in almost a fringe, see her thick calves, her narrow ankles, her worn sandals—without that dream he would never have seen his mother when she was young—in his daytime memory his mother was imprinted only as a heavy, talkative, and not-too-intelligent woman, with curled and dyed hair, gray at the roots. And then, awakening and believing that the nightmare was accurate, as nightmares are, he would consider his mother's action, who was afraid of being left behind somewhere in the Volga steppes, who knew that her seven-year-old son could run but the little girl couldn't. . . . But his mother had died six years ago, and Sergei had had time only for the funeral itself. . . . And now he, Ivan, who had never had a mother himself, felt gratitude toward another's mama, who had never run with him after a departing train and who had never frightened away a terrible bumblebee. At the same time Ivan understood that now he was closer to that woman than Sergei was, because Sergei had never had that nightmare, which had remained hidden deep in his mind.

26

"You're having an affair with him, and that bothers me," her mother said.

They were watching a boring mystery on television. Nina was so tired after her day's work that she did not have strength to do battle with her mother.

"First you say I'm having an affair with Sergei Rzhevsky," Nina said, "and now you foist his son on me."

I should go to bed, Nina thought. I have to get up early tomorrow and in the freezing dark rush to the institute. Maria is sick, Faleyeva has a cold, and she promised to type up the annual report. A crazy job.

"An affair with an artificial man is even worse," her mother said. "He's not normal."

"Not again, Mama!"

"And that suicide attempt in the boiling water! Don't you see that he had a destructive nature?"

She had to get up and go to her room. Without tea, but it wasn't the first time. She washed up, then got into bed.

The walls were thin, and Nina could hear the conversation in the other room.

"I loved him," her mother said.

"I don't believe it. Don't spoil the show."

"But I didn't understand myself."

"You had your mother to look after. And Sergei was a student, without an apartment, without money, without a future. You were caught in the middle—on one hand, Sergei, on the the other, your mother. And then I came along."

"You rotten good-for-nothing!"

"Quiet, the kid has to get up early. . . ."

27

Sergei stopped by in the morning, asked how things were going, reminded him about the commission the next day. He left new journals. He said he would drop by later. His look was inquiring, he talked with Ivan in a different way than the others. As though he were guilty before me, Ivan thought. I know his thoughts, his hopes for immortality, his reasoning about my carrying on his work—all that is in my memory. But today's Rzhevsky isn't there. We started at the same point and are now headed in different directions.

He opened a book but did not start reading. He would go out to the outside lab, where Nina was sitting; at the sight of him she would jump up, her face would break out in a happy smile—like a playful kitten. To think that Elsa had a grown-up daughter. They had a piano at home, and Elsa would play it with bravura. What was I thinking about? So what was I thinking about? My worn copy of Shepman—the genius who learned how to separate the ectoderm from a salamander embryo—the ectoderm survived and grew into a salamander without a nervous system. It seems the mesoderm controls the differentiation of nervous tissue. And that is how I was made—from Shepman through Goltfrater and Stewart to Rzhevsky. Ivan tried to will away his headache—he was already overloaded with medicines, and started leafing through the book, with page corners bent over by his father. He realized that he himself wanted to bend the corners of the same pages—once again Sergei had beaten him to it.

Ivan went to eat in the institute cafeteria. He had won the right to do so after a pitched battle. I can't live on a balanced diet. If you, my father, gave me your brain, you must acknowledge my claim to a place in human society. . . .

Elsa sat at the next table and tried not to stare at Ivan. The cafeteria was not busy—both of them had come earlier than the rush hour.

Elsa turned away. She envied him her own youth. So then, you want to pierce me with your gaze! It's not right—the pride of the institute, the first artificial man in the world sits there eating his goulash and staring at the library director. Elsa did not respond to his stare but twiddled her fingers nervously, started to tell a woman sitting with her back to Ivan a story, quickly and with great mirth, then suddenly jumped up and ran out of the cafeteria.

When Ivan went out several minutes later, Elsa was standing by the stairs, smoking nervously and clumsily. She met his gaze and asked, "Is there something you wanted to say?"

Ivan took out a cigarette, lit up, and did not answer. Then Elsa began to speak, quickly, in a high-pitched, ringing voice.

"You don't know me. We have never met. I do not believe Rzhevsky. You have fooled everyone. And I don't understand why you're harassing me."

"I'm not harassing you, Elsa," the young man said in Rzhevsky's voice. "We've known each other for a very long time, so you don't have to pretend otherwise."

"I still don't believe it," Elsa said. "You're only a few months old. Rzhevsky told you about me, because he needs you to satisfy his outrageous vanity. Maybe your game will work with the higher-ups in the Academy of Sciences, but you're not going to convince me."

"That wouldn't be too hard," Ivan said. "You can test me."

"How?"

"Ask me something that only you and Rzhevsky would know."

"And the answer would be that he told you about it. It's revolting, you know, very revolting—a person can do what he likes with his memories. But when they involve another person, it's a form of betrayal. Just gossip."

"Go ahead and ask anyway."

Elsa frowned. But she did not leave. And then she suddenly asked, "We were riding on the river bus. In the summer. It was cold and you gave me your coat. . . . Do you remember?"

The memory lay somewhere within. Until that moment Ivan did not know that he had gone for a ride on the river bus with Elsa, there had been no need to remember.

"You were wearing a blue sarafan. You told me that you wanted to have champagne and sunflower seeds, and I answered that it was a strange idea of the good life."

"I didn't remember that. Is that all?"

"Yes."

"You're lying." Elsa ran up the stairs.

She did not want him to remember, was afraid he would. And he did remember. Only on the river bus Elsa had tried to prove to him that Liza was not worthy of him. That he would never feel close to her intellectually, that Lizetta could not even finish the tenth grade—and that he had to understand the difference between infatuation and family life. You'll never be able to love her child, I'm saying this as a friend, she will always feel closer to the father of the child. You're still a kid, Seryozha, you don't know women. She needs to get married—and she'll do whatever is necessary to get a husband. Understand me right, I like Lizetta. Lizetta is a good person. But she'll ruin you, devastate you. . . . Run away, save yourself before you get stuck in that petty bourgeois quagmire. . . .

28

"Ah, I've finally found you," Rzhevsky said. "I thought you had gone to the cafeteria. I have instant coffee in my office—how about a cup?"

They walked up the stairs in silence, and the staff they met stopped to stare, because Sergei and Ivan were more than father and son: They were two halves of the same person.

Back in his office, Rzhevsky got to the point. "I'm upset by the fact that our relationship has developed in a way I don't like."

"What do you want? For me to replace you in this office?"

"With time, I had hoped for that, too."

"I can substitute for you today. There's no question about my experience."

Lena brought in the coffee. They held their cups and sipped the coffee in precisely the same way. And most likely experienced its taste in exactly the same way. Ivan kept his little finger down, but Sergei did not notice.

"You must go on, ahead, beyond the point where I left you. That's the meaning of you, me, our experiment."

"But what about the past? I have more in me than you do."

"How so?"

"Tell me, how was mother dressed, your mother, when you almost missed the train in nineteen forty-one?"

"We almost missed the train . . . it was in the steppe . . . the train was standing on an embankment . . . no, I don't remember."

"And there was a little girl there, very little. When Mother started running, she picked up the little girl, because she could not run fast. And you got mad at your mother and shouted, 'Drop her!' "

"I never did any such thing!"

"You did. How was Mother dressed?"

"I don't remember. I can't remember after more than forty years."

"But I do. Do you understand, I remember. Why?"

"Why?" Rzhevsky repeated the question.

"Because I am not you. Because you gave me your memories but did not give me your identity. Because I know that these memories were never mine! I can delve into them, I can see them. One time during your childhood you ran after your mother—she was wearing a blue sarafan and sandals. You think you have forgotten about it forever. But you haven't! But only I can remember, because I want to. And you seem to have forgotten. . . . Do you think that is the only difference between us?"

"Are there other things I have forgotten?" Rzhevsky attempted a smile.

"There are many things you've forgotten—I still don't know them all."

"Instead of trying to find resemblances, you are trying to distance yourself from me."

"Have you thought about the fact that I am the only person on Earth who has not had a childhood? I remember that as a child I walked through a meadow with my mother, and at the same time I know that I never walked with my mother through a meadow—it was you who did, and you've stolen my childhood, you know, you've robbed me blind, and now

you sit there content with yourself—you have an intellectual heir, a remarkable son, who resembles a human being in every respect."

"You are a human being. An ordinary human being."

"You're lying! I am not a human being and will never be one, because
I do not have my own life. I'm a bad copy of you, I am forced to do your
business, to handle your relationship with Elsa for you, and she is afraid
that I'll remember more about the past than you do. You don't understand
that and are still not afraid, but she is. Apparently the survival instinct is
more strongly developed in her than in you."

"What does she have to be afraid of?" Rzhevsky stood up and poured
himself another cup from the thermos pitcher Lena had brought. "Do you
want some more coffee, Son?"

"Shut up, Rzhevsky! A son has to be cared for, you have to get up in the
middle of the night for him, wipe his tears. You have not created a son but
yourself. A son is a continuation, and you wanted a repetition. If you were so
bothered by childlessness, why didn't you adopt Katya? You and Liza could
have had children. . . . Or was Elsa right when you were riding on the river
bus and she maintained that Liza was not right for you?"

"What river bus?"

"You have gifted me with this memory, but now you're unhappy with
it. Didn't you know what you were getting into? Did the chimps teach
you anything? Or did you think that I would inherit only your passion for
science?"

Rzhevsky got control of himself.

"You're partially right. . . . But I too am having a hard time. I have
the feeling that I am transparent, that people can look inside me and see
things I myself don't want to see."

"I don't want to look anywhere. It does not give me peace. You would
like me to refute the Gordon effect and take up mathematics seriously.
But all I can do is think about Liza."

"I thought that once the commission had finished its work you could
move in with me. I live alone, and we wouldn't bother each other."

"You should know better now. But you're right. You cannot live with
yourself. Let us go our separate ways. I can't feel myself your son, since
I am older than you are. Giving me your memory, you allowed me to
judge you."

"We'll return to this conversation at a later time," Rzhevsky said drily,
as though dismissing an employee who had committed an error. When
Ivan looked surprised, recognizing the intonation, he suddenly banged his
fist down on his desk. "Oh, go to hell!"

Ivan laughed, stretched his legs, and sprawled out in the easy chair he was sitting in. Alevich, who had just stepped in to discuss some business matters, came to an abrupt halt in the doorway. The young man from the experiment was acting just too insolently—Dr. Rzhevsky would not stand for it.

29

Nina was sitting with Ivan, and he was helping her with chemistry— winter was drawing to a close and it was time to think about getting admitted to school. Then Ivan ran out of cigarettes and Nina said she'd go out for them. Ivan stood up.

"I wouldn't mind getting a breath of fresh air."

Outside it was a dry cold, not too bad, and the snow crunched under foot resonantly, even cheerfully.

"We never did get to go skiing," Ivan said. "The winter is almost over, and you and I—"

"I'll bring skis from home," Nina said. "They've been sitting in the closet for ten years."

The barracks had already been torn down. But their absence was not felt so keenly in the winter when the trees were transparent and the gaps left by the old buildings were not so noticeable.

"Did you know that he lived here one time?" Ivan asked.

"Yes, a long time ago."

"In the third building from the end. It's too bad I didn't have a chance to see it."

"Why? You're struggling with Rzhevsky. To the point where it's ridiculous."

"Not everything is clear to me. And I feel tormented."

"Oh, what a simpleton you are," Nina said. "You want clarity? Even I have learned that sometimes things are simpler without clarity. It's remarkable that there are any secrets left. Before you were a secret and now you're. . . ."

"What am I now?"

"A researcher at the institute."

"No one can be friends with me," Ivan said and grinned. "I am potentially dangerous. Anything unknown is dangerous. And suppose I just give out?"

"That's not going to happen," Nina said. "An entire commission went over you with a fine-tooth comb."

Nina took a running start and slid down a long patch of ice on the sidewalk. Ivan, after hesitating a moment, followed her. He often hesitated before doing something quite ordinary for his twenty-year-old body. It was as though Rzhevsky, sitting inside him, was too embarrassed to slide down the ice or to jump over puddles, judging the obstacles facing Ivan with his aging bones and muscles. Even now he got in the way. A good thing Sergei was not eighteen—that would be some fun!

At the end of her slide Nina lost her balance and almost fell into the snow. Ivan caught her and pulled her against him. Nina froze. Ivan smelled the scent of her hair that escaped from under her knit cap.

"Well now," Nina said, "if anyone sees us, they'll think this is part of the experiment."

"Of course." Ivan let her go. "You are performing a special assignment for management."

For a while they walked on in silence. Then Nina asked, "What is the secret of the barracks?"

"Secret? There's really no secret. Rzhevsky lived here, with his fiancée, Liza. She was a friend of your mother's. They went to school together, but then your mother went to library school, and Liza fell in love with an actor and ran away after the ninth grade to join the theater, where she became a makeup girl. She was lighthearted and happy, while Elsa was already thinking about life and listened to her mother, who told her not to kiss anyone before marriage."

"Is it you with the sharp tongue, or is it your Rzhevsky?"

"The tongue is mine, and I take full responsibility for it. But the information, as always, is another's. Should I go on?"

"Of course, it's very interesting. No one has ever said anything about this Liza at home. Only once I overheard them say that Rzhevsky had killed Liza. But of course that is in the figurative sense."

"I don't know."

"It couldn't be! Do you remember?"

"Unfortunately, I remember everything," Ivan said. "But everything is much simpler than you think."

They went into a store near the bus stop. Ivan bought a pack of cigarettes. He was thirty kopecks short, so Nina gave it to him. Under an agreement with the academy, from the very first Ivan was listed as a research scientist—a healthy young man could not be kept as a guinea pig. Of course, he could direct a laboratory. But both Rzhevsky and Ivan himself knew enough not to count on such generosity from the academy. For the time being Ivan was the subject of the experiment, and even in the sage conduct of the members of the last commission Ivan had noticed a hint of timidity and caution. But he was used to overlooking it.

"Tell me more," Nina said, when they left the store and headed back to the institute.

"Elsa introduced them. Sergei was living in a dormitory, and Liza in a single room with her mother, brother, and most important, Katya. Katya was her daughter by that actor."

"How old was the little girl?"

"Katya? About three, she was still very small. Liza and Sergei fell in love."

Nina suddenly felt jealous of that distant Liza, which was ridiculous, but Ivan still remembered kissing her. And perhaps it would have been better if he hadn't mentioned Liza, but he could not stop.

"And then. . . . While Liza was a poor and flighty friend, your mother watched over her, adored her. Oh, those confessions in Elsa's kitchen!"

"Hold on," Nina said gloomily. "You and Rzhevsky can't understand—"

"My memory has the advantages over Rzhevsky's in the sense that I can always draw back and say: That is not my love! That is not my pain! You, Father, are wrong because you did those things. I see more, because I am an observer. And I judge."

Ivan took a running start and was first to slide along the ice. He turned and held out his hand for Nina, but she refused, skirting the ice.

"Tell me more," she said. "What happened then? And please limit yourself to the facts, as Maigret would say."

"He and Liza rented an apartment in one of the barracks, bought a daybed, made a little bed for Katya, and went about their lives. They loved each other . . . and then in my memories, hitches develop."

"Why?"

"I think that our dear Dr. Rzhevsky overestimated his strength and his love but did not want to admit it even to himself."

"Did he stop loving her?"

"It was more complicated than that. First, their circle of friends was broken—"

"Why?"

"Imagine yourself in your mother's place. You have a young friend, who is irresponsible, with a child on her hands, and there are the talented Rzhevsky and the ordinary Viktor—"

"Again?"

"And then it seems that Rzhevsky is seriously intending to live with Liza, to marry her . . . and then your mother, excuse me for saying so, comes to detest Liza, repudiates her, the traitor."

"That's a lie!"

"I spoke with your mother the other day. She wanted to know whether I remembered a conversation with her about Liza."

"She was hoping that you forgot?"

"But I remember. And better than Rzhevsky."

They entered the institute and met Gurina in the corridor. She was leading the chimpanzee Lev by the hand. He made a face when he recognized Ivan.

In the laboratory Nina stayed in the outside room. Ivan, feeling awkward about having said so much, went to his quarters.

But in five minutes Nina burst in.

"Why didn't you tell me how it all ended? Trying to spare my feelings?"

"No."

"Then tell me."

"Okay. It came time to enter graduate school. He and Liza had lived together for more than half a year. Rzhevsky waited on line to get Katya milk and worked nights while the child slept. Liza cooked, did the laundry, and was happy, completely unaware that Rzhevsky was exhausting himself—his last year in school, his thesis, but he was still a kid, on whom worries about his family fell."

Nina nodded. She took out a cigarette and was about to light it. Ivan took it away from her.

"Rzhevsky was tired—that's the main thing. He didn't like the soup Liza prepared for him, without meat, since they did not have money for meat—she worked during the day in a factory. Without that they would not have been able to get by, and every other day Rzhevsky was left with the little girl and couldn't get anything done—in those days it was hard to arrange for nursery schools, in the early fifties. Rzhevsky wanted terribly to be alone—without Liza, without Katya, without anyone. He felt like a caveman whose life was over before it had begun. And he would never be a scientist. He was irritable and unfair to Liza."

"I can understand him," Nina said. "Liza also should have understood what she was doing to him."

"You don't understand a damned thing," Ivan said. "What could Liza do? She tried to keep Katya from crying when Papa was working. And she hoped that Sergei would get into graduate school, they would get an apartment at the institute, and everything would work out. Somehow he met your mother and did not tell Liza about it. Elsa oozed sympathy. She understood him!"

"Easy on the commentary, please," Nina asked.

"You're right, okay. Then one fine day your dear Rzhevsky announced to Liza that she and Katya were ruining his life."

"Just like that, without any cause?"

"No, he had been told that his moral image—that means his liaison with Liza—was blocking his acceptance to the graduate program. In those days they were very strict about those things. And she hadn't gotten divorced from that actor."

"Who told him about graduate school?"

"It's not important."

"It is. My mother, right?"

Nina already believed it and therefore became aggressive and ready to defend Elsa.

"No," Ivan said, not looking her in the eyes.

He hadn't thought about it before but suddenly he remembered. Elsa hadn't told him—it was Viktor. He was working at the institute then; he knew everyone and had some kind of official responsibility. Of course, he mentioned it in the corridor, near a window. They were smoking, and Viktor looked at him sadly and said aloud, "The director is unhappy. They will probably give the position to Kruglikov, I overheard someone say. Old man, you have to choose. Love or your duty to science. You understand how it is." Ivan had forgotten about the conversation, because even then he hadn't decided on anything. Viktor could say what he wanted and it wouldn't have mattered unless Rzhevsky himself had been ready to separate.

"And how did it end?" Nina asked.

"Liza left him. And she moved away from Moscow."

"And he couldn't find her? Or didn't he try?"

"At first he felt relief. But soon he missed her. He went to Liza's mother. But she refused to help. Elsa told him, and she was mistaken, that Liza had returned to the actor."

"Was mistaken? Or was it on purpose?"

"I don't know. A few years later he learned that Liza had gone to Vologda. And that she had been run over by a train, or something like that."

"She jumped in front of a train. Like Anna Karenina! He did kill her!"

"It might have been an accident. Ever since, Rzhevsky has been convinced that he was responsible for her death."

"He was responsible," Nina affirmed. "And Mama was sure of it."

"With your mother, everything is in order. But the main thing is that he feels guilty himself. And when he planned me, of course he did not take into consideration the fact that I would remember everything about Liza. Not only about genes and mutations, but about Liza, too. He would have wanted me to stick to genes."

"And what about the little girl . . . Katya? Your sister?"

"My dear, many years have passed. Now she's older than either of us. She's probably living in Vologda, with children of her own."

"I wouldn't want to be in Rzhevsky's place."

"Please forgive me for telling you all this."

"You had to tell someone. You're jealous of your father."

"Jealous?"

"Of course. You think he took away your love. He kissed her, and you remember, as though you were a Peeping Tom. It's terrible!"

"An Oedipus complex, Freud squared. Don't make things more complicated."

"That's not it." Nina put her hand on Ivan's and he covered it with his other hand.

Nina froze, as though she were a little bird that Ivan had covered with his hand.

"And I," she said after a pause. "I was not there. I am only here today."

"I'm not sharing you with anyone," Ivan agreed.

"Are you thinking about something else?"

"No, not at all. . . ."

Nina pulled away her hand, jumped up, and ran to the door.

"I feel so sorry for you!" she shouted from the door. "Enough to cry."

"Forgive me," Ivan said. "I was thinking of something else."

"I know, I know, I know."

Nina slammed the door. Then opened it again and announced, "When you fall in love yourself, then you'll understand."

"It's hard for me to count on someone reciprocating my feelings," Ivan smiled, "with a biography like mine. I don't even have a passport."

"You fool!"

This time Nina slammed the door so hard that the test tubes in the white cabinet by the window jingled.

30

At the end of February it suddenly got very warm. Ivan was sad to see the snow shrink, turn dark. A warm winter is messy. It's a pity, especially when it's your first winter.

Ivan stayed away from the Museum of History. He went to GUM, the big department store, and bought Hungarian shoes and a tie. His problems with his wardrobe were catastrophic. He did not want to borrow things from his father, who was not all that well supplied himself. Ivan discovered a certain foppishness, a great man's coquetry: He would carefully pick out a worn jacket while standing in front of his mirror, so that everyone could see how much above it he was. His father, of course, was not aware of his coquetry—it was only visible from a distance. From a distance and from inside.

Low clouds stretched over Red Square, colliding with the star on Spassky Tower. Snow was threatening. Or rain. The Museum of History looked like an unassailable castle. Ivan decided that it must be closed. But in front of the heavy old door stood a crowd of bored visitors. They had the look of people who were already regretting the fact that they had been tempted by culture, while others were taking care of their material well-being.

Ivan bought a ticket. He even remembered the smell of the museum—he doubted that any of the visitors would notice it. The smell of a huge castle filled with old, old things. You had to get used to it, ignore it, forget it, and then remember it after many years. When was the first time he had come here? He was fifteen; his grandmother had a box with an ancient coin, seemingly cast out of platinum, undoubtedly ancient and incredibly valuable. He had entered through the door by the Kremlin wall, the service entrance, and had called the numismatic department, number 19, was it? He had held the coin tight in his fist. A girl came running up, and her name was Galya. Then later he was sitting in a room on the second floor that could be reached only through a jumble of narrow corridors. The walls of the room were covered with bookshelves. Another woman, an older one, brought out a thick catalog with a dark leather binding. He even remembered what she said: "A barbaric imitation." The words struck him as funny.

Ivan tilted his head as though he wanted to shake water out of his ear. He had never been in the Museum of History before and did not know how a castle filled with old things would smell.

Ivan stood in the Stone Age room. A large painting showed ancient hunters killing a mammoth. In a glass case was a collection of arrowheads, chipped skillfully and accurately, slightly jagged at the edges.

He had to move on to the next room. But there, as if to spite him, half of the room was cut off by a cord on which green pieces of paper were hung to frighten off the visitors; on the floor were several Greek vases; and seated on a chair, with a pile of papers on his lap, was Pashka Dubov. Pashka had aged terribly, put on weight, but aside from that hadn't changed. Ivan said, "Pashka!"

And then he realized. He had never met Pashka.

Ivan turned toward a showcase and concentrated on the colorful map

of Greek colonies on the Black Sea coast. He could see Dubov's startled
face reflected in the glass—the same old little mustache and sharp nose.
Although back then the mustache was just sprouting. Dubov used to say
that a real archaeologist shouldn't shave—it was a savings in time and
effort. His mustache was well sprouted now, but he still had no beard.
They had sat on the bank of the Volkhov in the city of Novgorod, not far
from the bridge. It was a cool, long, silvery summer evening. The sun,
even though it had long since set, managed to cast a dim light on the
dome of Saint Sophia. Sergei told Pashka that people like him had been
thrown off the bridge into the Volkhov when Novgorodian democracy had
triumphed. Pashka was in a hurry to grow a mustache and beard because
he was fatally enamored of a graduate student, Nilskaya. The difference
in age was enormous—at least six years. In addition, Nilskaya had her
eyes on Valya Kanin, who had the promise of a Schliemann. Then Valya
Kanin himself had come and told them that the birch bark they had found
that morning was blank. No inscription. Pashka looked at the bridge
and evidently wanted to hurl his talented rival into the Volkhov.
But Valya did not even suspect such a danger and proceeded to tell
them with gusto that the seal of Danila Matveyevich should be dated
from the very beginning of the fifteenth century. Sergei looked at
the young Schliemann with infatuated eyes. He shared the feelings of
Nilskaya. Valya Kanin was talking to schoolboys, who had come
along on the Novgorod digs during their vacation, just as he would to
academicians. What was important to him were intelligent people
who shared his ideas. Rank was something that would come with
time.

Pashka Dubov returned to his papers. I wonder if he's happy? Three
decades have passed since the evening they sat by the river. Valya Kanin
was now a member of the academy, and the birch-bark documents, which
in those years had just begun to be discovered, now numbered in the
hundreds. The elderly Pashka Dubov, it seemed, was working in the
Museum of History, counting pottery fragments.

Dubov sensed Ivan's glance and turned around. What did he see? Just
a young man who had wandered in on a gloomy day?

Dubov straightened up, put his papers on a chair, smiled timidly—his
usual smile, and asked, "Excuse me, but—"

"No, I'm not," Ivan answered. "Even though I do bear a strong resemblance to Rzhevsky in his youth."

And he walked quickly out of the room and practically ran out of the
museum, almost forgetting his boots in the checkroom. He was embarrassed at having acted like a child. Like a real child.

31

In the evening he dropped in to see his father. Unannounced.

His father had a visitor, a saggy old man, the academician Chelovekov. His father was surprised and delighted.

"So this is what you're like," Chelovekov roared. "I'm jealous of your father. He did a fine job. What's the matter?"

They were drinking tea. Two respectable men, an academician and an academician-to-be. Rzhevsky was too embarrassed to ask why Ivan had come. He acted as though Ivan spent all his days and nights there.

"Have some tea?" his father asked.

"No thanks. I'll get what I need myself."

"What do you need?"

"Some books," Ivan said.

Chelovekov had apparently decided that Ivan lived there and continued the conversation, not bothering about Ivan's presence.

Ivan adjusted the stepladder. The shelves were high, and there were journals stacked on the outside. He threw some down.

"Easy does it," Rzhevsky said. "The people downstairs."

"Funding I can guarantee," Chelovekov boomed. "I wouldn't come to you with empty hands. And a grant for Japanese equipment. You do need it, don't you?"

The books in back smelled of dust. When had he put them there? Six years ago, when the repairs were done. He hid them away to avoid re-membering. Ivan pulled out a collection of essays on dendrochronology, with a white paper cover. The cross sections of logs used to pave Nov-gorodian streets were drawn delicately and accurately.

"In any case," Chelovekov rumbled, "you're not going to stop with the first specimen. Don't frown. Specimen is no insult. Is it, young man?"

"I'm not insulted."

"See, he's smarter than you are," Chelovekov said. "But you're not going to get any more money right now. You're going to be tortured for a few years by commissions."

Behind the dense wall of books on archaeology was a box. His collection from childhood. The box opened with a creak. It was heavy. Ivan lowered it with difficulty to the floor. He sat down next to it and took out fragments of pottery and flint wrapped in white paper. He read the data—where, when—written in a round hand.

He didn't even hear at first when Chelovekov said good-bye.

"So passes the glory of this world," the academician said. He towered over Ivan, who was blocking his way. "My grandson wants to be a historian. I try to dissuade him. The past doesn't exist until we have built the present."

Ivan stood up, and Chelovekov marched out to the foyer and spent a long time putting on his coat. Then, studying Ivan carefully, he shot quick glances at Rzhevsky, then back to his son.

When, finally, he had put on his coat, he suddenly asked, "Young man, do you feel like being the continuation of your father?"

"I still don't know," Ivan said. "Most likely not in everything."

"Good lad!" the academician was pleased. "When we make mine, I'm going to tell him to study something different."

"Why?" asked Rzhevsky.

"I have given fifty years to my cursed science. I am tired. I have practically no time left. But what right do I have to force my son to spend another fifty years doing what he has already done in his mind with me? Don't pay attention to me, I'm just joking. I, too, have my doubts."

When the academician had left, Sergei said, "He asked me to do . . . it. With him."

"I figured that out," Ivan said. "But when he saw me his confidence seemed to diminish."

"Even with his influence he won't have the money," Rzhevsky said.

"That's his problem."

"What do you remember about your childhood amusements?"

Ivan held in his hands a half of a deep blue glass bracelet.

"Do you remember how you almost went over the edge of the cliff?" he asked.

"I remember. Of course I remember."

"I was in the Museum of History today. Do you know who I saw?"

"I can't imagine."

"Pashka Dubov."

"Really? What was he doing there?"

"Working. In the classical antiquities section."

"A good guy," Rzhevsky said. "But I thought he'd quit. You know, he was terribly afraid of mosquitoes."

"I know."

"Chelovekov is lying."

"About what?" Ivan carefully wrapped the bracelet fragment in paper. He unfolded the next packet. He had never felt such a pleasurable discovery. Even something in his belly turned from the joy he would feel in meeting an old friend. Of course—the handle from an amphora? From the Crimea.

"Chelovekov is lying," Rzhevsky repeated. "I am ready to continue what

I am doing for another fifty, another hundred years. And you must understand me better than anyone else."

"But Dubov has gotten fat," Ivan said. "But he still has his mustache. He was sitting in the museum, checking some papers."

"So he didn't get very far. Without an advanced degree," Rzhevsky said. "When you're finished, fold everything up again."

32

At the beginning of March the chimpanzee Lev died. From general exhaustion of the nervous system, as the veterinarians cloudily put it. During the last weeks he refused food, threw senseless hysterical fits, hurled himself against his cage, as though he wanted to break through to his father and tear him to pieces. Jon snarled, growled, but he, too, was subdued, as though he knew that Lev was not long for the world.

Rzhevsky was very much upset by his death. And not so much by the fact alone—experimental animals had died before. The worst thing was that none of the medical people could determine the cause of his death.

But then an unexpected complication occurred. When Lev fell, Jon went berserk, and rushed toward his dead son. Lev's body was carried away. Jon did not sleep all night. Gurina did not leave the vivarium but dozed off toward morning. Jon was clever enough to break the lock, without waking Gurina, and escaped from the institute. In his search for his son he made it almost to the center of Moscow—the hour was early and there were few vehicles on the roads. But at the beginning of Volgograd Prospect he was hit by a trolley. And killed. The driver had no time to figure out what was happening—he just saw someone fall under the wheels. And thought that he had hit a human being. When he stopped the trolley and saw that it was an ape, he felt such relief that his legs gave way and he sat right down on the pavement.

Ivan and Nina did not know about it. They went to Nina's parents for dinner. Elsa had told Nina to bring him. Nina was amazed and did not take the invitation seriously but with a smile conveyed it to Ivan. He accepted immediately. And said, "I haven't been there in ages. Many years."

"Is it simple curiosity? Or an excavation of yourself?"

"Archaeology."

"That's what I thought. I'll go tell my mother that you're coming. She won't believe it herself. If I don't tell her, she won't call my father. If she doesn't call him, no one will buy the grub for the dinner."

Her mother carefully put on her makeup, took the good china, a wedding gift, out of the buffet; it had some missing pieces by now but was expensive. Her father was late of course. And the guests heard an angry tirade against him.

Ivan paced the big room, studying various objects, many of which had lived for thirty years in the apartment, which had never been remodeled. Several years before they had saved money for remodeling, but they had had a rare chance for a trip to an artists' colony in Koktebel. Elsa spent a month in the very center of cultural life while Viktor rented a cot with Galina in the country and hiked in after breakfast to see his Puss. Ivan could not imagine why he had wanted to come so badly. He went into the kitchen. The ceiling was darker, the oilcloth on the table was new. How many times had he sat in this kitchen for interminable conversations until the wee hours. He had come here after Liz had left. . . . And Elsa, shaken by Liza's treachery, would repeat that you might have known. . .

But then the path to science opened to Sergei.

Nina hurried into the kitchen.

"Are you looking for something?"

"The past," Ivan said. "But it wasn't worth finding."

Elsa also came into the kitchen and began peeling potatoes.

"Excuse me," she said, "but I couldn't get off early. Everything will be ready soon. Ten minutes. Nina, wash the herring."

A pale and overworked Viktor straggled in.

"What a resemblance," he said to Ivan, "like two peas in a pod."

He put the bags on the table. Then he pulled a bottle of vodka out of one and several bottles of mineral water. He quickly shoved them in the refrigerator.

"Didn't I ask you?" Elsa started in threateningly. "I asked you to do something for your home once in your lifetime—"

"Hold on, Puss," Viktor said. "Don't get mad. I have just seen something you wouldn't believe!"

"Did you buy butter?"

"I bought it, I bought it. Can you imagine, a monkey fell under a trolley. What a sight!"

He goggled his eyes at Ivan, as though he was telling him alone.

"What monkey?" Nina asked, alarmed. There were hundreds of monkeys in the city, and she didn't know that Jon had run away.

"I saw it when it was already dead. Huge," Viktor said. "That's no more common than a fight between two lions on Gorky Street—you can figure out the odds. It must have run away from the zoo."

"His name was Jon," Nina said. "It was him, right?"

She took Ivan's hand.

"What?" Viktor asked. "Your monkey, from the institute? Well, all the more reason to have a drink. And let's not waste time. To her memory. She probably cost a pretty penny."

"One of ours?" Elsa was surprised. "From the vivarium?"

"Yes."

"Artificial or real?"

"Real," Nina said angrily. "Very real."

"A chimp suicide," Viktor guffawed.

Nina led Ivan out into the living room.

"Are you upset for Rzhevsky?" she asked him quietly.

"He's feeling bad now."

"But it was an accident."

"An accident," Ivan repeated.

Smiles and good humor reigned at the table. True, Ivan did not drink, not at all, and everyone agreed that he was right, it was better for a young man not to drink.

Viktor quickly got soused. The last few years two or three drinks were enough to do it, and now, taking advantage of the fact that Elsa's attention was riveted on her guest, he managed to toss off five. He soon became aggressive.

Nina did not like to see her father that way—as though another person was hiding in him, not the polite and soft father she knew, but a nasty-tempered, envious person who concealed his envy behind an ability to distort the truth.

"We and your father, Ivan," Viktor said, "were friends. Can you believe it?"

Ivan nodded. Viktor was close to the truth.

"And we'd still be, if it hadn't been for his careerism. He wanted to get to the top at any cost. For the sake of fame he was ready to kill. And I . . . I couldn't walk all over people."

Elsa went for the baked potatoes, and the oven door squealed. Viktor leaned over to Ivan and said, "I envied him. Always. But I was wrong. Now I don't envy him, you understand? He has gone all the way to the tragedy of solitude. And you are his retribution."

Ivan nodded obediently. His cheeks flushed. Nina did not know how to get him away from the table.

"Rzhevsky will be worried," she said.

"He knows your telephone number," Ivan said, not budging. He looked at Viktor attentively, as though inviting him to continue.

Elsa brought in the potatoes. She banged the plate down on the table.

Viktor stood up, walked over to Ivan, and bending down, seized him by the shoulders.

"I don't like you," he said loudly. "But it's not you, it's him, understand?"

"Papa!"

"Quiet! Maybe he himself wouldn't understand, he robbed me, and after so many years he comes back. Isn't Elsa enough? Isn't Lizetta enough? Do you have to have my Nina too? I won't give her up! I won't, you understand? I never gave you anything, and I never will!"

"Quiet!" Elsa screamed.

Nina jumped up.

"Let's go, Ivan."

Elsa started crying. Viktor followed them into the foyer.

"Don't take me literally," he mumbled.

Fortunately they found a taxi right away.

At the institute Ivan immediately went to bed. He felt terrible.

33

A crystal-clear nightmare came to Ivan that night. One of those nightmares that left no corner of Sergei Rzhevsky's memory in the dark, forcing Ivan to know more about him than he himself did.

He entered a room, in the barracks, seething with rage and hurt, and Liza, still not suspecting a thing, raced to him, with her thin arms embraced him in his rain-dampened coat, quickly and warmly kissed him with soft yielding lips, started to pull off his coat, saying, "Come on, take it off, why are you resisting? I'll iron it right away." Then, the coat in her hands, she froze: "Did something happen? At work? Some trouble?" She spoke with such a guilty voice, as though the problems at work were all her fault. He looked at her, realizing that she was not to blame, but everything— her nearsighted look and her trembling lower lip, and even the motions of her hands to fix a loose strand of her hair that had grown long and was pulled back with a rubber band—did not cause the usual surprise.

"I'm not hungry," he said, walking into the room from the little foyer— two yards, but then he went back—he had totally forgotten that Katya had been sick for three days, hadn't even asked about her when he came in— but that only increased his annoyance.

They were standing in the foyer quite close but without touching each other. Out of the corner of his eye Sergei saw, on the table, a dish, and bread and meat alongside it.

And so they stood in the foyer. And they could not leave. Ivan understood that in that immobility was hidden the dream's terror. And until the conversation came to a conclusion, they would not move out of the cramped foyer.

"Tell me what happened."

"You can't help."

"But I want to hear. You used to tell me everything."

"I'm not being admitted to the graduate program."

"It can't be."

"It's all right," Sergei said. "I'll get into a high school, teach biology."

"Why won't they take you? You're the best they have. And your thesis is going to be published."

Seryozha was silent, thinking that Liza had a forehead that was too slanted and cheekbones that were too wide.

"Because of me?" Liza whispered. "Tell me, tell me the truth."

"It's all my own fault. Mine. You understand—my own fault. We should never have met," he said finally.

In the foyer—six feet across—it was cramped and stuffy, and Ivan knew that Liza would start gasping for air. Liza had a bad heart, she was very sick, here in the stuffy air she wouldn't have air and she would die. And then it would all be over, they would accept him, all he had to do was endure just a little longer . . . and then things would be easier.

And Ivan felt, although the guilt was not his and the pain was not his, that he had to save Liza, open a window, break down the door, even knock out a wall . . . and he woke up. It was quiet. Now no one stood guard during the night. And really, why should a human being live at the institute? Like in a vivarium. They had brought him wardrobe, assigned to a lab, and the clothes he kept in it absorbed an acid smell. Should he rent a room? In what barracks?

Ivan picked up a journal and began reading. It was a Spanish publication. Rzhevsky did not know Spanish. Ivan was studying it. That was important. He read for several minutes, then he was overcome by drowsiness.

34

"Stop your studies," Professor Volodin said. "You'll drive yourself crazy. I'm being serious. Before, they used to call it brain fever. Now we have invented a more contemporary name, but we can't help you. Young man, your blood pressure is jumping around like an old man's. More fresh air, and you can go jogging."

"Even when I was young I never went jogging," Ivan said. He shook his head and added, "I'll try it."

The next morning Ivan climbed into a sweat suit, with a white stripe down the side of the pants, and jogged around an asphalt path, then turned off into a passage between the former barracks, fell in a hole, got his feet wet, and got mad at himself. In his early youth he was a lot more fit. And he headed back. He had to do something.

Ivan remembered that Nina was waiting for him. They had to study. Since he had promised.

Studying with Nina got Ivan out of his rut, but he could not admit to his pupil that it was because of her. He compared himself to a professional driver who is teaching a neophyte how to drive. Nina was average in her abilities. But no more than that. Without the spark of inspiration. The hours that he spent with her were exhausting—all he had to do was glance at a page in order to understand more than the author of the textbook had in mind. But he could not allow himself to hurry—Nina had to understand what was for her a sacred mystery but was for him old hat. And the feeling of time slipping by, precious time, irreplaceable time—that was from Rzhevsky. It would seem that he, Ivan, should be closer to Nina, for whom each day did not have any special value because the future held an infinite number of them. But in Ivan there was an inner haste, a desire to be in time. . . . Was there something he had to do? To do, despite the warnings of the good Professor Volodin. What did Volodin know about monsters? He had never treated any before. For doctors it was important to keep his fragile body intact. For his father it was important to make use of his head. Make use of it mercilessly, like his own. But what did Ivan want? Was he fit to live? A poor self-image, melancholy, outbursts of hatred toward the journals that his father slipped onto his night table—this characteristic of his as yet unstabilized personality and organic weaknesses that were characteristic of all such monsters? Lev and Jon had died—they were no more, although related. Experiments on humans had been halted for the time being—the scientific world looked at Ivan with varying degrees of goodwill and envy. For all of them he was a column of statistics, X rays, a few lines in a report. And next to him sat the lovely Nina, who was trying to comprehend the Hardy-Weinberg law, and population genetics were a mystery—she wanted to go to the movies, no matter what percent of alleles in the population of Baltimore were recessive. And in this terribly depressing life Ivan has only one bright spot: the look on Pashka Dubov's face and the dusty packets of his old collection.

"There's a week-long series of French films opening today," Nina announced to him suddenly. She couldn't hold out. Now he had to arrange it so she did not drag him with her to the movies, because he wanted to take a look at a book he had bought yesterday at a dealer's: an account by the most curious Bishop Evgeny of Novgorodian antiquities. For the book he had paid all his wages as a junior research scientist—except for a little set aside for cigarettes.

35

The brain is a system that has limits to its power. Only a small fraction of its cells are active. This is the result not of nature's oversight but of her wisdom. The brain has to be guarded.

In the accelerated creation of an adult individual the entire life experience of the parent is transferred to the brain. The more highly developed the donor, the more actively the brain works, and the closer it is to the limit of its capabilities, the less of a reserve it has. Consequently, Ivan's brain, his nervous system, was overloaded with information from the very first instant of life. Rzhevsky's fatigue, the exhaustion of his nervous system, were inherited by Ivan.

But once he was "born," Ivan quickly began to absorb information. He did not only continue Rzhevsky, he hastened to make himself unique, to assert himself, to fill his brain with his own information, and not gradually, over many years, accumulate it, as most people do. Feeling the overload, becoming aware of the danger, warning signals went off in the brain—and the brain began to fight desperately against the alien memory of Sergei Rzhevsky.

My God, Ivan thought, how much rubbage accumulates in each brain over half a century. Cheating at math in the fourth grade, and the glance Zina from next door threw me, and the report on the improvement in living conditions from Sinyukhin the carpenter that was handed in in October of last year. . . .

The struggle with Rzhevsky turned into a struggle with his own brain, and it splashed up thoughts and images from the past—cells inhabited by Rzhevsky's information shouted out that they were the real masters.

What should I do now? Ivan thought. Take a tranquilizer? Stop reading and writing? Or load my brain with new thoughts? That is impossible. I might as well hang myself. And the great conscience of Professor Rzhevsky, so heedlessly transmitted to his illegitimate son, reflected peace. It might end with Ivan breaking down, and Rzhevsky not being able to bear the failure—not only failure of the experiment but his failure as a human being. Everything was clear as day. In order to spare Rzhevsky, he had to survive himself. And to survive himself, he had to rid himself of Rzhevsky's mixed-up past—a vicious circle.

36

Ivan waited for Pashka Dubov by the service entrance. He came out with a shopping bag—the neck of a bottle of mineral water was sticking out.

Dubov was not surprised to see Ivan.

"Why didn't you come over and talk?" he asked. "I figured it out immediately: You're the son of Sergei Rzhevsky. Right? A remarkable resemblance. Even in the way you act."

Ivan did not argue. Later they sat for a long time in a restaurant in Aleksandrovsky Park, and Dubov obediently ticked off the expeditions he had been on, and even told why he had recently married a young student and how it had negatively affected his position at the museum, because his ex-wife—or maybe it was his two preceding wives—worked there, too. Dubov, it seemed, had the bad habit of falling in love during expeditions. And seriously. And that led to alimony, which put a real crimp in the salary of a junior scientist, and one who was not trying to get ahead.

"And how's Sergei?" he would ask from time to time, but Ivan would skillfully change the subject to expeditions and Dubov would obediently continue his story.

"Do you want to come along with us this summer?" he asked. "We're not going far, to the Smolensk region. I'd go to the Far East but Lyusenka is expecting, so she objects."

"I'd like to," Ivan said.

"And Seryozha, what about Seryozha? He could take a vacation."

"No, he's busy."

"Are you a student now? I didn't even ask."

"I'm a biologist," Ivan said.

"I was sure that Sergei would become an archaeologist. And an outstanding one."

"I'll take his place," Ivan said with a smile.

"Even if you only spend your vacation there," Dubov agreed. "I'd be happy. I really liked Sergei. It's a pity that our paths parted. But he won't object?"

"He probably will," Ivan said.

"He's against you taking time off, right?"

"Yes."

"But you're drawn to it?"

"I found my father's old archaeology collection. And I had the feeling that I had collected it myself. I don't have that feeling about my father's other activities."

"My father wanted me to become a lawyer," Dubov said. "But I was stubborn. I told him that you can't make your son a continuation of yourself."

"Why?" Ivan asked with curiosity.

"Because a father cannot know which of the possible continuations is the right one. In each person there are several possible persons. And until the very end of his life, you can't say which has prevailed. I am convinced that Sergei could have become a good archaeologist. But he became a good biologist. Neither you nor I know what happened in his life that made him take a right instead of a left at one of life's many crossroads. And perhaps even now he sometimes regrets not being on a dusty archaeological site, taking a brush and cleaning the edge of a pottery shard. And who knows what stands behind that bit of clay? Maybe a giant Buddha, like the one Litvinsky found? Maybe an unknown layer of Troy? Maybe a whole epoch in the life of humanity, the discovery of which will make us doubly richer. . . . Oh God"—Dubov looked at his watch and got very upset—"Lyusenka is going to tear my head off. She has a seminar tomorrow, and I haven't fixed her dinner. Write down my telephone number."

37

He hadn't felt like eating all day. He drank up yesterday's cold coffee straight from the pot, looked with anxiety at the pile of new journals. Then Rzhevsky called him.

He thought to himself that Rzhevsky had seemed to age during the last few weeks.

"Look at these," he said, pushing a folder of medical reports across his desk. "This is what the patient is not supposed to know. But you seemed determined on self-destruction."

The reports contained nothing new. True, there had been a certain regression. The impression that he was an old man with several organ systems out of whack.

"Physiologically I'm overtaking you," Ivan said indifferently.

"Let's call in consultants. We should transfer you to a clinic."

"There I'll just go down the tubes."

"But you don't want to help yourself."

"In the clinic they can treat only those things they're familiar with. And I only appear to be the same as other people."

"But you are constructed the same as other people."

"I don't believe it. Every person is programmed for a certain life span. At least approximately. Possibly the program is developed in the mother's womb. You don't know how that system works either. All these years you have been driving for practical results. You didn't take the time to consider the philosophical aspects."

"The philosophical aspects?" Rzhevsky said irritably. "And what about the mystical aspects?"

Gurina peeked timidly into the office, to get some papers signed for supplies for the new apes. Rzhevsky signed them without reading them.

"What were we talking about?" he asked after Gurina had left.

"About the fact that you, my father, are more afraid of the failure of the experiment than of my destruction. Don't worry, no matter what the final results, the experiment is sensational. You have done everything to perfection."

"Don't be stupid! You are my son."

"How long have you realized that?"

"Remember how you stopped by a few days ago, and rummaged around with the old pottery fragments? I didn't want you to leave."

"I saw Dubov again. He promised to take me along on an expedition. He also invited you. He is still convinced that you would have made a great archaeologist."

"Perhaps. Only it's boring."

"I don't think so."

"At your age I still had occasional regrets about having to sit in a laboratory. We both had the same childhood hobby."

"But suppose it is important for me even now?"

"Don't get distracted. We have more serious problems."

Ivan shrugged his shoulders. If indeed a person did choose his path his whole life long, his father had gone very far on his. And could no longer understand that the problem of a choice at the crossroads that he had decided could not be decided by Ivan once and for all. But to speak about that now would be to push his father into a fit of indignation.

"You are more authoritarian than I," Ivan said. "Before you is a series of problems. That is your life. You solve one, then the next, and the well-being of your guinea pigs does not concern you."

"Self-destruction is more than arrogance."

"I wasn't talking about myself, Father."

Ivan stood up and walked over to his father. Snow remained only under the trees and in the building's shadows. Over the white buildings at the horizon tall fluffy clouds drifted. Clouds like that did not exist in the winter. If you lay down in the steppe in the morning and looked at the sky, you would find it fascinating to follow their modulations, the changes in form, and to guess their transformations, imagining yourself a heavenly sculptor.

"Then about whom?" he heard the insistent voice of his father. "About whom? Do you hear me?"

"About your old experiment. With Liza. When, thirty years ago, Viktor told you that you had to choose between Liza and science. But you didn't have to choose. It was just more convenient that way."

"What does Viktor have to do with it?"

"He seemed to give you a scare at just the right time."

"I don't remember."

"I could write a study on the nature of human memory. How skillfully it manages to toss aside anything that inhibits its master's peace of mind."

"I really don't remember."

"You could have found her and brought her back."

"How could I find her, if even her address—" Rzhevsky suddenly fell silent. And Ivan understood why. He answered another person and then remembered that he was speaking to himself. The cloud outside the window finally stopped reminding Ivan of Alevich—it pulled his nose back inside. A wind struck up, and the trees in the park submissively leaned to one side, waving their crows' nests at their tops.

"That's not right," Rzhevsky said. "Of course, at first I was afraid she'd come back. But I got used to living without her. If I had wanted to find her, I could have gone to Vologda. But I don't remember any conversation with Viktor."

"He really was not the decisive factor," Ivan said. "The decision was in us. You throw something out of your conscious mind, hide something in the cellars of your brain, cover things up with a heap of old rags. But I can't store your goods in my brain. The oppressive past is for you like an old toothache. No more. But what if in each person, independent of his perception of his own life, there is hidden a scale of the importance of actions? And on that scale your breaking up with Liza was extremely important. You felt like abandoning everything and running after her. . . . But instead you rushed off to a very significant conference in Dushanbe."

"Hold on." Rzhevsky got up and joined Ivan at the window. He looked at the clouds. "How they change shape! I used to love to watch them.

. . . Where was I? Oh, yes, you are constantly trying to separate yourself from me, become an independent personality. I understand you. But you are getting in your own way! As long as you rummage around in my past, you are connected to me. So convince yourself: It is not my past! It is Sergei's past!"

"I cannot live until I uncover your cellars."

"But why?"

"Because I am your genetic copy. If you are a thief, I must understand why, so that I do not become one. If you are a murderer, a cowardly traitor, an egotist, I must understand whether I have inherited your traits or whether I can avoid them."

"So you, too, think that I am a murderer?"

"I inherited your memory, but I haven't understood a thing."

"Isn't there anything in my past that gives you joy?" Rzhevsky tried to smile.

"There is," Ivan said, turning to him and looking him straight in the eyes. "There is an evening on the banks of the Volkhov, when you sat with Pashka Dubov, and then Valya came with the seal. . . ."

"That was all nonsense," Rzhevsky said confidently. He did not believe Ivan. He returned to his desk and flipped through his desk calendar. He sighed.

"Be a friend," he said. "Rest today. Tomorrow we'll see the specialists. Do you want me to ask Nina to go for a walk with you?"

"She has to study," Ivan answered.

38

If he were in the doctors' place, he would not take any chances—he'd send himself off to the clinic and that would be the end of it.

If he tried proving to the doctors that the problem was an overload on the brain, they would either not believe or treat him for it. . . . No, he could not give in.

In the morning Ivan submitted to all the tests, then announced to Nina that he would not be needing her care. Nina sensed that all was not right but held her tongue, like an obedient little girl. Then Ivan shoved his pay and his institute identification papers into his pocket, dressed very warmly, and went out into the garden.

From the garden, sliding on the melting snow, he took a familiar path over to the bus stop. He felt miserable, but he had to pull himself together.

The sun came out. It was quiet and some bird of spring was twittering in the trees.

For some reason he remembered that Viktor always went to eat at the restaurant on the corner of Chernyshevsky and Khlopotny; all the waiters there knew him. Ivan headed there. Viktor was not there. Then Ivan went outside—it was stuffy in the restaurant, and Ivan felt dizzy from the smells—quite ordinary ones. That was another bad sign.

Ivan stood near the restaurant entrance, leaning his back against the cold wall. The idea came to him about shortening the process for cleaving RNA, and he began in his mind to construct the equipment, but right then he caught sight of Viktor strolling down the street. Viktor was about to walk right past him but then recognized him. He stopped cautiously.

"Hello," Ivan said. "I've been waiting for you."

"I understand," Viktor said quickly. "Of course, why shouldn't we talk?—even though things didn't work out last time, I'd like to very much. There's a bench in the courtyard—I have a beer there once in a while during the summer. Let's sit a while, okay? No one will see us."

Viktor reached the bench first and wiped the snow off with his glove.

"Are you sure you won't catch cold?"

Ivan sat down and lit a cigarette. He smoked more than Rzhevsky.

"Please understand me correctly," Viktor said. "I don't have anything against your relationship with Nina. Please don't think that."

My God, Ivan thought wearily, he's decided that I'm planning on marrying Nina—they discuss it in the kitchen and are afraid. It's something forbidden, but flattering.

"I wanted to ask you about something else. Something that happened twenty-five years ago."

"Twenty-five years ago?"

"Why do you think Rzhevsky left Liza?"

"He didn't leave her," Viktor answered quickly. "She left herself. She was a very proud woman—she had been hurt and she left. I guarantee it."

"But how did it come about that Sergei hurt her so much?"

"As a matter of fact, he did kill her—I'm not afraid of exaggeration. For his sake she had given up everything—"

"What did you do at the time?"

"I understood that Sergei was an egotist. No, not in a bad sense, but for him science was everything. He felt that Liza was in his way.

So he removed her from his path. . . . She had nothing left to do but leave."

Viktor was smoking furiously, inhaling deeply. Oh how he hates Sergei, Ivan thought, and can't forgive him even now, after so many years. But perhaps the anger has been accumulating all these years.

"Why did you tell him that he wouldn't be accepted into the graduate program?"

"Me? I never said that. It never happened."

Viktor cast Ivan a quick, cold glance. Ivan had not expected any other answer.

"Did you see Liza again after that?"

"Why do you want to know? Did Sergei send you?"

"He doesn't know anything about it."

"I'll tell you then. Liza called me, in tears, her voice trembling. Seryozha, she says, is abandoning me. I met her. Katya was sick, so I said, where will you go? But you don't know—once Liza had decided on something, tanks couldn't stop her. I, she said, won't be in his way, he wants science more than us. So I took her. . . ."

"Where did you take her?"

"Where? To the station, of course, to go to Vologda."

"And then?"

"She died several months later. I think she committed suicide. . . . After that I could no longer be friends with Rzhevsky. But what does all this have to do with you?"

"I have to know the truth."

"The truth?" Viktor seemed amazed. "Is there such a thing? It dies with people. There are as many truths as people."

"I need the one truth," Ivan said.

"Go on looking. But don't blame me later."

"Where did Liza's mother live?"

"You know, it was twenty-five years ago."

"You were there. You know the address."

"I've forgotten. Really."

"Think."

"No one lives there anymore. Ekaterina Georgiyevna Maksimova, that was her mother's name—she died ten years ago. There's no one there now. And her brother moved away."

"You've gone back?"

"Here, write it down: Arbat, house number. . . ."

Viktor watched as Ivan wrote down the address. Then he said, "Maybe we should have a glass of beer—I know all the waiters here."

39

It turned out that Viktor was right. Liza's mother had died a long time before, and strangers were living in her apartment. No one could help. Struggling against his headache and overcome more and more by the hopelessness of it all, Ivan went from apartment to apartment, but everywhere the old tenants had moved out long before. He went down to the building manager, finally, having lost hope. He stopped in the middle of a courtyard near a table where two old men were playing chess and several others kibitzing. One of the chess players, who had been glancing at him from time to time, suddenly spoke to Ivan, just as he picked up a pawn.

"Go down to the food store, number thirty-two. Go down to the corner, and on your right is a blue sign. Ask for the stevedore Valya. Got it?"

He immediately turned away, put down the pawn, and said to his opponent, "Your move, Edik."

Ivan was so tired that he did not ask any questions—he was told to go, so he went. Once in the store he asked the saleswoman, "Is the stevedore Valya here?" She motioned with her head to a counter. Ivan went behind it; there was a dark hallway, then stairs down to the basement, where the lights were burning. In the basement an elderly man was sitting on a crate and drinking beer from a bottle. His face was worn, and although at one time it must have been handsome, it now expressed insignificance.

"Hello," Ivan said. The man's face was familiar. Valya resembled Liza, and Ekaterina Georgiyevna. "Valya, you don't know me. . . ."

Liza's brother got up off the crate, wiped his eyes with the back of his hand, and swore softly.

"An exact copy," he said. "Absolutely identical. Must be the devil out of hell, how'd you get in here?"

"I'm Rzhevsky's son."

"You don't have to explain. It's clear enough that you're his son. How did you find me?"

"Your neighbors told me."

"You were lucky. I haven't lived there for ages—my footsteps were lost in the sea of humanity, as they say. So your father got married after all, one of his scientists, most likely, from the institute?"

Valya Maksimov was nervous; his hands were trembling.

"Sit down," he said. "How long it's been! I don't have anything against your father. Lizetta felt like a real person with him. What a business! How is he? Not sick? My mother died. In seventy-two. She wasn't lucky with us."

"I want to find out what happened after my father split up with your sister. It's very important to me."

"I wasn't there," Valya said. "I wouldn't want to talk about causes and effects. But if you're really interested, you can go talk to Katya. She doesn't consider me to be a real person, but she does send me a card at the holidays."

"Liza's daughter?"

"Yes."

40

In the airplane Ivan passed out, fortunately not for long. From the Vologda airport he called Moscow, the institute, not Rzhevsky but the lab. Nina picked up the phone.

"Tell Rzhevsky that everything is fine with me. I'm getting a breath of fresh air."

It was already dark, after eight in the evening, and tears trembled in Nina's voice. Ivan imagined the panic that must reign in the institute.

"You didn't tell anyone."

"Important business, kitten; every man has things to take care of. Tomorrow I'll be back and tell you everything."

He hung up and went to the taxi stand.

Katya was home.

She lived in a small apartment, in a new five-story building near the river. From her windows you could see the quais, the lights on the other side, the bright walls and cupolas of the coquettish churches.

"I recognized you immediately," she said. "As soon as you walked in, I recognized you."

She spoke slowly, evenly. She had a long braid, very old-fashioned in appearance, and the braid lay over her chest.

"Come into the kitchen," Katya said in a muffled voice. "Otherwise my Liza will wake up."

Katya put up the teapot. Ivan felt relaxed. He anticipated with pleasure the strong, fragrant tea. Liza had also known how to brew tea. Ivan admired Katya's smooth and accurate movements.

"Where is your husband?" he asked.

"I don't have one," Katya said. "I left him. He drank. He was a good engineer, very capable, but he drank and began beating me . . . and I am not a person who takes that kind of thing." She smiled, as though she could not really understand how anyone could beat her. "You've come all the way from Moscow?"

"Yes."

"Did your father send you? I used to call him Papa-Seryozha. He was kind, always brought me candy. You can't imagine how I cried for him at first."

"He didn't send me. I came on my own."

"Where are you staying?"

"I'll go to a hotel later."

"You're not going to get a room without a reservation," Katya said. "You can stay here. I'll fix the folding bed—if you don't mind a folding bed?"

"Thanks," Ivan said. "I've had enough trouble today."

"You're pale, terribly pale. Let's have some tea, it's whistling."

The tea, strong and fragrant, made Ivan feel better. He and Katya had known each other a long time already, thirty years.

"What is it?" she asked. "Is your father still suffering?"

"He thinks he's guilty of your mother's death."

"How terrible! If I had known, I would have written him about how things were. Mama wasn't mad at him at all. Not in the slightest. She used to talk with me a lot—when I can remember it now, it seems curious that she talked to me like an adult. We lived together for several years. . . . With my aunt. My aunt was a good person too, not prying. We had a hard life—my mother worked, my aunt did, too, and I went to the nursery. Of course, Mama missed Papa-Seryozha, missed him very much—wrote him letters, a whole pile of letters, maybe a hundred—I saved them, I'll show you. I even thought, after my mother's death, that I should send them. But I didn't. The man has forgotten, I said, and I'll just be torturing him. He'd married and had you, and it wouldn't have been right for him to get letters like that. And your mother would have gotten upset."

"Sergei never got married."

"But. . . ."

"Katya, I'll have to tell you everything. But first finish your story. After all, I'm the one who came to see you, not you me."

"True," Katya said. "What should I tell you about?"

"Why did your mother . . . die?"

"Accidents like that happen—she was crossing a street, a truck hit. The driver was drunk, took a wide turn, and hit her."

"I was told that she threw herself under a train . . . and that's what my father thinks. He looked for you. . . ."

"Apparently not that hard. You managed to find us. Don't be insulted. Mama was waiting all those years. And Viktor Gulinsky knew the address. He wrote Mama a letter. And then my aunt wrote him about Mama's death. Do you know Viktor Gulinsky? He was your father's closest friend."

"Do you still have his letters?"

"There were only two of them. One was just a note, the other was long. He wrote Mama that he loved her and wanted to marry her. But Mama refused very strongly, even harshly. And he understood . . . Mama loved Papa-Seryozha very much."

Suddenly Katya broke out crying—tears flowed out of her gray eyes and down her tan cheeks. She jumped up and ran into the bathroom. She did not return immediately, then came in with a box.

Inside were greeting cards, some kind of tickets, receipts, and letters. A packet of letters in blank, unaddressed envelopes wrapped with a ribbon.

"These are Mama's letters," Katya said. "All of them are to Sergei. Don't think that she was accusing him of anything—she felt she was in his way."

From under the packet Katya took out one more.

The handwriting was familiar. Viktor's small, femininely rounded handwriting hadn't changed in thirty years.

> Dear Liza,
> During our last conversation you refused to meet me. Are you right? It's not for me to say. I can't do anything about my love for you, which I have never mentioned because it is hard to declare your love to a woman who is living with your friend. And for me it is doubly tormenting since I saw that your life was going downhill, that it was doomed. He didn't love you, haven't you realized that? You were convenient—please don't be insulted, but that's the way it was. He never intended to link his life to yours. You were blind, but now perhaps your eyes have been opened. The whole business about him not being accepted as a graduate student is just your attempt to justify him—I swear to you that there were no problems—he just chose a convenient moment to cut himself off from you. How naive women are, even ones as intelligent as you. . . . The last few months Seryozha has been having a mad romance with Elsa. I knew out it but was afraid to tell you for fear of hurting you. . . .

Ivan realized that he did not want to read more. Maybe his father would read the whole letter. And maybe he shouldn't see the letter at all. How mean and rotten!

"Did you know," he said, folding Viktor's letter, "that he later married Elsa?"

"And he wanted Mama to leave Papa-Seryozha?"

"If it hadn't been for him, everything would have worked itself out in time."

"No," Katya said. "They would not have gone on together. He loved her, of course, but not strongly enough. He loved his work more. And Mama knew that. Maybe that's why she couldn't get mad at him. You know, she remembered the whole thing with gratitude—how the two of them went to Leningrad, how they used to go to the movies. He gave her Veresayev's biography of Pushkin—have you ever read it? I'll show you, if you want. She saved that book as though it were a Bible."

Katya fixed the folding bed in the kitchen. He could not sleep for a long time. But Katya went to sleep immediately and he could hear her gentle, even breathing in the quiet of the apartment. Then little Liza tossed about and cried in her sleep. Ivan thought about seeing her in the morning.

And then he began to shake violently. His teeth even chattered. He thrashed about, trying to prevent it, so that Katya did not wake up, but then he apparently forgot himself and his groan awakened Katya. Ivan began hallucinating. Katya was frightened and called an ambulance. Ivan was taken to a hospital.

Katya took Liza to nursery school, then went to the hospital.

When Ivan regained consciousness, he saw Katya's gray eyes very close to him, reached out with his hand and touched the tip of her braid.

"Hello," he said. "Thank you."

"For what?"

Ivan wanted to explain, but it was impossible—his tongue did not obey him, and he realized he could tell her everything later. Now he could not let one important thought slip away. He asked her to call Moscow, Rzhevsky.

Sergei flew out for Ivan that same day, with Professor Volodin. Rzhevsky strode into the ward. Ivan had a fever, but he recognized his father and said, looking at Katya, "Let me introduce you."

"Sergei Rzhevsky," Rzhevsky said as he stretched out his hand.

It was strange that he did not recognize her—she did resemble Liza. But Rzhevsky was thinking only about Ivan. And even when Ivan said, "Katya Maksimova" he still did not understand.

"Katya Maksimova," she repeated.

Only then did that piece of the mosaic fall into place. "Katya," he said softly.

"The letters," Ivan said. "Don't forget to give my father the letters. He needs them. Because a chimpanzee died at the institute."

"I have them with me," Katya said. "I don't know why but I brought them with me."

41

After Ivan had recovered, there was still another meeting, and not a very pleasant one. One morning before visiting hours, Viktor barged into his room; how he got in was anybody's guess.

"Just a few words," he said. "I know everything, Nina told me. Just two words."

He was drunk and pitiful.

"I have a daughter," Viktor said, "the only person I love, you still don't know that but try to understand. If she finds out, I might as well die. I swear to you that I loved Liza, and honestly, the feeling overpowered me. The business about graduate studies and what you might consider my slandering him is more complicated. Elsa gave me the idea. She didn't want to give up Sergei to Liza. She's a destroyer, you know. And I was after Liza. And I was suffering. You wouldn't understand." Viktor spoke in a quick, loud whisper. He bent over the bed; his breath smelled so heavily of vodka that Ivan had to turn his head away. But Viktor did not notice, he was hurrying his repentance.

"She would never have gone, she kept hoping, but I went to her the next day, to her mother, as though Sergei had sent me, and she never told anyone. And I told her he didn't want to see her anymore. That's why she left. And amen. You want the truth? The truth is that I would have been a good husband to Liza. She did not understand. I ended up in Elsa's claws, and she died. But please, don't say anything, okay? If you think anything of Nina, don't hurt her."

"Go away," Ivan said. "I won't say anything."

He left. And just in time. Five minutes later Nina arrived, bringing a dish of strawberries and a supply of institute gossip.

Two days later Ivan began walking. The crisis had passed. Volodin asserted that his organism had to overcome a biological incompatibility. As in an organ transplant. Only in this case it was a question of two personalities. The theory of memory overload did not arouse Volodin's sympathy. "You haven't taxed your brain at all, my colleague," he said. But Ivan remained of the same opinion. The alien dreams were no longer so horrible. Even though they had not disappeared entirely. Nina's feelings seemed to have thawed: She wanted to spoon-feed Ivan, she blushed easily, and took offense at trifles. Sergei proposed once again that Ivan move in with him.

"No," Ivan said, "we're too different."

"Nonsense."

"Yesterday I spent a whole hour solving a problem you missed on the tenth-grade state examinations."

"So you can see that there are problems to be solved. And there are a million others that we could solve together."

"You don't even remember the problem. You know how to forget your failures, but did not give me that ability."

At this point, when the argument threatened to become a quarrel, Dubov walked in. Again with the shopping bags. He greeted Rzhevsky awkwardly and noisily, then remembered that he had brought a gift and dumped everything out on the table, separating what was to go home to Lyusenka and what was for Ivan the invalid.

"What luck," he said, "that Ivan has decided to become an archaeologist. Lyusenka agrees—she says he will pick up where you left off. It's a shame I don't have a son like him."

"What the hell is this about archaeology?" Rzhevsky roared.

Nina fluttered into the room but froze near the door; she was holding a little basket of berries.

"I'm going on the expedition. In two weeks," Ivan said. "I'll be back in the fall."

"You're crazy! Who would give you permission?"

"Professor Volodin has no objections. He is even delighted. He says that the fresh air and dust from the excavations are the best medicine for a homunculus," Ivan said. He was now much stronger than his father and was using that strength.

"You could have told me sooner," Rzhevsky said.

"We still have three weeks. Tomorrow bring me the new journals. I still haven't decided. I don't want to make a mistake."

"Okay," his father said. "I'd better be going."

He turned to Dubov. "Pashka, drop by and see me, either at the institute or at home."

"Sure thing," Dubov responded. "We have a lot to reminisce about. Suppose I go with you now—I was just about to leave."

"Father," Ivan said to Rzhevsky as he was leaving, "is Katya coming?"

"I sent her a telegram," Rzhevsky said. "If she wants to move to Moscow. . . ."

"Go ahead," Ivan said. "Go and reread Liza's letters. And Nina, please, put down your present before you stain your blouse."

A Tale of Kings

OLGA LARIONOVA

The building was the last in the town. Beyond it was a field, where nothing had yet been built—a neutral strip of no-man's-land, not quite urban but certainly no longer rural. The field was overgrown entirely by burdocks because during the coming summer it would undergo the great torment of becoming civilized, and nature was reluctant to sacrifice even a blade of sweet clover or clump of daisies to be chopped to pieces by countless harrows, treads, scoops, or ordinary shovels. Nature therefore garbed itself in burdock.

At the far end of the field greenhouses, or more precisely what once were greenhouses, were visible. The *sovkhoz* responsible for looking after them had received new lands and, after prudently removing the glassed frames, took off for parts unknown. They remained, like skeletons of gigantic herring, letting through their trembling ribs the free wind from beyond the city.

At night it was totally dark in the field. On the other hand, alongside the building itself where the field was no longer really a field but because of the planting of a dozen half-dead barberry bushes had been transformed into a pocket park for the area—out there lay squares of light from the windows. But up above, from the ninth floor, this pattern was not visible, and at night Artem felt that somewhere out there, in the impenetrable darkness, the sky did meet the Earth, just as rails that have never yet met do finally come together in sidings; the sky temporarily joins the earth, and the black flash freezes over the world until the blade of the first sunbeam splits them apart like the shells of an oyster.

But sometimes, when things were really rotten, he had the sense of the absolute loss of space out there, beyond his window, and there was not just no longer earth or sky—there was nothing, just primal chaos, not yet separated into land and waters. Today was one of those days.

He entered his apartment quietly, as though he might awaken someone. But there was no one to awaken, and annoyed with his needless precautions, he was deliberately noisy, stamping around the kitchen and plopping his shopping bags with all the cans down alongside the refrigerator. He squatted down and started, very dejectedly, to take the cans, packages, and boxes out of the bags and put them into the white frost-velveted refrigerator. If you are such an idiot that despite a great desire you cannot make a model of the simplest family life, then that should be no concern of your friends. Tomorrow is the housewarming, and they will be gathering in your most beauteous apartment. And you will greet them. With the appropriate expression of benevolence. Especially with regard to the ladies. And with that in mind, here is the apricot compote. Look at that! he knew enough to buy apricots for us. Ah, Artem, you're a darling! What a shame that you look like Alain Delon!

And then his friends would realize how bad off he was.

"Artem," his friends would say, "you are dull, sodden, a bourgeois fathead. How, in this most beauteous of apartments, can you get by all alone? You have your aperitif and your salted peanuts," his well-read friends would say, "but you are in need of a Zizi. Thank God the situation is remediable. Just look at all the beautiful women (as they point to the women hovering over the apricot compote). Take your pick!"

And perhaps he should take his pick. After all, none of them would refuse. Beautiful women seemed to degenerate into self-clinging mechanisms in his presence. *Basta*. He had had enough.

Artem slammed the refrigerator door and headed for the living room. He did not bother to turn on the light but just walked over to the window and the barely glowing ashen night sky. An indistinct reflection of his own face appeared in the glass, and Artem looked at himself with hatred.

Imagine that next door to you lives a young man as irresistible as Alain Delon. Well, that you can imagine. And what his life is like—that too you can imagine. But Artem's problem was that he was much more handsome than Alain Delon or any other imported movie star. The comparison is not all that helpful, but there are not that many models available these days. Long ago, they say, the comparison would be to a king (as in Dumas). Slim and dark-haired, he was filled with the true Russian beauty, the type that the noble and unbelievable women of Venetsianov were famous for, with noses just barely touched with the hint of a hook, and inspired brows, with the heavy purity of innocent eyes of Raphael, and the sinful puffiness of lips of the Virgin of Kazan. Unfortunately, nowadays this type of beauty has been squeezed out of our minds by another, the epic hero of Novgorod, with the obligatory straw-blond curls and a reckless clarity in his gaze that for some reason we now accept as the truly Russian type. And incidentally, blue eyes and blond hair were considered obligatory for handsome men in medieval France, if we are to believe the eleventh-century codes of love.

However that may be, a noble appearance combined with a first name that is almost unique today created such a complex of irresistibility in Artem that despite his most ardent wishes he had not yet, by the age of twenty-four, succeeded in establishing a solid and secure family life. The man just had no luck whatsoever. And if he had been an actor or television anchorman, at least, he might have acquired an immunity against being goggled at and pointed at. But he was just a plain engineer and had still not gotten used to women stopping on the street and turning around to stare at him.

In the blurred reflection of his face Artem could not distinguish his features, but nonetheless he stared at it with a fixed hatred.

Until he suddenly realized that with the lights off there could not be even an indistinct reflection.

From out there, from the blackness of primal chaos, another person's immobile face was looking at him.

Artem remained motionless for several seconds. Then it occurred to him that it was not really a window but a door to the balcony, on which the stranger was standing. The idea that it was simply a burglar was absurd—a burglar would not just stand there calmly and stare at the owner of the apartment through the door window. And what would a burglar get from a young engineer who had just spent all his savings on the cheapest two-room apartment on the top floor?

And the face kept staring, motionless, without blinking, without coming closer. Artem stepped forward. He reached out, groped for the bolt, and opened it with difficulty. The door had settled during the winter and creaked harshly. The second door opened more easily, and Artem, hunching over from the wind's resilient blows, stepped out onto the balcony.

The dark face, hanging somewhere off to the side, began to float gently away into the darkness, the balcony railing flared up in a phosphorescent flame and disappeared; Artem stretched out his arms and squeezed himself against the rough brick wall, but it was too late to find the door behind him because the entire darkness in front of him suddenly came alive, started to move toward him like a huge black cat, and Artem felt a soundless immeasurable paw seize him, pick him up, press him against its furry warm belly, and in that tickling warmth he began to suffocate, but he had no strength to struggle, or even to cry out.

The nightmare continued, magnified tenfold by its endlessness. Artem was tossed about, softly pushed from side to side, but there was no way he could float up to the ceiling or down to the floor—every time a firm blast of air changed his movement, and he continued to float, fall, soar, and the worst torment of all was precisely the absence of anything solid whatsoever that he could grab onto. The air was terrifying in its thickness— it burst his body from within, and Artem felt like a deep-sea fish tossed into a tub of distilled water. He felt no hunger or thirst—on the contrary he was stuffed to the brim with something sickeningly sweet, and all of it together—the space around him, the air, the forced feeding—it was all nonhuman, unthinkable. *Not right.* In all likelihood, he was in some kind of sleep or unconsciousness, but everything around him and within him was such a torment for his body that he constantly regained consciousness and, unable to bear it, blacked out again. And so on without end.

His cheek hurt from the cold, and he awoke. Ay-yay-yay, he thought, so this is how young engineers die from overwork. Sitting on the kitchen floor and hugging the refrigerator.

He yanked the handle on the refrigerator toward him, and took a bottle of not-yet-chilled beer. His hand was shaking so uncontrollably that he had to lean against the refrigerator and slurp out the beer while holding the bottle with both hands, like a bear cub drinking milk from a baby bottle in a circus act. He automatically put the empty bottle in his shopping bag and stroked his chin. He should shave today, but tomorrow was a holiday; he stroked one cheek, then the other—a day and a half of whiskers had disappeared. Well, maybe he had stopped off at the barber's on the way home?

Artem got up and wandered into the living room, still rubbing his chin in confusion. He stopped in the living room and groped for a long time along the wall, trying to find the light switch. For an instant his glance stopped on the ashen, dimly outlined square of the window. A kind of oppressive memory stirred in him, but did not rise to the surface, did not take shape. His fingers found the switch, there was a click, and Artem was crushed to see that the hallucination—perhaps insanity—was still going on.

A woman, as small as a lizard, was lying on his daybed.

She was sleeping. Artem tiptoed over to her and quietly, so as not to awaken her, moved away the chair and sat down on it backward, resting his mysteriously shaven chin on its back.

The woman did not move. Her slender body looked as if it had been thrown there, and thrown quite carelessly, as something no one has to be careful about is thrown. No normal person would sleep in such an uncomfortable position.

It was only then that Artem realized she must be feeling bad and he should help, and that the need for help was the most important thing, and he rushed over to her and raised her up slightly by her thin, strangely sloping shoulders. For a split second he froze and gazed in amazement at the shoulders, because such shoulders did and could not exist in nature, but then before his eyes he pictured the watercolor portrait of Natalya Goncharova. And he, forced to believe in the verisimilitude of those shoulders, let them go and headed as fast as he could to the kitchen for water.

But the water served no real purpose, because he could not figure out what to do with it. He was too timid to sprinkle it over her head, and there was no chance of pouring it in her mouth—the woman's lips were tightly shut. True, from literary sources he had learned that in such circumstances the jaws could be separated with a dagger. But to hell with literature! What should he do about this person right here? Yell? Call for help? Call for help—emergency. Damn, if there were only a public telephone in working order nearby! But Artem knew that there was none around. And how could he leave her alone? Oh, the helplessness of the contemporary civilized twenty-four-year-old!

And then he saw her eyes come to life. Not her eyelashes, just the eye beneath the bulging eyelid; and then the eyelashes had their turn, but they were too gigantic and heavy to move. Well, he would prompt her—as though her opening her eyes would be a cure for all of today's ills. The woman was the most improbable of all the things that had come to pass this cursed evening—not her appearance, but she herself, resembling no one in the world, *not right*. What it was exactly Artem did not have time to determine, because at that moment he saw her eyes.

"Ugh," he said with relief and sat down on the edge of the daybed. "I was. . . ."

But she had already thrown up her hands, covering her face, and there, in the narrow gap between her palms and her lips, a desperate, almost childlike, scream was throbbing: "*Non, non, non, non, non.* . . ." He grabbed her hands—and now the scream filled the room to overflowing, bouncing off the walls, resounding from every direction. And then broke off. Oh, damn, Artem thought, again! Without standing up, he leaned over and pulled a woolen blanket out of the chest. That was right. What he should have done long ago. He covered her shoulders, the lily shoulders of Natalya Goncharova. After all, where today can you find a woman who faints at the sight of a handsome man? It's unthinkable.

He bent over her, staring intently at her face, then leaned back and whistled softly. Well, I'll be, he said to himself—before him lay a beauty with disheveled and luxuriant hair and arrow-long lashes. Why didn't he notice right away? Probably, he was fooled by the expression of unceasing suffering in that remarkable face. And then, just the fact of the woman's appearance. . . . If it was a woman? He looked again. And almost whistled again. She was no more than fifteen, just a girl, a schoolgirl, most likely. A schoolgirl? Or a witch, that's what she was. Or an agent of the Intelligence Service. After all, she yelled out in fright, "Non, non, non." That means she isn't Russian. Maybe an Estonian, or Latvian—they're also blonde.

The witch, or the secret agent, began to sob softly in her sleep. Artem fixed the blanket. The poor tormented foundling, from who knows where. She had taken shelter, and was sleeping now. She probably could use a good hot cup of tea.

Artem got up, and still feeling a cottony unsteadiness in his legs, went into the kitchen. After all this action from the *Tales of Hoffmann*, he really felt like something—not exactly to eat, or to drink, or to fling open the window and hang from the ledge. Deciding on the simplest thing, he opened the refrigerator. To hell with his guests, he'd worried enough about them. If worse came to worst, he could always run over to the delicatessen. He pulled out ham, butter, and apricot compote—to let it warm up, not give her in her exhausted state something straight from the refrigerator. And the ladies tomorrow would have to make do without.

He started eating without any appetite and began thinking about the sleeping arrangements. He still had not equipped himself with a folding bed, although he had been meaning to for a long time, in order to put up stay-late guests without taxi fare. Of course, the couch was wide enough for two, but the uninvited guest seemed to have scruples. In all probability she had not been to any all-night parties where everyone ended up sleeping side by side. He'd have to sleep on the floor. He went back toward the living room, stopping on the threshold because unblinking, terror-widened eyes were staring at him from the couch. Were he to take another step, the resounding scream would break loose again. Artem leaned against the doorway. However difficult it seemed, they had to talk things out. After all, every school teaches some kind of foreign language. "Non." She had screamed, "Non."

"Speak English?"

Her eyes did not even blink.

"*Sprechen Sie Deutsch?*"

Well, thank God she did not answer because that was the limit of his German, picked up while watching a movie. Well, what then? He shrugged his shoulders expressively. She looked at him for a long time from under her blanket, then whispered something inaudible. He stepped forward—

and her eyes fluttered in fear. She repeated it, but so fast that the only thing he could understand was that she was speaking French. He did not even have a single sentence at his disposal.

"Paris," he said furiously, "Notre-Dame, the 'Internationale,' revolution, the 'Marseillaise.' Henri the Fourth. That's my entire vocabulary, beyond that we'll have to make do with gestures. Marcel Marceau, you understand? Although we can leave the explanations until tomorrow, and today just get to know each other. We'll have to do like the savages and poke each other with our fingers, 'Me Tarzan, you Jane, Jane, Tarzan'— do you remember that scene?"

Establishing contact between two such erudite people is going to be rough, he thought angrily. And this during the space age. It's not very pleasant to be remembered as an absolute fool by such a pretty woman.

"My name is Artem," he said. "Artem!" And for greater clarity he pounded his chest with his fist. Like an orangutan, he thought, annoyed.

"My name is Denise," a voice came from under the blanket. "But I speak Russian poorly."

"Thank heavens!" A load dropped from his shoulders. "You speak as well as King Solomon, like Cicero, like Assistant Professor Vasilyev lecturing on the international situation. Only let's put off our talks until tomorrow, otherwise my head will split, and I can see your eyelids drooping. Sleep well, and dream of home."

"*Mon Paris natal,*" she whispered softly.

"So Paris, then." Artem couldn't care less, as long as he could lie down and sleep. "It's a question of taste. Although, of course, to dream about what you'll never see in real life."

"I was borned there," Denise said slowly, choosing her words with apparent effort. "*Mon Dieu, je confonds des mots simples,*" she whispered very, very softly.

"Was born there," Artem corrected her without thinking. And only then did he realize what she had said. "Aha, so it is the damned service after all."

"I don't understand. . . . What about 'service'?"

"Don't mind me. Are you hungry?"

"No."

"Too quick an answer to be true. Let me bring you something."

The can opener had disappeared, and Artem was busy in the kitchen for a rather long time, opening the can of apricot compote with a penknife. When he finally succeeded, he sprinkled the contents into a dish and carried it out to Denise.

"Here you go," he said as he walked up, but she had already put out her arm, defending herself from him.

"Oh, damn it!" he set the dish down angrily on the chair that stood between him and the couch. The shiny apricots with a piggish self-satisfaction were strewn over the narrow dish, eloquently dividing his own room into French and Soviet territory. "All right, then, as you wish."

He wiped off the blade of the knife and tried to fold it, but his hands were still trembling from the recent hallucination, and the knife, still unfolded, slipped out of Artem's hand and flew downward, blade first. Both of them saw the blade flash through the air like a silver minnow, touch the floor, and . . . go into it. All the way. As though it were not a wood floor but custard. A barely detectable ring expanded over the surface; its weak shadow slid under Artem's shoes—and everything had disappeared.

Artem, stunned, stared at the floor, at the spot where the latest miracle had occurred. Then he raised his head and crossed glances with Denise. They looked at each other as though the other were the most malevolent of demons in human form; they immediately hated each other for all of the evening's senseless impossibilities, for the nightmare of the pointless miracles, for their unasked-for meeting—and each one thought that the other was responsible.

Artem regained his senses first. That was the limit. He had had enough of all these tricks, and he was fed up. He dashed to the foyer and pulled a coat off the coatstand. He had no idea of what he was going to do— sleep over at a friend's, wander the frozen streets until morning, or find a public telephone and report the incident to the appropriate authorities— but he could no longer tolerate the mockery of his own mind.

If she had been just a tiny bit different, he would never have had the idea of accusing her of what had happened, but her unbelievable beauty in itself made her an accomplice in all the madness. He threw open the door and flew out into the hall—and saw around him a silvery evening garden.

And then he felt calm. Damn it anyway, he said to himself, it's not every day that you get to see such a magical, colorful, wide-screened, stereoscopic and stereophonic dream. Might as well take advantage of it. The thought made him laugh. So then, let's have this dream in full and complete detail.

The black little cartoon pyramids of the trees, glued evenly to the lower border of a dull, lifeless sky; the dark lines of straight paths—like rails— and between them shimmers of bright gray mother-of-pearl colors seeming not to grow from the ground but to overflow from a magic pot that instead

of the Grimms' porridge kept cooking an infinite colored mass until it
filled to overflowing this little toy world.

And in the middle of this garden, bewitched by an ashen half-light, the
total absence of any odors whatsoever, and a unique, sticky silence—right
in the middle was a little Disney house, sitting there totally naturally. Its
irregularity of form suggested the floor plan of Artem's apartment; it had
been built out of traditional brick and had a pointed straw roof. A cute
little hut. There was no chimney, but a touchingly white number shone
on the front door. Artem quietly, almost on tiptoes, went around the
house, keeping his arm and shoulder against the rough wall—for some
reason he was afraid to take even one step away from it. A turn—and
wallpaper rustled under his fingers. Of course, right here would be the
magnificent apartment belonging to his neighbor Vikentich, the four-
fingered butcher who had already managed to stop by for a cigarette. But
all that was left was the lonely wallpaper, already scratched in places by
Vikentich's watchdog.

And around the next corner were the windows. His windows—first the
kitchen window, with the scallions lying on the sill, and then the lighted
double balcony door. The balcony was resting flat on the ground, and
grabbing its ugly iron railing, Artem suddenly and vividly imagined that
the entire hallucination of the deathly garden had vanished, and the soil
dissolved beneath his feet, bringing back the old nine-story abyss between
his balcony and the ground. His terror over that imagined emptiness was
so great that Artem almost leaped over the railing and burst back into the
room through the balcony door, but through the pane he could see the
daybed and on it, Denise, lying face down. He forced himself to let go of
the saving railing and trotted around the last wall; pushing with his whole
body against the front door, he found himself in the foyer.

Denise did not move, as if she had not heard his steps. But the fluffy
texture of the blanket breathed evenly and infrequently, like the fur on
the back of a sleeping kitten. Artem walked over to the daybed and plopped
heavily on the edge.

"I was just out there," he pointed with his thumb toward the window.
"A regular hanging garden of Babylon. In the middle of the garden is an
open space, and in it is our little cottage. Do you want to take a look?"

She raised her head, looked indifferently out the window, then murmured barely audibly, "*Mais c'est égal,*" and once again dropped her head.

And now he finally got really frightened, because it wasn't just himself
but another person having the same dream. Whoever she was, he was still
a man, and older, and stronger. He didn't know a word of French, but

understood her perfectly—it didn't matter, to such a degree that she would not eat or drink but just roll up under her blanket into a little ball, like a baby bird abandoned in its nest, who would die without any ado. And he would not know what to do for her, since now there was no question of running to the nearest phone and calling for help.

"Come on now," he said firmly, "you're going to have to listen to me. We're going to have supper now."

The water in the kitchen worked beautifully—both hot and cold. So did the gas. Artem made some tea and almost forcibly made Denise drink it. He himself did not feel like anything after all the revelations, but his position made it his duty, so to set a good example he crammed down a few plump Moroccan sardines. Finishing his gastronomic feat, Artem felt that he could do no more.

"My watch says ten-thirty . . . Damn it! It stopped. We'll have to keep track from an arbitrary beginning. Outside it's pitch-black, not a single light on the horizon, so we probably won't be able to figure out anything that way. And accordingly, in my capacity as leader, I am putting off all questions until tomorrow and ordering everyone to get to sleep. Personally I'm dead tired."

He carefully locked the doors and checked the windows, then took out his toolbox and found a small but recently sharpened hatchet. As a weapon it was a joke, but it would have to do.

"Move over," he said to Denise. She blinked in confusion. "Move over, move over. You said nothing matters."

She flattened herself against the wall in fear. Artem shoved the hatchet under his pillow and stretched out blissfully next to Denise.

"We Russians have a nice proverb," he muttered as he closed his eyes. 'With your love, even a hovel is heaven.' Have you heard it?" The pillow under his cheek moved—Denise must have been shaking her head yes or no. "So then, heaven is at hand, our hovel is quite comfortable, you'll just have to imagine that I am the love of your life." Once again Denise quivered fearfully, but she could not move away any further. "Come on now, don't be afraid—I said to imagine. And my hovel is European. But you know what's the most terrifying thing in all this insanity?" Denise held her breath. "I think we're absolutely alone—"

He woke up.

He felt astonishingly light. The air tickled him inside each time he inhaled; his arms, when he raised them to put his hands behind his head and stretch, seemed to fly up by themselves, as though each had a dozen brightly colored balloons attached to it. And generally speaking, things couldn't be better, life was great, no need to sweat anything. But if something was not quite right, it was just so that he could overcome, surpass, redo, rebuild. And achieve.

A state of mild intoxication. Careful now, Artem. While you were sleeping, something happened to you. And maybe not to you but to everything around you. To the air, for example.

Artem groped in his pocket for a box of matches, crushed during the night, and lit one. The flare was brighter than he expected. Or maybe it just seemed that way. He lit another and only then remembered Denise. What a fool, I'll scare her.

He carefully put his legs over the edge of the daybed, stood up, and almost skipping—it happening of its own accord, not because he was particularly happy—made his way to the foyer. Okay, let us determine once and for all where we are. He opened the door and went out into the garden. The merriness, artificial and imposed, remained, but his confidence steadily evaporated. Yes, where are we, really? Into his head popped all kinds of boyhood nonsense about moss on the north side of trees, or anthills, which were usually on the south slope. But in the paradise garden there were neither mosses nor anthills. The gloom of night melted abruptly, but nowhere among the even spaces between the trees could he see even a dim spot of a hidden sun nor the rosy hues of dawn. The sky was covered with light but unusually low clouds; they hung motionless and, just beyond the trees, descended all the way to the ground. It seemed as though the garden with the tiny house in its midst was covered with a translucent jellylike bell jar. Not a single rustle, not a single breeze.

He went back.

"Get up," he said as he sat down on the edge of the daybed. He put his hand on the blanket where there was a hint of a slender shoulder. "Just don't pull any nonsense about being scared, the way you did before."

She turned her face toward him, shuddering with the unforgotten horrors of the day before, and Artem was suddenly terrified as a person can be terrified only in childhood, when he or she meets, while awake, something that cannot be, that cannot exist, like the Big Bad Wolf or the Wicked Witch of the West.

Right then he was struck by the inhuman beauty—the beauty not of nature but of art—of her face.

"You overslept," he said deliberately loudly, destroying the spell. "We have to determine our location by the stars. The north, south, and so on. But it's foggy." She looked at him, apparently not understanding what he was saying, and he himself did not hear or understand his own words.

"Fog. Clouds right over your head. Behind the trees they were lying on the ground. Just fog, and in the middle of the fog, us. You and I."

He was shielding himself from her with words, as though if he were to remain silent he would be defenseless against the demonic power of her beauty.

"So come on, get up," he shouted in desperation. "I have enough problems without you."

She obediently stood up and went into the bathroom, stepping fearfully and lightly, as though the floor, which had so mysteriously swallowed up the unfortunate knife last night, might once again give way. On the threshold she stopped short, listening with amazement, but not to sounds outside, because all around the same persistent silence reigned, but to something of her own, within her skin, something stirring within.

"That's strange," she said. "I'm all . . . *légère* . . . light. All I have to do is breathe out. . . ."

"And what then?" Artem asked, for some reason whispering.

"Then I could fly."

"Yes," he said, "yes. . . ." And he had no doubt that she would really be able to.

And he imagined her going out onto the balcony, leaning out over the railing—but damn it, he had forgotten that the balcony was flat on the ground. But all the same, all the same. She would stand up on the railing, take a little hop and without even flapping her arms, would begin to rise gently, toward the jellylike gray bell jar that covered the garden. The contours of her body would be vague, blurry; and then she would. . . . A door slammed—Denise disappeared into the bathroom.

Artem let out a deep and noisy breath and shook himself, like a duck coming out of a pond. Indeed, whenever he looked at Denise, all sorts of crazy ideas popped into his head.

Well, here's the plan: Grab something to eat, get his things together, and go scouting. After all, this garden of paradise could not stretch on for miles and miles. It had to end somewhere. Get to the end, and you could tell what to do next.

"Are you ready?" he asked Denise as she came out. "Sit down, have something to eat. You'll stay here, and I'll take a look around the area."

She shook her head in desperation.

"Listen when people are talking to you. If anyone had wanted to take you away . . . now don't look so terrified! Look, since you and I were put in this little cottage, it means that someone wants us to be together. And if they wanted to do anything to you, you'd better believe that they've already had their chance. So sit here and don't go away from the house. The hatchet is on the daybed, just in case. And don't make those faces."

He felt like slapping her on the shoulder buddy-buddy but stopped himself in time. Damn it, but he had nearly forgotten that she had shoulders that weren't made to be slapped buddy-buddy.

Woo, damn it all. He had to shake his head again.

"Keep up your courage, princess," he said in an unnaturally cheerful tone and stepped out the door.

Right at the door a good dozen paths led away from the house in a fan pattern. Choose the simplest variant: Go straight ahead, so that the cottage remains at your back the whole time.

He took several steps and realized that he could not go straight ahead. The path twisted and turned like a snake, losing itself among the noiseless masses of high bushes, which wove into each other with three-tined thorns the size of a chicken's foot. Artem unconsciously turned around—the thatch roof of the cottage had already disappeared behind a turn. A spool of fishing line or even of ordinary wire, two hundred yards long, would have come in handy. And Denise could hold one end.

He imagined the picture from a distance: a tall lanky guy on a fishing-line leash, like a house dog. So we are cowards, it seems? He walked decisively forward. The narrow path kept looping, slipping out from under his feet; it was strewn with large-grained red sand. Artem still could not figure out what was unusual, what was *not right* about the sand, and then he realized: he was not leaving footprints. None at all. To confirm his observation he squatted down and wrote a capital *D* in the sand with his finger. By the time he raised his hand it had disappeared completely, as though it had been written on water. Not a dimple, not a bump.

Only the red and gluttonous sand, in which things disappeared without a trace.

He ran back. A turn. Another turn. He collided with a grabby branch hanging over the path. He thrashed loose and started running again. Faster. Still faster. He tripped. A root. Damn it. What kind of root? There hadn't been any roots. There hadn't even been any trees. None at all. He must have turned off somewhere. Without noticing that the path forked. Back!

Back. But how far? He had already been running for more than a mile and hadn't seen a fork, and it was nothing like the first path. A grove all around. Why had he turned around? What had he been afraid of? If he had kept on for a while, maybe there would have been trees after all. By now he would have been home. Back!

Back. More and more trees. Easy does it. No running. But he was dying of thirst. Walk slowly. Slowly go back. That's the way. He had been going back for a half hour already. How many times had he turned back? And where was his house? How many times this morning had he turned around? If he only had a landmark, no matter how trivial. He did not even dream about the sun. The smoky belly of the mousy gray sky dropped right over the treetops. He slowly strolled forward. Forward? If only he could be sure.

An hour passed before he thought of climbing a tree and looking around. The helplessness of a civilized milksop, he thought with a masochistic saitsfaction.

He chose what he thought was the tallest tree, forced his way to it through the underbrush, and kicked off his shoes. The trunk was smooth, and climbing up to the lowest branches proved to be fiendishly difficult. But after that it was easier, and near the top he stuck his head out past the leaves and looked down.

He saw what is called a virgin forest: a sea of greenery, remarkably single-toned greenery, without even a patch of a slightly different shade. As though a helicopter had sprayed the forest with a poisonous-emerald vitriol. If it hadn't been for the path, neatly strewn with the large-grained, ferri-ferous sand, he would have said that no human had ever set foot in this region.

But was that really a path down there? He would not have been at all surprised if it had totally disappeared. But the path was still there, and leaping onto it, Artem once again could not determine the direction from which he had approached the tree. But did it really matter? All he could do was follow his instincts. Or not go anywhere. What was the sense of rushing back and forth, if the magic door had closed shut? What new and unnatural marvels had been prepared for him at both ends of the path, and most important, for what reason? Ever since that damned evening when he let the bags fall to the floor with a thud in his new apartment, someone was persistently and methodically playing games with his sanity. He remembered that in one of the concentration camps they tried to determine how much time a man could endure in a rarefied atmosphere. Or how much cold he could stand.

Was he the subject of some monstrous experiment to determine how many marvels the ordinary human brain could stand? And who was Denise— an accomplice or a fellow guinea pig?

It was strange, but the thought of Denise did not call forth the memory of her face. Indistinct memories of something beautiful—that was all. And after all, what was so unusual about her? With difficulty he forced himself to remember each feature in isolation—her lips, eyebrows, hair. It was all beautiful, no doubt, but the perfect components fit together into an ab-solutely expressionless, flat face. Nothing exceptional, and if he didn't ever

see her again, he would feel no great disappointment. But to find her now?
He was not about to budge from where he was. If anyone needed him,
let them come find him. He plopped down on the ground, kicking up the
sand with his shoes, and at that very moment he heard a pleading call
coming from nearby. It was Denise calling, not loudly, as if from pain or
fright, but slightly confused, pleading, as though asking, "Where are you?"

And once again, "Aaaah," but now the voice did contain fear.

He leaped to his feet, and without thinking rushed into a thicket, straight
at the voice. And when he forced his way out onto the clearing, the cottage
was standing about ten yards away, and in the doorway, her legs folded
and gray flowers strewn across her lap, sat Denise in a bucolic pose. He
understood very well that the whole picture was just a little bit too much
like a Christmas card in his grandmother's old album—all that was missing
was the cooing doves—and along with that sober thought he felt that he
would grab her—only her delicate shoulders would move—and just the
way she was, with folded legs and flowers in her lap, embrace her . . . he
was only a step away from her when he managed to overcome the delusion.
Slowing for a moment and catching his breath, he took the last step and,
pulling up his trouser legs, squatted down in front of her.

"What happened?" he asked. "Afraid?"

"Yes," she agreed readily. "You were so long . . . *dans ce fourré* . . .
out there," she waved vaguely with her hand. "I wanted to call. . . ."

She hesitated and lowered her head. A confused suspicion once again
arose in him; she did not want to let him go. She was keeping him near
her. He went away, and right away she raised a fuss.

"So then," Artem fixed her with his gaze, "you wanted to call me. And
then?"

"I wanted to call . . . and then . . . I forgot your name."

He had prepared himself not to believe her. No matter what she said,
he should not believe her.

But these words, uttered with a childish helplessness, in some strange
way coincided with his recent mental state. After all, he himself could not
remember her face.

This was the last thing he had expected.

"Artem."

"Artem."

"Say it again."

"Monsieur Artem."

"Forget about the imported titles. Just Artem."

"Artem, Artem, Artem."

"Now that's a good girl. Is there anything else bothering you?"

"I'm afraid of tomorrow"—not without reason, Artem thought, I'm afraid to today—"I'm afraid I'll wake up tomorrow and you won't be there. Not even a memory of you. Nothing."

He looked at her, stunned, as though she were the eighth wonder of the world.

"I thought it didn't matter."

"That was while you were near me."

So that's it!

"Don't be afraid, I won't leave you. Of course, it was stupid of me to go by myself. If you hadn't called me. . . . Why don't you ask what I saw out there?"

"That is something that doesn't matter."

"It's just a garden. An endless, lonely garden, and if we leave our little house, I don't think we'll be able to come back."

"Then why leave?"

He stood up and went into the house without saying anything. He wanted to avoid explanations.

"Get ready," he said.

From the doorway Denise watched in confusion as he shoved bread and canned goods in a bag, and folded a blanket.

"This is for you," he threw her his sweater. "It will be cold at night."

He left the door ajar and did not even look back.

"You go first." He let her ahead of him on the path, too narrow for two to walk abreast. "It's time for us to have a chat."

She did not answer.

"Who are you, anyway?" he asked.

She walked on several steps in silence, as though she were thinking over her answer, then turned around in full stride, and he saw her calm beautiful face: I am what I am, as I was born. More literature.

"Are you Russian?" A stupid question—Russian faces don't look like that.

"Mama was."

"That makes sense. A victim of prerevolutionary migration."

"No, the last war. My father and mother met in a camp and could not leave each other."

Well, if Denise looked like her mother, you couldn't blame her father. Although that might just be a convincing story. A story. And one from a B movie. And what spy would be interested in him, a fledgling engineer? It was ridiculous. To block off a forest like this, drag him out to this wilderness, and set him up with such a beauty, an underaged Mata Hari?

Nonsense, absolute nonsense. The girl was like any other girl, an ordinary schoolgirl, although a real knockout. Looking at her from the back, he was dumbfounded. She should be an actress; in the West they say it's easy for an amateur. But maybe she is a professional actress. Her fright before, and the shrieks, and the helplessness? If she were an ordinary schoolgirl, Russian or French, she'd be dragging along exhausted by now. But she's still going strong. Should I ask her a question? She'll answer. When she was born and what her concierge's name is, and what kind of stone is used to pave her courtyard. And she'll name the street, too. Should I ask, when I'm not going to believe her answer?

And she kept walking, without leaving tracks in the coarse sand that did not crunch underfoot.

"Maybe you're getting tired?"

She kept walking, and didn't even look back. Well, he did not have any right to be concerned about her. No right at all, as long as she still had strength left. When the strength comes to an end, the right would come into being all by itself. A strong right. A right to be concerned, to help, to—

Oh, damn it!

"Maybe I should go first?"

Then he wouldn't see her in front of him. But once again she did not answer and continued to walk noiselessly ahead down the red winding path on which no footprints remained.

They walked, walked, walked, and their heads were already spinning from the countless turns, and they felt like collapsing and lying there the way she was lying when he first saw her on the daybed in his apartment, to lie there as though you had been thrown there, and not even attempt to change the position of your body.

Denise stopped so suddenly that Artem had to take another step and grab her by the shoulders—the path was so narrow that they could not stand next to each other. She looked back.

"That's it," she sighed. "I've had it. That's all."

He had been waiting for it to happen, but now he suddenly felt confused.

"Just a little farther, Denise," he mumbled, as though a little farther would make a difference. "Maybe up ahead there will be at least a clearing."

They had now been walking for several hours, but there had been no clearings, only a wall of thorny brambles and the coarse sand of the path.

"I'll carry you."

She shook her head no.

"What do you suggest, then?"

Her shoulders gave way beneath his hands; he squeezed them harder, but nothing helped—she had disappeared, melted right out of his grasp.

But he did manage to catch up and lift her. Such a light body, even lighter than he had imagined. Aha, he caught himself, so you, it seems, had already imagined carrying her. And how long has it been? He tried to take long, even steps. Like a camel. But the lightness of a body was deceptive. Even hers, apparently weightless, would, after two hundred yards, become a terrible burden. That he knew for sure. He knew it from his day-before-yesterday life, that had remained alongside the refrigerator with the grocery bags that had clattered to the floor.

"Artem," she said loudly right into his ear, "let me go."

"What is it now?" he asked, carefully taking a breath between his words. "Having a conversation when you're carrying someone is a lost cause."

"Let me go. Completely." Artem walked on in silence, trying to keep his hand over her bare knees so that the gray-blue claws of the thorns would scratch them as little as possible even though they stretched out to the middle of the path. *"Si vous ne me laissez partir aussitôt. . . ."* she shouted in a high and harsh tone.

"Don't yell in my ear," Artem requested.

She pressed her face against his neck and fell silent.

"Wait just a little, maybe we'll find a clearing. Then we can rest."

And then around the corner a level velvety clearing appeared obediently.

He squatted down, still not letting go of Denise, and felt the grass—it was light and dry, like hay.

"Here we are—now you can rest."

Denise remained silent. He set her down on the warm grass, in which not a single grasshopper was chirring, not a single beetle was creeping. Dead underbrush, a dead clearing.

And the totally wiped out, pinched-looking face of Denise. That was no act. Even if she became a famous actress, even then she'd never be able to act so realistically.

But wouldn't it be funny if a dozen years from now he recognized her in the latest Hollywood superfilm and could casually toss out to his buddies: "I sure had a hell of a time when I had to haul that *mademoiselle* in my arms. That was when we were lost in—"

Lost in . . . , that was problem number one. Really—was it the Andes, the Appalachians, Burma, Venezuela, Herzogovina?

Maybe she knows? Catch her unawares—even if she doesn't say, maybe she'll betray herself in her confusion.

"Where are we?" he asked quickly.

She turned her calm face toward him.

"You're asking me?"

She did not know. She could not know and lie so well.

"We're not in Europe."

She did not object.

"They've taken us somewhere, and it must have taken them quite a while. We're not in Africa—it's not hot here. No sounds reach us, no wind. That means we're in a small valley, surrounded by mountains. High mountains. Are there such mountains in Australia? I don't believe so. But we're not high up in the mountains—otherwise it would be hard to breathe. Logical? Now, the heavy fog points to the nearness of water. There's water nearby, and a lot of it. Perhaps an ocean? But I don't seem to recall any uninhabited mountains on the Asian coast. Damn, and I got an A in geography. So that leaves South America, the Andes. Are you very tired?"

Denise just shook her head yes.

"It would be good if we could make it to those mountains by the evening. The valley must be tiny, otherwise we'd feel a wind."

Her hand automatically went up, and her fingers moved, as though the wind was something tangible, something that could be caught. Her hand fell back down.

Such damned sentimentality, such cheap chivalry! His tongue would not budge to say, "Well, let's get going." But they had to, they simply had to! They couldn't wait there for the next magic trick to be played on them.

"Denise . . . ," he said almost guiltily.

"Yes?"

"Let's get going, Denise."

She sighed very gently and stood up.

And so they walked and walked until it got dark—first Denise strolled ahead, then she began to glance around, and Artem carried her. Then they happened upon a clearing. They lay down next to each other and stared at each other, because overhead was an immobile sky, seemingly congealed during its fall to the ground, and it was terrifying to look at it.

Then they got up and walked on.

Darkness set in suddenly, too suddenly, as though someone had pushed a huge rheostat as fast as it would go. They walked for a while in the dark, but there were no more clearings to make life easy.

"It's okay," Artem said. "It's not the worst thing that could happen. The sand on the path is warm."

He began to unbutton his jacket, when a light shone up ahead. They did not run toward it, and not because Denise could hardly drag herself along—no, that evening they felt a certain caution. They soundlessly crept ahead, until the light became a bright window; seizing the railing of the tiny fence, Artem sprang over, and staying to the side of the window, peeked in.

The rumpled daybed with the check blanket, the empty dish on the chair in the middle of the room, and near the door on the floor, the black sweater, which Denise had ignored.

"Who's there?" Denise asked timidly from behind.

If only someone were there!

"No one," Artem said, letting her look for herself. "You don't have to be afraid of anyone."

No one, just the same house, empty, awaiting their return. Like a trap. Behind him the door slammed shut, and Artem automatically reached back to see if it would open again. The door swung gently open. Today they had tried to do just that. Well, tomorrow they would try once more.

"Just don't go to sleep," he said to Denise. "I'll make some coffee now, or otherwise tomorrow you won't be able to stand up."

But she was already lying on the daybed, just as she did the day before: as though she had not lain down herself but been thrown there like a dress. He turned around and on tiptoes, so as not to awaken her, and went to the kitchen. Here, too, everything was the way it had been. The loaf of bread in the waxed bag, a heap of cans on the bottom of the refrigerator. Even the apricots. Maybe he didn't really open them? No, he definitely had, and then there was the knife. . . . The penknife lay on the table. The penknife that cost two rubles fifteen kopecks—exactly the same one. And the coffee? The coffee in the can was up to the top, as it had been last night.

He no longer felt hungry.

He went back to the living room, carefully moved Denise over against the wall, and lay down beside her. She opened her eyes halfway.

"Incidentally," he said in a whisper, "we really are in the garden of paradise. And the refrigerator is our manna."

She frowned slightly—annoyed and indifferent. "No . . . not a garden," she muttered, falling back asleep. "In a garden there are flowers . . . and in paradise . . . *des pommiers*, apple trees. . . ."

Artem chuckled loudly, then squinted. No, it was okay, she hadn't awakened. Now he grinned in silence—mister teacher, I should have your problems. She wants an apple tree. That's my Eve for you. Is she an Eve? He examined her face. Whom did she resemble? Each separate feature reminded him of someone, sometimes quite definite—the shoulders of Natalya Goncharova, the hair of Catherine II, the chin of Audrey Hepburn. . . . Although . . . Helen of Troy was only ten years old, they say, when Paris abducted her. Juliet was thirteen. Eve herself was probably not an adult and certainly not a great beauty. Look at the painting by Jean Eiffel—the primordial featherbrain who's dying to get her hands on the paradisal McIntosh. No reason to expect her to turn out like this one here. The good Lord God, when he created Eve, didn't have any model at his disposal, and in his ignorance didn't even have the slightest inkling of the basic principles of industrial design. A primitive craftsman.

Tens of centuries had to pass before such a marvel could be born on Earth. And finally the marvel was born, but to what end? Heaven only knows that it would have been better if they had provided him with his kind of girl. At least he would know how to act. He'd get her to learn elementary tourist tricks, so that she wouldn't ask to be carried every hundred paces. They'd go crashing through that lousy paradise singing popular songs, and when they reached whoever it was who arranged all this, you wouldn't have to be afraid even if things got rough.

But this one? It was hard even to call her human. In the old days they would say "A face carved of alabaster." The feeling of something unearthly in the image remained, even though the average person does not have the slightest idea what alabaster is.

But all the same—a face carved from alabaster, there was no getting around it. A capricious dimple at the corner of her mouth. An apple tree she asked for!

And when they woke up the next morning it was already light, and through the window they could see a huge pentagonal flower bed, in flaming color, the kind that ornament the central squares of provincial towns. The bed was crowned by a green flower of unbelievable size.

To the left and right of the bed stood two grapevines covered with tomato-red apples.

"Arise, princess," Artem tried to talk as gaily as possible so that she would not notice his fear. "Something must have prompted the local Merlin to grant your wish. Let's go take a look."

They went out to the flowerbed. An unprecedented outburst of colors, every shade of red and purple, but the flowers were identical—five primitive petals, a tiny bottle of the pistil, and the bristles of black stamens. It was simply a flower. Not a camomile, not a rose, not even a buttercup. A botanical diagram. He tried to remember the trees he had seen yesterday, and with horror realized that they too were not poplars or birches, but something average, impersonal, dead in their absolute correctness.

But the thing they had taken for a huge light green peony was not even a flower at all.

In the center of the flowerbed a huge head of cabbage asserted itself insolently.

"Artem," Denise said, raising her calm, completely unfrightened eyes to him. "I'm terrified. This could be done only by . . . ," she did not even try to find the word but just waved her open hand near her head.

Artem was terrified himself. He had long since guessed that they were in the power of some insane but omnipotent maniac, and the only question was how long the insanity would remain within the bounds of the harmless.

Artem leaned over to her and quickly put his finger on her lips. Then he pointed to his ears and made a vague circular motion, intended to mean: Ears could be everywhere.

Denise understood. How could she fail to: After all, what she wished for last night, uttered barely audibly to her pillow, had been heard.

They were being listened to. And maybe even watched. Denise pulled Artem back into the house. They ate hastily and got ready without saying a word. They went outside.

"Yesterday we went straight ahead," Artem broke the silence. "Let's take a different direction, even though I have the impression that the house is not where it was."

He spoke aloud because it was clearly no secret. The grapevines with the tomatolike fruit were wedged into the monotonous greenery of the bushes, and the paths were significantly fewer than yesterday—just three. They chose the one that turned to the left. They walked slower and rested more often than the day before, but all the same by noon it was clear that dragging Denise along was just inhuman.

A plush meadow, dotted with rainbow splashes of primitive five-petaled flowers, was at their service. Artem opened the immortal jar of apricots and spread out the sandwiches. He made Denise eat. And that seemed to be the pattern, making her do things—eat, walk, stand up, lie down. She followed orders submissively. Now he suddenly realized that it took incredible courage on her part. After all, she most likely had been carried through life by helping arms, and fed with the proverbial silver spoon. She could not have grown into what she had become without some such special treatment. Totally a girl yet totally a woman. Completely pampered yet infinitely firm. Beautiful to stupefaction and in her extraordinary beauty fit only to be gazed at starry-eyed. And that was all.

He squinted and carefully looked down—Princess Dream was lying on the grass, rolled up into a little golden ball, like a reddish-brown sea urchin.

"So?" he asked, knowing in advance what she would say. "You're done? You can't take any more?"

"I can," he heard her answer, "but I don't want to. Why bother? We won't get home—ever."

"Come on, now," he said loudly, growing cold from the awareness that she was right. "Knock it off, princess"—he bent down over her and put his hand under her head, where the warmth of her hair was indistinguishable from the human warmth of the dry silky grass.

With a by-now familiar motion he picked Denise up in his arms.

"Why?" Her voice sounded as though she were at least fifty years old. "I ask you, why? Let's stay here."

"All right, then," he slowly let her down. "We'll try staying. Evening isn't far away."

Evening came even sooner than they had expected, and when it had gotten totally dark, about thirty yards away a bright window glimmered ghostlike. The same house as yesterday, the same house with the same jar of apricots in the refrigerator, like a dab of cheese on the mousetrap.

The next day they set out again, this time heading to the right, but by the end of the day they were back at the house. For several days they attempted to escape from their persistently arising house, and every day at evening they would find the bright window and the unlocked door. The place changed. The cabbage patch alternated with the tomato vine, a stream bank with marine algae gave way to rough cliffs overgrown with ten-foot ferns; but the house itself was immutable as it awaited them at the end of their day's travel.

"That's it," Artem said finally. "Tomorrow we're not going anywhere. We'll sit here like fools and wait for whatever they want to do with us."

They waited the whole day, and the most frightening thing was the fact that no one tried to do anything to them. They waited, and the wait became unbearable.

And then Denise found the only way out.

"*C'est assez!* Enough! Everything here is dead: the grass, the sky, us. . . . *Nous sommes au fond.* This is our fate, do you understand, Artem. We're going to die. But to sit and wait. . . . *C'est insupportable,* do you understand? I tell you, better to do it ourselves! Isn't that so?"

Artem looked at her attentively. "Decisively spoken."

He thoughtfully stroked his chin. Denise, of course, blurted that out not because of her great intelligence but because of the hysteria-proneness of her female nature. But still, out of the mouths of babes. . . .

But then maybe a little experiment, just a little courage and restraint on the part of the princess. . . . The goal? To force the enemy to reveal himself, when he evidently did not choose to do so; force him to make a move when he was intending just to observe. The experiment was, of course, not at all subtle, but the enemy—clearly a psycho—might fall for it.

"You won't be a coward, princess?"

Denise lifted up her face—not a sign of desperation, nor a trivial injury to her pride, an unchildlike readiness to submit to his will and reason.

"Then here's what," Artem took from a shelf several old newspapers, crumpled them and piled them on the floor, near the front door.

"We were dragged here," he continued loudly and theatrically, "we apparently have turned out to be of no use. They are not planning on returning us. I agree with you—better to die immediately than to live in ignorance and without any hope of return."

He lit the paper and returned to the daybed. He sat down alongside Denise, took her hands in his so that she would not be frightened. Denise was not looking at the fire but at him, her eyes attentive but not frightened in the slightest.

The newspapers flared up, the first tall tongues of flame were already licking the doorway. Well, now, an elegant move. If they had been dragged here, and this demonic pavilion created for them, and they were fed and every reasonable desire was satisfied, that meant that someone needed them very badly. So now this "someone" would have to take steps to save his living exhibit.

In the room there was the unexpected odor of scorched meat, although both the door and the walls stubbornly resisted burning. A tremble ran over the gray surface of the door, as though someone had blown on the surface of a puddle, and then it flowed away, all at once, as though it was made out of a huge lump of butter. A nauseating lilac smoke rushed through the gap that had been formed, and in the semidarkness of the rapidly descending night they saw the distinct outline of a man standing at the end of the path.

Artem leaped to his feet and jumping over the smoldering heap of newspaper, flew out of the house in hot pursuit of the stranger. If only he did not disappear, if only. . . .

And just then he flew up against a resilient invisible wall. The transparent surface was springy and tossed him backward. On his hands and face he felt an annoying sticky film, as though he had plunged into the body of an enormous jellyfish. Artem automatically lifted his hands to his face to wipe off the sticky slime, but the sensation had been deceptive—his skin was dry. Trying to rid himself of the feeling, Artem started rubbing his cheeks and forehead, and when he took away his hand, he saw the stranger standing a yard away from him, on the other side of the invisible fence.

For a split second they stared intently at one another; but the stranger apparently had already studied Artem very closely, because his eyes betrayed not the slightest sign of a suppressed curiosity; Artem, on the other hand, had nothing to scrutinize, since the stranger's face seemed to represent an average of all the ordinary men's faces. Just a face. Like an anatomical model.

The stranger moved his lips, and it seemed to Artem that the words, pronounced remarkably correctly, sounded with a slight delay with respect to the movements of the lips.

"What is it you need?" the stranger asked slowly and deliberately.

Artem stepped forward and leaned with his hands against the sticky surface of the wall that separated them.

"We want to know where we are and who you are. We want to know what right you had to kidnap us. We want to know what the hell you need from us."

Once again the stranger moved his lips. "Tomorrow morning at dawn," his voice reached to Artem—"I shall speak with you."

The wall clouded over, shook with a tremor like the hide of a threatened animal, then became completely transparent. Artem heard steps behind him—Denise was carefully walking to him.

"What did he say?"

"I think that was the face that appeared on my balcony to lure me outside. When you were abducted, did you notice anyone?"

Denise wrinkled her brow.

"I was sleeping. Then I opened my eyes—I was flying . . . like . . . like between rooms. . . . Not right? I was flying, everything around was dark, and a man, I don't know him, was doing this with his hands"— Denise put her hands up with the palms out and gently waved them, the way someone fans a cloud of smoke—"and I was floating, faster, faster, as though I . . . what's the word? . . . was *un duvet de peuplier*, a tree, no, a poplar—oh yes, dandelion," she sighed with relief. When she had to put together a simple sentence, everything went smoothly, and he was even amazed at the correctness of her speech, but as soon as she tried to go into detail, she floundered in a mixture of Russian and Bas-Gascon in which any sense was hopelessly drowned.

"But there, at home, was a different man. A different man," she glanced at Artem quickly and carefully corrected herself, "a different face. Like . . . a jar."

"Your Russian is improving by leaps and bounds. However, what are your mama and papa going to say when you get home?"

"My father and mother translate your prose . . . what is it? . . . *contemporaine*, contemporary. There they don't have these words . . . someday

I'll tell you. All at once, you will correct me. All right? But when I return. . . ."

Her shoulders suddenly slumped, and she quietly turned around and went back into the house. She stopped in the doorway and without turning around, as though she was not at all concerned whether Artem heard or not, in a whisper, very correctly enunciating each word, said, "I know that I will never return home."

Artem guessed more than heard what she said. The poor little waif stood with her back to him and cried in silence, just trying not to tremble, to keep her shoulders from giving her away.

Don't be so insensitive, go do something, pat her head, or something—a fellow human is crying.

He walked over. And leaned down to her.

"But if we do return," Denise asked, raising her calm, dry eyes to him, "won't you marry me and take me with you?"

"Of course."

What was there to say in a situation like that?

Denise was breathing heavily in her sleep, her face buried against his left shoulder.

He had to free his arm to look at his watch. It took him a while, because the last thing he wanted was to wake up Denise. The conversation he would have was too serious to involve this child in it. The child smacked her lips in her sleep and quietly murmured, "Artem." Well now, not "Mama" but "Artem." Maybe this was not a result of the constant, daily terrors, but maybe. . . . All right. This was not the time to think about it. The hands on his watch were just barely visible, so in another fifteen minutes or so dawn would instantaneously and irreversibly descend. He had to go. And try to remain the master of the situation. Artem walked to the foyer, and looked dubiously at his pants—all these days he had slept without undressing, and this had left his suit in a distressing state. He did not feel, of course, like appearing before the representative of a foreign power in such an unpresentable condition, but it was getting lighter with every minute and there was no question of lingering to polish his appearance.

He went outside. Mornings here were not fresh, just as there was no noonday heat or evening coolness. The broad meadow was empty, and Artem slowly wandered among the insolent and tasteless flowerbeds until he reached the brush. There, near a distant turn, unseen from the house, yesterday's stranger was already waiting for him.

"Sit," he commanded.

Artem cast a sidelong glance—to the left of the path appeared a bench. Artem shoved his hands in his pockets and rocked back and forth, from heel to toe, with a challenging expression. He himself would remain in charge, and he, too, had questions to ask.

"Come closer," he said in the tone of voice that is usually reserved for police headquarters. "And now if you'll make the effort to answer: Where are we?"

The stranger moved his lips and his words came through clearly: "Not on Earth."

Artem thoughtfully stroked his chin. . . . Not on Earth. All his questions evaporated. Not on Earth. That would take some getting used to, that would have to be accepted and digested, and until then nothing had any meaning. True, in the first instant Artem had almost asked, "But are we far from Earth?" but he had realized in time that it was a stupid question.

"Why are you quiet?" the muffled voice asked. "I have received authorization to speak with you and to answer any question."

"We're not on Earth." Artem just shrugged his shoulders. "Nothing else means a damn."

"Is that an idiomatic expression?"

"Exactly. At least tell me why you did it."

"We needed you."

"Us? Denise and me?"

"You and she."

"Two guinea pigs, a black one and a white one. . . . Do you plan on drinking our blood, or what? What can we expect from you—you almost killed her when you dragged her here! What's the matter with you, couldn't you have found someone a little older? Why did you pick on a little girl, that's what I'd like to know!"

"You already care about her?"

Artem stamped his heel dramatically. "The leaders of an alien civilization! Couldn't you have found a different solution?"

The stranger maintained a haughty silence.

"So then, in the future please understand that the question of our rights is not subject to discussion. That's the way it is with us, on Earth."

Something in the stranger's face wavered. Was it a sarcastic sneer? Artem could not tell.

"What is it then that you need from us?"

The stranger pursed his lips, and the lag between their movement and the production of sound increased even more.

"Once we were like you. Now we want to know what the difference between you and us is."

Artem just shrugged his shoulders.

"You have flown to Earth in a ship that we couldn't even dream of. You have the ability to create all this—a tiny quasiterrestrial paradise with the most contemporary of cottages. So couldn't you have constructed a computer that would have calculated the differences between us down to the last atom?"

"Simple quantitative analysis was unproductive. We required direct observation in conditions that maximally approached natural ones."

"So you reached out and took us just as you would take frogs out of a terrarium. You can congratulate me—I can see quite clearly the difference between you and the people of Earth."

"Yes?" said the stranger, and Artem was annoyed by his tone of voice. "Incidentally, I have spent some time near your planet and have observed the life of its inhabitants. These observations have convinced me that the transfer of two inhabitants of Earth, under conditions most favorable to them, would not be the most inhuman action of all those that take place on your planet."

"Your civilization can't be that great if you justify yourself by taking examples of the worst cases on a planet that lags significantly behind yours in development."

"Why are you trying to accuse us of a crime? If we had requested that you voluntarily fly here because we need your help, would you have refused?"

"Of course not. But you have Denise mixed up in this business."

They glanced quickly at each other.

"Our conversation has come full circle," the stranger observed. "Do you want to ask any other questions before your Denise wakes up?"

Your Denise. The tactfulness of this superman was beyond belief.

"I could go on asking questions forever. But this is enough for the first time. Will we see each other again?"

"Whenever you want."

"Well, when I want, how do I call you?"

"Call me."

"But I don't believe I know your name."

"You would find my name unpronounceable in your language. Let's agree to use something simpler. In your language, what do you call a being who is on a higher level of development than a human being?"

Artem shrugged his shoulders. "A god, I guess. One, Zeus, Ahura-Mazda, Jupiter. . . . If it really doesn't matter to you, I'll call you Jupe— that was the supreme god of the ancient Romans."

And also the humanoid ape in Jules Verne, Artem thought to himself.

The stranger pompously nodded his head in agreement. "Your food supplies will, as formerly, be renewed daily. What else do you need?"

"Something to do."

"Oh, we just wanted to let you rest after the trip. Just down this path, in two booths, you will find sound-recording equipment. We would request you to dictate in detail everything you know about life on Earth—first of all, about yourselves, your families, childhood, education. . . . Don't try to be systematic—dictate in the order you find easiest to remember."

"You don't have thought-recording equipment?"

"Not for alien beings."

"Why so poor a showing? Create them. After all, you did build the ship."

"The ship was built many millennia ago. We don't build things like that anymore."

An awkward silence set in. It was gradually becoming clear why the "gods" needed to find the difference between themselves and normal human beings.

"I think Denise has awakened," Artem said. "Until tomorrow, Jupe."

"Until tomorrow."

The transparent film whose existence was hinted at only by the muffled sound of Jupe's voice turned lilac, then purple, then a blackish purple, and then dissolved. The path was empty.

He went back to the house knowing that Denise had indeed awakened but had not gotten up but curled up in a ball under the blanket.

He was terrified of being alone. When he did not see her before him, he could think of her totally calmly, as a tenth-grade girl. Only an extremely beautiful tenth grader.

And then each time he found her completely different from the way he remembered her, and that unsettled him. He had to make an effort to come out with some neutral statement.

"Still dozing, my charming friend? Time to get up, my beauty!"

She stared at him without blinking, as a person looks at a miracle. In the same way, probably, as he had stared at her the first evening.

"What's the matter? Has someone frightened you?"

"No. But I woke up alone, and suddenly felt that you had never existed."

"But I do exist. That's the problem!"

"It's not a problem. Don't talk that way. But now I'll have to get used to you all over."

"Then let's begin with a good breakfast. Then we'll get ourselves in order. Have you ever held an iron? No? Hm, that's bad. I'll have to take care of everything: ironing, washing, wiping your nose."

"Artem, what are you trying to hide from me?"

"Absolutely nothing. It's just that today will be our first normal workday. Sit down, have something to eat. Are you sick of the apricots yet?"

"What I am going to do?"

"The same thing as me—remember and dictate. The being that invited us here—let's call it that—is interested in having our intimate memoirs. The cradle, kindergarten, school. How did you do in history?"

"Quite well."

"Oho, we'll complement each other nicely. So then, we have at our disposal sound-recording equipment. We are supposed to try to remember everything, from the very beginning of our Mother Earth. From far back and in the greatest of detail. The chronology should be exemplary. And try to limit yourself, for the time being, to the most ancient history. Charlemagne and Pepin the Short is okay, too. And who was there in England at that time? Yes, the Tudors."

"Oh, my," said Denise.

"Don't act surprised. I warned you. The average level of a dull-witted engineer. Nothing too new. They wouldn't be interested. Do you get me?"

"Yes," Denise nodded. "I understand you very well. They're only interested in history."

"Actually, they're interested in everything. But it's better to begin with history—it's harmless. As for geography, they probably thought to take some pictures of Earth when they came to get us."

He stopped short but it was already too late. After that, she would have to be incredibly thickheaded not to guess what was going on. But had she?

Denise was sitting with her eyes still lowered.

"Look at me, Denise. Please. The thing is, we're not on Earth."

"Yes," she answered calmly. "Yes, you feel so light here, too light, as though you could fly."

He stared at her, dumbfounded.

"So then . . . you guessed? From the very beginning? But why didn't you tell me?"

"At that time it didn't make any difference."

"And now?"

"It doesn't make any difference where we are now either."

She was clever enough to construct her sentences and make her highly significant pauses in such a way that after each of them he felt like casting himself at her feet.

"Wash the dishes," Artem said. "We have to get to work."

Summer pavilions grown over with grapevines were already awaiting them on both sides of the path where he had had his discussion with Jupe. Inside each pavilion was a device that remotely resembled a helium flow-detector. Alongside the control panel was a low revolving chair and a one-legged table with the imperishable jar of apricot compote and a package of crackers.

"It's fortunate," Artem thought, "that I have such a well-behaved child to take care of. To notice that the force of gravity is different here—a good show! The difference is barely noticeable. And that regal calm! Any other girl would have been bawling her head off night and day, remembering her mother, the quais of the Seine, the pigeons in the square. But really, why hasn't she once mentioned home? Let us return to the hypothesis about her being a spy. What a lot of nonsense! I didn't bombard her with my memories of my only aunt Polina Glebovna, after all. And if I had started singing the glories of Leningrad it would have been out of place. Uninvited candor is worse than an uninvited guest. So why then does what is completely natural for me myself seem so unnatural in her? Perhaps it's just an intuitive desire to find something wrong in her in the absence of other faults—a desire dictated by the fundamental law of self-preservation. But self-preservation from what? Well, you might as well admit it, no one will know, and these machines don't record thoughts—you are afraid of her, aren't you?"

He had known for a long time that it was true. And it was not just her that he feared but himself. He knew that if he started to get carried away, why, then his sober engineering mind would be helpless. Therefore he did not allow himself to look at Denise as anything other than a schoolgirl. It was neither the time nor the place. He had to get busy. He leaned over his recording device.

"The earliest center of civilization on our planet was, I think, Egypt," he began, and multicolored lights bustled on the device's controls. "As early as the fifth millennium B.C.—damn, how can I explain 'B.C.' without going into the history of Christianity? Well, we'll get to B.C. later. The supreme leader in ancient Egypt was the pharaoh."

The only pharaohs he remembered were Amenhotep IV and Akhnaton, and there was some doubt in his mind whether they were actually the same person. And there was the high priest Herihor. And of course, Nefertiti. That's who Denise resembled! The same calm, implacable tenderness, the same striving from the line of the top lip to the temples, as though someone had carefully stroked their damp palms over the already carved face, and it bore forever the touch of the hands that had created it.

"The ruling dynasties numbered in the twenties, maybe more," he said, pulling himself together. The lights once again fluttered across the control panel, as though they had been awaiting the sound of his voice. "The priests were a powerful group that opposed the pharoah's might. . . ."

At noon Denise came running up.

"I'm a little hoarse," she reported. "How about you?"

"I got as far as Akhnaton. And Herihor."

Denise's face expressed unfeigned horror.

"You didn't forget to mention that Ahknaton's wife was queen . . . the queen of Sava?"

Artem tilted his head and looked on Denise's serious expression. He was slowly getting the feeling that he was being made fun of.

"Incidentally, the wives of great men don't have any bearing on history. Nor do the great men themselves. History is made by the people, you should know that."

Denise made a mournful face.

"Poor history!" She sat down in the doorway, her legs outside, her face half turned to Artem; a cinematic dialogue with her lines delivered over her shoulder. "If history were without women—what a horror! Anything without women is awful. Like war. Like drunk . . . drunkenness. Like police. Like politics."

"History and politics are two different things."

"Precisely! Politics are done by men. And history . . . men do it like this." Denise moved her hands in circles as though she was stirring up water.

"A fine model of historical processes! And what does the queen of Sava have to do with anything?"

"The queen of Sava could not make history, she had legs like—oh, like a bear cub." Denise propped her arms against the doorway and stretched out her little feet. "The queen of Sava," Denise continued, "was no one's wife. Not even Solomon's."

"Has anyone ever told you that you look like Nefertiti?"

"Oh, of course. Monsieur Levain—you don't know him. Nowadays they say that to all the beautiful women."

Such modesty—"to all the beautiful women."

"As for Nefertiti. . . ." Denise shrugged, as if to say, okay, I suppose, but nothing that special; she put her fingers together in a pinch and moved it vertically upward as though she were feeling a thin reed. "A dried fish— a whiting, is it?—"

"A whitefish," he automatically prompted.

"The shoulders—straight, dry towels on them. And her legs? Like this and this!"—a pair of pokers sketched in the air—"and here"—she kicked off her shoe, and revealed a small shapely foot. Denise patted it and then measured off with her hands a distance corresponding to a size fourteen—"and here it is a regular woody . . . wooden leg."

What a problem these women are—how much plain ordinary jealousy they have! Just out of the cradle and already whispering put-downs of a woman who ruled three thousand years before, and not because she was better—no, as strange as it may seem, Denise was more beautiful, and it was frightening to think what she would be like when she was twenty-five—but right now she was jealous because the whole world knew Nefertiti, and only her mama and papa and a certain Monsieur Levain knew her.

"Okay then," he said aloud. "But I feel less hostility toward her and more sympathy—Akhnaton, after all, abandoned her."

Denise's eyebrows arched in amazement—she did that often, as though asking, "Am I speaking correctly?" Interrogative intonations arose in her voice too often and too unexpectedly—somewhere in the middle of a truly epic sentence, she would begin to have doubts about the correctness of her words and immediately make excuses for any possible error. The result was very endearing, but if she had spoken Russian even just a little bit worse, these galloping intonations would have made her speech absolutely unintelligible.

"Hostility?" Denise's astonishment finally reached verbal expression. "What for?" (She always confused "what for" and "why.") "You just have to look, think. You look"—she always had a problem coming up with words when she began talking rapidly—"and this"—her hand went back and forth like a saw: probably meaning "sculptural portrait"—"and this is not true, it can't be that way—for everyone, really . . . Really you have to look at *des fresques*, sketches. That is for everyone, understand? Sketches are just a woman. But this—the head, this is for one person, understand, Artem? For him. Not for Akhnaton. No? It is Nefertiti for one person, one and only."

He did not even try stopping her although she had already reached maximum speed, when one word replaced the previous one, pronounced in a half-questioning, half-annoyed tone (Lord, how can anyone not understand such a simple thing!), without waiting for it to be comprehended by Artem, replaced by another more appropriate one, and the main thing, to seek the connection of that word with all the ones before it. Denise continued chattering, and he listened to her without being able to get over his astonishment—she spoke as heatedly as if the question affected her personally and was not three thousand years away.

"What an outburst!" he thought. But really, what was he to Hecuba?

He had heard the story of the pharaoh's unfortunate wife dozens of times and the repetitions put him to sleep. What had happened was that when he and Fimka Neiman had picked up some erudite girls they wanted to overwhelm with their intellectuality, Neiman would unleash the saga of the unfaithful pharaoh, who abandoned such a beauty for the luxuriously thighed, thick-browed Kaia, a cheap cocotte from the Nile riverfront. As soon as he heard the canonical introduction, "By the way, on the subject of male fidelity . . ." Artem turned himself off automatically, and Neiman's inspiring raving failed to reach his heart and mind. It was enough for the girls—one tale for the two of them. It had gone on that way until last year, when the novel *King Akhnaton* came out and destroyed the originality and sensationalism of Fimka's tale. But he did not give up—he acquired from God knows where a hypothesis about the origin of the Mona Lisa— that it was Leonardo's self-portrait in women's dress, and with the help of this elegant art history fabrication continued to maintain his reputation as an intellectual.

So now several confusing and hasty words from Denise were enough for the whole boring story of the rebellious but inconsistent pharaoh and his incomparably beautiful wife suddenly to shine in a new light and for the first time became comprehensible all the way through.

But of course Nefertiti was not, could not, have been the way she was depicted by the unknown sculptor—that was Nefertiti as she was just for that sculptor. And everyone else—even the pharaoh himself—saw a long-faced no-longer-young mother of six with an ugly sagging stomach—the way she was shown in several wall drawings.

"So it seems that Akhnaton did not know that his court sculptor was, so to speak, embellishing reality and depicting his lawful spouse as a goddess of beauty?"

"How could it be that the king did not know? He did. Once he went into the studio and saw it. And became such an unhapp . . . unfortunate? . . . pharaoh. And everything he did. . . . What's the word . . . oh, everything he did went up in ashes."

And all of Akhnaton's great endeavors went up in smoke, for he began searching for the Nefertiti that the court sculptor had managed to see but could not find her. She had passed by very close to him, right next to him, passionate and tender, regal as she had never been in her youth, and youthful as she had never been at the zenith of her queenly power. And he held back his mighty armies, ready to descend in a devastating attack on the neighboring kingdoms, and he stayed his hand from annihilating the willful priesthood, and he allowed an upstart from the court favorites to rule in his place, and, quite possibly, took himself a thick-thighed, abundantly browed Kaia, and maybe several of them. And that is the way it was, and only Denise had guessed it.

"Denise, how old are you?"

"Sixteen. The same age my mother was when she met my father."

This way of framing the question, or rather the answer, sobered him immediately.

"Well, since you're only sixteen, you, as a minor, are entitled to a shorter workday. So go back home and cook the potatoes—they're in the corner of the kitchen, in a cake box. And make sure you don't forget to wash them. I'm going to dictate some more."

Denise floated regally out of the pavilion. Nefertiti should have shoulders like that.

An hour later she came running up, or more exactly came hopping upon one leg, and with a joyous shout dragged him to the kitchen; at first he could not fathom the reason for her joy and only after a little while realized that it was the first time she had ever cooked potatoes by herself. Denise had become a little housewife, and Artem with disgust found himself comparing her to Audrey Hepburn in *Roman Holiday*, when she, playing a hereditary princess of an undetermined country, makes her first, and last, cup of coffee.

After dinner they went back to their pavilions, but when it began to get dark, Denise was not at her work station—she had probably gotten bored and decided to take advantage of her privilege as a minor. Artem found her on the daybed, sitting cross-legged and with a needle in her hand. His only special shirt made of Indian fabric was neatly quartered and spread out on the table.

"Have you gone crazy, Denise? What are you doing with my shirt?"

"Oh! Do you mind?"

"Of course not, but still—"

"You are much too curious." She set about cutting the sleeves into long strips.

She was busy the whole evening, humming a tune under her breath. Finally she announced triumphantly, "Ready!"

"A very cute little sarafan. I recognize my sleeves in the flounce. I hope you're not planning on trying it on in front of me."

Denise blushed.

"Excuse me for being so stupid. Our conversation today reminded me that you are after all French."

"I don't see the connection. . . ."

"Somehow I have the idea that French women speak in double entendres, undress in front of male acquaintances, kiss the first man who comes along, and always respond with an inevitable 'oh-la-la.' "

"You've seen too many bad movies," Denise noted with sadness. "I'm not even angry. But if we are going to live here . . . for a long time, I would like to have *des draps*, sheets. Can it be arranged?"

"Of course. But will you cut them up too?"

"For what? I'll sleep. To spend a whole week without changing clothes. . . . I'm simply ashamed."

"It's okay, you don't have to worry about me."

"I'm ashamed for the sake of my own dress. It's my only one."

"What about this one, the new one?"

"*Mon Dieu*, it's a dress for the night."

Now it was Artem's turn to be embarrassed. To hide the fact, he stuck his nose in the closet.

"Take these pillowcases . . . and this . . . and this—they're not perfumed, you'll have to excuse it. . . . What an idiot!" he exclaimed with joy. "Here's Fimka's air mattress right where he left it! My whole life I've wanted to sleep on a balcony!"

"Won't you be afraid all alone out there?"

"Silly, they're watching over us like a mother hen. And I won't shut the door tight, so if anything happens, just call."

He went out onto the balcony, and Denise heard him struggle with the mattress and a bicycle pump. After a while he heard a call.

"What is it?"

Denise did not answer, and he guessed that she was waiting for him to go in.

She was already in bed for the night, and Artem automatically smiled when he saw his shirt, with the sleeves cut off and the collar much too large for Denise.

"Nefertiti in a man's shirt. What a picture!"

She raised her eyes to him, not accepting the joke. "Good night."

"Sleep well, my child."

He bent over and kissed her on the forehead.

On the balcony Artem felt quite comfortable. He hung his things over the railing, stretched out blissfully, and looked upward. A dungeonlike darkness hung above him.

"Jupe!" he called in a whisper.

To the left, beyond the railing, something flashed.

"Are you satisifed with us, Jupe?"

"Yes," came an equally soft voice out of the darkness. "And you?"

"Completely. Although remembering is not as easy a thing as one might think."

"Are you objecting?"

"No."

"Is there anything else you need?"

"Not for me. But I don't think this will be enough for Denise."

"What else will she need?"

"Toys."

"All right."

He fell asleep without noticing and woke up only after it had dawned. He dressed quietly and climbed over the railing. He had already decided to go around the house and go in through the front door so that he could reach the kitchen without making any noise, but at the very moment Denise's muffled shriek reached him. He hopped back over the railing and burst into the room.

A pile of colored boxes towered from floor to ceiling, and alongside it, Denise was kneeling, her bare knees on the floor. The whole room was submerged in some kind of golden foam, and Denise was lifting the foam and rubbing it over her face. At the sight of Artem she jumped to her feet, and shouted out something in French. She raised as much of the transparent foamy gold as her two hands could hold above her head; then she turned in a circle, and the honeyed weightless streams wound around her with a rustling sound. Artem walked over to it, touched it with his fingers—a flexible synthetic film strewn in countless glistening little bubbles.

"So you got your toy," he said good-naturedly.

"*Mon Dieu*, a 'toy'! Do you know what this makes me feel like saying?"

"I know: oh-la-la!"

"Exactly. Oh-la-la!"

"Instead you should say thank you."

"Oh, it never even occurred to me. I'm . . . *un cochon de lait*, a little pig. Who gave me all this?"

"Most likely, Jupe."

"Who's Jupe?"

"Our host."

"Jupe is a name for a servant, not for a host, *n'est-ce pas*? But it doesn't matter." She ran to the balcony door, opened it wide, and shouted, "*Merci*, Monsieur Jupe!"

"Now you are behaving like a French woman in a bad film: You shriek 'oh-la-la' and run out half-dressed on the balcony."

Denise just shrugged her shoulders. "And is Monsieur Jupe very old?"

"He doesn't look old. But enough of your ecstasy. Let's have breakfast and get to work."

"And when does . . . Sunday come?"

"Count for yourself—yesterday was Monday."

Denise pouted.

"But taking into consideration your age and your household work, I am assigning you only a half day."

"Oh-la-la!" Denise shouted. "Long live unworking!"

"First of all, the word is *unemployment*. Second of all, it's only partial, and third, you're really laying it on thick with the oh-la-las. If you're not careful I'll end up thinking that you've been faking it up till now and only the sight of these rags has brought out the real you."

Denise flared her nostrils like a young antelope and announced with pique, "I'm going to change."

"Fair enough. That means that I am supposed to make the coffee. But remember that beginning tomorrow, that's going to be your job—and not to reduce unemployment but to instill good work habits in you."

During breakfast it occurred to Artem to take along a sheet of paper. He was good at drawing, and it made the work more interesting.

"Among the ancient cave drawings in central Africa are drawings of a man in a transparent helmet; see illustration number twenty-three. True, further investigations showed that it was just a gourd; see illustration number twenty-four."

And so on, in like manner.

In the evening, when he returned to the little house, he experienced a slight sense of vertigo. All the walls, windows, and doors were draped with silvery gray, cream, and cherry-red fabrics, and the table was covered with a stiff fabric worthy of a banquet at Versailles.

"Monsieur Artem, I invite you to a farewell banquet in honor of my old dress. Tomorrow I will go to work in Empire style."

"Has anyone ever told you that you look like Madame Récamier?"

"Naturally. Monsieur Levain, once again."

"You know, you would have been better off cooking some soup."

"You're mad, not so?"

"Not so."

She shrugged her shoulders, because he actually was angry.

"Why don't you draw a dress for me. One you'd like to see me in."

I'd like to see you on Earth, he thought.

Then she got ready for the night, while he, seated on a kitchen chair, obediently sketched one of Natalya Goncharova's dresses. Denise called him.

"What's up, Denise?"

"I want to say good night."

Her bed was covered with black silk.

"Did anyone ever tell you that you look like Marguerite Valois?"

"Naturally. Once again—"

"Monsieur Levain. Watch, you'll fall—silk is slippery."

"Good night."

"Sweet dreams of Monsieur Levain."

He turned around and headed for the balcony.

"Artem!"

He went back.

"Good night," Denise repeated.

"Sleep well," He bent over and kissed her.

Then he went out in the darkness and stood still, leaning against the rough wall.

"Jupe," he called out, "today are you satisfied with us?"

There was a long pause. Artem had already decided that there was not going to be any answer, but then right alongside him came a dry and not completely confident voice: "Yes."

It was so dark that even if Jupe had been standing only two yards away—as you would assume from the closeness of the voice—you would not be able to make out the expression on his face. Not even the dim silhouette. But he was there.

"Jupe, tell me if you can, why out of all the millions of people on Earth did you pick us?"

"Look," he heard in answer, and immediately a screen appeared about ten feet away. Two motionless figures appeared on it, and Artem had to study the image hard in order to recognize himself and Denise.

When, during what happy time, had the aliens seen them like that? Both ran forward, he with a tennis racket, she holding shut a swimming robe; neither knew that they were running to meet each other, and it would have been better if one of them had stopped his light and thoughtless running, for the meeting was fated to occur not on Earth. But they flew forward, through worlds and spaces, and if Artem had not been one of them, he would have maintained that the aliens' choice was correct, because these two were the most beautiful people Earth had to offer.

"What then do you really want from us?" Artem asked softly.

"Be the way you are," came the equally soft answer.

The two people running to their inevitable meeting dissolved silently into the darkness. Artem reached out along the wall, felt the door, and pushed it open.

Dim glimmers of an unextinguished light barely penetrated the room. Artem stopped over the sleeping Denise. How frightening it was—the black bed. Her slightly turned-up face seemed to float in emptiness and might disappear at any moment into it. Now I will awaken you, Denise, but will your face be the way it was the day you ran along holding your robe closed with both hands? Will you run toward me, the way you ran before you knew me?

Right then it appeared to him that Denise's eyes were open. Could she see him in the darkness? Perhaps not; but she knew that he was there. "Why are you here, Artem?" "I saw the two of us together, and now I know that for me there is only you, and for you, only me." "But perhaps there's no one here but me?" "No, Denise." "This is paradise, our nice little house, although there's no phone if you want to say hello to a friend, is there?" "I don't know, Denise." "And I am so close, and no one sees, no one hears, and tomorrow my eyes won't be red from crying, because every night I call out for you?" "I don't know, I don't know, Denise." "And I'm the same age my mother was when she met my father; and we have already looked at each other so long that you can no longer just turn and leave me."

He bent impetuously over her—and then froze; her eyes were closed. The delicate balance of sleep was protecting her tired face, and it seemed that just one slight touch would destroy the calm—and the whole world would split in two.

He bit his lips to keep his breath from touching her. Just don't wake up, Denise, I implore you by all we both hold dear, don't wake up right now.

He carefully made his way out of the house, went around back, and tumbled over the balcony railing, plopping onto his mattress. Be what you are, was it? A son of a bitch was what he was. That was what it was!

In the morning, when he got up, he did not have nerve enough to go in the house. He was afraid that Denise was not awake yet, was afraid of her sleeping face. He rushed down the crunching path until the door flew open and Denise, wrapped in white, appeared on the threshold.

"Hello-o-o? Where are you?" she shouted and waved to him. "The bathroom is free."

He did not budge.

And then she ran up to him, holding her home-sewn robe together, and even from a distance he recognized the joyous face, and understood that no matter what walls he erected between himself and her, no matter what prohibitions he placed on himself and her, nothing would be of any use.

Strange fairy-tale days set in for them. The hours of work, easy and at times even enjoyable, flew by unnoticed; all the rest of his time was filled with Denise alone. She knew an unbelievable number of things, and every night, putting on a fantastic oriental costume, she would sit on the daybed with her legs folded and begin with the lines he had taught her: "This I have heard, O King. . . ." Denise's days. Like honeycombs, golden and heavy with their richness. Days that ascended silently toward night, toward the long rustle of capricious costumes tried on before sleep, toward an infinite tenderness that had to be contained in two tiny words: "Sleep well"; but that was not yet the end of the day.

For the last thing was the black night sky hanging over the balcony at a distance of an outstretched arm, and—in a quiet whisper so that the drowsing Denise would not hear—"Are you satisifed with us, Jupe?" And in answer a similarly quiet whisper, slightly uncertain: "Yes." Only with every passing day the pause between the question and the answer grew longer.

And then, finally:

"Are you satisified with us, Jupe?"

A long—very long—pause.

"No."

Artem had long been expecting it, but it was still damned hard to take, and he did not feel like getting involved in questions and answers. After all, they were to blame. Out of three billion people they decided to go for two pretty faces. If they had nabbed two full professors, then they might have received their complete picture of life on Earth.

"You want too much," Artem said with annoyance, folding his hands behind his head. "My school courses have vanished from my memory years ago, and I don't intend on telling you anything about my work. And Denise is capable of presenting the fashions of peoples of all times and places, but that's it. You made a bad choice, Jupe, and now you're trying to squeeze apple juice out of a carrot."

"We haven't made a mistake," was the dispassionate answer. "You were precisely the ones we needed, and we took you."

"Yes, and what right did you have?"

"Right?" The voice fell silent, as though Jupe was trying to remember the meaning of the word. "Right. . . . As though the basis for our action might change your fate. But since you feel I have to justify myself before you, I will do so, and as convincingly as possible."

His voice came closer and sounded as though it was coming from above, as though Jupe was standing right alongside the balcony railing. Artem could not restrain himself and unobtrusively stuck his hand between the bars, but his fingers hit the same sticky protective barrier. He's afraid. But maybe not, just a different atmosphere.

"Many tens of thousands of years ago we were just like you. However we were most likely even then wiser and more cautious. We reached the limits of human knowledge—at our disposal were ships that could take us to any point in the galaxy and even beyond. We knew how to extend our lives indefinitely, having conquered all diseases and even aging itself, we could . . . however, you wouldn't be able to follow me if I were to list all that we learned. So then, in our greedy striving to see everything, understand everything, and know everything we once flew to the third planet of an ordinary little out-of-the-way star. Incredibly, we found there conditions analogous to those on our planet at the time a rational being appeared. And we encountered this new being. Half-ape, a savage. And from that time on we carefully observed your planet. We destroyed wild animals that threatened the first human herds, we taught the savages to use fire and tools, we presented them with information they would never have obtained by themselves, and they began to develop faster, remembering our lessons but forgetting us. We helped you at the dawn of your humanity, we were your nurses and your teachers. . . . Well, how does this explanation appeal to you?"

Artem just shrugged his shoulders. "No wet nurse, to say nothing about teachers—has the right to infringe upon her ward's freedom. And as for the handing down of knowledge, to judge by the way you have treated Denise and me, I am sure you instructed primitive humans in goodness, justice, and respect for neighbors."

Jupe's dispassionate face expressed neither annoyance nor confusion. He just began moving his lips once again and after a second's delay his monotonous voice was heard.

"Then I will offer you a second variant. We found on your planet conditions in which reason could develop. But we did not find rational beings. And then a group of our people . . . even though they were refugees who had fled our planet for political reasons, decided to found a colony on your Earth. Unfortunately, they overestimated their resources and after several generations had returned to primitive conditions. Four groups of refugees, arriving at different times, created the four races on Earth. Isn't this version realistic?"

"Not especially. And it still does not explain why you permit yourself to dispose of us like your personal property."

"Several times you tried leaving your house, and each time found the

very same house again, only in a different place. Finally you stopped
leaving it and just stayed there. Well, I have to provide one hypothesis
after another until you stay with one. This time the hypotheses will be
different, but they are all in the same mode. Here's another for you: We
did not leave people on Earth. But having returned to our planet we
supposed that at some future time we might need beings that were similar
to us. We could not foresee everything that awaited us in the future, but
a dim anxiety gnawed away at us. We were at the peak of our knowledge
and abilities, and in addition we were very cautious. And then we created
biorobots, yes, self-developing biorobots, taking your apes as our foundation. That is why you could not find the missing link between the last
ape and the first human. We planted you on each of the continents in
the hope that at least one group would survive. And all of them survived.
Survived and developed. Developed and started asking questions: Why
does a human being live? What does humanity exist for? True?"

Artem made an ambiguous gesture—in general, yes. To hide that made
no sense.

"So then," Jupe's voice resounded passionately, "you exist solely so that
we can, whenever we choose, return to our past, to our youth. Our
humanity has become decrepit. We know everything, can do everything,
but we want nothing. Whoever we may have been for you—midwives
standing over your cradle, older brothers, fathers, or even gods who created
you out of dust—we are now asking of you only what is ours by right, and
indeed we are asking for very little. About one hundred billion humans
have passed over the Earth, and we have taken only two, you and Denise.
That is our right. Render unto the gods the things of the gods."

"But render unto Caesar only Caesar's. And even if we accept that you
are gods, then what in hell ever happened to you to make us lead such
lives?"

Jupe was silent for a while, then Artem heard something sounding like
a human sigh.

"We were very careful of ourselves. Too careful. And in order to provide
maximum protection for each individual, we cut our birthrate drastically.
Decades passed, centuries, and then only old people were left on our
planet. We stopped space travel, we stopped exploring ocean depths and
volcano craters. We were so afraid for ourselves! But one after another our
comrades perished, perished in absurd, unimaginable ways. And then we
made our last mistake: Instead of trying to give birth to a new generation—
perhaps that would have succeeded, since our medicine was, and still is,
for that matter, on an advanced level—we decided to make up for the lack
of people by creating biorobots in our image."

"Faces like tin cans?" Denise's expression popped into Artem's mind.

"Hundreds and thousands of years passed, and on the entire planet only one man born of woman was left, and that is me. But is it still me? My body has been renewed countless times, and even completely replaced—only the brain preserved. Externally I am exactly the same as all the inhabitants of this planet. But I alone feel that we are perishing. It cost me great effort to convince my comrades"—he pronounced this last word with a slight hesitation—"to send the last remaining starship to Earth. Using our ability to become invisible—you wouldn't understand how we do it—I spent some time near Earth, familiarized myself with its past and present, and most importantly selected you. The rest you know."

"Yes," said Artem. "In ancient times, they say, there were several half-insane kings who tried to restore their youth by drinking the blood of babies. Is that the way you're trying to rejuvenate yourself?"

"We are people, too," Jupe said haughtily.

"Excuse me, but you're tin cans! I really feel sorry for you, and we will do anything we can to help. Render unto Caesar. And now, good night."

Jupe did not answer. He was insulted and vanished. But no, long ago he must have forgotten how to be insulted. He simply felt the conversation was finished. And what a conversation it was! Another half hour of revelations like those, and he would be totally confused.

As long as Denise did not learn about all this. Not on Earth—that was a problem. But the fact that they were not with humans. And right then he felt that the balcony door was opening slowly. He could not see but guessed that there, on the floor, Denise was sitting, leaning against the doorjamb and hugging her knees against her chest.

He had to say something, make up some story to calm her down, so that she could go to sleep, and do it quickly. Just remember, drag out of your memory words after which nothing is frightening, after which you remember nothing else; well, go ahead, blockhead, go ahead. . . .

"Denise. . . ."

A hand, invisible in the darkness, found his face. The hand was gentle, like a tiny bat. What nonsense—a bat? Where could it have come from? Ah, the stony air of a pharaoh's tomb. Here too was that kind of immobility. Tiny globs of gray nothingness, coming to life from human breath, from the rustle of human lips. And where were they from, those globs? Probably from childhood, when you believed that in the morning all the night darkness was gathered inside the streetlights and hid there all day long, and if you looked closely, you could see inside the globs a thick heavy fog, and heaven help you if the glob were to explode—then the darkness would rush out like the genie out of the bottle in the tale of Aladdin, and in broad daylight would drown the city the way it does at dusk, when the streetlights go on, and the darkness, terrified, flies out onto the streets. . . . Oh Lord, what was he thinking about, what was it?

"Denise. . . ."

It was childhood again, just not like with the lights but later, with Larissa Salova, and if he could only remember what he said then, although it wouldn't help because what he said was "I'll take your lousy cadet and make hamburger out of him." And she laughed because his words were nice and flashy, the lousy cadet went to military school and was a head taller, and had a belt buckle with an insignia, and she stopped smiling so it would be easier for him to kiss her, and then he said, "I'm going to punch that Lymar of yours out" and kissed her again, and she said, "Granny is taking the garbage out" because they were near the front door, and he answered, "I'll shove your Granny out the door" and kissed her for a third time and then gave up, because he was bored and it seemed pointless.

"Denise. . . ."

And then it wasn't childhood, it was the last time, when everyone else had left but he could stay, and he was about to refuse but he stayed, four sheets to the wind, and the woman was smashed, too. And he undressed her without saying a word, and then she—maybe she took a better look at him, maybe she decided to be modest—started in, "You're my first real—"—"Hey, knock it off," he told her, and that was the last time.

"Denise. Denise. Denise. . . ." Like a prayer, like an incantation, like a chalk circle on the floor to divide what was now from everything that had been.

"I'm here," her marvelously calm voice sounded out of the darkness. "Reach out, I'm here."

He shuddered inside from her words, simple, meaning nothing in the ordinary literal sense, but now turning to him with all the oppressive nakedness of their one and only meaning. And so it was not he but she who first offered the only remedy for the terror of the dull and immortal ahumanity that surrounded them. And that "reach out" was the first thing she had said to him one equal to another, and it meant "reach out and take me."

He stood up slowly, scratching his chin against the brick wall. Somewhere below, by his feet, the invisible Denise was sitting on the floor.

So that is how it is. Don't torment yourself, it's inevitable, no matter what. You'll be a real bastard. It's fate.

"You seem afraid?" the cursed voice said, hurt, totally childlike. "No one can see. It's dark."

He felt as if he could kill. On the spot.

"Maybe I'm not beautiful enough for you? Monsieur Levain said—"

"Shut up!"

The air moved without a sound, and Artem guessed that Denise had stood up, her head slightly tossed back. Out of the darkness, her breath, in gentle spurts, floated up to his face. She was closer to him than an outstretched arm.

"Why did you tell me to shut up? I love you, Artem."

Lord, how could that 'I love you' sound so slow, so right, so calm?

"No, Denise, no! It just happens that we're alone together here, you and me. And so you think. . . . Why not? Girls tell stories, *maman* forbids it, your bald admirer talks about Nefertiti. It seems that it's love at first sight and forever. And that's the way it seems. Your admirer doesn't fit the role, he's old and the girls will laugh. But here's a young Russian, and it's a different planet. Oh-la-la! And since no one can see—"

"It's dark here, or otherwise I'd slap your face!"

"And you'd be smart to do it. I won't even ask your pardon. That's for tomorrow. When I'm capable of thinking about what I'm saying."

"You talk but don't listen! Every word you say is like a . . . *crapaud* . . . I don't know the Russian: cold, ugly, wet! Yes—a toad. For what! For what!"

Denise, my poor little one, not "for what" but "why."

"Because you should not say, 'It's dark, and no one can see.' " And you should not say, "Reach out." And you should not stand so close to me in the dark that I could reach out and grab you.

The rustle of footsteps. Farther. Still farther. Four steps in darkness between them. One large step for him if she called. Don't dare call me, Denise. I love you.

Silence. A long silence, in which Denise neither sleeps nor wakes. So it was not over. He still had to go over, find her calm forehead in the darkness, and "Sleep well." Can you? Now I can.

And her face was wet. All of it, even her eyebrows. And her hands, her narrow cold hands.

"Come on now, silly, my pumpkin, my little girl"—any word, any name, as long as it was tender because it did not matter which, put tenderness in them, all the tenderness in the whole wide world, the tenderness of every man who kissed a woman's face from Nefertiti on. "Oh, my little one, my brown-haired beauty, my love. . . ."

Denise went to sleep, happy, continuing to squeeze his hand as though it were a favorite toy. How little you needed, to be warmed and lulled. "Reach out and take me"—some idea! My silly little one. And now sleep sweetly and breathe deeply, you've cried enough, and I am going to sit here all night on the floor, like a total idiot, with my head on the edge of your bed just so I can see your face when dawn breaks.

If only Jupe could see this picture!

"Well, Jupe, you old tin can, are you satisfied with us today?"

Darkness. And the near and distinct: "Yes."

There was a short segment of time when Artem almost broke out laughing. Sometimes a person is in a mental state when his first reaction to everything is happy laughter. But that lasted only several seconds. Then— puzzlement; had he really been eavesdropping? The swine!

"Jupe!"

"I'm listening."

"Jupe, are you . . . are you satisfied with us today?"

"Yes. You understood what was needed of you, and I am satisfied."

"Did you hear . . . everything?"

"Of course. Since the first moment you arrived on our planet we have seen and heard absolutely everything."

"Even in the dark?"

"For us the dark doesn't exist, nor the walls of the house, nor your clothing. We see everything we want."

Could a twenty-four-year-old Earthling punch an alien degenerate several millennia old? However, they had already answered that question in the affirmative—otherwise the protective film between Artem and Jupe would not have been there, and then. . . .

"But Jupe, you're a human being, even if the rest of them are just tin cans—but you!"

"First of all, it's not completely accurate to call me a human, for you consider yourself one, and we stand on too different levels of development. Second. . . ."—the dispassionate computer voice, and word after word dripped on his skull and spread over it without penetrating deep into consciousness and without divulging its secret and carefully evasive sense— "second, the difference in level is in our favor, with the exception of just one question. It is information concerning that question that we intend on receiving from you. You have, of course, realized what is needed of you, and I am satisfied with you."

"Listen, Jupe, can you explain to me in plain language what the hell you're talking about? I listen to you and don't understand—my human reason is incapable of extrapolating your natural—for you at least—and most likely quite simple thought. What in hell is it that you're driving at?"

"Please. We have a variety of self-renewing biorobots, some of which are modeled on humans, some of which are much more advanced. But nonetheless the life of our humanity is dwindling away implacably. Development has ceased. There is no reason for us to develop anymore. For that we would have to love knowledge. There is no reason for us to explore space. For that we would have to love the stars. For all practical purposes we are immortal, and we do not have to continue our species, nor do we have to concern ourselves with each other. So each person is occupied with himself. And only himself. To help someone else, you have to love them. But we have long since lost any idea of what that means."

"And you, you yourself, Jupe?"

"It was so long ago. . . . I don't know, I don't remember, if I ever loved anyone."

"But you want to help them—so all is not lost. I just can't understand what we are supposed to do."

"I gave you a garden of paradise, your home. I gave you the most beautiful girl on Earth. All the necessary conditions have been created for you. Love each other!"

A punch. In the dark. The resilient surface threw Artem backward, to the front door. An impotent wild rage.

If I had known from the beginning what you wanted, I would have preferred to die beneath one of your paradise's apple trees.

Wait, what about Denise? No one is prohibited from dying under the apple trees, but what would she do all alone with these tin cans? Have you thought about that? Alone, they'll have no need of her, and. . . . Around here they don't hang onto unneeded things. Whether it's information or a human being. It's not economical. And once again the invisible starship would head for Earth to pick out another pair of nice young guinea pigs, and then—all the necessary conditions have been created, love each other!

And so the monstrous trick would be played for a second time.

"Why are you silent?" the voice asked out of the darkness. "What are you thinking about?"

I'm thinking that you are a computer son of a bitch, immortal perverts who call themselves gods but who are powerless to force me to do their bidding. You have achieved only one thing—you have taken Denise from me.

And before his eyes, like a curse, like a hallucination—the white swimming robe.

Carefree little Denise, enraptured with the unearthly synthetic fabrics. Tender impulsive Denise, running to meet him through the unreal flowers in their made-to-order heaven.

Love each other, all the necessary conditions have been created for you!

But you will see!

"You have not answered. What are you thinking about?"

I'm wondering if I should cut this comedy short right now, tell you in plain Russian what I think of you, and walk out into the darkness, into the labyrinth of nonreturning paths—to leave before dawn comes to show me Denise's wakening face. And never see her again. And then?

But then—the same old variant: You will consider the experiment a failure, and there is not the slightest hope that your conscience will trouble you. You will not return us to Earth. And here we will no longer be needed.

And so out of the countless number of choices, it all comes down to one thing: another pair of guinea pigs to take the newly vacant spot in paradise.

In paradise, from which Denise will disappear without a trace. . . .

"What are you thinking about?"

"I . . . I am thinking how happy we will be in this garden of paradise."

This lie was the price of several days in which to find a way out. Find it before you guess that you can render neither unto the gods nor unto Caesar.

The easiest thing was fooling Denise. "My dear, we're engaged now, and I have to worry about our future. You're a smart girl and realize that we can get married only on Earth—unless of course you reconsider. So I have to communicate the information our hosts are interested in as quickly as possible. Be sensible and don't bother me. The sooner I finish, the sooner we'll return home."

"So we are going home?"

Good God, Denise, if I only had the courage to ask them!

"How can there be any doubt? They are intelligent beings, after all."

She accepted his reserve easily and without concern, as a person accepts the rules of a new and amusing game. If she only knew how grateful he was for that agreement. If she knew how bitter the lightness of her agreement was to him!

And then every game is limited in time. Sooner or later the moment comes when one of the players says, "I win" and the game is over.

How many days can this game last, Denise? Because time is passing, and there is no way out.

No way out.

The days were transparent, colorless, one smaller than the other—like glass eggs on grandmother's dresser. Days that were tightfisted and powerless, each of which could fit in an old woman's fist. Damn literature for making people expect magical deeds of supermen from Earth as they burst out into the openness of space! Who could imagine that the first humans to reach an alien planet would not create a new society, or transcend the space-time continuum, or lead the way, at the head of alien masses, to a prompt and victorious galactic revolution.

Perhaps that is the way things would be. Someday. But not now. Because now the only thing he could do was *to do nothing*.

Nothing except feel—every minute, every second—that everything that had not yet been between him and Denise was gradually becoming everything that would never be between them.

And the days, which should have belonged to them both together, belonged to each one separately.

Do you know, Denise, that a day together is two days? We are wary of clichés, we are arrogant, have an immature scorn for quotations from the classics that have been beaten into our heads during literature courses. We were paid in full for these quotations; the checks were the A's and B's in our notebooks, long since gone the way of scrap paper, and so we're quits, we have every right to chuck out, to expunge from our minds everything that is clear, elementary, unflavored with the vinegary taste of paradox. Try sitting at a cafeteria table where a bunch of chattering engineers has gathered and saying that a person should be ready to die for his principles. Or that a person's dearest possession is life. You'll be laughed at.

But, Denise, that's the way things are: The most important thing is life. . . . Only the classics have fouled up one very important thing: You get more than one life. Because if you love, you live two lives. And that is why it is so great when you have the good fortune to really love someone. If I hadn't met you, Denise, I would never have known, because until now, it seems, everything I did was messed up. From Larissa Salova right up to the last one.

So what is to be done, what is to be done to break loose from the paws of these—pardon the expression—gods? What can I do so that each of my days is your day, so that each of your moments is my moment? I really want so little: just to be together, until we both have gray hair, like those mythological Greeks . . . what were their names? We used to make fun of them. . . . Ah, Philemon and Baucis. What did we understand, little snotnoses, brave d'Artagnans? Hopeless immaturity, which could have lasted until old age, until the loss of the ability to feel at all, if something terrifying hadn't come along, if the ground hadn't been knocked out from under our feet, like now, when we hang in airless space and cannot even twitch or yawn out of fear—they're watching!

But it did exist, Denise, it did, right there in the palm of my hand, it did, it did. . . .

To throw oneself headfirst against the blinking control panel, to knock it to pieces.

Yes? And what about the invisible starship once more sneaking up on the Earth. And two more prisoners in this paradise.

And then—suppose those two, out of ignorance, out of slow-wittedness, or just because they didn't give a damn, suppose those two gave the aliens what they were after? That they showed them, taught them, how to love?

Laughter through tears. That was the only thing he could no longer fear. And if Jupe remembered nothing—there was nothing to worry about with the other aliens.

But maybe. . . .

Memories float up unexpectedly, often against one's will. Suppose Jupe suddenly remembered that he was once a human? That suddenly he remembered what it was to love?

Perhaps that was their only hope to return to Earth, their way out.

"Jupe!"

And for the first time there was no answer.

"Jupe! Can you hear me, Jupe!"

Well, now. He dreams up the whole mess, runs this Gestapo experiment, drags them here—and now disappears into the bushes, the son of a bitch.

"Jupe!!"

But perhaps they are not permitting him to come? After all, the first time he said, "I've received authorization to answer any question." Or something like that. Perhaps they took away his authorization. Because the experiment had been terminated, for example.

Then there was no hope left. What then? Then—however strange it might seem—they would do just what Jupe wanted: to remain human. Remain human until the very end. And indeed what else was he doing? Just be human. And that was all.

But that turned out to be so little.

"You're bored with me, aren't you?" Denise asked. "Thirty days with the same woman and you're not interested anymore. Just don't tell that we're engaged again. I'm engaged—oh-la-la! Look at me—my gown, ready to go to the altar. White as snow. A dead white. But I'm engaged!"

"Denise, calm down!"

"I'm engaged to . . . what's the word? . . . Wood, Pinocchio. But what for, what for?"

"You mean 'why.' We haven't told each other very much about our-

selves, about our childhood. But just a while ago I remembered something
funny, and if you want I'll tell you the story."

Denise just twisted her mouth in a grimace, afraid that it was a trick to
avoid answering her question.

"I was very small, and my mother and I went for the summer to a resort
on the Baltic. In the room we rented there was a strange picture hanging
on the wall: a mysterious forest—not a real forest but the kind you find
in happy—very important, Denise—fairy tales. And in that forest there
were two old kings, one black and one white. With ashen beards and
tarnished crowns. And in these two kings' hands lay a tiny fabulous world.
You understand, Denise, a whole world, but perhaps only a single kingdom. A minuscule but very real city, with a forest around it, below it new-
grown grass, and people, so diminutive that their faces could be made out
only by the kind and sharp eyes of the wise kings. In the fall my mother
and I left, and I never saw the picture again—of course, it was only a
reproduction; but throughout my childhood I dreamed of having a toy
kingdom just like it. A tiny, living world that I could look at forever and
never get bored with. . . ."

"And what was it called?" Denise asked unexpectedly.

"The picture was titled *The Tale of Two Kings.*"

"And it makes you sad?" She broke out laughing. "You, too, need a
toy. But it's so simple. Just ask Monsieur Jupe. He will give you the fairy
tale. We'll be the two kings. Monsieur Jupe! Two beards, two crowns!"

My silly little one, you haven't understood a thing. For it's we who live
in the toy garden, and our unreal little world is not in kind hands.

However, when you love for the first time, being foolish should be
overlooked. He suddenly raised his head and studied her features. A tear-
stained, sagging face, circles under her eyes, and a greenish tinge because
she had taken it into her head to dress in a furiously red iridescent dress.

Her chin twitched, her eyes narrowed, became ugly. "Another fairy
tale? About a fish?"

When you love for the first time . . . where did he get the idea that she
loved him? Ah yes—the necessary conditions had been created. . . . And
then there was that calm, remarkably correct "I love you"—that night,
the last one; he just couldn't understand whether it had been out of curiosity
or out of fear. And he himself was a fine one to talk—the conceited dandy.
He believed it.

The old story, for thousands of years: He loves her, but she doesn't love
him. Then she loves him, but he doesn't love her. More literature.

But nothing is lost yet, Denise: I could just walk over and take your
face in my hands, and kiss it, and gently blow on your eyelashes and just

barely audibly smooth the beginning of her hair on her temples—the only
thing necessary is my lips and your face.

And right by the window, the sky, dull gray, like a huge tin eye.

I love you Denise, I love you more than the whole world, more than
the sun in the sky. I love you, but if I had a grenade that could blow this
entire world to bits, I would set it off right beneath us. They say love is
a creative feeling. That's the cliché. And what wouldn't I give now for my
love to become a hellish bomb? A thousandfold hydrogen bomb, able to
tear apart this whole superintellectual civilization! I don't know whether
it is humane or not—to destroy a whole race like that, because the mind
of an Earthling is not in a condition to decide such problems; faced with
such problems the mind of an Earthling just collapses. But for such a
grenade, for such a bomb, I, without hesitating and without haggling,
would give my life. And your life, Denise.

Because a world that has forgotten how to love cannot, should not, exist
in the universe.

The control panel of the dictaphone? Lights—one next to another, like
tin soldiers. How many were there? at least one hundred by one hundred.
At the sound of footsteps they turned sky blue, as though a tongue of dim
blue flames was licking the panel. And sit here until the end, because in
all that literature you love so much the true hero always goes down fighting.
Or at least where duty calls. True to his principles.

And really, he didn't want to see that nasty and indifferent face.

"Your face and my lips."

The lights on the panel submissively blinked. Blue, purple, lemon.

How many more endless days in front of this panel, how many more
lectures, stories, poems, traditions, how much more lying?

"The bear went over the mountain. . . ."

Blue, purple, orange.

Artem reached out and pulled out a bulb. A colorless sharp shape, like
the ones for Christmas trees.

The bulb in his hand flashed lilac, then emerald. So, it reacts to sounds.
And it doesn't need current. Artem stepped around behind the dictaphone,
found a door panel, pried it loose with his pocket knife, and looked inside.
Nothing.

A sham. "You need work. . . ." A primitive device to create the illusion
that they were busy. Enough of these cheap illusions.

A thin amazed ringing. Slivers of the bulbs tickled his hands without
even scratching them. And in the doorway the impersonal pink face of an
anatomical model. So he showed up after all, the bastard. As though
nothing were the matter.

Maybe he should fall to his knees and cry, plead, beg? From the beginning of time gods have loved it when people humbled themselves, crawled on their bellies.

For Denise's sake he could take even that.

"Jupe, I beg you. . . . Every experiment must have its limits. The limits of what is reasonable, limits of what is humane. You are wise and kind gods, Jupe, and if you have a drop of gratitude for everything we have done for you, help us to return home."

Then came what he feared more than anything else—that slight pause.

"You are asking for the impossible."

Now things seemed easier.

"If you need a human being for further experiments, keep me. But send Denise back to Earth."

"You'll get everything you could ever dream of. Things you would never have on Earth."

"But this will not be Earth."

Jupe did not answer.

"Jupe, I beg you, believe me: We have books, Shakespeare, Pushkin, Goethe. . . . "

"That information is incomplete and in most cases out-and-out lies. A single experiment with living subjects will give us more than all the literary data on the subject of human emotions. And then, don't forget, that I alone obtained you, but I am not the only one to control your fates."

He was not the only one. . . . Does that mean that he would return them to Earth if it were in his power?

"Jupe, my friend, you were an astronaut, so you should remember what it means to want to go home. You have a ship, Jupe. As far as I understand, you alone control it. I am not asking for myself. . . ."

"You are now in the hold of the ship."

Artem's mouth dropped open in disbelief and he chewed on the sterile dehumidified air.

"This is the leisure deck of our last starship. My starship. As you see, here we can create any conditions whatsoever, any environment. Only one thing is impossible: to reach the end of this room, even though it is comparatively small in size. When this ship, many centuries ago, made regular trips to other stars, we set off on many adventures right here to amuse ourselves, even though we really did not leave the room."

Well now, a squirrel on the wheel. But how the effect was achieved—"that's something you wouldn't understand."

"Thousands of years ago, when civilization on Earth was just being born, the composition of our atmospheres was practically identical. We did not count on the difference being so great that you would have to be kept in a special barochamber. On board it is easy to create any required conditions, but on the surface of our planet we would have to erect a special building with a mass of complex equipment."

Jupe apparently had finished.

"For you omnipotent ones it must have been a piece of cake," Artem could not resist.

"It was indeed quite simple . . . but no one wanted to make the effort. We *could* but *didn't want to*. We have forgotten how to create, and at best we can only copy. Then I proposed leaving you on board the ship."

"So we're in space? In orbit?"

"No. The ship, it is true, was not equipped for landing on the surface of the planet, but it was no longer needed, and I used the most powerful antigravitation equipment to lower it into one of the uninhabited plateaus on our planet. Our last ship is at anchor."

Oh, where are you when we need you, resourceful space superheroes? All the conditions have been created—you are on an alien ship, just get to the control room, spend a couple of hours learning how to fly it, push a button and *zoom*, back to Earth.

"Ah . . . how about lifting it?" Damn, what an idiotic question he must think it is.

"To lift it? But we do not have a powerful enough antigravitator to carry such a large mass into orbit."

"How about taking off from the surface?"

"You have no idea what you're saying. The takeoff of a cruiser-class starship would blow up the atmosphere and destroy all life on the planet."

Well, that's it. Perhaps there's a way out, but to find it you have to be more than a simple engineer. Now there's only one thing to do—hold out as long as a human mind can, and then die, not fighting for principles— no way!—but at least with dignity.

Now at least we don't have to fear a second invisible ship rapaciously stalking the Earth, and we won't have to anguish over our replacements in the experiment.

They were fated to be the first—and the last. If he had only known earlier! He stood there, staring thoughtlessly in blank space, just repeating, "If I had only known. . . ." The pink-faced god, shaded by the pavilion's arched roof, seemed to be a figure for a primitive Italian master. Only his lips were alive—they moved amusingly with a total lack of synchronization with the words, as though each sentence passed innumerable filters on its way from his lips to Artem's ears and was therefore hopelessly delayed.

"Try to begin your conjugal life," Jupe muttered placidly.

"There is nothing for us to begin," Artem said, forcing his mouth to form the words. "There is nothing for us, period. Except for losing."

The lips on the pink face froze in midword.

"We can only lose," Artem repeated.

And then somewhere quite close by, right next to his face, a shout rang out: "Shut up!"—the shout seemed to come from everywhere now, as though someone was shouting in both ears simultaneously—*"I'm not the only one listening."*

He stared at the face's motionless mask, not understanding what he had said that was so terrible; but then the face contorted, and in total silence the lips moved, silently repeated the words that had just resounded.

Artem rushed to the doorway. The figure on the threshold did not budge, did not step aside, and Artem, instinctively expecting to encounter the usual sticky film but not hitting into anything, went sailing right through Jupe, just as a person runs through a sunbeam. But he didn't have the nerve to try to understand, or even to look back. He raced to the house, knowing that with his words, to which he had not given any significance, he had produced some kind of hellish chain reaction. "The only thing left for us. . . ."

Denise was lying face down, and the scarlet tongues of her weightless clothing, like the artificial fire in a phantom fireplace, trembled over her. Her hands had time to be surprised, and shot upward in a gesture of defense.

"The only thing left for us is losing."

If on her face there had been even a hint of terror or suffering, he would not have dared touching her; but it was only surprise, a patient surprise and expectation, as though something slow and not at all frightening was floating up toward her.

So that is the way it was—the gods had decided to sit through to the end of the play. And he himself had hinted at the contents of the last act. They could not have cared less about the meaning of love. But on the other hand, how fascinating they—the immortal gods—found the idea of losing.

What had they done to her?

He picked her up in his arms, carried her to the daybed. No marks on her body. A world in which everything just came about. The trees just came about, the flowers just came about, and faces just came about.

And death just came about.

No, not that simple. It was a theatrical death, death in buskins, in a purple synthetic robe.

Artem took his pocketknife and cut the slippery, like fish guts, red silk.

Gently, as though he were afraid to awaken her, he undressed Denise, throwing the pieces of her fantastic costume on the floor. Sacrilege? No. Purification.

An ordinary sheet with a black seven-digit number in the corner and the earthly smell of laundry detergent. Mama used to say that they wrapped Aunt Pasha in a sheet and dragged her to Smolensk Cemetery on a small sled. But the burial ditch had been dug not at Smolensk but farther away, over the river, but Mama didn't have the strength to go there, so she sat down alongside the old tram line and waited until a soldier came up with the same kind of sled, only his corpse was wrapped in a fine blanket, and he silently tied Mama's sled behind his own and went quietly over the bridge, and Mama watched until he passed the old tram terminus, where still another cemetery began, a small one and apparently not Orthodox, and the ditch was behind that second cemetery, and then Mama remembered suddenly that she had given the sled away, and that there were still two sisters left.

He knew the story by hearsay, as he knew about the thousands crucified along the Appian Way, the tens of thousands burned by the Inquisition, about the millions tortured in concentration camps, about the tens of millions killed in the war. He knew these things with the light forgetful knowledge of a contemporary young booby that allows a person not to turn gray from horror, not to go mad, not to bang his head against the wall.

Those were the minutes when he was still in a condition to think, to suffer, to remember—maybe not minutes but hours, because when he took Denise's hands into his own they were already as heavy as if they had taken up the torment of the eighty billion deaths that Earth has endured.

He tried to fold those arms across her chest—they would not fold.

And nothing was left but the endless horror before those unbending arms. Denise was no more.

Denise was no more.

He kissed her body. Sacrilege? Even if it were, a thousand times over, could there really be anything that mattered anymore. There was no more good, no more evil. No night, no day. No you, no me.

No Denise.

He wrapped her body, as little girls wrap their dolls. He took her in his arms and went out into the blinding glow of day, which today had not been replaced by the dark of night.

The foliage of the trees unmoved by any wind, the loops of the narrow path, the carpet of the lily clearings. He was carrying her to a grove of trees, as animals carry away their prey, but there were no groves, and there was no getting away from the decadent fleshy roses, from the brooks stinking of amber, from the saccharine sweetness of the marble pavilions. He walked straight ahead, gasping from the burden, from a blind rage, from the impossibility of finding in that glittering rainbow world even a single dark corner where he could conceal Denise.

He had already stopped understanding what was happening around him, and only his feet, which were sinking in up to the ankles, told him that he was no longer in the garden.

All around was sand. Yellowish-gray, dull, without end. Artem set his burden down and sat for several minutes trying to suppress the trembling of the exhausted hands that no longer seemed his. Then, remaining on his knees, he started to dig the sand. The thin flowing mass would not do what he wanted, pouring back into the the narrow, long pit. A little more. That was enough.

Full handfuls of sand. Huge, heavy handfuls. Enough for a whole city, a dream city with pyramids and labyrinths, a hospitable city with milk and honey in the streets. In the sand by the river we cooked *pirozhki*. By the river, by the river. Before dying of thirst, before going mad. . . . We baked. . . .

He was really not dying of love or sorrow—that takes much longer— but from thirst, but there was no force in the universe that could make him take even one swallow of water from this cursed world. In the sand by the river.

The red-hot sand beat under his skull, and a tiny barely quivering thought was enough to make the sharp hot crystals pierce his brain, and then there was short cool unconsciousness. And then again the sky swollen with a gray superheated steam, and a sinking pillow under his head, and Denise's calm face turned to the sky.

Hours passed, and days, and years, and he could not raise two handfuls of sand to cover that face. He lay and looked as long as he had strength, and her death was his death. That was her entire legacy.

And then thousands of years passed and he no longer had strength to look, and he did not see, to his left and to his right, lilac tornados rise up and sweep up the toylike world. And only the thunder, pulsating, increasing, and remaining somewhere to the rear forced him to regain consciousness for an instant, and he realized that Jupe, who had not had the good fortune to remember what love meant, had remembered something else.

He had remembered the meaning of loss, and moved by the bitter and a just force of that memory, turned on the deadly photon reactors of the mammoth starship, wiping from the face of that exhausted planet the long-lived gods and with the whole might of the takeoff blast rendered unto them what belonged to the gods. The first thing he felt was the wind, a real wind, damp and biting; then, the rawness of the earth, covered here and there with goosefoot, and right next to his cheek, the icy mosaic of a tile slab. Artem got up. Ten yards away his building towered, improbably huge, sending its antennas into the fall morning sky. But the building was no longer the last one in town. Right beneath his windows, insolently creeping over onto the narrow strip of lawn, was a new construction site, with the inevitable piles of broken bricks, crushed stone, and sand, with lime-smeared boards awaiting their doom in the pyre, with a disconsolate backhoe, from a distance resembling a dinosaur with a fractured neck, with the street faucet and the piercing rusty drip.

The drops clattered against a piece of tin, as though they were beating on it with silvery hooves, and Artem got to his feet and headed with difficulty toward that noise. Something strange had happened to him, but he could not think of what it was and could not even describe coherently his condition, because it was the way it is only in childhood when you cry your head off and for oh, so long, so that you fall asleep and then wake up all light and bitter, and at first you can't remember what it was you were crying about.

He walked over the tile shards, happy with his ignorance, with his eyes searching for something torturous but miraculously forgotten, he walked and prayed—just not to remember, not to remember; but his fear was in vain, and everything that lay between his spring holiday and this September morning was stored behind seven gates with seven locks, and no effort of memory could get past.

He walked over the broken bricks and fragments of still not mounted but already broken glass, and each step over that rubble-choked piece of ground that was giving birth to a building that was destined to be for a short while the last one in town—each of these steps was a new infinity separating him from the black abyss of the seemingly forever-vanished summer.

And then he stopped.

Because there, behind the clattering tin was some sand, fine, yellowish-gray, a sloping pile, and Denise's calm face, turned up to the fall Leningrad sky.

The piercing pain of memory touched him, and squeezed him, pressing harder and harder until it became unbearable, until it would remain with him for the rest of his life. And then he said, "Thank you, Jupe."

No one answered him, and he realized that the last of the immortals had sacrificed himself along with the others.

Tower of Birds

OLEG KORABELNIKOV

Yes, man is a tower of birds
A receptacle of shaggy beasts,
In his face are millions of faces
Of four-legged and winged creatures.
And many beasts dwell within him,
And many fish from ocean depths.

—N. ZABOLOTSKY

1

That summer the taiga was burning over an enormous expanse, and the airborne firefighters were assembled near the center, but all the same, despite their efforts and sacrifices, the flames slowly crawled forward in the wake of the wind, and only the rivers would not let them pass, held back their implacable advance, absorbing the fiery avalanche in their coolness. Everything in the taiga that could move, everything that had legs or wings, moved away from the fire, and only the trees and grass, which had become a part of the earth, died in silence, but even they attempted to send their seeds out on the winds, on the claws of birds, in the fur of animals—as far as possible from the fire and destruction.

Explosions boomed throughout the taiga, bulldozers roared violently, human beings worked in the smoke and fumes. And Egor felt out of place here, a stranger to these people, and to the taiga with its immobile trees and its running, crawling, and flying inhabitants. He ended up in the fire region by accident, and his goals did not coincide with the heavy labor that these people performed. He wandered through deserted taiga villages, seeking spinning wheels, samovars, and dark, crackled ikons. All those things died with the passing of time, crumbled into dust, and Egor strove to hold back even the tiny bit that fell into his hands. A fire nearby stopped him, and now he waited for it to be put under control so that he could without risk move on, upstream. His vacation was coming to an end, and he was annoyed with the unexpected delay and moped around the small village where the firefighters were staying, too.

During these two weeks of voluntary exile he had learned much and understood much, and all the problems of his city life—his divorce, his leaving the institute, his confusion and restlessness—here seemed trivial and unworthy. Faced with the huge expanse of perishing forest, with the inferno of a crown fire, boiling streams, the charred bodies of burnt animals, and black miles of dead taiga, faced with all this, the whole past with its woes and suffering seemed unreal, a human invention.

When his patience was exhausted, on a windless day, he decided to go to a forsaken little monastery, where according to the tales of local residents no one had lived but where the treasures that had brought him here lay in boarded-up *izbas*.

He traveled light, only an ax in its sheath, a knife in its sheather, a box of matches, and a pack of cigarettes. And a compass on a strap.

The morning was quiet, which meant that the fire would advance slowly and would not jump to the crowns—so, so terrifying and more amenable to taming. Making his way over a damp slope, cursing the thick underbrush, Egor suddenly felt that the fire was getting close. That did not coincide with his original plans, but the smell of burning, a low but still-thin smoke, and a barely audible crackling of burning trees spoke unequivocably—the fire was near. Egor stopped, listened carefully for a long time and realized that the fire was moving at him and that he would have to run before it was too late. In front of him, with great noise, without looking where they were heading, some elk leaped into a narrow gully; seeing Egor, they turned abruptly and breaking through the brush, disappeared into a grove. And still unseen by Egor smaller creatures were fleeing the fire, birds were screaming loudly, bushes were swaying, and fallen trees cracked under the feet of many animals.

Before reaching the end of the gully Egor began to climb gradually up the steep slope on the hill, presuming that the fire, overcoming the last barrier, would roll more slowly down below, held back by air currents. The damp grass slipped under his feet, the thick underbrush blocked his ascent; gasping for breath, Egor reached the top and saw from there that the fire was right next to him—on the top of the next hill, and that meant that there was little time to save him, at most fifteen minutes. The crackle of branches, trunks, broken and crippled by the fire, became louder and louder. It was pursuing Egor. Seeming to roll down the opposite slope, from somewhere in the middle, he suddenly heard a song.

Someone was walking down there and calmly singing in an incomprehensible language, and the song was echoed by an indistinguishable chorus, as though mourners were following a coffin and lamenting, wailing piteously, each in a different key. And Egor thought that it must be the local inhabitants walking through the gully, and if they were so calm before the fire, then the danger could not be that great. Egor could now distinguish individual words but still did not understand them, and between the song's rhythmical repetitions he heard the sharp crack of a whip. After each crack the chorus's lamentations increased, and Egor could not free himself from the feeling that he had heard something similar somewhere else. That long howl, not divided into words, was familiar. He slid down through the tall grass and saw something that amazed him and forced him to stop.

Along a narrow path a short old man was walking with a short whip in his hand, and behind him, stretched out single file, were a pack of wolves. Ten or twelve of them, of varying ages but all with hanging heads, and they all minced along, their tails between their legs, and howled in different tones in time to the cracking of the whip. The old man sang the incomprehensible song, and Egor, frozen still on the slope, could find nothing better to do than shout, "Hey, shepherd! Don't you see the wolves behind you? Clear out while you still can!"

The old man turned his face to Egor, slid an indifferent glance over him, and without stopping the procession, turned aside. The wolves did not even look in Egor's direction. For a short time Egor saw the old man's face and, judging by the yellow, wrinkled skin, concluded that he was an Evenk, since many of that ancient people lived in the region.

The wind blew on the nearby fire, and Egor, turning up his hands in despair at the procession, cut across the gully at a run, a yard behind the last wolf, and still running, without decreasing his speed, ran down the low ground in the opposite direction. He realized that the fire had jumped to the crowns, and its speed now exceeded any one imaginable for a human being. It became noticeably hotter, the roar of the fire grew, and Egor saw the crest of yellow leaping flames slowly roll over the hill and begin to descend the hill in a suffocating heavy wave. In despair and hopelessness Egor raced along the gully, gasping from smoke, seeing almost nothing behind except billowing clouds that filled the low ground, and then suddenly he heard a woman's voice calling him by name. Someone out there in the smoke was calling him, calmly and tenderly.

"Egor, follow behind me, hurry. Not that way, my little fool, not that way."

And the woman laughed. Her voice was not loud but somehow was not swallowed up by the noise around him, as though she stood behind him and spoke right in his ear. Egor looked around at the voice and saw a narrow strip leading from him into the depths of the burning taiga. And the strip was untouched by fire, as though someone had sealed it off with an invisible wall. On both sides fire raged, but on it trees were growing and dew was on the flowers, and the spiderwebs did not tremble in the wind. And he stepped on the strip, felt the coolness of a summer morning, and set off running along it, not looking to the sides, feeling that the wall of fire was closing behind his back and burning branches crashing down on his footprints. Ahead something flashed, someone's head glanced out from behind a pine, a naked arm waved to him from behind a currant bush, a quiet bell-like laugh floated to him from behind. Egor was afraid to stop, the fire was pursuing him, and there was no time to think or to call out to whomever was running ahead.

Fear distorted his sense of time, and while crackling was heard all around, and trees were falling, and branches breaking, it seemed that several hours passed, and Egor, short of breath, ran and ran, until the noises of the fire were behind him and at the sides of the strip were no longer burning trees. He slowed down to a walk, and then stopped entirely. And the saving strip disappeared into the trunk of an enormous cedar, and there, behind it, the burnt-out zone began. Egor turned around. Behind him as far as he could see, stood a smoky, black taiga, and tongues of flame slipped up between the trees. Egor sat down at a small patch of green grass under the cedar, slumped back against it, and wiped the sweat from his forehead. Something rustled, a green twig floated down, a green cone bounced along the ground and buried itself in ashes. Someone above his head laughed.

"Who are you?" Egor asked, tilting his head back and trying to make something out in the trees.

The quiet laughter changed into a squirrel's chatter and a minute later into the cry of a jay. And then Egor saw the cedar change before his very eyes. The green foliage turned into gray ashes and fluttered down, the branches twisted and turned black, and the trunk became charcoal, without fire; now it was like all the other trees. An owl's guffaw was heard above, invisible wings rustled gently, and a soft tender voice reached him from the distance:

"Go, Egor, go. The way is long, and life is short. Go to the river."

Within twenty-four hours he had finally made his way to the side of the wedge of fire. It was marked by a little river, and on the other bank everything was green and quiet; it was strange to see living taiga after all the ashes and char. He fell into the water, which smelled of mint, drank long and greedily, then carefully washed and even rinsed out his shirt. He lay on the green bank and looked across at the burnt side, as at an alien planet. The deformed and disfigured taiga, black and gray out to the horizon.

The glass on his compass had broken and the needle fallen out. Egor threw away the useless case, determined the direction by the lichens on the trees, and headed north. He was not afraid of getting lost, somewhere nearby was a village, and other people. He carefully searched for a path made by human beings, but all around was only tall grass, the name of which he didn't know, bushes, trees, mosses, and lichens. His feet fell into invisible holes filled with water; he was plagued with a foul feeling, and most important, hunger came. Egor walked and walked toward the north, remembering that on the map in that direction there had been a river and a village on its banks. Peeling off the bark on pine trees, he chewed the sweetish soft tissue, ate the meaty stems of tall grass, and dug up tubers of arrowroot. Now rare in the taiga, they were floury and tasteless. But his hunger was not satisfied, his weakness grew, and his fatigue not alleviated by short halts.

And then came his first night of solitude.

He started a fire, using up six precious matches. He still had ten. His torn and seared clothing did not keep him warm, so he lay close to the fire, with the flames burning his face while his back froze. Then he cut down some fire branches, spread them out below, covered himself above, taking care that the boughs did not catch fire.

His thoughts were not particularly cheery, but he was still hoping for the best, and it never occurred to him that he might never get out of the taiga. He dozed off and dreamed of the city, which was now strange to him but still made him homesick, particularly now. In his dream he was walking down an asphalt road and a sterile wind was blowing in his face. At the side of the road grew nickel-plated trees with aluminum leaves. And someone was walking toward him, not exactly a beast, not exactly a human being, and someone was shouting or singing in the distance.

In his dream he was glad to hear a living human voice, and was at the same time afraid of it, as though it could harm him.

And he awoke with a sense of impending catastrophe that seized him by the throat. The fire was going out, and he stood up, piled up the branches, and right then heard a human voice.

2

Egor moved away from the fire slowly, so that its crackle would not disturb his hearing, and held his breath. Someone was shouting in the distance. A resonant voice, apparently a girl's, and it even appeared to be happy. He could not make out the words, only the long vowels: a-a, u-u, o-o! As though she were singing. Egor determined the direction of the wind, stood up, and shouted himself. The hills swallowed up the echo, and the sound of his voice was soon extinguished. But it seemed to him that the invisible girl was answering him on a higher note and slightly louder. Then he put out the fire and strode off in the dark in that direction. From time to time he gave a shout and convinced himself with joy that he was being heard and answered, as incomprehensibly as before but still in a human voice. He had to go straight ahead, across a high hill, and in the pitch-dark it proved to be a severe problem. Several times he slipped on the steep surface, fell, rolled down the dew-heavy grass, swore loudly to keep his anger strong, to urge himself on, and when he reached the summit he realized that the voice that had been calling him was now gone. He yelled loudly, in every direction, listened carefully, but no one answered him. Then he sat down, worn out, felt like spitting in disgust, but his mouth was dry. He just sat there, listened to the taiga, and it spoke in the language of crawling and flying creatures, but not a single word resembled anything human.

He decided to start a fire again and sleep even for a little, but again he heard the voice, and so close that he was startled. This time he could make out the words, or more accurately, one word. The unknown girl was shouting, "Ego-o-r!" she was calling him by name, and the voice was tender, young, excited. "Ego-o-r," she called, "come here!" And he could not resist. No matter how absurd everything that happened may have been, he was so hungry, so tired that he could not resist the gentle voice calling out to him. In a low, damp gully he stopped, listened, and yelled at the top of his lungs, cupping his hands like a megaphone, "He-e-y! Answer me!"

But he heard only the splash of the river. He groped his way to the low bank, washed his face, drank his fill, and yelled again.

"Egorushka," the voice called to him softly from behind.

He turned around abruptly and lost his balance, falling to the ground. In the dark he heard a laugh, cold, muffled, as though the mouth was covered by a hand.

"Well, what are you laughing at?" Egor asked, turning to the darkness. "Who are you? Was it you who led me out of the fire? Why are you hiding?"

"Ego-o-orushka!" the langorous voice drawled. "I am here. Come to me. Come."

The voice fell to a whisper, provocative, almost passionate.

"Are you making fun of me?" Egor asked angrily. "Well, go ahead. I'll wait."

He sat down on a damp log, not afraid of wetting his pants. Even without that his clothes were soaked through. Egor was not afraid of evil spirits, even less of human beings.

"Why are you sitting there?" the girl whispered right in his ear.

He felt her breath on his neck, cold for some reason, like a gust of river wind. Without turning around, he reached out suddenly behind him, leaning back. Something soft and cold slid beneath his fingertips.

"Well then, I am waiting, come here," the girl whispered, then giggled.

The moonless night, the dampness, the splashing of the river, and the invisible girl reminded him of something seen or read, but he did not feel fear. A girl, that was all. How can you fear a girl? But still there remained a feeling of near danger, so he preferred to stand up and face the possible danger. He saw something whitish, as though a wind-washed fog, which flashed briefly before disappearing onto the darkness.

"Why are you running away?" Egor asked challengingly, putting his hand on his ax. "I come to you, but you run. Come closer, let's introduce ourselves."

And right then something poked him in the chest. Egor was caught by surprise and fell on his back, striking a stone painfully. The ax fell out of his hands but, held by the strap, remained attached to his belt.

"Egorushka," the girl whispered in his ear. "Egorushka, my love, my darling, my handsome one."

A cold hand slid over his face.

"Away, get away!" Egor yelled, jumping up. "Whoever you are, get out of here while the going is good!"

He struck a match. The dim light shone on shoreline rocks, the water, and clumps of grass. Nothing else. Then he decided to move away from the shore and light a fire. While he was wandering in the dark, the invisible girl circled around him, touching his body with her hands, each time in a different place, and Egor tried to brush her away, like an uncatchable fly.

He collected some branches by feel and peeled off some birch bark. The fire flared up brightly, baring a circle of stones. Egor sat down close to the fire, not relaxing, expecting some monkeyshines. And they came. The fire hissed loudly, the flames shot up high, and the burning branches flew off in every direction, sending out sparks that the heavy dew soon extinguished. Egor barely managed to roll to the side.

And he heard laughter. Loud, ringing, unrestrained. At first it seemed to him that the girl was to the right, and he turned in that direction, but the laughter switched to the left, and then behind him, and then even above him. No footsteps, no rustling of wings. Egor completely lost his temper.

"Hey, you evil spirits of the night!" he shouted in a flash of rage. "Just let me catch you, just try coming close to me!"

"Oh, my mischievous little boy," the girl said in a loud whisper, and then an icy, burning weight fell on Egor's back, strong arms encircled his chest, squeezing his arms flat against his body. "How playful my little one is, my dearest, oh, how dear you are to me, come with me, let us go."

Egor always considered himself strong, but no matter how he struggled, the embrace grew stronger and stronger. He bent forward abruptly and kicked with all his strength. His foot hit something soft, yielding. Panting and shivering from the cold, Egor fell on his side but freed himself from the bearhug. He quickly rolled over on his back, bent his knees, tensing his legs, and positioned his hands holding the knife so as to beat off an attack. In the almost absolute darkness fighting was hard, particularly with an opponent who surpassed him in strength and cunning and, most important, was invisible and unknown. His foe, it seemed, was not tired, her voice was just as even and langorous.

"What's the matter, Egorushka? Why do you spurn my embraces? Am I not dear to you? Embrace me, my caresser, I am cold, oh, so cold."

A cold hand slid over Egor's face, and he barely managed to strike it, but the hand immediately tore his collar, and for an instant he felt a touch of ice under his arm.

"Oh you treacherous bitch!" Egor said through his teeth. He began flailing out with the knife, making circles over his chest.

But it did not help. The icy hands touched him now here, now there, and once he felt the touch of firm lips against his cheek—as though liquid nitrogen had dripped on it. The girl laughed, without malice, resonantly, but in the laugh was such confidence that Egor finally became terrified. She's only playing with me, he thought, and while she's only playing, a grown man like me can't handle her. What would happen if she really applied all her strength?"

"What do you want from me?" he wheezed, short of breath. "What did I ever do to you? Why are you tormenting me?"

"Do not spurn me," the girl said. "Embrace me."

"In the morning," Egor answered, "as soon as dawn breaks, I'll embrace you."

"No, only at night."

"I'm tired. To hell with embraces that send shivers through your body. Let's make a fire, and I'll agree."

"No, my dear, no."

And something cold, heavy, like a block of ice, fell on Egor, pressed him against the ground, and in vain he attempted to free himself from that living, tenacious ice. It was very heavy, and his own helplessness infuriated him most of all. He put his arms around whatever had fallen on him and felt a human body, cold and wet. Streams of water flowed onto his face; it smelled of fish and algae. Overcoming his disgust, choking, he wound up and plunged the knife into the body. The knife entered the body unexpectedly easily, as if it were water. He threw it away, grabbed the back with his hands, and began to knead it, icy, amorphous, viscous, sticky, trying to push the body away, if only partially.

"Harder, darling, harder," the girl whispered. "Ah, how warm it is, my love." Streams of supercooled water lashed him in the face, as though they were the girl's hair. Egor no longer paid attention to her kisses that froze his skin—he kneaded her back, sides, but could not rid himself of the weight or tear away even the slightest part of her body. And then he noticed that her body was becoming warmer while he was freezing, and his exhausted arms were numb, despite the movement.

"But you're killing me," he said. "Why must you?"

"Warm me and I will leave," she whispered and kissed him on the lips. The kiss seemed warmer than before.

Egor choked, gasped, his arms were numb, and his body had lost sensation. And it seemed to him that he was lying on the bottom of a river and two hundred feet of water pressed down on him, washing away the warmth, dissolving his body, carrying it away in the current, destroying his integrity and indivisibility. He prepared for death and cursed desperately, but his throat gave out only short gurgles.

Right then a horn sounded beyond the river. And Egor saw that the night was becoming light and gradually flowing into morning.

And he still saw the face of the girl pressed against his face. It was beautiful but seemed to have been sculpted out of dense fog, white, it radiated in the darkness like a phosphorescent spot, and the transparent eyes looked at him blankly and calmly. He butted the face with his forehead and sank his teeth—the last weapon of the doomed—into the left cheek. The warm flesh let his teeth through without resistance, and they clacked together.

And once again the horn sounded, louder and more melodious. He could already distinguish the silhouettes of trees against the sky and river, and the stones on the banks. Egor went limp, his strength was gone, and he felt only a winter cold penetrating his body and a freezing breath.

And the girl grew lighter, her face shone, her hands stroked his chest a last time, and he felt relief. She stood up straight, and he saw her from head to foot. Even the soft contours of her body were beautiful and graceful, her long flowing hair streamed down to her feet, her gaze was indifferent and deep. Egor tried to stand, but his body would not obey him. The cold had penetrated deeply and would not leave. Egor felt snow and ice in his belly, a dank rawness in his chest, and such an incredible weakness that he seemed weightless and his body nonexistent.

"You have warmed me," the girl said. "You have dissolved in me. Now you are mine, you are ours."

And she walked away; she stepped inaudibly toward the river, and he saw the dark waves cover her feet, and only a splash in the river told of her departure.

Then he lost consciousness or just fell asleep, but when he awoke it was day already, and the turbid sun stood at the zenith. He was lying on his back, warming himself, remembering the night's events as a departed but still nearby nightmare. He raised his hand and rubbed his face. The hand seemed to belong to someone else, dry and wrinkled. Egor was frightened, tried to leap to his feet, but his body refused. His hand fell back, and separating itself from his body, to the side. Egor followed its movement with a dismayed look. It was really not his hand, but the hand of the Evenk who had shepherded wolves. Yellow-complexioned, seemingly withered, with two fluid pigtails, he looked at Egor with an indifferent expression, pursing his dry lips.

"Ah, the wolf shepherd," Egor said quietly. "Give me water, I'm thirsty."

The Evenk walked away, sat down at a distance, and began to repair his whip.

"Do you understand Russian?" Egor asked. "Give me water, do you hear? Wa-ter!"

He made a sucking gesture with his lips, motioned with his eyes toward the river.

"Lie still," the Evenk answered in a high-pitched, nasal voice. "You'll die soon, however, Mavka took all the warmth from you, so you die."

"Well, let me drink my fill before death."

"I won't give you it, however."

"Is it so hard for you? The river is near."

"I have eyes, I see. All the same, you'll die."

"What have I done to harm you, old man?"

"You have done nothing. What can a corpse do?"

"Don't bury me alive!" Egor said angrily.

Evenk dispassionately finished weaving the tip of his whip, got to his

feet lightly, and left. In the distance his song broke out, followed immediately by the dissonance of the wolves' howling.

Anger gave Egor strength, and he turned on his side and rolled down
to the nearby riverbank. He plunged his face into the water, drank deeply,
slowly massaging his sore body, positioning himself to catch the sun's rays,
cold, cold within. He was very hungry, and when he could stand, the first
thing he did was stroll over to a nearby currant bush, pick a handful, and
chew greedily.

He lay on his stomach, having taken off his shirt, absorbed the warmth
with his skin, following the sun with his eyes as it sank toward the horizon,
and decided that one way or another he was going to live, he was going
to go on, to find people. The river splashed, and he turned toward it, on
guard, and saw that a large fish had hurled itself onto the shore and was
thrashing its strong body against the stones. Egor jumped up, knowing
that he was going to fall but timing his fall so that he would land on the
fish. It was a salmon, and Egor had to hold it down for a long time before
it ceased moving.

"Trying to bribe me?" Egor asked the river. "Well, all right, to hell
with you—I'll get even, my beauty. I'll return, I'll return, even so. If I
survive, that is."

He recounted his matches—there were eight left. And with each match
he used he felt life flowing out of him, warmth and hope for rescue. From
the night dampness the heads of them had fused together. He lovingly
separated them, set them on the warm stones, warmed them in his hands,
blew on them, waited patiently. He ate the salmon raw.

He ascended a knoll and looked around, searching for smoke from the
fire. But the taiga from horizon to horizon and undulated in low hills,
green, thickly overgrown, untouched by human beings. He carefully put
on his shoes, placed the dried matches in the box, and strapped on his
knife so it would be easy to pull it out quickly. Following the reddening
sun, he piled flat stones in a pyramid so he would remember the place.

"Hey, Mavka!" he yelled in farewell to the stream. "Look out here, my
beauty, let us say farewell!"

The river carried its waters past him, ringing out in the shoals, and did
not answer. Only in the distance, beyond the hills, the horn played a sad
melody and broke off on a high note.

The following day Egor realized that he was totally lost. He did not
have any high hopes of their searching for him, but still pricked up his
ears when, in the morning, he heard the distant chirr of a helicopter. The
noise of the motor diminished, then disappeared; it did not return. Ap-

parently Egor had wandered too far from the fire to a place where no one was searching for him, thinking that he could not cover such a great distance. He himself could not understand how, during the night he ran across the taiga after the invisible girl's call, he could have gone so far; it seemed impossible to cover a good fifty miles in a few hours.

Struggling through almost impenetrable windfallen trees, he remembered his being saved from the fire and the near-fatal embraces of Mavka. He found no rational explanation but could not believe in the unbelievable: that Mavka was straight from Russian folklore, a *rusalka*, a spirit of a betrayed maiden who returned to take revenge on men. He knew that in the mountains the mysterious abominable snowman wandered, that in far-off Loch Ness a monster lived, and that flying saucers were circling the Earth, and he believed in all these wonders that existed far from him, but in ancient pagan myths about *rusalkas* he just could not believe.

He was firmly convinced that amid the blind, self-absorbed nature, he, Egor, was a rational man, and the master of all that existed on Earth; even though he had been bested, crushed, he was still the master and was not about to share with anyone, not even in his thoughts.

The river, which had not been gifted with a name, flowed amid nameless forests, where forest spirits hallooed to each other in the groves, *rusalkas* in deep pools grew intoxicated on the fat of fish, the water spirit picked its teeth with a rusty fish spear, *baba-yagas* turned in their narrow graves to shake loose the aspen stakes driven through their bellies, *oborotens* with knives stuck into them leaped over stumps and changed into wolves, bogeymen blinked their owllike eyes in his tree hollow, *kikimoras* squatted near paths as they lay in wait for passersby, the ancient Slavic Belbog, whose face was red with squashed mosquitoes, gorged himself on bear flesh, the ordinary man chopped down pines, and the chips lay at a distance from the dying trees. Wolves listened to the distant ring of metal and rubbed their ears. They did not like human beings.

3

Despite his dread of the river he was afraid to go too far from it. Following its twists and turns and walking in the direction of its flow was still easier than taking a chance on walking straight through the brush. And Egor decided to tie together a small raft and make the river carry him. He chose a spot on a cliff so that he would not have to roll the cut-down trees far, sharpened his ax, and selecting appropriate pines, set to work. His hunger and fatigue soon made themselves felt, and he had to sit or lie down often to rest his still-numb hands and to catch his breath. His sense of hearing, which had become very sharp during the last few days, caught the sound of footsteps. Soft, cautious. Egor clasped the ax firmly and stood with his back to a pine. The steps died down, and then behind him he heard snapping and chattering, like a squirrel. Egor turned abruptly and saw the familiar Evenk sitting on a knoll, his short legs crossed; he stared disapprovingly at the fallen tree.

"Well, I'm healthy," Egor said, flashing his ax. "So you were wrong? See, I'm alive. And where are your wolves, shepherd?"

"Why are you killing the trees?" the Evenk asked.

"What's it to you? When I need to, I chop them down. Who are you?"

"Dyoyba-nguo is who I am," the Evenk answered. "Why, didn't you know? Everyone knows me. Why don't you fear me? Everyone fears me."

"I spit on you," Egor said and, turning around, swung his ax.

"Oh-oh!" the Evenk shouted. "It hurts! Why do you make it hurt?"

"When I hit you, that's the time to shout. I'm just chopping the pine."

And once again Egor struck the ax against the unyielding wood. A chip flew behind him.

"Oh-oh," the Evenk cried out again and squinted, as though from intense pain. "You are killing my forest, however. What did it ever do to you?"

"It's just that I want to live. Clear enough?"

"Then live, however," the Evenk counseled. "Since you didn't die, live. To live is good."

"Thanks for the advice, but I know myself that living is good," Egor said and struck a third time. "I don't need stupid advice."

"Ah, what a bad man!" the Evenk said reproachfully. "Everyone wants to live. You cut down the forest, and kill me."

"And did you have pity on me? You refused me water. I spit on you now. Is that clear?"

"And why do you need pity? You're a human being, there are many of you. I am alone, an orphan, poor Dyoyba."

The Evenk gestured with his hands to show how many people there were, and how alone he himself was.

"One person more, one person less," he said, "changes nothing. You kill each other. But I am alone, an orphan. You burn the forest, and it hurts me. You chop down a tree, and it hurts me, you kill animals, and oh, how it hurts."

"What can I say?" Egor answered. "It's the same way in your forest: Everything kills, and that's how they live. Why put the blame on people? After all, what are you?"

"Dyoyba-nguo, I already said."

"So if you are, what about it? Go shepherd your wolves, if that's what you like, and leave me alone."

And Egor deepened his cut.

"Mou-nyamy, Mother Earth, gave birth to us all, and all have one soul," Dyoyba said. "You, human beings, Syarada-nyamy, the Mother of Underground Ice, gave birth to you. Your souls are cold. You have pity on nothing. The forest is large, its soul is one. You thin its body, it hurts the soul. You kill the body, the soul dies. You are foolish."

"Don't be offended by fools," Egor said, swinging his ax. "And don't bother me with your fairy tales."

"Didn't Mavka torment you enough?" Dyoyba asked. "You were pitiful, so you were spared, Litsedei did not permit it. If he had not sounded his horn, you would be dead."

"Go your way, Shepherd Dyoyba," Egor said, lowering his ax. "Don't keep me from doing my work."

"The forest is mine," he insisted. "If you kill the body, the soul hurts."

"Soul? In you yourself the soul is barely alive."

"Humans have done it," Dyoyba complained. "They burn the forest, kill the animals, poison the rivers. It hurts."

"So what's it to me?" Egor said and swung his ax.

"You are bad," Dyoyba said, wincing from pain. "I will make you heal the tree, then feed you to the wolves. Wolves don't like men, they are very angry with men."

"So what?" Egor said, doing his work.

"Heal the tree. Tear your shirt in pieces and heal it."

"I forgot to bring the drugstore," Egor said and heard the buzzing of a bee by his ear.

He waved his hand at it, but it returned, and soon a whole swarm was buzzing around him.

"Will you heal it?" he heard above the buzzing.

"No way!"

The bees hurled themselves at Egor. The more he struck at the amorphous swarm, the more fiercely the bees attacked. His eyes swelled. Enraged by the pain, Egor rushed toward the river, rolled down a steep slope in a cloud of dust, and dove in.

The water was icy, unbearable for long, but leaving it was impossible—the swarm was circling overhead. And then something under the water bit his leg sharply. And again, as though cutting it with a hacksaw. Egor struggled in vain against his new enemy; each time it came up from a different direction and nipped him on the legs with its sharp teeth. Forgetting himself in pain and anger, Egor leaped out on shore and started digging in the sandy slope. But as soon as he had covered himself with sand and clumps of grass, something burrowed to him from under the ground and, squeaking, bit him on the stomach, and again, on the back, and again, on the thigh.

"Heal it, however," Dyoyba said.

"Call off your assassins," Egor said, barely keeping himself from screaming the words out.

He lay there, gathering strength from the damp earth, stood up, tottering, swollen, dirty, with bite marks on his body, climbed up the bank grinding his teeth, sat down with his back against the half-chopped tree, and spat out a gob of thick saliva.

"You vermin," he said, unsticking his lips.

"Tear your shirt," Dyoyba said, "and heal the tree. Then you will wash the river."

"Are you crazy? Wash a river?"

"People sprinkled a powder in the river, killing fish. You will wash the water."

"Fool!" Egor said, and grinding his teeth in humiliation, tore up his shirt.

The material was ancient, tore easily into short, unequal strips. Struggling to keep his swollen eyes open, Egor wrapped the cut in the pine, sticky with resin and sap, and tormented by his consciousness of the idiocy of his task, tore more strips and used them, too.

"If I get to you," he threatened Dyoyba, "you'll dance to a different tune."

"Heal it, however," Dyoyba counseled peacefully. "It hurt me before, and you did not show pity. Have pity on yourself now. When you heal, you will be healed yourself; if you cause pain, you will feel pain. You, people, do not understand words, you understand pain, and you understand death."

Dyoyba clicked his tongue as a sign of regret.

Egor finished his foolish task and tied the ends of the cloth in a bow.

"Well, how about it?" he asked. "Am I a good pine-tree healer?"

"Let's go, however. You will wash the water. Oh, how dirty it is!"

"There's no soap," Egor blurted out.

"Why soap? You will wash without soap."

"Show me how! You do half, and I'll do half."

They went down to the river.

"You're not going to set the fish on me, are you?" Egor asked, fixing his ax so it would not hit against his leg.

"I won't," Dyoyba said. "Get in the river."

"Okay," Egor said and took a running dive, trying to swim as far underwater as possible.

The rapid current carried him along, and when he climbed out on the other shore the spot where he had been chopping the pine was around a bend. This bank was low, covered with thick grass. Egor lay down and rested, catching his breath and inspecting his wounds. They were not deep but were still a cause for concern. No medicines, no bandages, and the merest trifle in the deserted taiga could be fatal.

Egor washed his wounds in the river, looked for some plantain, but it did not grow in the taiga—there was no one to carry its seeds, no human beings at all. He took out the water-swollen matchbox, twirled the bare sticks between his fingers, and threw them away indifferently.

"So here's the story, Egor," he said to himself, "they've burned you with fire, drowned you in water, frozen you with ice, attacked you with bees and animals, and you are still alive. Just keep it up."

He set off through a swamp. He stopped in a dry spot and saw the beginning of a narrow path. He crouched down, crawled along it, and saw what he had been waiting for—a human footprint. A narrow, shallow impression in the moist soil, a single footprint.

"Hey," he shouted, straightening up. "Hey, anybody around?"

He was answered by some owls. They created such an uproar of hoots and clucks that Egor did not hear the person who walked toward him on the other side of a clump of honeysuckle. He felt someone's glance upon him, turned in that direction, but saw no one.

"Come out," he said. "What are you afraid of? If you're a fellow human, I won't harm you."

"Throw down your ax," a girl's voice said melodiously.

"Is that you, Mavka?" Egor trembled. "Off with you, then!"

In the bushes there was laughter, gentle, not at all menacing.

"No," the girl said, "I'm not Mavka. Your ax, though—throw it down."

"Okay," Egor said and threw his ax a short distance away. "You picked a fine person to be afraid of. There's not an untouched spot on me. Is your village close? Maybe there will be something to eat? I'm really starved."

And out of the honeysuckle a girl stepped. A very little girl, thin, cute, her cheeks stained with raspberries, wearing a red sarafan and a white kerchief.

"Oh," Egor said, relaxing, "where did you come from? For a while I thought I'd never see another human being."

He lowered himself to the ground and sat there looking at the girl, admiring her, even to smile with his swollen lips.

"Well, what are you staring at? Am I so terrible? Don't be afraid, I'm no forest spirit. I'm Egor, I got lost in the taiga, and the evil spirits set to work on me. I'm surprised I'm still alive. Sit a little, let me rest, and then let's go, all right?"

The girl did not answer but stood near the bushes, smiled gently, and her face showed she did not fear him at all. Most likely adults were nearby, he thought, and gave a sigh of relief. The tension of the past few days, when he had to struggle every minute for his life and the consciousness that the chances of survival were not that great, slipped away and left an emptiness and enormous weariness. He looked at the girl and after days of isolation from people, felt with joy a sense of belonging to the human race, strong, beautiful, and magnanimous.

"Bring me something to eat," he asked, "and call some adults. My strength is gone, I can't move."

The girl did not answer. She stood and smiled, pursing her lips as though she were about to whistle. Then she bent over and picked up a basket of raspberries. She handed it to Egor.

Egor took a handful of raspberries, held them in front of his mouth, inhaled the scent, and trying not to hurry, swallowed them without chewing.

But then he realized it was still not raspberry season. He had walked through the taiga and encountered bushes with green, astringent berries. But these were ripe, juicy, strongly scented, and just picked. He said nothing to the girl and accepted the absurdity with ease.

"Do you have bread?" he asked, handing her the empty basket.

The girl once again reached down into the grass and picked up a chunk of bread. Egor was amazed, but ate the bread, every last crumb.

"And what else do you have in the grass?"

The girl shrugged, smiled.

An unchildlike smile, Egor thought. The taiga matures them early.

"What would you like?" she asked.

"To sleep," Egor said honestly. "I'm awfully tired. Will you bring some adults here, and maybe find some clothes? You can see I'm practically naked."

The little girl nodded her head and disappeared into the bushes. Not a sound of footsteps, not a rustle of her dress, not a crackle from a twig beneath her feet.

"Hey," Egor shouted. "Don't disappear, come back! I'll wait!"

He had just enough strength to pick up the ax and put it under his head. Ignoring the hum of mosquitoes, he fell asleep, as if he were in a deep pool.

4

Egor lived inside a tree. Not in a hollow, not separate from the trunk, but within the wood itself, and his body ended with the bark and leaves. Through him the earth's juices passed, inside him an annual ring was growing slowly, and it was he, Egor, who groaned with his whole body during gusts of wind. Egor was not surprised by his new state of being; he considered it natural and even convenient. He was growing in a large clearing, and his roots sank deep into the ground, intertwining with the roots of other trees.

It was dark, warm, comfortable. Egor sensed his existence, and he needed nothing more, just to grow without thinking about a thing, awaiting the day when the birds would arrive, settle in him, as in the cornices of a tower, and begin to sing their songs in languages he could comprehend. He knew that it would happen and was therefore calm and patient.

Something touched his side. He moved and thought lazily that it was probably a woodpecker hammering at his side, and was not alarmed. The woodpecker seemed to be a continuation of himself, like the beetle larvae that lived under his bark.

"Egor!" he heard a voice calling. He shifted his body, his eyes still shut tight.

"Get up, Egorushka," he heard again.

"Is it time already?" he asked and did not recognize his own voice.

He opened his eyes and saw that he was not really a tree but a human being. And he was lying on a soft bearskin, on the floor, near an oven. A bearded man in a red cap pushed forward over his forehead was bending over him and tugging at him.

And Egor remembered that he had fallen asleep on the bank and realized that they had picked him up and carried him here. He finally shook the cobwebs out of his head, sat up, and looked around. He was dressed in a broad fur shirt, his pants were new, and also made of fur. He rubbed his hand over his body, and nothing hurt anywhere: His hands did not ache, his feet were not sore, his head was not spinning. He was young, healthy, and being a human being seemed the most pleasant thing on Earth.

"Thank you," he said and smiled joyfully.

"Look, he's thanking us!" someone above said in a tiny voice.

Egor was not embarrassed, got to his feet, and held out his hand to the man. He was dressed in an old-fashioned way. His coat was a cross between an *armyak* and a *zipun*. Egor was not well versed in old styles of clothing and could not tell exactly. The soft cap with white piping, the reddish-brown beard, the white *kosovorotka* instead of a regular shirt.

"Thank you, good people," Egor repeated.

The man smiled good-naturedly, but did not shake hands, went to the window, and sat down on a bench.

"Look, he's holding out his hand!" someone above said.

Egor stood in the small *izba* with unhewn walls, narrow windows covered with something translucent, a table, benches around the edge, and a huge oven near the door that was made out of flagstone. On top of it sat a small child, kicking its legs, sticking its tongue out, and making faces at Egor.

"What is the name of this village?" Egor asked.

The child broke into a laugh, and leaned back and stuck his legs up toward the ceiling.

"What say?" the man questioned in a deep bass. "What village do you mean?"

And Egor realized that the *izba* stood by itself in the taiga and his question about the village was funny, and he also thought that these must be Old Believers, living in the woods all these years—that would be why the man did not shake hands. It was not permitted by their laws. And Egor did not take offense at them, for the good they had done far outweighed their eccentricities.

"Okay," Egor said, "God be with it—the village. At least point out the road for me. I'll just rest a little, then be on my way. I don't want to intrude."

"There is no road from here," the man answered in his calm bass.

"Well then, are you telling me I have to stay with you?"

"Very good, stay, if you wish," the man said and turned away, looking out the dim window."

"And if I don't want to?"

"Then leave, if that is what you wish. The taiga is big, enough room for all."

"Let's get down to business," Egor said. "Where should I go if I don't know the way?"

Here the man suddenly turned around, facing Egor directly, threw out his right hand, its index finger pointed at Egor, and quickly said in a squeaky voice, "The path is known unto you, it is known, known, oh, but it is known!"

The man seemed to lose his dignity. He pushed his cap back, dropped onto all fours, and hopped around the edge of the *izba*, making faces and chanting shrilly, "*Shivda, vnoza, shakharda! Indi, mitta, zarada! Okutomi im tsuffan, zadima!*"

In answer the child on the oven rolled with laughter.

"How now? Are you afraid?" the man asked, getting to his feet.

"Not at all," Egor sighed and sat down on the bearskin, folding his legs. "Why clown around? I'm not fooling."

"Well, this should scare the wits out of you," the man said confidently and stood up tall against the light.

And he began to shrink, flatten himself, bend himself, deform and distort himself. Egor automatically jumped away from the oven. A severe illness contorted the man, warping his body, now stretching it in spirals, now compressing it into a formless lump, his head inflated, then shrank into his body, his legs shortened, spiraled, fused into one fat leg, and on his chest a huge toothy mouth was slashed, and from it a fat pink tongue stuck out, as though it were teasing him. The child on the oven bounced up and down in delight, and shifting his gaze from the man, Egor saw the child, too, deform himself, ooze in a dull spot over the oven, like an ameba, transforming himself into heaven knew what, heaven knew how. . . .

Egor felt like jumping out of the *izba*, but he forced himself to sit still and watch everything, overcoming attacks of nausea and regretting the absence of his ax, which would have lent him courage.

Meanwhile the man's shapes had begun gradually to be organized, the longitudinal waves that had contorted his body calmed and the diffuse forms solidified, and Egor saw an old man. Small, wrinkled, with a long, dirty beard, dressed in a shaggy bearskin. The old man hopped up and in place, as though trying to shake his body into form, blinking both eyes at the same time, and breaking into a smile.

"And now are you frightened?"

"Not at all," said Egor in a hoarse and deliberately raised voice. "So then, once again it's nonhumans. . . . Well, thanks for your kindness. I'll be going, if you don't mind. Give me back my ax and knife. I can't do without them."

He felt so bad that his mood can only be described as blue. And so blue that he could get down on all fours and howl at the top of his lungs. If he had not thought himself saved and back with human beings again, then he might have found what he saw more bearable. But he had imagined himself back among people, dressed and fed, solaced and warmed, and when he became convinced that these were not humans and he could expect no help, he realized that he was alone again, facing by himself the whole taiga, the taiga that was indifferent to people, to their woes, to their lives, to their sufferings and their deaths.

"I'll go then," he repeated stubbornly and strode toward the door.

"Wait a moment, Egorushka." He heard a familiar voice, turned around, and saw that the boy on the oven had become the little girl, neat, beautifully dressed, with a red ribbon woven in her braid.

"A series of magical changes," Egor growled and without looking back walked out of the *izba*.

It was gloomy and quiet in the taiga. The flowers and dry grass smelled sharply, scorched by the blistering heat, the sky was dull, and there was a sense that rain was coming. Egor went down the high stoop and looked around. The place was totally unfamiliar. Wind-fallen trees and a grove, damp, dark, with huge pines covered with white lichens and mosses, with boulders towering amid tall ferns, and no paths, no ruts, no fires, no leveled places. As though no one had ever lived here. The *izba* stood in the middle of all this and seemed to have grown out of the ground, like a tree, with a life of its own, sucking up sap with its deep roots, alien to human beings, a mockery of human beings' cozy habitations.

Egor straightened his shirt, which had slipped to one side, and tied the lace at the collar more tightly, and set off at random.

"Ego-o-r!" the little girl called out to him melodiously. "Where are you headed?"

He could not hold back—the anger and fury that had accumulated in him demanded release. He turned toward the *izba*, toward the girl standing in the doorway, and shouted a curse accusing the taiga, sky, and sun, all the spirits who were hostile to him and who dared stand in the way of man—the king of nature, its master and rightful owner. Let them do with him what they may, suck the warmth out of him, set wolves on him, torment him with hunger or plague him with mosquitoes, let them even take his life—all the same he, a man, was higher than any of them, for he, not they, had tamed, at the cost of enormous sacrifices, a blind and cruel nature, subordinated it to his will, and the death of one person would not deprive people of their power over her.

And when the words dried up and only an emptiness remained in his chest and a numbness in his vocal cords, he started picking up sticks and hurling them indiscriminately at the *izba*.

The whole time the girl stood near the door, leaning against a mossy railing, stood there and was silent, unsmiling, serious, totally adult. The sticks did not reach her: Following a short arc, they slowed in midflight and, turning sharply, flew backward with a whistling, like boomerangs. The first blows brought Egor to his senses, and when a hefty stick hit him in the chest and he almost fell, he stopped his useless attempts, sat down, devastated, on a fallen tree, and turned away.

"Our little calf has decided to catch a wolf," Egor heard the old man mumble. "His face is white, his mind not right."

Egor did not even feel like answering. He had to formulate new plans for his rescue, he had to survive no matter what, survive and return to the human world. Let the forest spirits mock him as much as they wished; after all, that small, forgotten tribe had reason not to like humans, who were stronger, wiser, and more adapted to the struggle for survival and life. Egor wanted to show them that he was a man and not about to give up. He became ashamed of his weakness and once again became furious, this time at himself.

"All right," he said to himself, "I flipped out for a while, but that's enough. Just get moving, Egor."

He walked slowly back to the *izba*, stopped in front of the girl, looked her in the eye—her eyes were light blue with dark flecks around the pupils—and said, "Give me my ax, my knife, matches, and some food. I don't need anything else from you. Thank you for everything and farewell."

The girl did not answer; he admired her pretty face, her clear skin, not tanned at all, and added, "It is a shame that you are so beautiful but not human. Who are you really? Do you have a name?"

"Call me what you wish," the girl said with a smile. "It doesn't matter."

"All right, I'll call you Masha. We humans have fairy tales where girls named Masha live in the forest with bears."

He tried to remember what he had read or heard about forest spirits, surrounded by legends and tall tales, but recalled very little—only an ancient charm came to mind: "Uncle Spirit, appear to me not as a gray wolf, not as a black raven, not as a fire—appear to me as I myself am."

They had appeared to Egor in human form, and perhaps in exactly the form he expected: Masha, the favorite of Russian fairy tales, the rough and clumsy grandfather spirit, the kind man with a cap tilted, an impish boy. . . . Theater, stage settings, makeup, impersonation, deceit, mirage. . . .

"And might you not be the one they call Litsedei?" Egor guessed.

"That's one of the names they use," Masha answered. "What does a name matter?"

"And do you know Dyoyba?"

"How could I not know Dyoyba? We know him well. Dyoyba has lived here all the time—we are the newcomers."

In the doorway there appeared a strangely dressed lanky young man, wearing a stern black suit, polished shoes, a gaudy shirt, and bow tie, and round dark glasses pushed down on his nose.

"How about this?" he asked boastfully, straightening his jacket. "Are you afraid now? How about it?"

And blinking both eyes simultaneously, he broke out laughing.

"I am not afraid," Egor answered. "Why should I fear you? Even though you are spirits, you are still like people."

"Oh, don't say that!" the man said with a drawl. "Don't confuse us with yourself. Our clan is no match for yours. We are more ancient than you humans."

"Then why are there so few of you? Are you dying out?"

"Need you ask? You are a human, it is your desire that there be few of us, and of animals, and of trees. But do you know how your conquering of nature will end up? You know, of course; how could you not know? We, on the other hand, an inseparable part of all that lives, we are not against nature but with it. You destroy nature and us along with it. Isn't that clear?"

"No," Egor said, "it is not clear. What is the point of your life? What have you created throughout your history? You declare yourselves the soul of nature, you garb yourself in various guises, now as a bird, now as a spider, now as a fir tree. And that way is good for you—you don't have to think about a thing, you live like the trees, today is the same as a thousand years ago. And what would change if you died out completely? Who has need of you? No, Litsedei, only our path was the right one, even if hard, even if we err. Only we humans have taken responsibility for ourselves and for nature. It is not you but we who are the soul of nature, flesh of its flesh, blood of its blood. You are just hangers-on. Now it is clear to me. Well, then, farewell Litsedei, I'm off."

"But you can't get away from us anywhere," the man said calmly and became foggy, distorting his body, swelling, then sprinkling down in pieces.

Egor turned away from the unpleasant sight.

He did not feel like guessing what Litsedei had changed himself into.

He had turned himself into a flock of brightly colored butterflies, large and small.

And the butterflies, maintaining their formation, flew up to the treetops and were lost from sight.

"May the birds devour you," Egor shouted after him, then turned to Masha. "Well, what are you waiting for? Go ahead and change into a lizard, a beetle bug, a *baba-yaga*, a bear, an elk, a horned demon. Why are you just standing there? After all, girls like you don't really exist."

"And what about this?" she asked and, wavering in the air, turned into a large bright bird with a girl's head.

"They really exist," Egor said firmly without turning away. "They are called the Sirin Bird, or the Alkonost. That's nothing! Now you must sing me your song and enchant me. I'm still not afraid of you."

"I will sing."

And indeed she did. She sang well, although there were no words to her song. To Egor it seemed that the taiga around him changed, that he himself dissolved into it, into each vein on each leaf, into each and every creature, each grain of sand, and the sensation was new to him, unusual, strange, but still pleasant, and he did not even feel like resisting the song, so he listened to it, and then—he was no longer himself, Egor, and his body was gone, and his soul spread out among the trees. . . .

5

Someone was walking in the darkness, making the floorboards squeak, sniffing, snuffling, shuffling bare feet on the floor, and from time to time tiny paws touched Egor. Egor's eyelids were heavy, he opened his eyes with great difficulty, and saw that he was lying on a bed, in the apartment he moved into after his divorce. It was night outside, the moon was visible in the window, everything was quiet.

"Nina!" Egor called. "Nina, do you hear me? I'm awake!"

He saw that someone was leaning over the head of his bed, gray and vaguely outlined in the semidarkness, bristly, rumpled, the eyelashes like tangled fluff. It blinked, breathed heavily, its teeth bared, its arms outstretched.

"Who are you?"

Egor leaped to his feet.

He was terrified, pressed his back against the wall, tightened his fists. But it loosened its lips, started mumbling, in a cottony voice: "Do not be afraid. I'm a *domovoi*, a house spirit. I live here, the only one left in the whole city, and I feel lonely. I looked for a living soul, and finally succeeded. I'm bored without people, hungry. Give me some *tyurya*, Egor. Soak the bread in the *kvass*, make me some tyurya. I'm hungry."

"What's this about *tyurya*?" Egor said angrily. "Your tribe gives the city no peace. Where's Nina?"

"There's no one," the *domovoi* said, and began sobbing, wiping his nose with his hand and smiling through his tears. "Everyone must have died, everyone, and you are left alone. Give me *tyurya*, Egor, or *pierogies*. I am hungry."

Egor pushed him away with his hand and started pacing the room. Everything was in its place, his clothing was draped over the chair, covered with a thick layer of dust. He opened the refrigerator, and everything inside was covered with mold; apparently the electricity had been turned off long ago. The faucets were rusty, and dust and desolation were everywhere. He glanced out the window and suddenly felt sick. Not a sound, no honking of automobiles, no lights in the windows. Deserted, gloomy, like the steppe.

Egor went outside to the street, and it was littered with garbage, weeds were growing alongside the buildings, the asphalt had been split by poplar sprouts, and not a single window was lit, not a single shadow moved across the windows. It was totally eerie, and he ran down the street, yelling, the echo bouncing off the empty buildings. There was no one. The street turned into a highway, but the highway was turning into a forest. Dawn came. The sun rose, the robins sang, grasshoppers fled in front of him. He waded across a stream, and sunfish tickled his feet. And Egor felt lonelier than he ever had. Suddenly he heard human voices. He ran toward them, out into a large clearing, and people were there. They walked slowly, conversing. And Nina, radiant, delicate, walked to him. She put her hands on his shoulders, looked straight in his eyes. And Egor almost broke out crying, embraced her, light, warm, alive.

"It's so good," he said, "that you are alive, that people are alive."

"But we're not people at all," Nina laughed and motioned with her head. "Now we are forest spirits. I am, too. You're the only one who's remained human."

Egor felt terrible and he collapsed to the ground, lay there, cried, bit the earth, and Nina on her knees stayed next to him and stroked his head.

"If you want," she said, "I'll become an apple tree. Or a bird? Or maybe a fish? Would you like that?"

Egor just shook his head no, he couldn't say a word. Nina stood up, laughed, grew roots out of her legs, clothed herself in leaves, and became an apple tree. And Egor felt that his legs, too, were going into the ground, seeking a path between the stones with his roots, stretching upward, dividing into branches and leaves; and he became a poplar, and he felt good, and he felt alarmed.

"Don't cry, Egor," someone said to him. "You are asleep but still crying. Your face is all wet."

It was Masha leaning over him and touching her cold fingers to his cheek, wiping his tears away, comforting him. And Egor felt himself so tired, so weak and small, that he did not feel like snapping at her, did not even feel like saying anything. He was lying on his back, staring at the sky without moving, and crying without a sound, just with tears. And Masha changed form again, and she was no longer a little girl but a grown woman with a heavy light brown braid fastened around her head, and a necklace jingled around her neck whenever she moved. And Egor was lying in the clearing, among tall camomiles, and the bees hummed, and the sky was cloudless, and it smelled of honey.

"Look, Egor," Masha said. "Is it really so bad here with us? Look around and dry your tears."

"Eh-hey!" came the voice of Litsedei, right beside her. "So tell us now, Egor, why have you come to us in the forest? Isn't your city enough for you? We don't go calling on you."

Egor did not want to argue and felt too lazy to roll over and look at the man to see what form he had taken now. But he had stopped crying, wiped his eyes and let them dry in the sun.

"What can I say?" he said after a short pause. "We will never understand one another. Live as you please, and don't bother us. Show humans the path home. I need nothing more from you."

"But we are not bothering you in the slightest," the man said from somewhere in the camomiles, "but you are certainly bothering us! So why should we love you and spare you?"

"How am I supposed to answer you in the name of all human beings? Well, do what you want, but I'm not going to give in to you that easily."

"A lot of good you are!" Litsedei said scornfully. "If we had wanted, we could have turned you into food for the grass a long time ago."

"Thanks for that," Egor answered him, piqued, and got to his feet.

"Can't we talk?" Masha asked.

"About what? What do you want from me? Or are you just bored without anyone to talk to? Well, go ahead, talk!"

Now Litsedei was tiny, no bigger than a camomile stem, and he had woven himself a nest in a clump of grass and sat there, his little legs crossed.

"Here's what amuses me, Egor: You intend to fit all of nature under you. Everything that lives in her, you consider your possession. And you go teaching your nonsense things like a bear in a circus. You put pants on him, a hat, sit him on a bicycle, and feel pleased with yourselves. And all your fables are foolish. They're still about people, just the names are animals'. And why do you do it? I will tell you why. You find it amusing when a beast resembles a human. Even though the resemblance is there, he is still stupider than a human. That's what makes him funny. But isn't it a mockery?"

"Listen here, my forest spirit friend," Egor said, shaking yellow pollen off his sleeve, "no, it's not a mockery. Just the opposite. It's because of our loneliness, because of the injustice of our being alone on the earth and having no one else to talk with. So we lend animals human form, human speech, and actions. But your clan has never liked humans, and there is a good reason why some call you evil spirits. What good have you done on the earth?"

"And what good have you done?" Litsedei quickly interjected.

"True, humans have brought much evil, to themselves, and to nature, but no less good. You, on the other hand, are neither here nor there, neither good nor evil, neither black nor white."

"And there you are wrong!" Litsedei exclaimed, hopping up and down in his little nest. "We are both here and there, good and evil, black and white, fish and fowl, and grass and bugs—all of that is us. And you are just yourselves and no more. In nature there is no evil and no limits that you try to impose on it. In it everything is one. And we make one whole with it."

"Stay with us, Egor," Masha said simply. "If you want, you can be like us."

"Like you?" Egor almost whistled in surprise. "What on earth do you need me for, or I you? It's no great treat to turn into a caterpillar and munch grass all day long, or become a bird and flutter from branch to branch. . . . I don't want to be a tree, or a woodpecker, or a bear. I don't want to be a forest spirit, or a devil, or a god, or an angel. Nor the gray wolf, nor the white hare. No, I live quite nicely in my human form. I am a human being, and no one on this earth is higher than me."

"Just try it, Egorushka," Masha said. "You might find that you like it."

"No," Egor answered, "I wouldn't like it. I have no need of your charity."

He tossed the ax in the air and caught it with one hand. A sunbeam glanced off its blade.

"At night," Masha said, "at night, you can see everything and understand everything."

"Eh-hey," Litsedei agreed, "at night you, too, might understand. Don't be late for the celebration, Egor. Be proud, you are the first human to see it. And do you know why? Because you are no longer entirely human. You only think that you are, but in reality—barely half. We are making a fuss over you, to pull you over to our side, and well will, you will see."

"I will only cease being human when I die," Egor said. "As long as I am alive I am human, and I plan to live for a long time. Is that clear?"

"At night," Masha repeated, making herself thin and bending to the ground, "at night," she repeated still more softly, covering herself in brown fur, "at night," and she became a wild goat, looked at Egor with moist eyes and slowly walked into the forest and said nothing more.

"Eh-hey," Litsedei shouted, growing transparent wings. "Eh-hey!" he repeated, and flew up into the air. "Oh, the night, beloved night!"

And they left the clearing, dissolving in the forest grove, elusive, formless, diverse, inscrutable, like the forest itself, like its rivers and mountains, like its birds and beasts, like nature itself.

6

The human calendar and the division of a homogenous flow of time into minutes and hours lost all meaning for Egor. He floated in the undifferentiated flow that carried along with it the forest with its unceasing transitions, the overflow of the living into the dead and of the dead into the living; and within Egor himself something old was constantly dying and something new being born, at first imperceptibly, foreign to him but increasing more and more, filling him and spilling over the edges, growing to the soil, the grass, making him akin to this infinite, ununderstandable world, previously alien to him.

In his former, urban, life he would never have believed seriously in forest spirits, or *rusalkas*, or in any of the other supernatural beings familiar to him from childhood tales but always conceived of as an invention, the fantasy of a folk gifted with imagination and inexhaustible creative powers.

And now he himself had made contact with that ancient legendary horde, who inhabited Slavic lands from prehistoric times and lived side by side with human beings, dying out as Slavic paganism itself died out, disappearing into nothingness, dissolving into the Russian forests, fields, and rivers. He had made the contact with the soul of Slavic nature, with the sources of his own tribe, who had gone further and further from nature.

And to merge with these mythological beings—would that not be to regain one's lost roots, to go back to one's forgotten homeland, where *rusalkas* play nursemaid to perch and raise fry, where forest spirits live inside trees and water spirits are dissolved in lakes, where the forest, turning its soul into a girl, brings fruits in its hands, which smell of fresh water?

To merge with them and cease to be human, or perhaps, on the contrary, to find the torn bond and return to the times when humans, too, were one with nature, and had not yet set themselves apart, and their bodies were inhabited by the souls of animals and birds, and their souls were devoted to everything that lived. . . .

Egor did not know what would become of him, but of one thing he was sure—death would have a long wait.

He walked through the hushed forest, and not a single owl rustled above his head, and not a single leaf fluttered in the wind; only dry twigs cracked and withered grass rustled beneath his feet. He did not select a direction, but wherever he went, no matter what direction in the infinite taiga he chose, his path must meet human beings, and that inspired him with hope.

Evening found him in a broad hollow covered with dense clumps of ferns. Damp, fragile, with delicately patterned leaves, they were waist-high, and hindered walking. He broke them, crushed them with his feet; the dew wet his clothing. The sun went down, and dusk came rapidly, but he could not get through the ferns. The hollow seemed to stretch out forever, the ferns to grow taller and thicker, and he had to cut a path with his ax. Egor cursed himself for cutting through the hollow rather than circling it, but there was no sense turning back. He walked on, but was actually going in circles, getting lost in a place where going astray was unthinkable.

He did not want to believe that spirits were leading him around again, but apparently that was what was happening. Then, knowing that resistance was hopeless, he cleaned himself a dry place, sat down, and waited.

The ferns began to tremble, their sap-filled stems wavered, and once again the horn sounded; it was followed by another, deeper and louder, and the thunder of a drum made the air sway. The ferns came to life, danced from side to side, the underside of their leaves swelled with bumps that immediately burst with a muffled sound, and blue flowers, never before seen anywhere by anyone, sprang forth.

The sound of wings, a hubbub of voices, and the stamping of countless feet filled the hollow. Egor lay on the ground and avoiding vain curiosity, hoped for just one thing: to become invisible. The flowers emitted a heavy scent that tickled the nostrils, inebriated, spun the head.

A curly cat's head shoved through the fern stems, shined a green eye on Egor, then vanished.

"It is Egor," a mewing voice said.

"Does he drink sap, too?" another voice asked, rustling.

"No-oo," the mewer purred.

A furry black cat with teeth too long to fit in its mouth jumped out from behind the ferns and landed softly on Egor's stomach.

"And who are you?" Egor asked calmly.

"Kurdysh," the cat answered and licked Egor's cheek. His breath smelled of honey. "And why don't you drink sap? Sa-a-vory sa-a-p."

Someone else crawled out of the ferns quietly, indistinguishable in the dark, rustling slightly, sighing like an old woman.

"And who's that with you?"

"It's Kikimora, of course," the cat answered; sticking out its neck, it bit off a blue flower with its sharp teeth and rumbled contentedly.

Egor rested his head in his hands. He had been found again: Hiding was useless.

"This is amusing," he said. "Well then, appear to me, Kikimora, appear."

He reached out toward the vague shadow and immediately received a flick in the forehead.

"Don't pester her," Kurdysh advised. "She always flicks nosybodies. If you want, she'll tickle you. She's good at that."

"Please don't bother."

"Whatever you say. Come along with me. I'll show you everyone."

Kurdysh bit off a flower again, neatly sucked out the sap, and spat out an amorphous lump. Egor stood up. He did not feel like going to the bonfire, but it seemed there was no escape. He sighed and, turning around, slowly wandered through the brush to where he heard laughter, shouts, the roar of horns, and the clatter of drums. Underfoot Kurdysh roamed, explaining as they went, "On the second day of the new moon the ferns bloom and everyone gathers here. Everyone from around here, everyone from a distance, everyone who has survived. You'll see them all."

"Ferns don't have flowers," Egor said. "They reproduce by spores. You're saying foolish things."

"Well, all right," Kurdysh was quick to agree, "It's foolish. But sa-a-vory foolishness."

He smacked his lips with gusto.

"You'll see Litsedei," Kurdysh went on. "There's no end to the forest spirits here. And Stribog is here, and Pokhvist, and Belbog, and Chernobog, and Lado, and Perun—all the old Slavic gods."

"And Mavka?" Egor asked.

"Mavka's here, too, and Mara, and Poludnitsa, and the *obiyniks*, and the *ocherepyaniks*, and the *boltnyaks*, and the *tryasovitsas*, and the *banniks*, and the *ovinniks*, and the *zhikhars*. They all love the sap. And there are a lot of locals too: Mou-nyamby, Dyaly-nyamy, Kou-nyamy, they're all here."

"To be brief, all the evil spirits," Egor said, cutting a path with his ax. "A witches' sabbath you're having tonight. Ah, the devil take you all, I'm not afraid of any of you."

"And why should you be?" Kurdysh calmed him, picking up the cut-down ferns. "Now you're one of us."

"I'm still a human," Egor grinned. "People have been looking for flowering ferns for a long time, but have never found them. Or aren't you afraid of me anymore and don't consider me human, since you're inviting me to your sabbath?"

"Oh, Egor, you're quite a person!" Kurdysh laughed. He meowed, he rumbled, he jumped up on Egor's shoulders, sticking his sharp claws into his shirt. "You don't have the smell of human spirit about you."

"That's the last straw!" Egor was indignant but did not throw the cat off. "You go your way, and I'll go mine. I won't bother you, and you can leave me alone. I don't need your ferns."

"Try it, Egor, just try it," Kurdysh suggested with a smooth tongue, breathing hotly in his ear. "Sa-a-vory, oh, how savory."

The ferns parted and Egor came out into a glade. A huge bonfire was burning, and in its light, in clouds of sparks, in blue smoke, hundreds of beings crowded, girdled with garlands and crowned with wreaths of the flowering ferns; they danced, they sang, they played their oaten flutes and blew their horns, leaped, ran around the glade shrieking, somersaulted over the fire, ripping the air with their light bodies.

Egor stopped at the edge of the circle of light.

"I won't go any further," he said firmly. "I have no reason to go on. I can see well enough from here."

"Ego-o-r!" called a familiar, tender voice, and Egor recognized Mavka.

She walked up to him, stepping soundlessly, and the grass did not bend under her feet. Naked, graceful, flowing like water, variable like water, and murderous and life-giving like water.

"Hello," Egor said, tightening his grip on the ax despite himself. "Still craving embraces, my little *rusalka*?"

She came close to him, and her body gave off coldness and dampness. She looked him in the eyes blankly and calmly and smiled.

"Oh, my dear," she whispered. "Have you missed me?"

"I almost died of longing," Egor answered and, turning to Kurdysh, said, "Listen, my friend, spare me her. I'll remember her forever."

"Who's going to spare you?" Kurdysh meowed thoughtfully. "From her, as from water, you can be protected. But don't you worry. Today she won't touch you."

"Let her go to blazes," Egor said and strode to the far end of the glade.

Indeed, Mavka did not pursue him. She flowed over the glade, babbling, and disappeared into the ferns.

A crowd of dancers descended on Egor, surrounding him. The cluster of beings seized him by the hands and drew him into the enchanted circle, shouting and whooping. Faces flashed by, furry, sweaty, elongated, flattened, lipless, and earless. All of them reached out to Egor, grimaced at him, giggled, and pinched each other. Egor did not try to escape, but when a nonhuman face came too close, he just turned his head. Kurdysh sank his claws painfully into his shoulder, but Egor did not abandon him.

"The forest spirits are swinging you in a circle," he said. "Litsedei is one of them. Recognize him?"

Someone in a familiar cap and dark glasses pressed close to Egor.

"How are things, Egorushka?" he shouted. "Ah, the cherished night! Dance, Egorushka, dance, relax your soul, calm it, the restless one, console it, the homeless one! Drink some sap, oh, how good!"

"I'm not going to drink your sap!" Egor shouted into Litsedei's face. "And you can't make me!"

"Oh, yes, we will, oh, yes, we will!" the forest spirits shouted. "To Perun with him, to Perun! He'll show him! He'll teach him!"

Egor was seized from all sides and carried to the fire. Kurdysh did not leave him, just held on tighter with his paws, and it was impossible to tell whether he was protecting Egor or helping the others.

"Don't fight it, Egor," he advised. "You're not going to escape."

Egor was pushed to a huge idol. His head was silver, his long gilded beard shone dimly, and his wooden body was set firmly on already rusted iron legs. In his right hand the idol held a long twisted bough.

"Perun, Perun!" the spirits wailed discordantly. "Here, teach Egor, strike him with your wand! Instruct him, the heedless one! He will not drink the sap!"

And the idol moved, and his wooden flesh cracked from the strain inside, the dry wood of his body groaned, his beard rang out, his silver eyelids opened, and clear blue eyes gazed at Egor.

"Drink!" he commanded in a loud, rasping voice and struck his stick against the ground.

"I do not wish to," Egor said. "I do not wish to and I will not. I do not wish to be like you. I want to be a human being."

"You were a human being, you will become a forest spirit! Drink!"

"After my death," Egor agreed. "But now you will not make me."

Perun's iron legs jingled dully, and his eyes sparkled, and the stick in his hand glowed yellow, then changing color, turned white hot. He struck it against the ground and scattered blinding but harmless sparks. The forest spirits ran away, shrieking, and Egor remained alone with Perun—not counting Kurdysh, who was slumbering on Egor's shoulder as though nothing had happened.

"How are you, my grandson?" Perun asked in an unexpectedly gentle tone, with creaking and snapping bending over toward Egor. "You are acting unseemly. Before you honored me, but now you put me to shame. Are we not of one root?"

"I don't remember," Egor said, rubbing his numb hands. "I do not remember you, Perun, and I do not consider myself your grandson."

"You have taken to philosophizing in strange and new ways, have moved away from the curly-headed and ox-eyed gods of your forefathers. Before you thought yourselves grandsons of Perun, and of Dazhdbog, but now where do you seek your roots? In the lands of the midday sun, in the lands of the setting sun? But your roots are here! Here, in Russian lands!"

And again Perun struck with his white-hot staff. There was a smell of ozone.

"We are of one blood," Perun said softly, moving only his lips. "Drink the sap of your native land, gain your patrimony."

And he held out a horn filled with blue, sparkling sap.

"Come now, you dawdler," Perun said like a kindly old man. "You won't become a forest spirit, but you will cleanse your soul, flow into the Russian earth."

"After my death," Egor repeated stubbornly, but took the horn. "After death we all flow into the earth. Do you want to kill the human being in me?"

"So become one. Become a human being. A human being without a country, a tree without roots. From where will he derive his strength? Drink, my grandson."

Egor lifted the horn to his mouth. The thick sap seethed, and its heady aroma stupefied him.

"All right," Ego said. "I believe you, Perun. My ancestors honored you, so I will honor you. Let it be as you wish, grandad. To your health!"

And he drank down the burning, seething sap.

"Drink to the bottom! Drink to the bottom!" the forest spirits shouted in triumph, lifting Egor up in the air and carrying him, laughing.

"Should have done it long ago," the awakened Kurdysh mewed and licked his cheek with his hot tongue. "You see, you did not die. But you were afraid."

They carried Egor, not giving him time to come to his senses, to pause, to feel in himself what was almost imperceptibly beginning to happen to him. They put him down facing the fire, and he saw a seated giant. His enormous body was covered with blood-swollen mosquitoes; he did not drive them away, only ran his hand over his face from time to time, leaving a red stripe. In his hand he held a large horn, filled with sap.

"It's Belbog," Kurdysh prompted. "Don't worry, he's kind."

"Well then, Egor, shall we drink?" the giant asked in a bass voice.

"Let's drink," Egor agreed and someone shoved a horn into his hands. "You drink out of a horn, and the mosquitoes out of you."

"They drink the bad blood out of me," Belbog answered good-naturedly.

"Do you think that it is easy to be good? These swarms suck all the evil out of me."

"Well, let us taste of good!"

And drank down his horn without blinking and without pausing for breath.

"How about some evil now?" someone asked stealthily. "Drink with me now."

Not exactly a beast, not exactly a human, with a shining, seemingly fused face that kept changing its contours, he held out a powerful lion's paw with a goblet clasped between its claws.

"This is Chernobog," Kurdysh whispered. "Drink with him, too. Good and evil are always brothers."

"I will know both good and evil," Egor laughed and drained the goblet and without looking tossed it into someone's trustworthy hands.

The forest spirits again picked him up, raised him in the air, and set him down on the broad back of some creature. Trying to maintain his balance, Egor waved his arms and hit a bearded face.

"Hold on!" some yelled to him, and the back under Egor shuddered, hooves clattered, and he raced around in a circle.

The bearded creature turned around, grinned, and Egor saw that he was sitting on the being that is called a centaur.

"How about a gallop?" the centaur asked. "My name is Polkan."

Without waiting for an answer, he leaped over the fire. There was a blast of fire, and Egor put his arms around Polkan's strong torso, and the inseparable Kurdysh hugged Egor around the neck with his soft paws.

"Fun, isn't it?" Kurdysh asked.

Someone with a snake's body and the wings of a flying bat flew by, and Ego saw Masha on its back. She was the same but not quite the same. Half little girl, half demoness, with her long hair loose, flushed, giggling. She waved to Egor and zoomed high into the air.

"That's Krodo," Kurdysh had explained meanwhile, still hugging Egor's neck. "And there's Yarilo himself. And that's Leda, very militant, very. . . . And over there is Lado, so, so. . . ."

Kurdysh sweetly blew a kiss.

"And those cutups are his children. Lelya-Raspberry. Dido-Snoball-Tree, and the eldest, Polelya. And the one over there with four heads is Svetovid, the good warrior. All of them have gathered here, all of them have survived. Now the taiga is the only place to hide from humans. But will it last long?"

"Forever!" Egor said and in his excitement kicked his heels into Polkan's sides.

Polkan reared, galloped even higher than before, and Egor was torn loose from his back.

"Don't be afraid," Kurdysh managed to say. "Fly yourself."

And Egor felt that he was not falling but continuing to fly in a circle, as though the earth had ceased to attract him. The forest spirits surrounded him again, circled him, began mumbling.

"Well, Egor, good wine is what we have, isn't it?" Litsedei shouted as he flew up. "Feeling good?"

"Scram!" Egor yelled, laughing.

He felt like giggling and somersaulting in air because of the lightness that filled his body. He wanted to embrace all these freakish monsters, join hands in a round dance, bellow songs without words, fly through the flames of the bonfire, and drink the sweet burning sap squeezed from the blue flowers.

And he shouted out in a strange voice, "Eh, night, beloved night!"

And he saw an old acquaintance, Dyoyba-nguo. He was sitting by the fire, his legs folded, surrounded by a circle of wolves; he was singing something, his eyes half closed, and the wolves seconded him with a soft howling. And he saw the ancient gods of the region—the soul of the taiga and of the tundra, squat, powerful, with faces shining with bear fat, dancing hand in hand with the Slavic gods and celebrating the abundance, eternity, and persistence of life.

Only Dyoyba-nguo, the Orphan God, sat alone, beyond everything. He foresaw the end of the eternal, the destruction of the indestructible, the disappearance of the abundant, and lamented them in his song.

And Egor drank sap from large horns and small, drank with Stribog, and with Dazhdbog, and Lado kissed him, and Lelya-Raspberry piped a tune for him.

"Hey!" Egor yelled as loud as he could. "Hey you, the dead ends of evolution! I'll see you're all listed as endangered species! Do you hear? From now on no one will touch you! Live as you like!"

And the forest spirits laughed in answer, Polkan kicked up his hooves, and the *rusalkas* tickled Egor as they flew by, pressing their bodies against him—cold and stiff.

Things flashed, spun, spread, fused into a huge fiery crucible, mixed, were born, died, disintegrated, united out of a million fragmented grains and split again, were buried, arose, ascended, and plunged down-ward. . . .

And when, exhausted, he sank down at the edge of the glade, he saw that Kurdysh had vanished, and Masha was standing near. Naked, delicate, without a smile, without a word, she was looking at him. And he reached

out to her, put his arms around her, pulled her against him, and she put
her arms around his neck, and he felt her enter into him, squeeze her
flesh into his flesh, disappear into him, dissolve, without leaving a trace
behind. And he did not try to reject her, he did not take fright, but embraced
her still harder, until he saw that he was holding his own shoulders. And
he felt that he was no longer himself, and that in him were two souls and
two bodies. And what people blindly strived for, pressing their lovers in
their arms, what they had lost and forgotten forever, now returned to Egor.

But it was no longer Egor.

The fur clothing had grown fast to his body: He pulled on the sleeve
and felt pain, as though he were trying to remove his own skin. And no
longer paying attention to anyone, he lay face down on the ground, pressing
himself into it, the life-giver, and grew roots and became a tree, and then
he grew fruit on his branches. The fruit of the knowledge of good and
evil, knowledge of the soul of nature.

In the morning rain set in. Stealthily, gradually gathering strength, it
fell on the taiga, watering the roots and leaves, setting the thickened sap
into motion, washing, renewing, saving from death, knocking faded blue
blossoms to the ground, flowing in even, resilient streams on the back of
the man lying on the ground.

Egor was sleeping in the middle of the glade, and there was no one
near him, and at the same time the entire taiga bent over him and lulled
him, whispering dreams, one better than the other.

And in those dreams beasts and birds, trees and grass came to him,
spoke to him in their language, and every word was understandable, and
there was no need to call living beings by names invented by humans, for
he himself, and all of them, were one and indivisible. Everything that
breathed, grew, moved, everything that is born, changes, turns to dust,
and is born again, all that, from the microbe to the whale, was him, Egor,
and he was all that—living, eternal.

I change, therefore I am.

The essence of life is in eternal change, and Egor had changed. He had
changed without being unfaithful to human beings, or to the forest. . . .

7

A week later some Evenks, crossing the river, happened upon him. Egor
was sitting on a riverbank next to a pyramid of stones and talking with
someone invisible. For a long time he did not recognize people and
rambled on about the fact that he was not himself, and that in him were

all the trees and all the animals of the taiga. They washed him, fed him, put him on a reindeer, and took him to their camp. While they were waiting for the helicopter, Egor roamed around the camp, talking to the reindeer, petting the dogs, who did not bite him. They were concerned about him and treated him like a sick man, crazed by his long wanderings through the taiga, who had lost his reason. He answered all questions monosyllabically but did not avoid conversation; it seemed that he did not see any great difference between a reindeer and a human being. The helicopter came and took him to a geologists' camp, and from there to the city.

He was put in a hospital. He lay in a light room with three other patients. One of his neighbors was the generalissimo of the galaxy, and at his command stars were extinguished and dreams became unsettling. Therefore at night Egor turned himself into a tree and slept dreamlessly until morning.

His doctor chatted with him freely, did not spend much time trying to get him to change his mind but treated him according to science, trying to split his multifaceted soul.

An accident occurred. The generalissimo was sticking a black hole into space and miscalculated, falling from his bed and breaking his arm. The pride of his rank prohibited him from crying out, so he sat on his bed and groaned softly. Egor did not bother to call the doctors. He took his neighbor by the arm, looked at it, unnaturally twisted and powerless, and saw sharp bone chips through the skin and muscles. With tenderness and, at the same time, strength, he compressed the arm and felt that something came out of his palms and flowed into the other's body; he sat there until his neighbor quieted down and the pain subsided. Then he carefully removed the chips, pressed the no longer painful spot with his fingers, and watched the weakly glowing aureole around his hand increase in intensity, flare up, and in short pulsating waves penetrate to the bone in the generalissimo's arm. In half an hour the bone had knit, and soon the generalissimo could move his arm freely. In his next proclamation the generalissimo awarded Egor the Order of the Supernova and appointed him to the post of Inspector of White Dwarfs. Egor thanked him for the honor, and from that day on they were friends.

The generalissimo had an ordinary human name: Vasily Petrovich. He was over fifty and previously had been a biophysicist. Of course, he did not consider his present state abnormal and continued to believe in his high calling. His own distinctive logic did not let him down: He proved in detail to Egor that the entire galaxy was one living organism, and he, Vasily Petrovich, was the focus of its reason, and an overwhelming sense of responsibility for the fates of billions of stars kept him from sleeping and was driving him mad. He wanted peace, but an echo of war reached him from the constellation Cygnus, where hundreds of stars were burning up. He wanted to sleep peacefully, but on countless planets life was developing, and breaking out into outer space, and twisting space, deforming time, and disobeying the generalissimo's orders. Then he would punish the rebels cruelly with bursts of supernovas, cast civilizations into black holes, turn stars into dust and light. But he was alone, and the stars numbered in the billions, and in the entire galaxy there was no place where he could lay his head down and rest.

"What would you like to become?" Egor asked him. "In what shape would you acquire peace of mind?"

Vasily Petrovich thought a moment and said, "I would like to be interstellar dust. . . ." And then added, "No, I'd like to be a hydrogen atom. . . . No, I'd like to be a quantum of time. . . . No, I want to be everywhere and nowhere, always and never." Then he said, "No, I no longer wish to be, I want peace."

That night he slept poorly again, hurled curses at the Sirius system, elevated someone to power, cast someone else down. A nurse came and gave him a shot. Vasily Petrovich calmed down, and Egor saw that the man was old and tired and needed help. He put his hand on Vasily's forehead, moved it to his temple, his crown, the back of his head, he touched his cheek to Vasily's cheek, and did what he had intended to do.

When Vasily Petrovich awoke, he lay for a while with open eyes, stared at the ceiling, and smiled.

"I've retired," he said to Egor. "My position has been taken by one more qualified. I'm a private citizen now and would like to have breakfast."

From that day on he made rapid progress, and soon the doctors recognized that he was cured. Egor and he were released on the same day.

Egor was invited to the office of the director, who leafed through his thick file, closed it, slapped him on the shoulder, and said unexpectedly, "Egor, you're a perfectly healthy person. I have the feeling that even healthier than you were before you got lost in the taiga. I'd like to think that it was we who cured you, but I'm not going to perpetrate an illusion. Unfortunately, in many things we are helpless. We are incapable of curing your so-called sickness or that of your neighbor. So I, as a doctor, am very curious about how you did it."

"I've already explained to you, Doctor," Egor said cautiously. "I'm not sure there's anything to add. I don't know how I do things, but I can do a lot."

"Bioenergetics?" the doctor asked. "Have you read about it?"

"I read something but don't really remember. All I know is that all living things on Earth are joined in one organism."

"Biofield," the doctor said. "There's a theory. Maybe you could show me something. Don't worry, I believe you're totally healthy, and will continue to do so, no matter what."

"All right," Egor said.

And changed into a flock of birds. Blue tits, flycatchers, larks, wagtails, pipits, shrikes, waxwings, chaffinches, goldfinches flew about the room and perching in the corners broke into song, each with its own melody.

"Interesting," said the doctor, leaning back in his chair. "Whatever else it may be, it is certainly interesting. Listen, Egor, what do you plan on doing now? Come on, knock off the singing, I can't hear your voice, and the whole hospital is going to come running."

"To live," Egor answered in a many-voiced chorus. "And to fight to save the forest spirits."

"Well, okay, okay, I believe you. No, it's not just a doctor's politeness—I really do want to believe you. But it is completely incomprehensible. I look at you and I am inclined to consider myself insane. How did you learn all these tricks?"

"Very simply," Egor answered, gathering all the bits together into a single, and human, body. "I overcame the limits of my body and ceased to be solitary. And, I believe, I have become immortal."

"Teach me," the doctor said. "Is it hard?"

"I will teach everyone," Egor answered. "It is very hard, but possible. Can I be free?"

"Yes, of course, I won't hold you. By the way, why didn't you leave here immediately? It would be very easy for you."

"And who would I leave here as?" Egor laughed. "You'd better give me a release saying I'm healthy."

He waited for Vasily Petrovich, and they went out through the hospital gates together. The former generalissimo was totally alone; during his illness his wife had died and his children moved away. Egor invited him to stay at his place.

Egor himself returned to his old job, and Vasily Petrovich managed to collect a pension; he sat home for days at a time and put together some strange equipment. In the evening they talked, sometimes argued, each arguing his own point but unable to convince the other.

"Man has created a second nature," Vasily Petrovich might say, "and that is the natural path of evolution, and living nature is only a necessary step, from whose heights man can attain omnipotence, the title of Cosmic Man. To be one with earthly nature? A trifle, a transitional stage—we will be one with the cosmos. Spaceships? Primitive. Man must travel through space without those tin cans. You can turn into any being, and man will learn to turn into light, a stream of particles, into a gravitational field, and who knows what else? Biofield? Beautiful. But that is only a part of the universe's single energy field. You are indignant that man has set himself in opposition to the surrounding living nature? I am indignant that he has set himself in opposition to the whole cosmos and intends to conquer it! It's funny. It really is, funny and naive. That's how man conquered earthly nature, and got so carried away that—well, you know as well as I how it turned out."

Once the doctor came. He searched out Egor's address, found him— not without amazement—in the company of the retired generalissimo. He said he remembered Egor's promise to teach him.

"Why do you want that?" Egor asked.

"I am a doctor," he said. "I want to heal people. It is painful to admit my powerlessness. It is not really honest if you can save patients and don't want to. Teach me, and if you have nothing against it, we can both fight to save your forest spirits. I am young and full of energy."

"All right," Egor said. "I will teach you."

From then on the doctor visited him every evening and bearing stoically Vasily Petrovich's skeptical grins, studied what he had never studied in medical school, or anywhere else.

He was learned, believed in all kinds of things, joyously found confirmation of vague rumors concerning Philippine healers who removed tumors without piercing the skin, and even came up with his own theory on the penetration of the body through the fourth dimension. The theory was greeted with deafening laughter by Vasily Petrovich; he still felt hostility toward doctors and could not really help himself.

Finally the doctor picked up a few things. He himself could not understand how it worked, but he found within himself the barrier, beyond which a human being ceases to be a human being and turns into something new, something different, a more perfect being.

In late autumn Egor could not stand sitting home any longer and went off into the taiga, to the very spot where he first felt himself a part of the single whole whose name is the Universe.

Vasily Petrovich continued to put together his wild equipment. He aimed his lenses at blue stars and dreamed in secret of the time when he would control the galaxy and all that limitless sky would be under his control.

The doctor continued his work; making further advances on his own, he cured the incurable and avoided the unavoidable.

Egor did not return alone. With him came a bearded man, who had the strange habit of blinking with both eyes simultaneously. The two of them would go off somewhere together, arguing loudly about incomprehensible things and even coming to blows, but Vasily Petrovich separated them and threatened to split them into mesons.

He himself did not live until the following autumn. Dying, he wrote a will to have his body sent into space, where it would gradually be drawn into the sun, land on its surface, and burned in its core. He would turn into a stream of photons flying to the end of the universe, alive and immortal.

And the doctor did his job, wrote appeals demanding that forest spirits be declared an endangered species, wrote articles that no one would publish, argued furiously, and believed that the day would come when the unity of humanity and the planet Earth, so small and so fragile, would be a reality.